THE
HEARTS
OF
MEN

THE HEARTS OF MEN

A NOVEL

NICKOLAS BUTLER

ecco
An Imprint of HarperCollins*Publishers*

FIRST EDITION

Designed by Ashley Tucker

Library of Congress Cataloging-in-Publication Data has been applied for.

ISBN 978-0-06-246968-7

17 18 19 20 21 RS/LSC 10 9 8 7 6 5 4 3 2 1

For my mom, and all the mothers who
place books in the hands of children

For my dad, who did his best

And for Regina, Queen of the North

Where stars that died gave out, gave up, gave in—
Where no one meant the promises they made.
Oh, and one more thing. I send my love
However long and far it takes—through light,
Through time, through all the faithlessness of men.

"DEAR MISS EMILY," BY JAMES GALVIN

"Have faith, old heart. What is living, anyway, but dying."

"KNOWN TO BE LEFT," BY SHARON OLDS

PART I

》——→

SUMMER, 1962
THE BUGLER

1

THE BUGLER NEEDS NO ALARM. IN THE MUSTY CLOSE
canvas darkness, his smallish hands fumble for the matchbox, scratch the
blue sulfurous tip against the box, the match catching and burning, and
finally the golden kerosene glow of the lantern, the wick burning like a
lung on fire. He yawns, rubs the sleep from his eyes. In this new light, he
seeks and finds his glasses, and now can make out the familiar particu-
larities of his tent, its shadows, his things. An owl hoots from the crown
of a nearby maple as the boy flaps open the tent and shivers in the predawn cold. His bare feet move lightly over the well-trod camp soil. He
tugs his white underwear down and, trembling, sends an arc of piss onto
the big accepting fronds of the unseen ferns. It is a pleasant sound. Like
rainwater bouncing off a canvas awning. Then back into the tent, now
that much warmer for the flame of the Coleman. It is a race until dawn.

The youngest in his troop of some thirty boys, Nelson sleeps alone.
His possessions are neatly organized into piles: socks, underwear, shorts,

books. Shirts and trousers hang from a line that he has erected to follow the tent's central pole. Mornings, he is glad of the tent's solitude, but at nights, the campsite and forest are alive with the low murmuring and high giggling of boys and their nocturnal conversations. This reminds him of his loneliness. It is the fifth summer he has visited Camp Chippewa, and the second time he has had a tent to himself. Sometimes, he creeps out around midnight, to watch the Kabuki theater of the other boys' flashlights, hear the pages of comic books turning and the plastic crinkling of candy wrappers, smell their contraband cigarettes. His father halfheartedly volunteered to bunk with him, but both parent and son recognized in this gesture something ultimately embarrassing. No, it was better for Nelson to be on his own. Perhaps at some point in the week, he might gain a roommate, some other young Scout badly homesick or alienated by his peers and in need of refuge. Some boy who'd accidentally wet his sleeping bag. Nelson would be ready. Ready to consolidate his belongings to one side of the tent as necessary, ready to assemble another cot, ready to be: *helpful, friendly, courteous, kind, cheerful.*

Now he carries a woven birch-bark basket out of his tent, toward the camp's fire ring of black-scarred rocks. He walks past tents whose canvas walls seem to ripple with snores and dream-noises rattling out into the night. Up above, the Milky Way spills out over the forest canopy, in tiny pockets as purple and sparkling as amethyst or as pale blue as the heart of a glacier. He bends down beside the fire ring, holds his little hands over last night's coals. Residual heat radiates against his palms, warms the soft pads of his fingertips. He lowers himself to his knees and leaning into the fire pit, begins blowing at the embers, his lungs well practiced from the bugle. After a minute or two of patient puffing, the fire begins to glow a drowsy red. From the basket he removes a ball of dried grass, some pinecones, and sets this tinder on the coals. And then he blows and blows again, until at last a fire licks up, small flames, like the petals of some primal night orchid. The tinder catches and now his hands go into the basket for more twigs, more pinecones. The fire leaps higher still.

He stands, so limber and awake, and begins making a teepee of fire, using larger sticks now, until the fire is crackling and pushing the darkness back, back toward the roof of the forest where the owl wings softly off, away from the roiling sparks and cone of fire reaching up toward the early morning sky. Nelson makes his way to the picnic table now, finds the grimy teakettle all covered in creosote and ash. He shakes the kettle, hears no sloshing. Walks all the way back to his tent and returns to the now-crackling fire with a heavy canteen. Fills the kettle and sets it on the fireside grill to boil. Finally allows himself to exhale. He has always been a good fire starter.

Nelson has no friends. Not just here, at Camp Chippewa, but also back home in Eau Claire, in his neighborhood, or at school. He understands that this is somehow linked to his sash full of merit badges— twenty-seven to date, allowing him the rank of Star. It isn't that earning merit badges is *uncool*, but the speed and determination with which he has added weight to his sash seems to be enviable, perhaps even pitiable. Possibly, his unpopularity is linked as well to his eyeglasses, though it might just as easily be his inability to dribble a basketball or throw a spiral, or, worse yet, the nearly reflexive way his arm shoots into the classroom air to volunteer an answer. Nelson likes school, actually enjoys it, strives to win his teachers' approval, the gratifying surprise in their faces when he delivers some bit of arcane historical trivia—the machinations of our legal system, say, or the rarer elements on the periodic table. He can't pinpoint *it*, that one thing about his personality, his being that, if changed, might win him more friends. But he dearly wishes he could. Wishes his mornings and afternoons weren't limited to hallway wanderings or endless games of solitaire at otherwise abandoned cafeteria tables. Then again, maybe this is just who he is, and sometimes, when he is feeling brave, he embraces this notion, imagines himself as a wolf without a pack, roaming, free as can be, a solitary forest creature.

At his thirteenth birthday party, he sat in the backyard on a sweltering Sunday afternoon in June, waiting for his fellow Scouts to arrive with their BB guns and coonskin caps, the wrapping paper of their presents dampened with summer perspiration and torn in places. The night before, against his better judgment, he'd allowed himself to imagine a stack of gifts: books and model airplanes, baseball cards and candy.

A giant glass jar of lemonade sweated profusely on a side serving table, as if under interrogation. The plate of frosted cupcakes had already moved back into the icebox, after sitting outside long enough to attract the unwanted attention of hornets and flies. He and his mother had sent invitations to each of the boys' houses a full month in advance. Yet, as the afternoon wore on, not one boy arrived, and so he spent the hours sending arrows toward the primary colors of a target's bull's-eye affixed to the trunk of the yard's noblest elm.

At supper that night, it was difficult restraining his tears, and when they came, they poured hot and wild down his sunburnt cheeks as his mother and father looked on from across the family picnic table, a red and white gingham cloth clinging to the redwood planks in the June humidity, two unmoving balloons framing him on either side in the close summer air, without so much as even twisting on their flat plastic ribbon strings. His mother moved around the table, sat with him, placing her arm around his shoulder.

"I don't understand," he cried, "we sent them the invitations! We sent them weeks ago! Where is everyone? Where *are* they?" Surely he did not want his voice to leak out as the whine it did, but there it was, higher pitched than the eight-year-old neighbor girl's, just then skipping past the house, barefoot as could be, trailing her beloved jump rope. He might as well have inhaled all the helium in the less than festive balloons beside his head.

"Oh, dear," his mother said, shushing him, "it's summertime. I'm sure they're all at their cabins or on vacation. And, why—well, you've had a wonderful day, haven't you? Here with your father and me? Hasn't it been a splendid day? And there are still presents to open, *aren't* there, Father?"

Clete Doughty looked on, through his own thick, thick glasses, the lenses murky as quartz. He swatted at a vectoring hornet orbiting his head.

"Now, Nelson," he said flatly, "this flubbering here—about this flubbering . . . Now, I'll tell you something, and it may sound harsh, but it's not. These boys, these so-called friends of yours? They won't be around for the long haul, so to speak. I can assure you of this. They never are. Look at me, for instance. You see me off gallivanting with a bunch of chums? No. There comes a time when you have to be on your own, see, and maybe that time is now, sorry to say." He harrumphed indignantly.

The boy, though, for all his efforts to stifle the hot, hot tears, the hiccups of embarrassment and loneliness and shame, wept that much harder.

"There'll be no crying, now!" Clete snapped. "You're thirteen years old, Nelson! Men don't—there will be no more crying! Is that understood?"

"Let him be," said Nelson's mother, as sternly as Nelson could ever recall, for rarely did Dorothy Doughty dare challenge her husband. "Poor boy. You let him be."

Nelson had noticed an air of tension in the house over the past year, an anxiety he could only manage to trace back to himself; something was awry. Doors slamming with greater frequency and volume. Father arriving home late for dinner and marching straight to the bedroom or plopping right down in his chair. Mother, weeping quietly over the dishes and then, when he asked her what was the matter, well, she would rush to the bathroom, close and lock the door, the only response the sound of the sink water spilling into the basin. In the backyard, the once-immaculate carpeting of fescue was steadily losing a battle with the dandelions and creeping charlie.

"But it's true, Dorothy. And you know it! Name *one* friend of yours from high school that you still see. One."

"Clete, this isn't about me—or you, for that matter. This is Nelson's day, and the poor boy—"

"I'll tell you where you make friends. You make friends in the military, in the trenches, on the front lines. Men that will take a bullet for you, that will share their only Lucky Strike, the last drops in their canteen. It's not about birthday cake and candles, Nelson. Being friends with someone is about loyalty. Lifelong loyalty. You're almost of an age when that will become more and more apparent. Soon, there will be no toys and no cake, no parties or friends. It will just be days upon days, stacked up so that you can't remember what you ate for breakfast that very same morning. Now, I'm sorry to have to say that to you on your birthday, but there it is. The truth."

Nelson was silent a moment. "I thought they liked me," he whined. "At least well enough. Well enough to come to a birthday party. And no one bothers to even show up? No one!" The volume of his voice was something he could not seem to control, like a yellow balloon untied and drifting up into the sky.

"Oh, darling." His mother held him closer, their bodies both so hot, and he aware of their garments sticking together, of how his own body did not feel small enough to be held this way by her, and yet, how his heart was not big enough to manage the breaking he now felt, the rejection. "I love you so," she whispered in his ear. "I love you so, so much."

"I just want people to like me. Aren't I a nice person? I mean, *aren't* I?"

"Of course you are, Nelson; of course you are."

"Aren't I? Aren't I a nice person, Mom?"

"Stop that flubbing now!" Clete ordered. "Stop it this instant!"

"Ignore that old grump, Nelson," she cooed. "We can sit like this as long as you'd like. Happy birthday, my sweet little boy."

"I'm sorry that I'm crying," he managed. "I don't *want* to cry. I don't want to at all."

"It's okay, baby."

"Stop it!" shouted his father. "Stop that crying!" His voice as sharp as the finger he extended toward his son's face, like a pistol. Sweat made his glasses ski down the slope of his nose. And then he was on his feet, unhitching his belt and trying to whip it loose of his slacks, the cotton of the belt loops moist, and the leather tacky. He yanked violently, as if ripping the cord on a lawn mower, but the belt stuck tight to his waist, his sweat-slickened glasses falling off his face to land in the green faux turf of the plastic carpeting on their back porch.

"Clete, no!" his mother said. "Clete, not today, okay? No, Clete!"

Clete's *disciplining* of Nelson had taken on a new intensity of late, causing Dorothy to absorb some of the violence intended for her son, a phenomenon that startled all three of them, even Clete, who on one occasion had stood over her body where she lay, near the kitchen sink, his hands trembling visibly, his bottom lip quivering.

But now the belt swung loose as a viper, its buckle a shining menace in the last of the afternoon light, its prong like a single fang, and Clete Doughty snapped the belt in the air to make it pop like a bullwhip. "Stop that crying, young man, you hear me? I won't have any more of it!"

How Nelson shrank smaller and smaller into the lap of his mother, so painfully aware of his own size, of the precipice he stood on—close to growing, to becoming something like a man, and yet, just a boy, still just a boy, cowering, whimpering against his mother's breast, waiting for the blow to come . . . *But surely he won't whip me here, in her arms, not here . . .*

They had been more frequent of late, the whuppings. If not the belt, then a wooden spoon, or a carefully selected switch from the weeping willow in their neighbor's yard. Nelson had never before hated a tree, a species of tree, until that willow; until he had been sent out there to select the very weapon that would make his bottom so sore that for the next two nights he could only sleep on his belly. Nor was choosing a weak switch a viable option, for his father would just have used that selection until it broke, and then demanded another.

"Excuse me," came a hesitant voice just then, the sound originating from around the garage, on the driveway, as unexpected as the telephone ringing, or every bell in the city sounding out in unison.

The sun, so hot where it hung in the western sky, seemed to have cooled its own furnace a bit. A pair of cardinals landed on the backyard feeder and began singing, as if they had accompanied the driveway guest. Wiping his hair back from his forehead, Clete stooped to retrieve his glasses, while Dorothy, relaxing her arms, looked up, her chest slowing its heave.

And Nelson's cries diminishing, but how? *How could, how could this be?*

"Golly, I'm sorry," said Jonathan Quick, appearing from around the house now. "I'm just . . . so sorry to be late."

"Oh, not at all, Jonathan!" Dorothy said. "Why you're just in time for cake and ice cream!"

Nelson madly wiped his nose, wiped his eyes. *Miracle of miracles!* Jonathan Quick, Life-Class Scout, fifteen years old, and already six feet tall. Varsity swimmer, junior varsity starting tailback, junior varsity backup shortstop, member of the glee club and the model railroaders. Jonathan Quick, standing in Nelson's driveway, holding a box wrapped all in newspaper funnies with a red bow sitting on top. He cast a furtive glance in Nelson's direction, the present in his hands like a hot potato he would so very much like to pass elsewhere.

"Well now," Clete said. "Jonathan. What a nice surprise." The belt sneaking its way back around his waist as he circled the picnic table to extend a hand toward Jonathan. "Delighted you could join us."

"I do apologize, sir," said Jonathan, now seeming to inch just slightly backward, retreating down the driveway from where he first appeared, "I can't stay too long, see. My granny had a tree limb come down in her backyard last night and I told her I'd be over to get that all cleaned up. I should've been here earlier, but my younger brother Frank was stung by bees today and we had to rush him off to the hospital. I didn't even know a person could be allergic to bees? Did you, Nelson?"

Nelson was just *so happy*, to be acknowledged in this way by Jonathan Quick, all the tears of just moments before this suddenly so trivial. "Want to shoot some arrows?" he blurted out.

"Ah . . . sure," Jonathan said. "Only—like I say, I can't stay overly long. 'Cause of my granny and all."

Nelson all but took Jonathan by the hand, leading him out into the backyard. Clete slumped down in a chair fuming, thrusting deviled egg after deviled egg into his furiously working jaws while Dorothy smoothed the tablecloth with her trembling hands. Smoothed it, again and again, as if her palms were two hot steaming irons.

Nelson's birthday guest stayed on for about twenty-five minutes. Enough time to shoot a few moderately well-aimed arrows, and then to join Nelson and his parents in an all-too-earnest rendition of "Happy Birthday." Enough time for a slice of cake and a scoop of melted vanilla ice cream. Time enough for Nelson to open the box and discover there a birch-bark basket.

"I made that, actually," Jonathan said. "I, ah, made it for you."

Nelson's hands held the basket reverently. "You made this for me?" he stuttered.

"Yeah, sorry the weaving isn't tighter, but . . . I've only made two. Yours was the first one." He blushed in the gaffe of this honesty. "I gave my granny the other," he added solemnly, though, in truth, his second attempt had been presented to Peggy Bartlett, a girl he hoped to ask to the Homecoming Dance that October.

"Oh, it's beautiful!" Dorothy exclaimed, making one, two, three small claps with her hands. "Such a talented young man!"

"Well," said Jonathan, extending the width of his hand to engulf Nelson's, "happy birthday, old chum."

"Thank you," said Nelson, still marveling at the basket. "Thank you so, so much."

And now the older boy fled back down the driveway while Nelson remained where he was, holding the basket, noting its lightness, the imperfection of its plait, wondering what he could fill it with that might be meaningful enough to complement his older friend's extraordinary generosity.

He set it on the picnic table, beside the presents his parents had bought him: a new pair of trousers, a build-a-working-clock kit, and a chapter book about the Civil War. But it was the basket his eyes kept coming back to, this beautifully imperfect little crown.

2

⤬

THE KETTLE HISSES AND NELSON PULLS IT AWAY FROM the flame before quickly bringing it into his tent, where he aims the kettle at his uniform, spitting hot water and sputtering steam out at the olive fabric. There are many ways to iron clothing without the aid of an actual iron, and Nelson is well practiced in a few different methods. His other preferred technique is to spritz vinegar on a wrinkly garment, though this lends both uniform and Scout a certain olfactory signature, and already he is struggling to gain friends.

Two times, he rushes with the kettle between bonfire and tent, applying steam to the shirt and shorts hanging from the line inside his tent. Satisfied at last that his uniform is impeccable, and aware that the eastern horizon has begun to faintly brighten, he walks the one-mile path to Camp Chippewa's central parade ground. This gives him time to warm up his lips, to practice his horn without fear of waking his troop, his leaders, or his father, who has agreed to act as chaperone for the week's stay at Camp Chippewa, though Nelson has seen little actual chaperoning from his father, who prefers to return to the campsite after each meal, where he sits at an aged picnic table reading a biography of the Chicago Cubs Hall of Famer Gabby Hartnett, of all people, or untangling the unruly knot of fishing line perennially dogging his reel. He does not even commiserate with the other fathers that much; the other fathers who follow behind their sons as the boys run from one camp activity to the other: perfecting their cooking skills, navigating an orientation course, fashioning a coin purse from a few ragged scraps of leather. For so many of these fathers, it seems to Nelson, camp may be a vacation from their jobs, their wives, the rest of their lives. Even the dads who go through the motions seem barely involved in the week's activities, rarely offering any kind of guidance or wisdom, except perhaps to say, "We could use some more wood for the fire." Or, "Careful, I heard a coyote last night." Always with a jocular elbowing, a conspiratorial wink.

Nelson has set a goal of earning no less than five merit badges during this week. He would like to earn the rank of Eagle Scout before his sixteenth birthday. Clete was a lackluster Boy Scout; Nelson has seen his father's moth-eaten uniform, its low-level badges of rank and honor. Deep into his cups, though, his father always reminds him of what counts: that he served with honor in the Second World War, moving north from Africa into Italy, and thence on to France, before being honorably discharged at the age of twenty-two with the rank of corporal. In his gut, though, Nelson feels that the skills accrued here at Camp Chippewa, and at his troop's weekly meetings inside the narthex of St. Luke's Lutheran Church, are already preparing him for a hallowed future in the United States military. He just needs his body to play catch-up with his brain. Maybe that would make his father proud of him, a life in the military, though Nelson has really no idea what such pride would even look like—let alone feel like. A hug, perhaps? More likely: a firm handshake and a grim smile to accompany it. Still, something to work toward.

The bugle in Nelson's smallish hands comes from his grandfather, who served in the First World War, a full half century ago. For the first several years of Nelson's life, the bugle sat on the fireplace's dusty mantel, beside a folded American flag, framed all in oak, and encased in glass. It had taken Nelson months of pleading with his father before Clete would allow the boy to play the horn, in his bedroom, with the door closed. It's been with him ever since, and he keeps its brass to a shine, a thing of beauty.

Most nights at camp, Nelson sleeps with his instrument, fearing the other boys might try to steal his horn; not because they are jealous of the bugle, but because they know how precious it is to him. He sees them pointing at him during meals from the other side of their mess hall table. Just as he sees that his own father does little to dispel their pointing, no more than the other fathers, or troop leaders, who sometimes eat with the boys, but as often as not seem to congregate at their own table. Nelson cannot imagine their conversation, these grown men in little-boy uniforms, eating the same chow, mumbling the same prayers and campfire songs, oaths and incantations. The only voice Nelson ever hears rise in his defense, as it does every so often, is Jonathan Quick's, and even he seems to react more out of irritation or boredom, revulsion even, or a desire to be contrarian, than any particular allegiance or compassion.

"Shut up, fellas," he'll say. "We're a troop, all right? Let's act like it." Or, "The next person who wants to tease Bugler can tease *me*, see how they like what happens next."

That is what the other boys call him, he now knows, *Bugler*. Not to honor the job for which he is known, but rather, just a nickname, spoken with derision. Another way to write him off.

THE PATH WENDS BETWEEN POTHOLE LAKES left by steamroller glaciers. From the safety of trees, deer spy on Nelson, fidget, and then bound off deeper into the woods. Once, a skunk scurried right past him, but thankfully left his tail lowered as he passed. The path opens up to the parade ground near the staff campsite, and already he hears activity coming from that direction: indistinct voices, cabin doors clapping shut, water splashing. Counselors and other staff live in small cabins, and there is talk that someday, even campers will move into such digs.

The fog is so thick he cannot see the flagpole some two hundred yards in the distance, the air heavy enough that he wonders if it was fruitless to iron his shirt. He marches forward, his leather boots slick with dew. At the flagpole, he consults his pocket watch, runs through a series of scales, and then, at precisely seven o'clock, slides his two feet together, stands perfectly erect, and raises his bugle to his lips to blow out reveille.

The horn sounds out over the parade ground, a plain of grass draped before the hillock where the flagpole stands atop a fieldstone base surrounded by a horseshoe of tall maples behind it. No matter what anyone else might think, Nelson revels in this responsibility. This sanctioned brass musical power he holds in his hands, blown deep from his belly and diaphragm, these bursts of notes that slice through the fog and into the forest, rip through those canvas tent walls, startle the forest creatures from their foraging, tingling even the dense white ear follicles of the camp's Scoutmaster, Wilbur Whiteside, a man aged some eighty years, who at the joyful sound of Nelson's blasts will practically leap from his narrow bed in the administrative lodge, towels jauntily wrapped around his neck and narrow waist, a giant pair of goggles making his eyes as oversize as a frog's, and tiptoe lightly down to Bass Lake, where, parting the cattails, he will lunge naked into those serene waters, there to swim one down-and-back, his old-man arms slicing the water. Nelson has never seen Wilbur's morning circuit, of course, but he's heard about it; an older boy, perhaps, up early to fish, startled by the sight of pale old Wilbur, cutting his way through the lake.

BY NOW, Nelson sees a few of the camp's counselors making their way toward the tent pole; stuffing shirt flaps into shorts, cinching belts, hiking olive-green socks high up on skinny-kneed legs. They come toward him talking hoarsely, laughing low. He can hear their boots squeaking over dewed grass, their pocket-change music, their hocks and loogies. If asked to label his admiration of these young men, he would call them heroes. But no one, of course, does ask him, and so his regard for them stays secret. A few of them consider him a brown-nosing toady, but most of them are affable enough and kind in their interactions with him.

They are, of course, what he is striving to be: taller, stronger, more sun-browned, more capable, ready with a joke, bold, devout, kind. Some of them serve as acolytes, others altar boys. Some are mock senators or UN ambassadors. Others are team captains, class presidents, newspaper editors. These young men, they do not cut him from the herd for his weakness, and they do not mock his otherness. They just move beside him at picnic tables, or on the archery range, instructing him, sharing the complex maneuverings of handy knots, how to tune a ham radio, where to divine water when there is none. They point to constellations in the sky, name certain stars, identify various manner of cloud in their west-to-east comings and goings, and what these celestial migrations mean for the next day's weather. They know the tracks of animals, the songs of birds, the husbandry of pigeons and rabbits. And, on most mornings, as they approach the flagpole, they acknowledge him with the kind indifference of an older brother. A few nods of the head, or perhaps a "Hey, Bugler" or a warm "Nelson." He has always longed for a brother.

Now he plays reveille for a second time and shortly thereafter more and more boys appear through the fog with their disorganized laughter, pounding feet, and play-punches. They assemble themselves by troop into two long lines facing the flagpole. Some idly twirl lengths of rope, or practice their knot tying. From Nelson's vantage they might be an army at the end of a long and desperate war when young boys and old men have become the only conscripts. Forming a separate line on the flagpole ridge, facing the downhill campers, are the counselors, cooks, and administrators, their posture noticeably stiffer, the hair on their kneecaps darker and coarser, their aftershave heavy on the air. Nelson notices his own troop take its position at the eastern edge of the parade ground and near the marshy shore of Bass Lake. His father is there among them, his morning beard not yet shaved, Scout kerchief askew, stretching his stiff arms in the air and offering the careless public yawn of a bored silverback gorilla with all the time in the world to forage.

Scoutmaster Wilbur is striding toward the line of counselors now, hands held at the small of his straightened back, and Nelson blows the final reveille. A few stragglers come bursting through the lifting fog as if fleeing some forest foe. They, too, stand at attention, now red-faced and out of breath. A color guard approaches the flagpole with utmost respect; Wilbur insists on this. And now, with the delicacy and deliberation of the nation's finest hotel staff making a bed, the flag is unfolded and then clipped to a lanyard and smartly, evenly raised up into the sky. Wilbur tolerates no herky-jerky movements as the Stars and Stripes makes its ascent, and it is something to behold, the flag rising so smoothly and purposefully it seems impossible to imagine that the machinery behind its flight is nothing but a team of teenage boys.

As the color guard retreats, everyone in camp raises a hand to his heart and recites the nation's pledge of allegiance. Then Wilbur delivers the morning messages. For many boys whose stomachs are grumbling quite loudly, these incessant messages are the most trying and mundane moments of the day. They simply cannot conclude fast enough for that mad dash to the mess hall, that great stampede of hunger.

"Scouts," Wilbur begins, "we have been blessed with beautiful weather this week and I certainly hope that you will all utilize your time effectively." He paces the grass near the flagpole, Nelson stiffening at his approach. "Because, as Benjamin Franklin once asked us, 'Dost thou value life? Then guard well thy time, for time's the stuff life's made of.' Scouts, I know that the sunset of your lives feels like a distant, distant thing, but I am here to tell you, our lives are mere instants, and I would hate to think any Scout amongst you would be spending his precious time here at Camp Chippewa idling away."

And now, a look of disquiet crosses old Wilbur's wizened face.

"I have heard some troubling reports, Scouts. Reports, truth be told, that predate your arrival this week here at Camp Chippewa, but nonetheless have reached my ears once again even as recently as last night. I don't have the full picture yet, but here and there have heard tell from upset and confused boys of clandestine meetings, vulgar happenings . . . It seems," and here he pauses, pressing a neatly clipped and filed finger to his dry lips, the very tip brushing his white, handlebar mustache, "that some amongst you have been participating in some rather disturbingly uncouth behavior, behavior totally unrepresentative of the Scouting Way. Behavior I find troubling, and, frankly, deviant. Furthermore, I fear this behavior is not being brought into the camp by young men, by young Scouts, but may in fact be perpetrated by my very own counselors—dare I say, my *staff*."

The parade ground is suddenly so, so, quiet. The sound of the flagpole's rope and lanyard—even the snap of cloth as the flag flaps in the slight breeze—seems deafening. There is an edge of gathering fury to Wilbur's voice behind a delivery that aches of crestfallen heartbreak. His small shoulders droop perceptibly inside his uniform.

"It may be," he continues, "that I cannot correct the behavior of those who I fear are organizing these most unfortunate events. It may be that something inside them is so twisted, it cannot be untwisted. But it is my duty as this camp's Scoutmaster to address those of you whose hearts remain devout, whose compasses remain true.

"It is a difficult thing, you see, to strive to be a good man. The whole world will try their level best to make you swerve, to bend your principles. I don't need to provide you with specifics. But if you've read your handbooks, you'll know what it is I'm talking about.

"Now, here is the thing: You are this nation's knighthood. *You* are the ones with a code, with a sense of duty, of right and wrong. It is *you* who will be challenged, asked to cheat, tempted to corrupt. And for those of you out there before me now, those of you true of heart, I want you to know, there is a reward in being good, in being decent, in being kind. It is this: You need not lie about your behavior, you need not hide anything, or be ashamed. You need never to apologize. You will be the leaders and the defenders. Those in our society who are weak, who are downtrodden or hard on their luck, their faces will turn to *you* for help or guidance. Which is why *you* must persevere, why your spirit must endure."

Now he turns his face toward the Boy Scouts of Camp Chippewa, and to his own counselors, to the secretaries of his office and to the cooks of the mess hall, some of whom have attended the morning flag ceremony in the stead of their peers, who even now are frantically scrambling eggs by the dozens and dozens, or frying pounds upon pounds of bacon and sausage.

"I am too old to even speak about the sort of behavior that has been reported to me. And too many of you young men out there, I fear, are too young, too innocent, too pure to be introduced to it all at this point in your impressionable lives. The truth is, I'm ashamed to stand up here amongst you, with this filthy cloud lingering over us all. It isn't Scout-like. My hope, then, is that my words this morning will be enough to put a stop to it—to put a stop to this abhorrent behavior. To make those of you complicit in the crime so ashamed, so chagrinned, that it will all come to a full and decisive stop."

He touches the waxed curls of his mustache.

"And now, to the wonderful volunteers working each evening after dinner on our network of paths, our canteen area, the Bass Lake lavatory facilities, and the old amphitheater, fixing its stage and seating," Wilbur says in summation, "I give you my thanks. There is no greater glory than that of a volunteer whose back burns with the honest work of labor given without reward.

"One final announcement. Please make your ropes ready."

At this, every boy in attendance holds his three-foot length of hempen rope in front of him, one hand on each end with the middle dangling below.

"Now," Wilbur says, "tie a square knot."

Hundreds of boy-hands begin tying. Nelson *wishes* with all his being that he could be included in this rite—who, after all, could tie one faster, or tighter?—but because he has been tasked with holding a horn each day, he is duly excused. Still, every part of his being recites, *Over under through; over under through: Voilà!*

By and by, boys begin holding their knots skyward, until every Scout has completed this most elementary task.

Giving a cursory survey across their ranks, Wilbur nods with satisfaction. "That is all, gentlemen."

THE PROCESSION TO THE MESS HALL is more somber that morning. No boys racing ahead of the pack to queue up outside the mess, huffing in the greasy smoke of sizzling bacon and hissing sausages. No younger boys kicking at puddles or hunting through the tall grass for garter snakes or frogs.

Nelson sidles close to Jonathan Quick, "What happened, Jon? Do you even know what Wilbur was talking about?"

"Who cares?" Jonathan shrugs. "You mixed up in it or something?"

"What? No—I just asked—I wouldn't dream—"

"Then forget about it, Bugler. All right? Anyway, everyone knows you're too busy earning merit badges to do anything even slightly wrong. Probably never been in trouble in your whole life, have you?" Jonathan doesn't even look at Nelson, doesn't even break stride.

Nelson feels his cheeks redden. He has never felt so acutely embarrassed by his own earnestness before. How stupid to have thought Jonathan might be impressed with his determination to reach Eagle.

"I'm sorry," Jonathan says, slowing his pace almost imperceptibly, "that was mean. You're a good kid. No, I don't know what Wilbur was talking about. I really can't imagine. I mean, guys sneak in dirty playing cards, and I've heard of one counselor who has a stash of *Playboy*s, but . . . I don't know. Could be somebody's smoking some mary jane or something."

Nelson stares up at Jonathan.

"Marijuana, you dolt."

"I'm sorry, Jon . . . What's marijuana?"

"Never mind."

The doors of the mess hall swing open and Scouts file inside to sit at their troops' assigned tables. Predictably, Nelson sits on the very end of his own troop's table until his father joins him, sliding his thick, pale legs over the table's bench and sitting down.

"Sleep well last night?" his father asks, scratching at the mosquito bites on his hairy arms.

"Yes."

"Wish I could say the same. Listened to an owl until damn near three in the morning. I would have shot it if I'd had a gun."

"I don't think you're allowed to shoot owls," the boy mumbles.

"What?"

"Nothing."

Nelson stares at the tabletop, mutters, "Scoutmaster Wilbur was sure angry this morning."

"Well, bear in mind, Nelson, Mr. Whiteside is of a generation that doesn't believe in smoking cigarettes or whatnot—sipping a little brandy, a whole laundry list of other so-called sins. I wouldn't worry too much about it. Probably some counselors gambling their paychecks away." Nelson's father peers at him strangely, through slightly squinted eyes. "See, it's his job to put that fear in you."

The food platters are nearly bare by the time they reach Nelson's end of the table.

"Mind if I join the other fathers?" Clete asks at last.

Nelson pauses as he bites into a blackened tongue of bacon. He *does* mind, does not want to be abandoned. "Okay," he manages.

"All right, then—I'm going to get more coffee, Nelson," Clete says, rising. "Could I bring you a glass of orange juice?"

"Yes, please," Nelson says softly. And now he is alone, a space between him and the next boy large enough to accommodate three Scouts.

All around the mess hall, boys are leaning into their tables, hunching over their plates, talking about Wilbur's speech. There is a conspiratorial buzz to this great room, with its pennants hanging from the trusses, its taxidermied busts of deer, moose, and bear staring down at the Scouts from the upper reaches of every wall. With its rustic but grandly vaulted ceilings, the building has the dark atmosphere of a Norse longhouse. Time creeps achingly slow for Nelson as, yet again, making silent lonely work of his cold eggs, he feels his neck and face grow red with shame. Then, just as the weight of his own alienation is about to overcome him, a hand settles on his shoulder, warm and firm. He flinches.

"We haven't had a bugler with your tone in years, son. Keep up the good work."

Nelson looks up to see Wilbur's pale blue eyes looking sadly down at him from above a mouth pursed into a woebegone smile.

"Thank you, sir."

"May I sit down?"

"Uh, sure." Nelson makes a small motion to indicate his father's vacant position. Beyond Wilbur, the boys of his troop seem to have collectively contracted, moving even farther away.

"Nelson, right?"

The boy nods.

"Where did that horn come from?" Wilbur asks. "Not likely purchased from any old downtown music store, I should think."

"Um, my grandfather."

"Get rid of these *um*'s and *uh*'s, my boy. It doesn't become you. Now, I know you're a young man—what—twelve, thirteen, but the thing is, you must answer a man of authority with force and confidence. If you need to hesitate, to gather your thoughts, that's understandable. But hide your pause behind a steady gaze, and then speak when you're ready and able. To me, these *um*'s and *uh*'s, they're like a rifle misfiring. And what good is a rifle if it can't shoot, I ask you?" The old man is grinning behind his mustache.

"Yes, sir."

"Was he in the First World War, your grandfather?"

"Yes."

"Is he still alive?"

"No, sir." Nelson looks at his plate of scrambled eggs.

Wilbur draws in a breath. "The world is a funny place. You would think a man must be invincible, immortal to survive a world war. But of course, that is ridiculous. We all die, in our time. If I may be so bold, Nelson, how did your grandfather die?"

Nelson hesitates, then looks at Wilbur with doleful eyes, "I don't know, sir. He just got sick. I went to visit him before he died, but—he wasn't talking then. He could only communicate by squeezing your hand. I was very young. Five, I think." Nelson remembers that hand, its coldness, the veins, his fingernails grown past their normal lengths, the cotton sheet drawn up to his grandfather's chin, and then, later, over his face.

His own father had never uttered a kind word about his grandfather, who, Nelson pieced together over the years, had been a bad drunk, and a failure at farming. Nelson's father, suffering the indignities of his father's flops, had apparently been forced to handle most of the farm's most tasking and onerous chores. The farm was eventually foreclosed and bought by neighbors for a song. It had been a beautiful piece of land, too, from what Nelson understood: four hundred acres of rolling fields and ridges, clear cold-water trout streams, and sandstone bluffs. There was said to have been an Indian burial mound even, a bear, and in the spring furrows each year arrowheads rose out of the loam and were collected by Nelson's father to be sold to a university professor for a nickel apiece. Rather than toil in the fields behind a team of horses, or even a tractor, Nelson's grandfather had seen fit to drink away his family's money at the taverns in Eleva and Strum.

"Well," says Wilbur now, his tone softening somewhat, perhaps as he observed Nelson's downcast eyes and sunken shoulders, "I'm sure that if he could see you now, he would be proud of how beautifully you play that horn. People forget it, but the bugler in a cavalry unit was almost as important as the general. Without the bugler, there was disarray, chaos. Communication is essential on a battlefield."

Nelson sits trying not to fidget, too nervous to touch his food, hyperaware of the eyes of his troop mates, the absence of his father, whom he can still see, standing at the coffee urn, casually stirring sugar and cream into a white mug. *My grandfather was a drunk*, he wants to say. *Dead far too young from drink. He stole this bugle from a dead German. He was a thief and a coward and a bad, bad man.*

"The other boys don't like you much, do they, Nelson?"

This time, something rises in the boy, and without the briefest hesitation, turning to look directly at Wilbur, he says, "No, they don't."

"Do you understand why, Nelson?"

"No, sir."

"It is because they see in you a challenge. *You* don't belong in the rabble, that mob. Which is precisely why *you* will be a leader. Your troopmaster, believe it or not, has communicated as much to me. As have some of the counselors here, who are impressed with your acumen." Whiteside scans the mess hall, exhaling deeply. "But, the truth is, not all of these boys will become good men, Nelson, good human beings. We do our best, try our damnedest to guide them, and instruct them. But in the end . . . Some boy in this room will become a murderer; another, a bank robber. Some of the boys in this room will cheat on their taxes, others, their wives. I wish it weren't that way. But when I hear you play that horn, I hear more than just a boy blowing air. I hear something echoing through time. Something that is good. Don't let them discourage you, Nelson."

The boy tries to process all of this, knows not what exactly to say, except, "Thank you, sir."

"When they are ugly to you, what they want most of all is to take that beauty from you, the beauty of that horn. They want to steal it, kill it. Don't let them. Be stronger than they are."

Wilbur cups his hand again on Nelson's shoulder, and this time the boy is aware of the hand's small size, no bigger than his mother's really, and in that instant, he longs for her. Longs for the one person who is always kind to him, always offering him something to eat or a book to read, always fluttering around their house, singing "Que Sera, Sera" or there again, sitting on their front stoop with the newspaper spread across her lap like a blanket, smoking her daily Pall Mall, hardly even drawing on the cigarette, but holding it just so, the smoke drifting over her face like a veil, and her beautiful fingers, peeling a small speck of cigarette paper off her lower lip. Closing his eyes for the briefest of moments, he feels Wilbur's hand on his shoulder and smells his mother's afternoon cigarette and the paper and ink smell of her newspaper and would give anything to be back home with her just now, even to be drying dishes or vacuuming the living room floor.

Then the hand is gone and Nelson opens his eyes.

"What did Mr. Wilbur want?" his father asks, standing over him, holding out the glass of orange juice he promised before.

Nelson accepts the juice, and drinks it down. Ordinarily, his first re-action to his father's voice is to glance down at his own feet, or the back of his own hands, but this time, he decides to employ Wilbur's advice. He looks directly at his father's face. Only, his dad is looking into his cup of coffee, then out the window, around the mess hall, anywhere but at his son. Nelson says nothing, almost as a kind of experiment, to see if his father really sought an answer at all. He stares up at his dad until finally the older man's eyes glance down and meet his. "What?" Clete asks.

I miss Mom, Nelson wants to say. "He was keeping me company."

"Who was?"

"Scoutmaster Wilbur."

"Oh, yes, of course."

"Dad?"

"What, Nelson?"

The boy wants to ask, *Do you love me?* "Thanks for the orange juice."

"Think I'll get myself another plate of eggs," his father says, before moving off again, striding toward the kitchen, plate held before him like a man begging alms.

3

X

THAT NIGHT, NELSON LIES IN BED READING HIS *HAND-book for Boys* by the light of his lantern. A moth bangs against the lantern's glass globe. Nelson rests the book down against his pale chest. Outside his tent are the sounds of laughter and of campfire flames sizzling and popping, of zippers yapping and outhouse doors clapping shut, the sounds slowly diminishing until the silence is punctuated only rarely by a cough, perhaps, or the long, low, wet note from a recently purchased dime-store whoopee cushion. The moth bounces again and again and again off the globe until reaching out a hand, and careful not to harm the creature, Nelson captures it in his fist. He feels the tiny thing, the hair of its legs, the tickle of desperation in its wings, the curiosity of its antennae. Opening his fingers he examines the moth resting in the palm of his hand.

For all his knowledge of knots, the constellations, poisonous mushrooms, rocks, minerals, and the trout streams of northern Wisconsin, Nelson knows next to nothing about moths. He blows a jet of air at the little creature and it alights from his hand, only to return to its fascination with the lantern. *What instinct is this?* he wonders. *Does it think it has touched the moon? The sun?*

Then: the sound of boots moving fast through the forest. Nelson's heart quickens. More footfalls, branches breaking, leaves tossed aside. Shrugging into a shirt, wrestling into trousers, and slipping on his boots, he readies himself. Then, calmly closing his eyes, he blows out the lantern, and counts to five. Slides his eyeglasses onto his face. When he leaves the tent, his pupils are wide, wide open, drinking in the light spilled by the moon and the stars. He holds his breath and listens. Far off he hears them, other Scouts, he supposes, crashing through the forest. He follows, moving low to the ground.

Thrilling it is, this night chase, and, *Where are their flashlights? Their lanterns, even some crude torch? Why the cloak and dagger?* Then he realizes, *These must be the deviants, the ne'er-do-wells Wilbur is in search of.* He moves all the faster for it.

How he navigates the wind-fallen sentinels, fuzzy with their thick green carpets of moss. Through groves of ferns, patches of raspberry canes sharp as concertina wire, and through aspen slash so young and tight it might as well be bamboo. And every few minutes, just to be sure, Nelson sinks to one knee, cups his hands around his ears, wills his own heart to slow, and focuses on the night sounds all around him. Only the flow of his own blood is nearly deafening: in the smallest veins of his ears, in his swollen hands and feet, but most of all his forehead and chest, where he feels his own circuitry sizzle with excitement.

But no sounds come to his ears. Not so much as a hoot from an owl, a tree frog chirping, not a single cicada rasping and rattling against the night. Nothing. And now, Nelson realizes, he is very far from his tent in a very dark forest, no path beneath his boots, no flashlight against the cold sweat of his hand.

His heartbeat seems to double in time now. With no idea even of what time it is, his first thought is the next morning's reveille. He cannot disappoint Scoutmaster Wilbur. And so, ever so silently he turns, hoping to retrace his steps, picking his way back the way he came.

Then: a sound—the snap of a branch.

It is not far off. Nelson ducks down, his head even with the fronds of the bracken. More sounds, breaking twigs, plants pushed aside. He lowers himself flat to the forest floor, where the salamanders and snakes and snails squirm, he knows, against the cool rot of the soil.

Whoever else is in the forest at this moment will not be his friend. Only now he cannot cry for help. Cannot expect his troop's leaders to protect him, or Jonathan Quick, or even his father.

Whispering. Two boys, perhaps three. Then, "*Buuu*-gler. Oh, Buuug-*ler*. We know you're out there. Should've stayed in your tent, Bugler . . ."

He holds his breath, dares not move so much as a centimeter.

"Tell us, Bugler. Do you know the way back to your tent?"

The beats in Nelson's chest intensify, even as his heart sinks. It is the strangest, saddest feeling. He imagines it is what a gambler must feel when the cards he has bet on don't stack up. When he realizes they've failed him.

"Because, Bugler. We *do* know the way. And, well, wouldn't it be a tragedy if poor Bugler's bugle were buggered before daybreak. Boo-hoo."

And now the woods erupt with snide laughter and sudden movement. For they are flying away from him. He can see their vanishing shoulders glowing white-blue with the moonlight filtered down through the leaves above, like epaulettes.

He rises to take chase.

This time, though, the woods seem to conspire against him. Every tree reaches out a sharp set of branches to scratch at his face. Each half-rotten log seems to roll toward his shins and knees and toes. The forest floor is now littered with dozens of glacial erratics: boulders and rocks, some as big as automobiles, looming up and out of the dark forest floor to impede his progress.

They would destroy his horn! His grandfather's horn! The only redeeming memento of the man!

Now he is out of breath, bleeding, sweating, and desperately afraid of his bugle being stolen or vandalized. Ahead of him, the boys seem to be opening a distance. Tears begin to craze down his face, but when he wipes at his cheeks, the backs of his hands brush no eyeglasses, no metal frames, nothing but the wet, raw skin of his hot, hot face. Stopping short now, he blinks out at the indistinct world, terrified, and sadder even than he'd been a moment before. His eyeglasses are lost then, too.

I want to go home, is all he can think; and: *I want my mom.*

He stops and sits down. There is no urgency now. They will beat him to camp, slink into his tent, find the bugle, and by the time he arrives, he will be lucky to ever touch the instrument again. He imagines them throwing it into the lake, or worse yet, taunting him with it, hanging it from a tree so that he's publicly humiliated into retrieving it. His grandfather's bugle, stolen off some dead soldier on a bloody battlefield and taken all the way home from Europe aboard a steamship in 1917. All the horrific nightmares it has already survived—mustard gas, trench warfare, cavalry versus machine guns—before being brought back across the ocean, and clear across America, all the way to Wisconsin and somehow not destroyed by Nelson's father or his aunts or uncles. Only to be presented to Nelson, who has now managed to lose it in this disgraceful fashion, stupidly leaving his tent in the dead of night to chase rule breakers through the forest. What was it he even hoped to achieve—or, more shamefully yet, to observe?

He sits there, swatting the hundreds of mosquitos that have by now descended upon him, and thinks of Wilbur, the old Scoutmaster who all but predicted this evening's happenings, told Nelson what to expect and why. *I have to be smarter, I have to be smarter than them. I can't fight all of them at once.* Finally, resigned to whatever it is he's going to find, he stands, and begins walking slowly in the direction he believes the camp might be.

4

IT IS AFTER MIDNIGHT AND THE HOUSE IS ABLAZE with light—every lamp, every bulb, every sconce—burning against the loneliness. The radio is on, loud. Having tuned the dial to some big-band music and at the kitchen sink, Dorothy whistles along to "In the Mood," makes a cacophonous clatter of washing and drying the few dishes she has dirtied. Her mother and father liked to dance to big-band music back in their day, and she has always felt a nostalgic pull toward Glenn Miller, Tommy Dorsey, Count Basie. She can see them—her parents—dancing in a crowded town hall, impossibly wide smiles on their faces as they swung and lurched, bopped and kicked.

This little house, in this cozy blue-collar East Hill neighborhood, the steady sound of the tire factory, even the noise of the train across the river—none of it is a comfort to her. She has locked every door and window of the house and even placed a dining room chair against the front door's knob. Sometimes, moving around the house, she laughs to herself, or sings—wants her voice to ward off any burglars or Peeping Toms.

Dorothy is, foolishly, she thinks, *afraid*.

"Don't be dumb," she mutters to herself. "More dangerous with him around, probably." Clete, she means. It is as if he has become another man, someone very different from the young soldier she fell in love with, honeymooned in St. Paul with, once shared a bed with. He is so frustrated, so bottled up with anger, such a bully. A few months ago, after church, he went into a gas station for a Coca-Cola, leaving her and Nelson in the car, and there was an instant when she considered crawling behind the wheel and leaving him altogether, driving away, anywhere, but then she was stymied by a ridiculous sense of hope. The hope that Clete would rise up out of this malaise, perhaps into a new job, or even enroll in a college—take advantage of the GI Bill, anything to escape sales and the frustrations that followed him home. Hope had held her hostage.

She vacuums the house for the third time since Clete and Nelson have left. Takes her time with the Hoover, making lines in the living room shag as deep and linear as furrows.

At two o'clock in the morning, the radio station signs off and she falls into Clete's chair, exhausted, and closes her eyes.

SHE WAKES TO THE SOUND OF RAIN hammering the roof and thunder shaking the china in her cupboards. Morning has come, darkly. All of the lights are still on, the radio back to its warbling. Dorothy is wearing yesterday's clothes. She teeters into the kitchen and percolates some coffee. Rubs at her shoulders. Her back is sore.

She sponges off her face, and brushes her hair, changes clothing. Taking a cup of coffee, she moves the chair away from the front door and finds the morning paper on the stoop. So she sits in the entryway, reading the paper, smoking a cigarette, and occasionally peering out at the street's gutters, where the rainwater gushes in torrents toward the city's two rivers. Daytime isn't so bad—she can see everything, for one thing, and, were it not for the rain, some of her neighbors would be about: hanging their laundry out to dry or weeding a garden, say, pushing a stroller, perhaps trimming a hedge. She thought that this week would be restful, time to sleep in, perhaps sit in the backyard and read a novel, or walk downtown and window-shop. She was unprepared for this loneliness. Perhaps it doesn't help that Clete and Nelson have their car, that she can't just drive around.

This is what it would be like. You would need a job, she thinks. *That's right. If you left him, you would need a job. Money for bills, groceries, an automobile . . .*

When she thinks about all the stumbling blocks, all the challenges involved in leaving Clete, her first impulse is simply to stay put, to absorb this man's frustration, to shield Nelson. She knows many other such women in just this position, and not a few of her aunts and cousins. Women biding their time . . . She wishes, for the boy's sake, that there was another answer, a surrogate for him. But her parents have passed on and she has no siblings. In six years he'll be off to college anyway, and then, she supposes, things will be quieter. Perhaps she can simply avoid Clete—why, they haven't slept in the same bed since before Nelson was born. Clete only seems interested in her to the extent that she can be counted on to provide meals and mix a strong drink.

Before the lunch hour, Dorothy spies the mailman, tiptoeing around puddles and dashing through the rain, water sluicing off his hat and poncho. She's always secretly admired Gordon, the mailman. Perhaps, she is even attracted to him; his face is square and soft, but deep dimples mark his cheeks and his eyes are bright and sincere. A man of seemingly infinite positivity, he wears a smile no matter the season or weather or the weight of his mailbag. A daily reminder to her that the world is *not* populated exclusively by men like Clete, but by optimists, too, happy men who whistle and sing as their shoes pound the sidewalks. Men who spontaneously throw the pigskin to neighborhood boys, or give golden butterscotch disks to the neighborhood girls. Rising from where she sits, Dorothy pushes the front door open, stands out on the porch, extends a hand beyond the eaves, feels the rain on her palm.

Rushing up the front walk, the mailman tips the brim of his hat. "A wet one out there!"

"Why, you're soaked to the bone, Gordon!" she exclaims. "Come inside and have a quick cup of tea."

"Oh, I couldn't, Dorothy," he says, shaking his head. "I'm near the end of my route, anyway." He peers around her, inside the house. "Say, where's that Nelson off to, anyway?"

"He's at Boy Scout camp," she says. "He and Clete. They come back in a few days."

"Bet you miss him," Gordon says.

She notes that it's the singular he's used, rather than the plural—rather than *them*. She nods.

"He's a good boy," Gordon nods. "You know, sometimes he'll walk my route with me. Not just a few houses, either. I mean, that boy will walk *for blocks*. Asks about foreign stamps and calligraphy. Envelope sizes and different inks, typewriters. The other day he was asking me about graphology. Had to explain to me what it was. I'm not talking kid stuff, you know? I mean, he was a good companion. Just curious about everything. Sharp cookie."

Dorothy feels a blush spread across her face. It's true, he is a good boy. "Thank you," she manages. Wonders what Gordon would be like as a husband, father. Then instantly feels guilty. No—she isn't that kind of wife, to be idly fantasizing about another woman's husband.

"Well," Gordon says, leafing through his mailbag. "Thought I saw only one letter. For Clete. From Wrigley Field, if you can believe that." He laughs, shakes his head.

"I'm sorry," Dorothy says. "Wrigley where?"

"You know, the Chicago Cubs. Ernie Banks. All that ivy on the walls. Wrigley Field."

She doesn't, exactly, but claps her hands in mock bemusement, "Oh, how silly of me. Of course, the Cubs." *The Cubs? For Clete?*

Gordon shakes his head apologetically. "Anyhow, here you go. The envelope got a little wet." He shrugs. "What can you do? It's a deluge. Anyway, my father was a farmer. I learned never to complain about rain. Have a good day now, Dorothy!"

And with that, the mailman charges back out into the storm, his head tucked against his chest, his uniform fairly drenched.

THAT NIGHT, at the barren supper table, Dorothy stares at the envelope, its flap all but open. She can't imagine what is inside. Nelson loves baseball, true, but Clete has never shown any interest in professional sports. The envelope is puffed out even, like it's inviting her to read whatever it is that may be inside, like it's holding its breath. She considers that even in its current state, Clete may accuse her of opening it. Maybe the best thing, she decides, is to quickly read what is inside and then seal the envelope back up, a little better even, lickety-split. And what if Clete has somehow ordered baseball tickets? Wouldn't that be grand? A father-son trip down to Chicago! How Nelson would love that! The Field Museum and Art Institute! Oh, a trip to the big city would be ever so stimulating for Nelson.

She reaches carefully for the envelope and with a tender fingertip, slides the flap up and open. This motion is slow and patient. Now the envelope gapes and she examines the flap. It is completely undamaged.

Inside, she sees, is a piece of letterhead. Her hands shake as she frees the paper, unfolds it, and reads:

1060 West Addison Street
Chicago, Ill. 60613
June 21, 1962

Mr. Clete Doughty
1325 Fairway Street
Eau Claire, Wis. 54701

Dear Mr. Doughty:

After careful consideration, the Chicago Cubs and Wrigley Field are pleased to offer you the position of Assistant General Manager of Concessions & Vending. Your employment is effective August 1st. Please report to the Clark Street entrance for employee processing.

Sincerely,
Mack Prior
General Manager of Concessions & Vending

Stunned by this, Dorothy delicately slides the letter back into its envelope, like the secret it is, and exhales deeply. The rain continues to fall.

After some time has passed—she's not sure *how* much, really—Dorothy rises from the table, searches through a drawer until she finds a small jar of glue, then gently seals the envelope shut. She carries it to a wire basket near the front door, where the rest of Clete's mail awaits his return.

She pulls a red box of Pall Malls from her apron, and lighting one, stands at the front door, blowing smoke outside.

"What am I going to do?" she whispers. "What the hell am I going to do?"

So the die is cast now, and some of her wishes seem to have come true, in the saddest of ways. Just like that; be careful what you ask for—because you just might get it.

She stubs out the cigarette, walks back into the kitchen, grabs a stack of plates from the cupboard, and for a moment stands in the middle of the room, holding all of that porcelain above her head, her shoulders shaking with fear and sadness, but she does not throw the plates at the floor. Can't. And so she lowers herself to the floor, the dishes carefully balanced on her lap, and cries. She was not raised to waste good things, especially in anger. And what a silly demonstration that would be anyway, with no witnesses, in a house otherwise ever so quiet. There is no radio that might console her now, no vacuum noise that might bury her sadness.

After a time, she breathes deeply, begins to think of answers to her question.

5

✕

HOURS LATER, FEET RAW IN SWEATY SOCKS, NELSON stumbles back into camp. It is his nose that led him the final thousand feet or so: the smell of the latrine overlaid with wood smoke. All is quiet; no one seems to have noted his disappearance. He skulks into his tent, removes his shirt and trousers, kicks off his boots, pulls off the socks wet with perspiration, and lies on his cot, so relieved to be at rest and free from the mosquitoes. He does not know how he will explain the glasses to his father, but is too exhausted to further consider it.

Reaching out to the right of his cot, where he hangs the bugle each night from a tiny nail hammered into a wooden post, he is shocked to feel cold metal, where he expected to only wave his fingers in the thick air. Clenching the bugle, he pulls it from the nail and holds it against his chest, feeling the cool contours of brass, which have been quite rudely deformed.

The bell is badly bent and crumpled in the edges, so that it feels like what he imagines the early stages of cauliflower ear must be like, something beginning to fold into itself. The mouthpiece, too, is now misshapen, though the coils seem blessedly intact. He runs his hands over and over across the metal, feeling every ding, every scrape, every dent.

And then it hits him: the bugle smells of piss, too. He imagines them, spraying their pee over his instrument. Who could say how many of them had emptied their bladders into his bugle? He shakes his head, no longer tired. Dawn isn't so far away and he cannot play the bugle in this state; it must be cleaned, perhaps repaired.

He keeps a washbasin in the tent so that he can avoid trips to the shower room whenever possible, not feeling safe in those claustrophobic stalls constructed of concrete block, with their well-mildewed tile floor, and the weak yellow light thrown by a single cobwebbed bulb, with the other boys amid the cacophonous sounds of jetting water, acerbic shouts, the snap of wet towels. No, his washbasin and mirror have always sufficed. Lighting the lantern, he sits on the cot and washes his face clean, then wets and parts his hair.

He is still a frightful mess: cuts, bruises, bags sulking beneath bloodshot eyes. This morning he will not tend their fire. With a spray bottle of vinegar and water, he spritzes his uniform, dresses, and leaves the tent. Already the sounds of whippoorwills and robins and wood thrush. The stars disappearing into the paling sky by the dozens.

Working the brass with his hands, he pushes out some of the dents, but the bugle is forever brutalized. No amount of coaxing will burnish out the scrapes and scratches that adorn it now, as if the bugle has just come through a war much worse than its first one. Nelson walks hard in the direction of the parade ground.

Low clouds almost meet the terrestrial fog and though it is early, rain seems a promise. Nelson is thankful; he'll be able to return to his tent between merit badge classes or assemblies and perhaps even sneak a nap in, unnoticed. He has never napped at camp before, like some of the older boys who practically sleep away their entire week at camp, but now he yearns to.

Halfway to the parade ground, Nelson takes a side trail toward Bass Lake. In his pocket: a small container of dish soap. At the shoreline, he unlaces his boots, hangs his socks on the limb of an alder, and moves out into the shallows.

The lake bottom is gravelly on his toes, the water morning-cool. He can see next to nothing, but feels the tiny tickles of minnows rushing around his ankles, and in one moment almost amusing in its sharp pain, the pinch of a crayfish at his big toe. Kneeling in the lake, he pulls the crayfish free and holds it up and out of the water, examines its ruddy armor and angry pincers, its inquisitive antennae.

Once, he and his troop mates harvested crayfish by the hundreds and then boiled them, spilling the well-cooked crustaceans out onto a picnic table and roaring with glee before busting their shells to suck at their tiny claws and thoraxes for meat. That seems an impossible memory now. He tosses the crayfish far out into the lake, then pours a small amount of soap onto the horn and begins washing off the piss tainting his beloved heirloom.

His toes are still wet when he pulls his socks on, laces up his boots, and begins the final march to the parade ground. Beside the naked flagpole, Nelson raises the horn to his chapped lips, tastes his mother's blue dish soap, and blows.

The music that limps out of the horn is pitiful, as damaged as the instrument itself. Nelson slumps, waits for ten minutes to pass, then blows again. By now, Scouts have begun collecting on the parade ground and the counselors beneath the canopy of the massive maple, the birds beginning to sing with more vitality, even as the sky darkens and a rumble of thunder rolls over the forest.

After his final muted reveille, Nelson steps away from his appointed spot and joins the line of counselors. He can sense a devious trilling from the Scouts before him, and almost does not blame them. He is a joke, his arms and face badly scratched and the bugle sounding less like a call to battle than some injured waterfowl. He hangs his head as the color guard raises the flag; everyone knows they will be rushing to pull it right back down any minute when the rain comes. For a moment, he is thankful he can't see anything, the world a smudged blur.

If Wilbur has noticed Nelson's off-key reveille, he betrays nothing, saying only, "Foul conditions moving in, boys, a real squall. Recall your weather safety tips. We'll stay indoors today, then, as best we can. A good opportunity to write your mothers, I would remind you, and read your handbooks. Keeping one's mind sharp is just as important as a fit body.

"Now, please ready your ropes and tie a bowline."

Nelson's mind comes into sharp focus, crystallizes: *Here is the rabbit's hole, out runs the rabbit, rushes around the tree, and hops back into its hole.*

One by one, several hundred lengths of rope rise into the air in the shape of a knot and Wilbur surveys the boys' efforts.

"Very well," he nods. "All right, then—dismissed."

Careful to camouflage himself amid a crowd of taller counselors, Nelson falls into the throng. In the mess hall, he takes his appointed place, at the end of the table, feeling his face go hot with embarrassment. He is so lonely right now, so utterly ready to return home.

His father sits down beside him without so much as a slap on the back or a rub of the shoulder—nothing. Nelson steals a glance at him. *He doesn't even notice my glasses are gone.* His father seems well rested, almost happy. This is quite at odds with his visage at home, always so haggard and angry looking.

"Morning, Dad," the boy offers.

"Good morning, Nelson," Clete replies, sipping at his coffee.

Are you having a nice time? Nelson wants to ask. He hopes so. Would like to imagine some idyllic weekend when he and his father could go camping together, just the two of them, without any of his father's office worries, without any bottles of brandy or newspapers or squawking television. Just the two of them exploring the backwaters of a state park or paddling a canoe down the Red Cedar River. Wonders if this fantasy was ever, or could ever be, a possibility. Or would such a trip actually be an expedition of frustration and anger, so much time in a canoe without any words, just fuming resentment?

Nelson looks down the table at some of the other boys. Even without his glasses, several of them appear exhausted, with mosquito bites decorating their foreheads, and forearms marred with the same sorts of cuts and bruises as his own. *The vandals*, he thinks. The boys ignore him, waiting restlessly for the morning prayer, scratching at greasy hair with dirty fingernails. *Barbarians*, he thinks.

Breakfast is pancakes, sausages, and orange slices. Nelson is famished, and when the serving plate comes to him, he serves himself greedily, eating quickly and ravenously, thankful at least to have a mouth full enough that he needn't struggle to manufacture conversation with his father. Not that there was much dialogue at home, true. Though Nelson knows there are, somewhere, fathers and sons who talk, who sit beside one another at ball games, who toss a baseball in the backyard, who rake leaves as a team. It's just that this is not his experience, his life. A normal evening at home is his father arriving late, retreating to his chair to read the newspaper, and then his mother entering the family room with a TV tray laden with Swiss steak or chicken Kiev and a brandy old-fashioned. Sometimes Nelson kneels to unlace and remove his father's shoes; other times, he simply sits in the same room quietly, waiting to be asked about his school day, but those inquiries rarely come, and almost always, his father falls asleep right there, in situ, mouth agape, highball drained, newspaper neatly folded into quarters and set beside the chair.

After breakfast is finished and the Scouts have been dismissed, Nelson rushes out of the mess hall and into the densely humid air. Now thunder booms out low and loud over the camp, with not a bird to be seen, nor a breath of wind to unsettle the leaves of the trees. He walks quickly back to camp and enters his tent just as the first slow, fat drops of rain beat upon the canvas roof like fingertips flicking the fabric.

Nelson crawls onto his cot, pulls a light blanket over his body, and biting a rolled-up pair of socks, begins sobbing until he falls asleep.

6

"HEY, BUGLER, WAKE UP. WAKE UP, BUGLER."

The words are like a rope, pulling him up and out of the deep waters of sleep, but slowly, for he is a very heavy anchor at the bottom of a cold, black northern lake.

"Bugler, wake up. You missed lunch."

Now he bursts up and out of his slumber, as if breaking through a crust of ice to gulp down breaths of cold air. Sitting erect, he instinctively reaches beside his cot for his glasses, only to feel nothing, momentarily panics, before remembering—they are gone.

"No, Nelson," says Jonathan Quick, "here they are. Right here, in my hand. Here you go."

Reaching out, he feels the shape of the frames, slides them on and over his ears, settles them onto his nose, perhaps a little askew, but still—he is grateful. One of the lenses is cracked, but at least he can see. "Where'd you find them?" he asks.

"In the woods. Totally by chance," Jonathan says, looking at his boots. "Listen, I'm sorry about that lens, it might be my fault. Then again, that's how I found them. See, I heard a little crunch, looked down at my boot, and . . . there they were." He peers around the tent. "Here, I brought you something." He hands Nelson what appears to be a peanut butter sandwich on Wonder Bread. "You haven't eaten since breakfast."

Nelson swings his feet off the cot and sits, perches the glasses on his forehead, and rubs at his eyes with his free hand. Chews the sandwich suspiciously, won't look at Quick.

"You found them in the woods?" he asks.

"Sure, well, I was out doing a little compass work and then, well, like I said, I apologize, Bugler, but I heard a little crunch, and sure enough. Figured they must be yours, since you weren't wearing them this morning at reveille."

"So you just—of all the acres and acres of land, you just happen to step on my glasses?" He chews slowly, his mouth very dry without any cold milk to wash the sandwich down.

Rain continues to drum the canvas as water drips steadily down the central tent pole to the ground below. It will be a wet night, Nelson knows. Jonathan Quick's light mood seems to have dissolved.

"That's right," Jonathan says. "I would have thought you'd be grateful."

"Somebody—last night—last night someone destroyed my bugle. Pissed on it. Bent it all out of shape."

Jonathan tries not to smile, not to laugh, his hands rising to his mouth.

"It's not funny."

"Come on, Nelson, it's a *little* bit funny."

"That's not just some ordinary horn, Jonathan. It was my grandfather's. It was in World War One. And they, those bastards . . . They pissed all over it! To hell with you all!"

"Hey, watch it now, Bugler. I'm the best friend you've got."

"Some good *that's* done me. Nobody talks to me, unless it's to make fun of me. Nobody eats with me. And now my bugle is destroyed. In fact, I'm of the mind that you were out there last night. With them. Maybe you pissed in my horn along with everyone else, huh?"

"Come on, Nelson. We were just out . . . Look, we were out smoking cigarettes, okay? And you scared them. That's all. I didn't know they were going to hurt your bugle. So . . . Listen, I apologize about that, I really do, *geez.*"

"So you smoke cigarettes, too?"

Jonathan runs a muscled hand through his long, thick, brown hair. Nods his head. "Some of the older guys might have been up to something else, but I wasn't invited to wherever they were going. I think you interrupted them."

"Why didn't you say something to me?"

"I didn't know it was you."

"Aw, horseshit, Jonathan. The other boys seemed to know pretty damn fast." He is not accustomed to cursing, but twice now he just swore in Jonathan's presence, and sees the power in that forbidden language. How it surprises the older boy, makes wide his eyes and straightens his posture right up. Nelson feels instantly older, wiser, hardened even. He likes swearing, likes that word, *horseshit.* It's a good one.

Jonathan lowers his head, examines the backs of his hands. "Sorry, Nelson. I've let you down."

Nelson can't remember the last time someone actually apologized to him. What's more, he recognizes that Jonathan is right; he is the best friend Nelson has at the moment.

"It's all right, Jonathan. Thanks for finding my glasses."

Jonathan glances up at the younger boy. "You can still see with those things? They're pretty messed up."

"Better than being blind—that's for sure. Last night I wandered around the forest for—I don't know—hours, trying to find the camp-site. Couldn't see a thing."

Jonathan shifts uneasily, clears his throat, seems ready to leave. Only now, Nelson is desperate for him to stay, this young man he so admires who, inexplicably, treats him with some degree of kindness. "I have chocolate," he blurts out, "and pretzels. We could play cribbage, or, I brought some baseball cards, just in case someone wanted to trade. You could look through them; I could even give you one or two."

Standing halfway up, the older boy parts the tent flaps, peers out-side at the wet, green world soaked under a deluge that shows no sign of relenting. Nothing stirs, except the leaves trembling with the steady pitter-patter barrage of the afternoon rain. He moves back into the tent. "Sure," he says, "we've got time."

THEY SIT ON OPPOSITE ENDS OF NELSON'S COT, the cribbage board between them, a Hershey's chocolate bar and some pret-zels arrayed proudly on a Scout kerchief. The lantern throws a warm, happy light over it all and by and by the boys pass a canteen back and forth. They play three games of cribbage—Jonathan winning twice—and then Nelson produces a four-inch stack of baseball cards rubber-banded together and stored in the same shoe box that holds his snacks.

"Do you collect cards?" he asks Jonathan.

"A little bit," the older boy shrugs. "I used to collect 'em more, you know, when I was younger." He blushes at the gulf in years between the two boys that he's just emphasized. "Right now," he shrugs, "I'm trying to save money for a car."

"Oh," Nelson says. The notion of driving an automobile seems light-years away, some unknowable parallel reality far out in a distant galaxy. "How much does that even cost?"

"More than *I* have," Jonathan says, unwinding the rubber bands and beginning to study the cards. "My dad says he'll help out, but . . . still. I gotta have a couple hundred, probably. Hey, you got any Eddie Mathews cards?"

"I think so. What I really try to collect are rookie cards."

"Why?"

"I think they'll be worth more."

Jonathan balances a little square of chocolate on top of a pretzel, then pops it in his mouth, seeming to relish every chew. "Worth more?"

"Well, I mean, if I hang on to these cards *long* enough, maybe they'll be worth something. You know? My grandma collects first edition books, and some of them are worth dozens, maybe hundreds of dollars. Maybe more. So I was thinking, if I can keep some of these rookie cards safe, maybe they'll be worth a lot of money someday, like those first editions. Because that's what a rookie card is, really, a first edition."

Jonathan peers at the cards with what looks like slightly more reverence. "Huh. I just thought you put 'em in your bike spokes, or used 'em for BB gun practice. Or bookmarks."

"I really shouldn't have them rubber-banded them like that, either," Nelson continues, "'cause the pressure, you know, leaves little indentations on the sides of the cardboard. Nobody else seems to care, but I notice. My grandma barely touches her first editions, and—you're not going to believe this—sometimes she wears white gloves when she does."

"No kidding," Jonathan says, shuffling slowly through the stack, and then scrutinizing one card at length. "What about this Pete Rose guy? He any good?"

"Nice choice," Nelson nods. "He might even win Rookie of the Year. I heard that earlier this season, he ran to first base on a walk. You believe that? A walk!"

"You only have one of his cards, though. Are you sure?"

"That's okay, take it," Nelson says. "Hey, thanks for finding my glasses. Really, I mean it."

Jonathan slips the baseball card into the breast pocket of his uniform shirt, exhales slowly, and dips toward the tent flaps.

"Jonathan," Nelson says.

"Yeah."

"We're friends, right?"

"Sure, Nelson—sure we're friends."

Nelson smiles at his cot, thinks, *I'm so glad.* "Then what were those guys doing last night, out there in the forest?"

Jonathan looks at him with sad, serious eyes, then exhales. "I don't know, old chum. But it wasn't knot tying or practicing their first aid skills."

And now Jonathan turns his back on the younger boy, moves his head out of the tent, into the rain, "Sometimes," he begins quietly, "I think you get mixed up in something, and it's like stepping into a river. The current takes you and the next thing you know, you're swimming . . ." He stands up fully and is gone, the flaps undulating behind him like green canvas curtains.

"Jonathan," Nelson calls out, still sitting on his cot, holding two handfuls of baseball cards. But by the time he peeks his head out into the rain, Jonathan is thirty steps away, hands buried in his pockets, chin pointed at the mud, and small puddles of water already collecting in his footsteps.

AFTER DINNER, several of the counselors perform a skit called "Iron-Gut." Then four Scoutmasters gather into a barbershop quartet and warble on and on for close to a half hour, and later, a radio is wheeled to the middle of the dining hall and every boy, every father leans closer to catch—an afternoon game *way out west,* in San Francisco—Warren Spahn pitching against Juan Marichal. Evening begins to drape over the forestland, though a steady rain still pounds the mess hall's sharply inclined roof. Even the Scouts, stir crazy as they are from being cooped

up inside all day, seem disinclined to leave their mugs of hot chocolate, sugary tea, or milky coffee. A fire is built in the grand fieldstone
hearth and the light inside the long room shifts toward a warm pump-
kin orange while deep shadows collect heavily in the corners. Now the
air smells of chocolate and peanut butter and sugary dough as the cooks
circulate baskets of still warm cookies, and when night is finally and
truly ensconced over the camp, Nelson's troopmaster, Mr. Blanton,
strides toward the two oversize doors of the mess hall, steps outside,
withdraws a hand from the dry warmth of his pocket, and offers it out
beyond the protection of the eaves, later returning to his troop's table,
declaring, "Come on, boys. I don't think we'll melt."

The steady, sometimes violent rain of the afternoon and early evening has been replaced by a dark, drizzling mist that seems to fall from
a bank of clouds just above the treetops. The wet air feels good in Nelson's lungs, as he walks with his troop, the boys recounting the baseball game, the two great pitchers. Across the asphalt road that snakes
through camp, frogs bound ahead of the boys, while steam rises off the
pavement to join the clouds overhead.

Nelson's father is suddenly beside him.

"You found your glasses."

He did notice! "Oh, yeah . . . They fell beneath my bunk. Just couldn't
find them this morning."

"Are they broken, Nelson?"

The boy fidgets, removes the glasses from his face, rubs at the bridge
of his nose. "Yes. I'm sorry, Dad. Guess I stepped on them in my tent
this afternoon when I was looking around. I didn't mean to."

"You've got to be more careful with your glasses, Nelson. How many
times have we had to have them repaired?"

"Three—no. Guess, this'll be the fourth."

"Christ, you think that's free? You think new lenses, new *frames*—
you think any of that is free?"

"No, Father."

"Christ."

"I'm sorry." Nelson shrinks slightly, leaning away from his father as they walk, ready for the blow to come, even here, even at camp.

"Is everything quite all right, Nelson?"

Now his father is looking at him through the darkness with a degree of concern that Nelson rarely witnesses.

"You have to protect those glasses, Nelson," his father says. "Okay? I mean, what if your mother and I couldn't afford to fix them, huh? Then what? What would you do? How would you survive? Do you understand?"

"Yes, Father," he says. *Although, why wouldn't his parents have enough money to fix his eyeglasses? That doesn't even make sense . . .*

His father hums a deep low note of dissatisfaction. "All right, then, sleep well, Nelson. Be well rested for tomorrow morning. Your bugling this morning . . . Why, it was as if you stepped on your horn as well . . ." And with that Nelson's father moves off without another word into the unknowable night.

BACK AT CAMP there is some excitement when a younger Scout encounters a porcupine at the outhouse, but the startled creature lumbers slowly off into the ferns and isn't seen again. Nelson starts the evening fire, stacks a load of kindling and logs next to the fire ring, and then slinks off into the near shadows and listens as the other Scouts discuss the baseball game they've all heard.

Mr. Blanton and several fathers stand tightly together, laughing, a silver flask flashing between their hands in the firelight as they pour a quick glug or two into their coffee mugs. Nelson's father stands off to the side, talking quietly to another father who stares into the fire, nodding from time to time. Clete's glasses glint in the light like mirrors and his hands move excitedly in a way that seems only to push the other man farther away, closer to the fire. Nelson wonders if he isn't talking about his work in insurance, perhaps trying to sell the man something, wondering if that wasn't the whole pretext for participating in the trip. Just what Nelson needs—not only is he a kid no one wants to be friends with, he's a kid whose father has spent summer camp trying to sell insurance policies to all the other dads who were just trying to have a good time. The boy shakes his head, and retreats to his tent. He is just . . . so very tired.

Nelson removes his clothing without the light of the lantern, shivers in the wet air of the tent. The temperature has fallen, and a slight wind rustles the bottom of the tent's canvas, sends big fat drops of rainwater sliding off the leaves above to land on the tent in sudden violent pats. He crawls into his thick, downy sleeping bag, happy as always to be alone when no one expects anything different from him. He curls into a small ball and rubs at his arms with clammy hands. Within moments, he is asleep.

7

HE WAKES TO RIPPLING LAUGHTER AND THE WET COL-
lapse of his tent all around him: a pole banging against his forehead, the
damp canvas slapping down onto his dry sleeping bag, and then, more
alarming yet, the lantern pitching over, the dangerous smell of kerosene,
the panic of imagining his bugle again stolen, his baseball cards suddenly sodden with rain and mud. Then, just as quickly, the laughter
is gone, and Nelson sits on his cot, spreading his arms to lift the wet
canvas off himself, trying to find the lantern with his feet then locating
the matches, only hoping he does not set himself on fire.

   The lantern hisses to life to reveal all of his belongings, which seem,
for the most part, intact and dry. Only his sleeping bag is already water-
logged. Dressing quickly, he manages to resurrect the tent, and then,
standing in the midnight damp cold, tilts his head to the heavens. Not
a single star, not even the searchlight of the moon to shine through the
gray wispy hair of a cloud.

Nelson does not feel like sleeping alone now. And so he walks through camp—starkly quiet, without even much in the way of snoring—and comes to his father's tent. He pauses, for it is always so difficult to announce oneself at the door of a tent: no door to knock against, no knocker, no doorbell. Just the straight line of a vertical zipper. He clears his throat, loudly.

Nothing.

He leans in close to the canvas and in a polite, hoarse voice, says, "Dad? Dad? It's me, Nelson."

Then, the distinct sound of his dad's snuffling, the cot protesting beneath his shifting body, the rustle of his sleeping bag.

"Dad?"

"Nelson? Are you all right, boy?"

"Can I come in?"

A zipper whizzes open. "Quickly," his father says.

Nelson crawls inside, zippering the night safely back out. *No one is going to knock this tent down*, he thinks, feeling instantly safer.

The tent looks remarkably like his own: impeccably neat, but with the dense canvas-scented air marked by pleasant hints of tobacco and aftershave. His father's effects are all in order: shaving kit, clothing, boots, an issue of *Life* magazine, his salesmanship books. Now Nelson lays his sleeping bag down alongside his father's cot and, crawling into the bag dressed in warm clothes, tries to fall asleep, but sleep does not come.

"Dad?" he whispers finally. "You still awake?"

"Go to sleep, Nelson. For Christ's sake."

He decides to plow forward. "I miss Mom."

He can hear his father turn to face him.

"Do *you* miss her, too?" Nelson asks.

"Of course. Now go to sleep."

"Dad, why are you so . . . Is everything okay at work?"

His father is quiet.

"Dad?"

"I told you to go to sleep."

"It's just . . . Mom cries all the time."

He hears his dad sigh, smells his breath. Then feels a hand, this thick, heavy hand on his head, rubbing his hair. Nelson waits for his father to say something, *anything*, but he doesn't. Just goes on touching his ears, his cheeks, his nose, his lips. It's as if he's a blind man, and Nelson some stranger, a new face to be memorized.

"Dad?"

His father's hand retreats, and there is the sound of his shoulder turning.

"Go to sleep, son."

Nelson closes his eyes.

NOT LONG AFTER FALLING ASLEEP, the boy may have dreamed, or imagined, he felt a warm hand resting again on his head, his shoulders, and the soft sound of a grown man crying gently.

8

HE SWIMS HARDEST THINKING ABOUT THE BAYONETS. In his worst nightmares, he feels the stick of a bayonet, plunges the blade into one body after another, at one point breaking the tip off between one brown-eyed boy's ribs. The machine guns sound like hell's snare drums and the wet *thwump* of bullets ripping through the boys behind him is nothing he can ever forget, a kind of psychic shrapnel, lodged in his memory.

Hardly an even match—entrenched artillery and machine guns versus bayonets and poorly aimed and sporadic rifle fire. At one point, Wilbur falls down into a bed of French wheat, and watches as his men, his *boys*, go screaming past him, their legs hurtling, their eyes far, far too wide, and the world so terribly loud, the air full of hot lead and blood and fire and the terrified bawling of soldiers dying, young men who are little more than children.

He swims harder, faster, cutting his way through the cold lake water.

How long did he lie listening as his men died all around him? Long enough for day to slide into night. Long enough for a flare to land not five feet away from him and begin to burn away at the wheat—that red-pink light, like a dragon's eye, and the smell of sulfur, too. Then an epoch of thirst as the smoke drifted over him, hanging, and the sounds of men dying, their wounds sucking or scorched or leaking into the ground. How many of them tried to pull out crumpled sheets of paper and blunted pencils to scrawl out a few last words to mothers, fathers, sisters, or brothers? No stars to shine the path to some other world. No craggy-faced moon to study. No night birds or bats or nocturnal beasts. Just ragged coughing and shameful crying. Gunshots here and there, almost disinterested-sounding, and then silence.

Wilbur pretended to be dead. Let dozens, perhaps hundreds of men run past him on that battlefield. Heard medics come toward him with their red crosses and white flags. They all died, too. Three days later—maybe more—delirious with thirst and hunger, he is discovered by some doughboys who proclaim him a hero, an uncommonly brave survivor. Every other member of his unit died, he learns, running forward while he survived on his back.

BACK HOME, in Durand, Wisconsin, he is appointed the grand marshal of a parade that processes straight through the center of town. Young women toss him roses, blow kisses. Little boys plead for his autograph. Politicians slap his back. A tailor offers him a new suit. For two years before he leaves Durand, he cannot depart a bar without being thoroughly drunk; nor will anyone allow him to buy his own beer.

He finds a job at Camp Chippewa, where it is quiet. Where his military background is considered a boon, though the boys he serves can have no real notion of what it is he is supposedly famous for.

Each autumn, when the Scouts leave, he drives the camp pickup truck, a navy blue International, up to Hurley, where he pays to lie with women. He cares not whether they are young or old, or particularly beautiful even. What is important, everything else aside, is that they allow him, if only for ten minutes, to rest his head on their breasts, their stomachs or laps. Sometimes, they touch his head, or sing to him.

He stumbles from bar to bar, drinking boilermakers, letting the miners up there take swings at him. Many of them fought in the war as well. Many of them lost brothers, uncles, cousins in the war. None of them, he imagines, rode down the main streets of their hometowns on a parade float.

After two weeks of this, he drives to the Porcupine Mountains in northern Michigan and wanders those virgin hemlock forests, drinks freshwater from streams, startles black bears. For the first five years or so, he chooses a high escarpment that overlooks a winding river that leads to a long, narrow lake. Beyond the lake are hundreds of miles of primordial forest. Behind him, Lake Superior. On that escarpment he places a pistol in his mouth and wraps a finger around the trigger. He closes his eyes. But he can never squeeze it, that sharp comma of metal.

Once, he opened his eyes and there before him sat a hawk with a freshly killed rabbit in its talons.

That was the last year he tried to kill himself. The first year he reconciled to start living a decent life, a life without vice, without debauchery or violence.

9

NELSON SITS FOR SOME TIME ON THE ROCKY BASE OF the flagpole, just after the sun has risen. The lanyard and rope ring against the metal pole intermittently, but otherwise, there is no sound, not even from the counselors' camp. He holds the bugle, still dented. He tries his best to push the dimples out of the metal, but his fingers are sweaty and small, and mostly slip right off the bugle's coils. Much of the pride he always felt in being the camp bugler has dissolved, and holding his grandfather's horn now feels like a farce. The merit badges on his sash, the uniform on his back, all of it—a charade he has so passionately enacted, only for someone to pull the curtain so that: there he is, alone. And for what?

"Can I sit with you for a while?" asks Wilbur, already ten paces away but closing in.

Nelson glances up, his face threatening to crack into that all-too-eager smile of thankfulness. He tries to keep his lips in check, the corners of his mouth from running toward his ears in relief, if not true happiness. "Please," he says, motioning to a space on the rocky base beside him.

Wilbur sits down with the ease and grace of a twelve-year-old boy. His legs are well muscled, the skin tan, the fine hair on his shins a downy white. He smells of pine-tar soap and another scent that Nelson can't quite identify, but which seems to emanate from the corners of his mustache—some kind of wax perhaps, that even now, Wilbur is twirling through the whiskers there, as he stares off over the parade ground through the lifting fog.

"And how is your week going, son?" Wilbur asks. "Couldn't help but notice that yesterday's reveille was a tad . . . balky."

With Wilbur, a boy certainly wishes to put his best foot forward. There is the sense that whining, bellyaching of any kind, would not be tolerated. Partly, this is because Wilbur clearly sees the Scouting movement as essential to a young man's growth, and as such, how can any sort of negativity be allowed to intrude? *A week at a Boy Scout camp in northern Wisconsin? What could be more beneficial, more therapeutic to a young boy's soul?* Nelson expects little sympathy, then, from Wilbur. This, after all, is a man who served in the First World War, and though he rarely speaks about his time in that war, there is the sense that he must have endured a bit more than Nelson's indignities at the hands of his fellow Scouts.

"My bugle . . . ," Nelson begins. "It got—well, it was damaged, sir."

Wilbur takes the instrument in his hands, turns it over, as if it were an ornate and alien seashell, these coils of brass, this instrument.

"This bugle has seen some action," Wilbur says.

"Yes, sir. Like I told you before, it was my grandfather's. He was in World War One." He does not mention the pillaging of the dead German.

"I see." He spins the bugle slowly in brown, veined hands; no wristwatch, no wedding band, no class ring. Fingernails perfectly trimmed, cuticles curtailed.

"Sir," Nelson says, "I . . . I appreciate what you told me earlier this week, in the mess hall, in regards to leadership and all—"

"Nelson," Wilbur says, not waiting for the boy to finish, "almost without fail, my body has served me well. That is because I have trained it to be strong. Not to give in to gravity or to the common complaints of so many other men my age, or younger.

"Every morning, I wake up early and swim across that lake. When I first began swimming, I could barely make it a hundred yards without drowning. By my fifties, I could do as many as five full crossings of the lake—down and back—without much thought.

"Each day, I perform two hundred push-ups and three hundred sit-ups. Ten years ago I was doing double those numbers. I'm embarrassed to say that I may be slowing down.

"Son, I know when a mutiny is afoot, when I'm losing my men to some kind of perverse rebellion. I can see it—something in their faces. Their eyes won't meet mine in that same way. Something is up, only I can't figure what it is. Oh, on the surface of things, everything is in order. The camp continues to operate like a very efficient ship. And yet . . ." He shakes his head. "I wish I could root it out, but I can't seem to."

"Could I, do you think?" Nelson asks. "Could I help root it out?"

"Son, you help me locate this evil, I'll make sure you are promoted to camp counselor next year. I'll personally supervise which cabin you are assigned to. You can select another counselor to be your roommate, or, if you so choose, you can sleep alone. I'll be honest, Nelson, you are not just on a highway to Eagle Scout; you may be on a fast track to Harvard or Yale—who knows—maybe even the U.S. Congress. I've known such men, son, and you are of their ilk, their caliber. I see them in you. In the burden you carry. You don't think I know how the others tease you? I told you in the mess hall, and don't you forget it: they tease you because they're afraid of you.

"Well, we'll give them something to be afraid of. Mark my word."

"Yes, sir," Nelson says, nodding.

"And, Nelson," Wilbur says. "I hope this will make it easier and not harder, but: this bugle here isn't military issue."

Nelson looks into Wilbur's face, locks on to the old man's sad, thoughtful eyes.

"There would be an insignia here of some kind," Wilbur says, holding the instrument for Nelson to see, "an army insignia, most likely, right here."

"Well, sir, to be honest, the story I heard was that my grandfather took it off a dead German. See, I don't think it's an American bugle, is what I heard. Sir."

Wilbur nods, still examining the horn. "Then we should expect to find some German engraving somewhere on the horn, you know? Some kraut manufacturer, some dour super-eagle or somesuch, but I don't see that, either. Son, this may very well be nothing more than a good ol'-fashioned Sears and Roebuck horn, if that makes it any easier. Something out of a catalog, or off a traveling tinker's wagon."

"So it's not my grandfather's?"

"Well, I'm not saying *that*," Wilbur says. "No, no, no. I'm just telling you, this particular horn probably didn't see any fighting in World War One. My guess is, your grandfather bought this for your dad, a long time ago, and cooked up that story so that your father would take care of the horn. And, look, it worked. The real bugle, though, if there was one, is probably somewhere much safer than this camp."

"Oh," Nelson says sorrowfully. "I suppose that's a good thing." *He probably pawned the real one*, the boy thinks.

Wilbur hands him the horn back.

"Don't despair, son."

The old man's small hand finds Nelson's shoulder, gives it a firm squeeze, and his eyes are bright as stars.

"Would you like to borrow a horn that is less damaged, son?"

The boy nods thankfully.

"Come to my cabin. There is time yet before your regular reveille. We'll get you fixed up."

"Thank you, sir."

10

AFTER BREAKFAST, AS THE BOYS ARE MARCHING BACK to their campsite, Jonathan Quick approaches Nelson.

"Hey, Bugler, better get ready, old chum. We've been challenged by Troop 16 to a game of capture-the-flag. Right after lunch. Should be a good match . . . We'll need you, old man. All hands on deck. Can I count on you?"

Nelson generally hates the games played at camp. Football, crack-the-whip, baseball, basketball, water polo. In almost every circumstance, his smallish frame, poor hand-to-eye coordination, and feeble athletic ability betray him, and he becomes a hindrance to the troop as a whole. A target for opposing teams. Imagines himself a lame impala on the Serengeti Plain. Capture-the-flag, though, he has always loved. Of all the camp games his troop participates in, it is surely his favorite.

"Of course," Nelson says. "Absolutely."

In capture-the-flag, a playing field is generally imagined out of a forest or grassland, and borders agreed upon. In the case of Camp Chippewa, it is best to play the game in the forest between the waters of Bass Lake and the road snaking through camp that leads out to Birch Road. Between the lake and the road are countless acres of forest, swamp, highland, trails, and then the broad, flat plain of the parade ground.

Across the middle of the capture-the-flag field, a center line is agreed upon, though here, as in the exterior borders of the field at large, the line remains invisible. On one side of the line, your territory. On the other, theirs. Somewhere hidden on your side of the center line is a flag, though it may not be hidden in such a fashion as to make the game impossible for the opponent; that would not be sporting. Generally, the flag is hung in plain sight from a tree branch, or staked atop a large pole in the middle of a clearing.

The object or goal of the game is to cross into enemy territory, steal their flag, and return it to your side of the field without being tagged by an opponent. For Nelson, this last bit is crucial. For once you've been identified as the flag thief, the opposing side is not apt to tap you politely on the shoulder to indicate that you have been caught. No, you are tackled brutally to the forest floor, there to be fed handfuls of twigs and leaf rot until you cry *uncle*.

NELSON'S MORNING IS UNEVENTFUL. For most of the other Scouts, camp is a week's worth of time to schedule sessions in which they will work with counselors to earn merit badges. But since Nelson has already earned so many merit badges, it is more difficult for him to find sessions that are useful. This summer, he is enrolled in: Ham Radio, Cooking, Canoeing, Woodcarving, and Archery.

Mornings, he and a dozen other boys meet at a small lakeside fire ring to practice their cooking skills. Early in the week, this meant demonstrating their acumen in building small yet sufficiently hot cook fires. As the week progressed, they learned about properly using a cast iron skillet, a Dutch oven, and cooking a piece of meat over an open flame. For the most part, Nelson's been bored, only feigning curiosity or attention. His mind keeps wandering to Wilbur's mystery—what could trouble him so deeply? Who was behind those supposedly dreadful acts? And what about the antics of Monday night?—were they related to all of this?

"That's a nice-looking peach cobbler there, Nelson," his cooking counselor says. "Very evenly cooked. Scouts, take a look at Nelson's cobbler here. See the brown along the cobbler's sides? Now, watch: say I poke at the center of the cobbler here with a clean stick, or toothpick. If the stick comes out dry, you know the cobbler's done. But if it comes out with some batter on it, well, then you'll know to cook it a bit longer."

"Goddamn, Bugler, you're a better cook than my ma," mutters an older Scout to a group of snickering and snorting others.

Later, most of the boys sit at a picnic table eating Nelson's cobbler. A few others crouch near the diminishing campfire. Nelson kneels within inches of the lake's placid waters, where cattails crowd the shore and pebbles congregate like millions of beautiful little eggs. No one's thought to bring their canteen, except him, and he passes his to the younger Scouts, who drink greedily, water sloshing down their faces. He could go for a tall, cold glass of whole milk, but of course, camp isn't the place for those sorts of conveniences. Even a sip of his father's coffee would be nice right now.

"Heckuva cobbler, Nelson," his counselor compliments him again. "Moist, rich, heck—I don't know if a centimeter of it was even burnt. Hard to do, cooking over a campfire."

"Thanks," Nelson says quietly.

"Would you talk to the boys about what you did, how you got it to turn out so beautifully?" The counselor's face is earnest and kind. A college boy, he is just far enough removed from the cattiness and immaturity of middle school to miss the faces of derision and contempt now greeting Nelson. The counselor is just keenly impressed with his camp proficiency. "And what are you doing over there, for crying out loud? Come be by the fire. The mosquitoes aren't so bad near the smoke."

"Thanks, Counselor Tim, but trust me, they don't want to hear *me* talk about the cobbler. They'd rather hear from you."

The counselor casually lets the moment pass, then hands his dishes to some tenderfoot to wash before walking over to Nelson and dropping down to a knee beside the boy. From the shoreline he sifts through the pebbles and rocks, as if looking for something he dropped there, a ring, perhaps, or a valuable coin. Then his hand rises from the water and still kneeling, he flicks a flat rock out across the smooth waters of the lake where it skips: one, two, three, four, five, six, seven, eight, nine—times.

"Wow," says Nelson, "pretty good."

"How old are you?" Tim asks.

"Thirteen, sir."

"Thirteen. You're going to be running this place someday, you know that?"

Nelson does not know how to reply to this compliment, so he aims his eyes at the ground.

"Can I ask you something?"

The boy nods, feels his throat tighten. Counselor Tim is conventionally handsome, of average height and build, but his eyes are very, very blue, and as he leans down beside Nelson, the younger boy notices that his face isn't just sympathetic-looking. It is sad, too. Tim draws in the soft mud of the shore, draws a figure throwing a spear. Bugler draws a crude buffalo.

"Some fellas and I are working out at the old amphitheater," Tim explains. "You heard old Whiteside talking about it during announcements. It would sure be grand if you baked a couple of those cobblers and brought 'em out. Heck, we sort of make a work-party out of it. Guys bring all sorts of stuff, if you know what I mean. I'll even buy the ingredients for you, pay you two dollars for your trouble."

Nelson stares up at him. *Two dollars! And an invitation to a party?* He struggles to compose himself.

"Um, sure," he says slowly. "The old amphitheater?" He's pretty sure he knows where this is.

"That's right," Tim says, rising from his crouch, and smoothing over his drawing with a boot tip. "I'll drop those ingredients at your tent tonight with further instructions." He holds out a hand for Nelson to shake. "Don't let me down, okay?"

Then turning his back to Nelson, Tim merrily claps his hands and calls for the other boys to assemble at the picnic table for a lesson in cooking homemade bread.

Mosquitoes begin orbiting Nelson's ankles, where his socks are puddled over the laces of his boots. He hikes them up, halfway to his knees, and swats at the bare skin above. With his pocketknife he cuts several low-hanging boughs from a nearby spruce and lays them over the campfire, where they are slow to ignite, but then do, making a festive sound as they burn not unlike sparklers sizzling and cracking on the Fourth of July. The air gradually becomes dense with fragrant gray smudgy smoke and the mosquitoes relent, at least for a while.

OVER LUNCH, the boys strategize passionately about their imminent capture-the-flag game. They pass trays of cold-cut sandwich meat— ham and bologna and salami and turkey, laid out in circular fans according to variety. Likewise with cheese, and later, lettuce, onion, and tomatoes. Baskets of white bread circulate, jars of mustard and mayonnaise, later a great platter of brownies.

"Jerks have a map!" Jonathan Quick snorts.

"And they're older," says Billy Bowden, a boy of about fourteen, smaller than Nelson, but already beloved for his ability to recycle his father's dirty jokes. "And bigger, too." A wrestler, Bowden sports a face smeared in acne, his body purportedly perennially accosted by ringworm, too. Everyone in school has heard the story of Bowden being thrown down to the mat on his back, where apparently, dozens of pimples were all violently burst, soaking his uniform and fouling the royal blue vinyl.

"Well, it's not an orienteering course," says Jim Tolliver, one of the troop's most senior boys, and off to Notre Dame the next year for college. "If it was, we've got Bugler. No, this is about strategy. We've got the same amount of Scouts. The question is, where do we place the flag? Who are our attackers? Who are our defenders? Or do we just forget about a plan, and go into this thing for fun? Every man for himself, so to speak?"

The boys begin shouting suggestions, only to be silenced by Jonathan Quick, who whistles loudly in their faces, drawing a chorus of laughter and applause from the rest of the mess hall, before he huddles the troop in close.

"Look," he says seriously, "we can't have anarchy. I've never been much of a planner, but maybe this is the time. I ain't much for losing, that's for sure."

The boys nod their assent, moving brownies into their mouths nervously, eyes wide, crumbs falling to the tabletop.

"We need a bet," Morris Redman suggests. "You know? Something to up the ante."

"The winning troop . . . ," Jonathan whispers quite to himself. He drums dirty fingers against a greasy chin. It is a widely known fact that personal hygiene deteriorates over the course of the week at Camp Chippewa, even among the camp's most fastidious boys. Hair becomes thoroughly untamed, shabby mustaches begin to dust the upper lips of older boys, the white of one's teeth dulls perceptibly, zits blossom red and white, like night mushrooms popping from the loam. "The winning troop . . ."

The boys, having fallen silent now, examine the hall's rafters and pennants, the dusty taxidermy and the dry pine beams. Around the mess hall, other troops are beginning to rise, returning to merit badge clinics, swimming, fishing, or quietly reading comic books, Mickey Spillane, or the like.

"The winning troop," Nelson says with uncharacteristic certainty, "should get twenty-five dollars to split between its boys for use at the canteen."

Twenty-five dollars is, of course, a fortune, especially this late in the week, after some boys have already blown most of their money on canteen Coca-Colas, popcorn, candy bars, cotton candy, and ice-cream cones. But it seems an appropriately lavish wager, a sum that can be achieved only through pooling communal assets. And it means that the winning troop will spend the remainder of the week living like kings, gorging on their favorite nosh. They will be famous.

Jonathan Quick reaches a hand out and slaps Nelson's shoulder affectionately. "I like it," he says. "Any objections?"

The troop is quiet, their eyes wide with promise, excitement.

"And the loser?" asks Morris.

The boys look first to Jonathan, then slowly turn their gaze to Nelson, the black sheep, who shakes his head, as if in complete bewilderment. *If we lose*, he thinks, *they will come for my head*. And, *Please, God. Let us win*. "Isn't it enough that the loser has to pony up money?" Nelson asks.

"Naw," Morris continues, "we hate these guys. Let's make 'em pay. Twice."

The mess hall is all but empty, cooks spilling out of the kitchen now to wipe down the tables, to sweep and mop the floors. Only Nelson's troop remains, and of course, Troop #16, arrayed shoulder to shoulder along one side of their table and upon the tabletop, arms crossed, staring at Nelson and his troop mates as sternly as a rugby squad.

Jonathan holds out his hands for calm. "Let me take this to Jack

Lovell," he says. "See if he's got any ideas for the losing troop. Are we agreed then?" he asks.

The boys give him their thumbs-up, confident nods, clapped hands.

Jonathan stands from their table, walks over to Troop #16, and shakes hands with another tall, lanky Scout, a boy with a red crew cut, freckles, and eyes that seemed to shine golden. The two older boys talk for a minute or two, then shake, and Jonathan returns to his table as Troop #16 bursts out into squeals of delight.

"We've got an accord," Jonathan says wryly. "But you won't want to hear what the loser has to do."

"Did you already agree to the deal?" asks Billy anxiously.

Jonathan nods soberly. "The deal is this: the winning troop chooses one member of the losing troop to . . ." His voice trails off.

"What?" Nelson asks. The other boys lean close to Jonathan, their captain.

"Go down into a latrine."

The troop gasps.

"For how long?" someone asks.

Jonathan gulps air, as if he is contemplating vomiting. "The winning team gets to throw a nickel down the latrine. Losing team has to find it."

"And you agreed to this?" Nelson cries.

"We have one hour to place our flag," Jonathan replies. "Now, how much money do we have? Come on, fellas."

They reach deep into the dark wells of their pockets for bills wet with rain and perspiration, folded tight as origami. They touch coins greasy and shiny, or fuzzy with lint and the decomposed scraps of Bazooka Joe wrappers. Each boy has to come up with about a dollar. With Jonathan acting as troop secretary, they collect twenty-three dollars and seven cents and he places the kitty in a leather pouch that he then hangs from his neck, in escrow.

"Wait a minute," Jonathan says. "You sure that's all your money?"

The boys pull their pockets inside out in a mugging display of full disclosure.

"Scout's honor?"

They raise their right hands in pledge, like senators taking an oath. "Scout's honor," they repeat, in chorus.

"Okay," Jonathan says, "let's get our flag hid."

"HERE," HE SAYS, "RIGHT HERE."

The boys follow behind Jonathan, swatting mosquitoes and wiping sweat from their brows. The afternoon is growing hot. Finally the rain clouds of the last two days have pushed on toward Michigan, and now the sky is opening its bright blue tarpaulin over the land and the sun beams down upon them with all its fire. Steam rises off the forest and asphalt trails.

Jonathan stands at the top of a small ridge, the only topography of consequence on their side of the playing field. A scattering of boulders lie strewn about, lichen barnacled over their quartz crystals. A young oak tree chatters its leaves above them and farther up—a red-tailed hawk wheels and circles.

"Here," he repeats. "Morris, pound our flagpole in here." He indicates a specific spot by disrupting the moss there with his boot. Morris summits the ridge and hammer in hand, pounds the flagpole into the rocky soil.

"Won't they be able to see it pretty easily?" asks Thomas Salkin, a boy of about Nelson's age. "Don't we want to, I don't know, hide it a bit more?"

"No," Jonathan replies. "We want them to find it."

"Why?" Thomas asks. He bites at a hangnail. "I'm not going in that latrine. I won't play. I'll call my mom and dad."

"Shut up," Morris says. "Shut up, you sissy."

"We'll split our numbers into three groups. One group will go along our western boundary. I want them to sit still and eliminate the chance of getting flanked. Same for the second group, only they'll sit on our eastern boundary. A third group will hide on the windward side of the hill and if anyone on their team gets close, why, we'll have a force lying there in wait to snag 'em. I don't want anyone going into enemy territory. No one! I don't care if this game takes us a day to win, but we're not going to force the issue. We'll let them come to us, and after we've captured most of them, we'll form up together and *then* we'll launch a counterattack. Is that understood?"

The boys salute their general.

"Morris, you count out six Scouts and take the eastern boundary. Jim, count out six and take the west. Whoever's left, come with me." He begins walking past the flag and down the windward slope, where scraggly jack pine, cedar, and juniper grow in stunted clumps. Nelson, passed up by Morris and Jim, follows Jonathan down the hill.

They hide in the sparse shadows of early afternoon, underneath the hems of coniferous trees where sharp dry needles jab the soft palms of their hands and sap sticks to their hair and uniforms. No wind stirs. Grasshoppers pop off the dry blades of grass, and flies trouble the air. Their hearts jump as if on trampolines and sweat runs into their eyes and down their skinny-boy spines.

No birds chirp, no chipmunks titter or taunt, and for what seems like hours, Nelson focuses on the rocks about him, waiting for a sunbathing snake to slither past. He runs his hands through his hair, combing for wood ticks and horseflies. He closes his eyes, sleeps. The dappled sunshine on his cheeks and forehead is like the warm hand of his mother, whom he misses so much in that moment, he smiles, thinking of her, standing at their kitchen sink, humming an old, old song and watering her potted herbs with a turkey baster.

HE WAKES TO SCREAMING. Scouts, crashing through the brush around him. Scouts, whooping and hollering.

Scouts, carrying their flag high overhead and pouring down the hill, well organized, a line of blockers like a stout arrowhead V preceding the bandits holding their stolen banner. Scouts, his troop, giving chase, their faces red with sunburn. Scouts, running fast through the forest, leaping over huge stumps of logged white pine, hurdling downed maple trunks, wailing as they tear through raspberry and thistle patches. Down the hill they hurtle, Troop #16's biggest boys pushing down the eastern and western divisions of Nelson's troop like an oafish offensive line flattening a team of pee-wees. He hears desperation in Jonathan's voice as he cries, "Stop them! Stop them, goddamnit!"

Out of the forest they burst, the filched flag held aloft as they run into the parade ground, Nelson's troop hot on their heels, but not close enough, because the thieves reach Camp Chippewa's central flagpole and in a roar of unity holler down at Jonathan Quick and his confederates, taunting, *"Now eat shit! Now eat shit! Now eat shit!"*

Their chants are only halted when a counselor emerges at the margins of the parade ground scratching his head and crossing his arms, and then, seeing the captured flag, waves at all the young boys and their silly shenanigans, before retreating to his cabin.

Jack Lovell, redheaded Jack Lovell, who ten years later will die as the result of stepping on a land mine in Vietnam, marches down the hill toward Jonathan Quick, holding his right hand out in search of his winnings. Jonathan removes the leather pouch from his neck and offers it to Jack, like an Olympian forfeiting a gold medal. The ginger smirks at Jonathan and the slumped-shouldered troop of boys behind him.

"Well," Jack asks, "where's that bugler of yours?"

11

"FOR GOD'S SAKE," JONATHAN SAYS, "LOWER HIM DOWN first, then throw the nickel."

"No," Jack replies. "You losers stand there. I'll throw the nickel down, so that only *I* know where it went."

Nelson stands in his white, white underwear, trembling with fear. Morris holds his uniform, as if, prior to his dying, Nelson had neatly folded and stacked his effects before jumping to his demise. The sun still rages overhead. Flies boil around the latrine.

"Are you sure that was all your money?" Jack crows. "You didn't even pony up all twenty-five bucks!"

"It's all our goddamned money, you asshole!" Jonathan cries. "Now throw that nickel and be done with it!"

Jack kicks the door of the latrine open with a boot, and in the midafternoon heat, the smell is pugnacious. Another Troop #16 boy holds open the door so all can witness the throw.

"Jesus," Jack gasps, "disgusting." He gags. "And awfully, *awfully* dark down there." And then he leaps up about a foot, as if he were about to spike a volleyball, and at the apex of his jump and with all his might, he throws the nickel into the darkness below. The coin makes no sound at all.

Troop #16 lets out a raucous barrage of belly laughter and hand-clapping, back-slapping, and foot-stomping. Jack-the-Ginger leaves the latrine and lets the door slam, walks directly up to Nelson, and taking the boy gently by the shoulder says, "Sorry it's you, bub. But, hey, at least you'll have more money than your buddies, right?"

Jonathan Quick pushes Jack away from Nelson, pushes the redhead in the chest so hard, in fact, that he trips over a tree root and falls down in the dust before scrambling back to his feet.

"All right," Jack says, determined not to give him anything, "time to pay the piper. Let's see him go down."

With several long lengths of rope, Jonathan and Jim create a harness that fits around Nelson's thighs and shoulders. The knots are expertly tied.

"I'm sorry, Nelson," Jim says, "I'm so, so sorry. This is just awful. Anything you need, I swear, I'm your man, okay? Anything." He kneels and checks the knots fastened to Nelson's legs. This would certainly not be an occasion for a knot to fail, leaving Nelson stranded.

Nelson's troop stands at a distance and many of the younger boys turn their backs and seem on the brink of openly crying, as much for themselves and their newly empty wallets as for Nelson. Most of the boys came from families who can ill afford to even send their children to camp, let alone lose a dollar bill on a stupid bet. Some of the Scouts are in danger of real lickings if their fathers discover their wager.

Jonathan hovers close to Nelson's face, surveying the knots and loops around his shoulders and arms. Then he hugs Nelson, and hold-ing the smaller boy's head in his hands, he whispers, "I've got a nickel in my front left pocket. No, no, no. Don't make a move yet. We can't give them any reason to think we've cheated. I need you to start crying, right now, really put on a show. It'll be our distraction. Right now."

Nelson sobs and sobs, and some of his sobs are authentic. He is still about to be dropped into the latrine, after all. But a bit of his crying is sheer happiness, because Jonathan Quick has just saved him.

"Now," Jonathan continues, "reach into that pocket. But when you do, do it fast, and keep that fist balled up tight. Do it."

Nelson dives his hand into Jonathan's pocket and sweeps the nickel into his palm. Continues sobbing.

"Hey!" Jack yells. "What're you nancies doing over there? Get 'em in the damn hole. Somebody'll notice if we don't have a bugler for taps!"

"Don't come up right away," Jonathan whispers. "You need to stay down there for at least five or ten minutes. The longer the better. You need to convince them you worked some goddamn miracle. When you hear me and Jack fighting, that's when you yell for us to pull you up, all right? That's your cue. They'll all be distracted. Only, our timing has to be perfect."

"Thank you, Jonathan," Nelson whispers. "Just please pull me up as soon as you can, please."

Jonathan rubs his hair affectionately, pulls away. "You ready?" he asks aloud.

Nelson wipes his cheeks with the backs of his fists, terrified he'll drop the nickel.

"All right," Jonathan says, "let's go."

They walk toward the privy, its stench intensifying.

"I'm so sorry," Jim says. "Jesus, I'm sorry."

"It's okay," Nelson assures him. "Someone had to go."

Inside the outhouse, the space is close, dark, the very air confused with flies and the fumes rising off a pit of excrement. Nelson has actually gone the last three days without having a bowel movement, so much does he despise the outhouse. He would rather squat in the forest, his thighs seated on a downed log, his ass pointed out, or cling to a small birch and do his business the way he'd once seen his mother do on a family camping trip up near Lake Superior.

Jonathan lifts the seat of the toilet.

"Christ," he says, "it's gonna be tight down there, little buddy."

The distance between toilet platform and the top layer of the pit is maybe five feet. At first, they lower Nelson slowly, mindful of their jerry-rigged harness, lest it fail the boy. But as he swings off the sides of the latrine, his feet, hips, and shoulders scraping all kinds of horrors, he shouts up, "Just drop me! Do it quick! Come on!"

So they do, to a gruesomely loud *plop,* and then the sound of Nelson vomiting. Now Troop #16 rushes to surround the latrine, Jack-the-Ginger pushing through the crowd of boys to enter the privy.

"Son of a bitch," he mumbles, glancing down at Nelson. "He actually *did* it."

"Well," Jonathan says, "we're not the kind of Scouts who welsh on a deal. And Bugler is a goddamned tough kid, isn't he, fellas?"

Nelson's troop mates cheer him on, suddenly his defenders, his brothers. Nothing insincere about the encouragements they rain down upon him now, even as some of them turn their racking shoulders, their gagging mouths, their red-rimmed eyes, and stumble out into the ferns to vomit their stomachs empty. Poor Nelson is coated, every bit of him, paper in his hair, and the sounds he is making . . . The awful, awful whimpers giving way to groans and sobs and then more vomiting.

How he struggles in that deep, dark latrine, his arms floundering, his eyes closed as his hands pretend to search through the muck and every time he delves deeply into those depths, he just as quickly wrenches his hands up to vomit. Every second an hour.

"Pull him up," some of the Troop #16 boys are saying now. "Pull him up for Christ's sake."

"No," Jack insists, "a deal's a deal." He leans down over the seat of the latrine, rubbing at his shiny forehead.

"We've won the bet; come on now. Pull him up."

"No!" Jack bellows, his newly basso voice pushing the boys back.

Now Jonathan grabs at Jack's shirt, a handful of fabric in his fist, and he pushes Jack out of the latrine, saying, "Pull him up now, or I swear to God, I'll knock your block off."

"And how will you explain that to Wilbur?" Jack grins. "That you made a big-money bet and agreed to a set of terms that would send one of your boys down a latrine? *You'll* be dead meat, too. Go right ahead."

Jonathan loosens his grip of Jack's shirt, takes a single step away from the redhead, and then turns back, slugging him deep in the stomach. The two troops erupt with the excitement and curiosity that always encircles a fight, and now Jonathan has tackled Jack to the dusty ground and is hammering away at him as he pins the other boy to the earth and pounds and pounds. And all the while, from deep down in the latrine, Nelson screams, "I *found* it! I *found* it, fellas!"

Jonathan runs back to the privy and begins pulling on the rope that a younger boy held in his small hands. "Help me, goddamnit!" Soon Jim is there, too, wrenching at the rope, until Nelson's head surfaces at the seat, his glasses streaked with shit, shit and paper in his hair, and smelling so, so very foul. But in his right hand, clenched between thumb and forefinger, a nickel, and despite the shit, Nelson smiling white, as if he's just dived to the very bottom of the ocean to collect the world's most priceless pearl.

12

NELSON'S TROOP UNIFIES AROUND HIM IN ALL THE
ways that they have been trained to, and yet for so long, failed to do.
Two boys snatch together soap, shampoo, toothpaste, and mouthwash,
and Jonathan escorts Nelson to the showers, standing guard outside the
building while he scrubs and scrubs. A pocketknife is donated, and a
pair of fingernail clippers, a compass, a leather belt, and even a watch.
These offerings are dropped into a hat stationed immediately in front
of Nelson's newly reassembled tent.

Jonathan leans into the doorway of the shower room and yells, "You
got about twenty minutes before taps, Bugler!"

Nelson turns the showerhead off and reaches for a fresh towel. His
eyes still sting in a disturbing way, and even after an hour of brushing
his teeth and gargling mouthwash he can still taste the latrine. He wonders if he'll ever feel clean again. Clutched in his right hand: the nickel.
He feels he will never let it go. Nelson dresses quickly, strides out of the

shower room, and walks across the campground to his tent. Jonathan follows him closely.

"Nelson," he says, "Nelson, I'm sorry. I should have never agreed to that bet. I know that. I just hope you'll forgive me, you know? And I hope this can stay, you know, between us. Within the troop, I mean. Nelson?"

Nelson disappears inside his tent, reappears a moment later, replacement horn in hand, walking efficiently toward the parade ground. Jonathan jogs a few paces to catch up to him.

"Nelson? Jesus, *Nelson!*"

But Nelson does not acknowledge the older boy—just blows out some test notes and occasionally spits into the forest.

"Nelson, remember, old chum: *I'm* the one who gave you that nickel. All right? I'm the one who saved you."

Nelson stops abruptly, lowers the horn, and with his back still turned to Jonathan, says in a quiet voice, "I remember."

"Just like you gave me that baseball card!" Jonathan's voice is almost frantic. "We're friends, see? We're in this together!"

"When I think very hard," Nelson says, running a hand through his hair, over the soft lines of his jaw, tugging at his ears, "when I really concentrate and try to remember, I don't know that I've ever had a friend. My mom, maybe . . ." He thinks of her just then, their time together in the mornings, before school, when she prepares him breakfast, always setting a piece of toast before him, slathered in marmalade or her homemade raspberry jam, her body just behind him, so warm, almost as if she radiated her own light and heat, as if her heart were a crystal emanating unabashed love . . .

He turns to Jonathan. "I should have held on to one nickel. We all should have. You were just the only one who remembered, but trust me, Jonathan, I'll never forget."

"Forget what?"

"The motto."

"The motto?"

"Be prepared. I don't think you were necessarily thinking ahead, Jonathan. I think you were being greedy." He held up the nickel like a talisman. "Tell me," Nelson orders, a new strength and sadness in his voice, "how much money do you have left in your pockets?"

"None, bu— None Nelson, I swear."

"Pull them out, then. Pull out your pockets. Show me."

Jonathan stares back at him.

"I heard you," Nelson says. "I heard you, as I was pulled up. I could *hear* the coins in your pocket, as you ran. I'm not stupid." Then, the rage rising, "I'm not stupid! I know now! I understand everything!"

"I'm sorry," Jonathan says quietly, staring at the ground. "We failed you, buddy. I failed you."

"And that's it," Nelson says. "That's the lesson."

"What?"

"That everyone will fail you. Everyone."

"I'm sorry, Nelson."

"Tell me something, was there ever any doubt that I was the one going down into the latrine? Ever any doubt that I'd be the sacrificial lamb?"

Jonathan looks at the ground.

Nelson, trembling, continues: "Because *you* sure as hell weren't going down, were you? You made the bet, but I was the one who kept it. *I* kept the bet. I kept your word. And you failed me. *Failed* me."

He turns and walks down the path, and for the first time that week, he blows his bugle loud—loud, as if he were rallying the cavalry toward one final, epic ride.

13

AFTER DINNER, NELSON DECLINES TO LIGHT HIS troop's fire. He doesn't need to. Another boy hurriedly gathers kindling and kneels down beside the fire ring, busily assembling the bonfire's structure. Nelson stays in his tent, staring at the central pole, up which a spider creeps. The lantern is a comfort, the steady low throb of its combustion.

Before dusk, Counselor Tim announces his presence by clearing his throat.

"Come in," Nelson says.

Tim lifts the tent's flaps and shrugs inside, sinks down to one knee, and then appraises the tight space.

"You've got a good spot here, Nelson," he says. "Real tidy. I shouldn't be surprised, though. Like I said, you'll be running this place someday."

Nelson sits up off his cot. Tim has brought a canvas bag full of provisions: two cast-iron Dutch ovens, flour, salt, sugar, powdered milk, canned peaches, vanilla, even a box of matches.

"Fine," he says. "The old amphitheater?"

"You know the way?"

"Not really," Nelson says, tiredly.

"I'll show you," Tim offers. "Here—follow me." He stands, and begins to leave the tent, then turns, "But play it cool, Nelson. I mean, it's okay to tell people you're volunteering to work on the theater, but don't broadcast it, okay? Our parties are sort of top secret. The labor isn't, of course, you can talk about that. But the parties are something different. Like a reward for our work, see? You're in the know now, sure, but we can't have just any old tenderfoot coming to these things, you understand?"

Nelson's eyes are clear and cool. "I understand," he says. "But does Scoutmaster Wilbur know about your . . . parties? How do you keep it a secret?"

"Oh, that old goat," laughs Tim. "C'mon, I'll explain when we get there."

Now the sun is sinking fast in the west, like a quickly collapsing magenta balloon. Tim and Nelson walk side by side down the canopied path toward the parade ground, Tim occasionally turning back to survey whether or not they are being watched.

"Did you tell anyone?" he asks.

Nelson shakes his head, exhausted. "No."

"Good." He pushes the younger boy into the woods. "Follow me."

The path is old, overgrown by ferns, but still there, like the bed of a very old, dry stream. Occasionally, they pass an ancient white pine, where Nelson touches a blaze carved into the thick bark.

"Did you know this trail?" Tim asks, pushing steadily forward.

"No," Nelson murmurs, "I don't think so." He knows many trails that even his older fellow Scouts do not, but he's only been to the old theater once, and it was along a different route. Still, he has made it a point, even before his first visit to Camp Chippewa, to study the topography of the land, so that if ever lost, he could orient himself simply by knowing the lay of the land. This is a path he has seen only on old maps, and knows leads to an old outdoor theater where once induction ceremonies were supposed to have been held for secret Scout societies, societies populated by older boys, their fathers and uncles, and even grandfathers, old men who had joined the movement in its earliest, purest days. Men, Nelson thinks, like Wilbur. The newer theater, complete with a modern sound system and lighting, was constructed just five years ago on the shores of Bass Lake.

It is difficult to measure time. Occasionally, Tim stops, and either backtracks or slowly peers around at the tree trunks close to them. Then, just as quickly, they march forward in the darkness, until, at last, the forest opens into a clearing and above them, the innumerable stars sizzle and blink, with some of them, suddenly unmoored, arcing out across all of that dark, dark blue, and Nelson stands, dumbstruck, as he always is, by the stunning immensity of it all, the stupefying gravity of suddenly having the cosmos illuminate your own smallness; to think that only hours ago, he was this putrid sewer rat of an organism, sent down into an unholy murk to go fishing for so small a treasure that many adults he knew would not trouble themselves to bend over to pluck its insignificant value off a clean, dry sidewalk. That was who he was. A star sliced loose from its berth and went scuttling out into the void, turning and turning without ever a hope of gaining traction again.

I am cut loose, he thinks. And, *To hell with them all.*

And suddenly there they are: ten rows of sun-bleached, weather-rotten benches rise up out of a gulley, and nestled deep in the depression, a small stage. There seems nothing nefarious about the amphitheater. Just a beautiful little place deep within the forest.

"I'll pay you tomorrow night," Tim says. "Just bring your famous cobbler here tomorrow night, nine o'clock. I'll have your money and if you'd like, you can even hang around."

"Hang around? What do you do? Smoke cigarettes?" Nelson stammers. "Some mary jane?" He feels proud to use this term, to know it, at least in name if not in meaning.

"Oh sure. But it's the movies, mainly. We really set it up. It's something. One of the counselors found these canisters of films in his dead uncle's basement. He took them. You'll see . . . Anyway, come on, let's get back."

Nelson still doesn't quite understand—*what's so taboo about some silly movies?* "Say, Tim," Nelson says, "how do you keep your parties a secret? I mean, Scoutmaster Wilbur knows you're all out here. He even commends you on your work. I don't understand."

Tim slaps him on the shoulder. "Aye, but that's just it. When he visits, he always comes at the same time. Just before dark. Like clockwork. So we don't begin our parties until well after he's gone. That way we can be sure. I mean, what are the chances an old soldier is going to break his routine? Why would he pay us two visits in one night?" Now he rubs at Nelson's shoulder. "What? You're not nervous, are you? There's no need to be. Heck, at the beginning of the summer we even appointed spies that kept eyes on all the trails around the theater. Nobody has ever even come close. This whole thing is both out in the open and way too far off the beaten track. It's perfect."

"Smart," Nelson says. "Very smart."

"We're prepared, is all." Tim grins. "Right?"

The two depart each other's company at the main trail and Nelson finds his own way back to camp, walking very deliberately through the dark.

WILBUR SITS BESIDE THE FIRE, alone, a stick in his hands nudging the coals, arranging flaming logs. His face betrays nothing. The boy sits down beside him, wonders where his own father is. The camp is quiet.

"I won't ask where you've been," Wilbur says. "Looking at the stars, maybe."

Nelson stares up into Wilbur's face, the old man's long, sharp nose outlined by the fire in crimsons and golds.

Nelson decides to more or less tell the truth: "I was with Counselor Tim. He was showing me the progress on the old outdoor theater."

Wilbur runs a hand over his face and nods obliquely. "Oh, yes," he said, "a fine job they're doing out there, those boys."

Nelson recognizes the truth in what Tim had told him. The old man suspects nothing of them, their parties.

"I sent four boys home today. You know why? One of them was pulling the legs off a live frog. Another shot an owl, not far from your camp—a barred owl. You imagine?" He shakes his head in disappointment. "The other two . . . It pains me to say, but they were smoking cigarettes. Cigarettes! Scouts don't smoke cigarettes. Not cigarettes, not pipes, not cigars, nothing. It is a boy's job, his responsibility to strengthen his body with exercise and games and a smart diet. Now, tell me how inhaling smoke is going to make your body stronger, Nelson? Please tell me that, because maybe I'm just too old, and I don't understand the way of things anyway. Can you explain it to me?"

Nelson kneels beside his bench, snags a log from the pile he's stowed there in the morning, and sets it on the fire.

"I'm sorry, Scoutmaster Wilbur."

"What for? You did nothing wrong, Nelson."

Nelson is quiet. Tries to decide whether or not to tell Wilbur about Thursday night's festivities, whatever they are. Unsure he wants to hand the old man another burden, another disappointment, especially without certain knowledge of anything inappropriate at those happenings.

"I never had any children," Wilbur says quietly. "Never been married. I don't know why. I became Scoutmaster of this camp after I came back from the war. It was nothing back then. A thousand acres of tamarack swamp and a rotten cabin we bought for a song. I put everything into this camp. Everything. Every drop of strength and smarts I have. And the thought of having children, of getting married, I can't say it ever passed through the transom of my mind. Because over time, more and more boys came to this camp. More young fathers. And *they* became my family. I could watch them grow, watch them change. Some of them became like sons to me, even invited me to their houses for Christmas and Thanksgiving.

"But if they were really my children, my own children I mean, I know that there would be something else . . . Something deeper, stronger. The feelings, the sensations I have, they would be more natural perhaps, more amplified, on some molecular level even. Something ingrained in me. I guess this is what people call *love*.

"But the thing is, Nelson, I know you don't love me. You might *like* me. You might respect me. But you don't love me, not the way you love your mother or father, or your grandparents. When I am gone, you will perhaps feel an absence, but it will be like a favored book lost from your collection, a space on your shelf. You will miss it, but you may find another. Or not."

Wilbur stands from the fire. "If you have something you need to tell me, Nelson, perhaps tomorrow morning would be a good time. Before reveille. In fact, there's something I would like to share with *you*."

Nelson nods up at Wilbur, and then listens, as the old man walks into the darkness, leaving him alone to tend the fire.

14

NELSON DOES NOT SLEEP WELL. THE WEIGHT OF THE
week's events weighing on him combined with a sneaking homesick-
ness form a new kind of unnamable existential uncertainty. And now
Counselor Tim's party—he has no idea what to expect exactly, but there
is the sense that the secret nature of the party itself, Tim's advance forest
spies, the way he talked about Wilbur—none of it seems to add up to
anything wholesome.

By the light of the lantern, he reads Ian Fleming's new *Thunderball*
for hours, until, not even realizing he's fallen asleep, he is stirred out
of slumber by the stealthy approach of soft footfalls. Since being am-
bushed in his tent, he has slept fitfully, shallowly.

"Come on now." It is the camp's Scoutmaster, whispering through
the canvas of the tent. "I want to show you something special," says
Wilbur.

The boy dresses quickly, unzips his tent, and meets the old man in
the predawn chill.

They set off through the woods, Wilbur nimble as can be, leading them deeper into the forest than Nelson had ever ventured before. The composition of the trees changes as they move along, the topography of the land seeming to dip and run downhill, everything draining away from the oaks and maples near the campgrounds to this lower forest of cedar and tamarack, where the trees huddle closer together, the air scented with pitch and rot. The canopy is shorter here, but denser overhead. Wilbur moves noiselessly, even as Nelson finds himself stumbling over knobby cedar roots and tamarack knees.

And then, they come into a boreal bog, bordered on all sides by dead tamaracks, and a little pond reflecting silver moonlight. The air smells of peat and the spice of cologne. Wilbur crouches down.

"I've been watching them, generations of them, come here to drink from this pool," he whispers. "I've never showed this place to anyone before."

As to just what Wilbur is referring to, Nelson has no idea, but the world is perfectly still. They wait together, close as can be.

"Scoutmaster," Nelson whispers, "I think—"

But Wilbur grips the boy's kneecap firmly, and with his other hand, points.

Even without the moon, the buck would have glimmered in the wan morning glow, but bathed in that lunar light, the albino deer nearly shines as it silently approaches the pond. A wide rack of antlers crown its thick head and there—pink eyes, *pink eyes*. It laps at the pond, sending out tiny corrugated ripples across the surface. Nelson trembles with awe.

Wilbur moves very close to the boy, inching his face tighter and tighter to Nelson's ears, until the boy can feel his whiskers against the skin there, skin seldom if ever touched. "Have you ever seen anything so beautiful?" Wilbur whispers. Now the old man scoots away, reaches for the boy's shoulder, squeezes, and grins.

Other deer move out of the forest and stand beside the pool, grunting quietly and chewing slowly on bog grasses. Nelson can hear the grass against their fur, their teeth gnashing, the wetness of their nostrils. More than a few of these deer are also albino.

"I used to visit this place once a week, on Saturdays, after the campers had left. I came here to meditate, to . . ." Wilbur's voice trails off though his lips still work, his eyes yet focused on the white buck.

"To what, sir?" Nelson asks, eyes still trained on the deer.

"To collect myself, son. To, ah, pray. I'd come here on Saturdays and simply watch these creatures. Some people call them ghost deer. Very rarely will a Scout spot a white one anywhere near camp, but it does happen. I tend to downplay their existence." Wilbur looks down, runs a hand over a thick carpeting of moss. "To acknowledge their presence would be to spoil this place, I suspect. And, no doubt, to entice some barbarian of a father, or a renegade counselor, into killing one of these creatures. Taxidermied, one of these deer might bring hundreds, maybe thousands." He smiles. "If a Scout tells me that he's seen an albino deer, I tell him it must be a trick of the light, some strange dappling of the forest leaves, or maybe a deer with more blondish fur." He eases out a small laugh.

"I worry about what will happen to them after I die," Wilbur says quietly.

"Then it is a good thing this camp is here," Nelson offers, "so we can protect them."

Wilbur glances down, exhales, and then looks at Nelson. "That's right," he says quietly.

The deer continue their browsing, and the moon descends toward the horizon, as if hurrying away with important news.

BACK IN CAMP, Thomas Salkin is hunched over the fire pit, blowing furiously at a huge log cabin of sticks, split wood, and kindling. No smoke arises for all his efforts. Nelson walks boldly to the fire pit and, without saying a word, disassembles the framework of Salkin's big fire, then reassembles a much smaller infrastructure: a single log, some pinecones, crumpled newspaper, and a handful of twigs. From the coals of the previous night's fire he discovers one still hot coal, and using a stick, he pushes it to the side of the pit and begins coaxing it alive again, blowing tenderly. It begins to glow: first red, then orange, then a whitish-blue. Now he touches the coal with a single strip of newspaper; it catches fire. He returns the newspaper to the nest of kindling and blows patiently, adding fuel, stick by stick, until the fire's health is without question.

"How'd you do that?" Thomas Salkin asks. "I had it all organized, only it wouldn't catch. I even squirted some kerosene on there."

Nelson dusts his palms off, then his knees. He is exhausted, more exhausted than any thirteen-year-old boy in the history of Camp Chippewa.

"It's easy to suffocate a fire before it even gets a chance to breathe," he explains. "Start small with the most combustible fuel first. Keep a nice pile of small kindling handy. Birch bark is best, or pinecones. Dried balsam boughs. Then, once it gets going, you've got to feed it, give it air."

"Sounds like you're describing a person or something," Salkin jokes.

"I don't know anything about people," Nelson replies, moving off to his tent.

NELSON SPENDS THE BULK OF HIS DAY away from the merit badge clinics and his camp, building his own fire beside a secluded bay of Bass Lake. He isn't sure precisely why he cares so much about the cooking of these contraband cobblers, but he does care; in everything he does, there is desire for perfection. And perhaps it is in the hope that when he and Wilbur appear at that derelict amphitheater, the Scouts assembled there will turn out to be covertly working on some miraculous surprise: a giant trebuchet, say, for launching water across the parade ground, or a chain saw carving of Wilbur himself— something other than what Nelson fears, which is what Wilbur had initially warned the entire camp of back on Monday, that if they were good and decent and honorable, they would never have any need to hide anything about their lives. And yet, certainly Counselor Tim, and apparently many other Scouts, *are* hiding something. But what? What are these movies Tim alluded to? Old James Cagney films? Pulpy gangster pictures full of tommy guns, the spray of bullets, loose women smoking cigarettes?

It is a beautiful day, and Nelson wishes, as he often does, for a friend to pass the time with. Some other boy to sit beside the fire with and discuss baseball or books . . . merit badges or school. But of course he is alone, the fire his only confidant.

THE KEY TO CONSISTENT CAMP BAKING is an evenly dispersed bed of coals; this ensures equal heating throughout the cast-iron pot. And because Nelson is cooking two cobblers, he sets about early that day gathering kindling and larger chunks of wood. Doing so close to camp would have drawn attention, which was why he set off on his own, and because of his time in the latrine, his fellow Scouts are treating him with a newfound respect and shameful distance. Before, he simply wasn't invited to share their space. Now they recognize in themselves something ugly and embarrassing, something that separates him from them.

He thinks about his father's words, about *true* friendship and loyalty. Wonders if he'll ever experience such a kinship.

Sighing, Nelson finally takes out the pen and pad of paper he brought to the shore of the lake and begins to write a letter to his mother:

Dear Mom,

This has been the worst week of my life. It feels like someone has lifted a blindfold away from my face, and now I can see. Father was right, these boys are not my friends. What friend would damage Grandpa's bugle? Knock down my tent? Send me down into the latrine after a stupid nickel?

Father hardly ever talks to me. Nobody does. I am so ready to come home. I have realized this week that I think you are my best friend. You have always loved me as I am, and defended me without question.

I do not write this letter to you in the hopes that you will feel sorry for me. I write to you so that you will know how much I love you.

Your son,
Nelson

He looks at the letter. Hears his cook fire pop and sizzle. Mosquitoes harass his ears, assault the back of his neck. He knows he cannot post the letter, and crumples it up, tossing it into the fire.

He begins another letter:

Dear Mom,

It has been a wonderful week here at camp, with Dad. The counselors have been very encouraging, and I am hopeful that by Friday afternoon I will have earned five new merit badges!

I have made a new friend. His name is Wilbur, and this morning he showed me the most amazing thing: a small herd of albino deer! I wish you could have seen them, Mom. Next year, I'll know to bring a camera.

I hope you are well. I wonder how your week has been, what

you are doing? I miss you. While it is fun here, I'm looking forward
to coming home too.

Love,
Your son,
Nelson

PS—I am (as I write) making two peach cobblers to take to a special party tonight! (Invitation only . . .)

He folds the letter into a small square and slides it into his breast
pocket. After dinner he will stop by the canteen, buy a stamp and an
envelope, and mail the second letter to his mom, who might receive it
Monday or Tuesday, by which time he'll already be home again, waiting
for school to resume in late August, though now with the goal of graduating early, and pushing into a new life, far afield. He will volunteer for
the army, become part of a new brotherhood, change his body, use his
skills, and prove to everyone, *everyone* that he can no longer be bullied
or ignored.

15

NELSON IS SO, SO PATIENT IN THE CRAFTING OF THIS
fire. He builds it large and wide and feeds the flames all morning long,
using what oak and maple he can find to set a base of reliably hot coals.
At lunchtime, he marches to the mess hall, eats without fanfare or conversation, and when the meal is finished, makes his way back to the
fire. He knows that to abandon the fire as he just did was reckless and
against every principle in Scouting—and yet, he does not care, the fire
was built beside a lake, contained on that side, and there was the day of
rain midweek. This fire was never going anywhere. He feels stronger for
having gambled with thousands of acres of forest, the lives of hundreds
of Scouts, and all the invisible creatures of the woods. He should, he
knows, feel ashamed.

At about three o'clock in the afternoon, he stokes the fire again, and
then, leaning against the trunk of a thick birch tree, falls into a troubled,
fitful sleep.

He dreams of the ghost deer. He dreams them in winter, when, though otherworldly, they seem perfectly suited to their habitat, the naked forest under snow. In the dream, Wilbur lies dying beside a small fire, and Nelson rushes between the forest and fire relentlessly, trying to build the flames up, with the thought that the fire may somehow keep Wilbur warm, keep him alive. The deer look on, blinking their eyes dumbly.

Back and forth he runs, back and forth, breaking branches off live trees, hearing their woody screams, and never enough fuel to beat back the cold that is frosting Wilbur's eyelids, his mustache, making fragile his thin, crinkled skin. What moisture his eyes held has now frozen, the lids forced forever open.

And Nelson, blowing and blowing at the flames, throwing more and more wood at the dwindling fire as daylight fades faster and faster, and night comes on cold and crystalline, perfectly silent, the stars suddenly dazzling and uncannily close, as if heaven were real, no farther than the treetops.

The ghost deer circle the dying fire now, gazing upon Wilbur's frozen corpse, and Nelson, aware of his own frailty, the cold slinking through his garments, pressing past his flesh, taking hold deep within the marrow of his aching bones. Distantly, the sound of a single wolf. Time stretching itself into boundless indefinite uncertainty and Nelson strains to hear it again—another long, low howl.

Only this time, a hundred howls, a thousand, all as close as the tree line, like a necklace of teeth waiting to snap shut on him and snuff out the stars forever.

Then the ghost deer screaming, as deer will do when startled, and just as quickly, the dream done, and Nelson awake and panting.

He removes his broken glasses, rubs at his eyes, wipes some coagulated drool away from his lips, restores the glasses, and examines his lush, green world.

The cook fire crackles contentedly, contained within its little make-shift ring, a thick bed of coals radiating waves of heat. Far off: boy laughter, the hollow clap and slap of lacrosse sticks, the sound of oars protesting inside rusty aluminum locks, a lifeguard lazily blowing his whistle.

He builds up the fire one last time, and returns to camp for his bugle. Soon it will be the time to blow taps.

DINNER IS ROAST BEEF left so rare that each time the platter is passed a wave of greasy diluted blood spills over the side and onto the table. Bowls of mashed potatoes with calderas of melted butter circulate from hand to hand, and peas, too, and hot white bread to wipe the plates clean.

Nelson has no appetite and waits patiently for the meal to con-clude. He has taken to sipping a cup of coffee as he listens to the other boys talk. Tonight they are whispering about him, about whether or not he is *okay* after the latrine, whether the experience hasn't *messed him up*. Some of the younger boys are talking among themselves; they want to go home. One boy leans close to another and seems to ask him something about a *new movie*, but Nelson can't tell which one they are discussing.

Maybe that's what he will do when he returns to Eau Claire. Have his mother drop him off at the theater downtown, all burgundy velve-teen grandeur and buttered popcorn; with the sizzle and fizz of Coca-Cola and the mad clamor of kid footsteps up thickly carpeted stars so very muffled; and, then, in secret dark corners and back-row sanctuar-ies, the new lovers draped over one another, their parents so far away. And then, a broken-in seat to settle into before that great rectangular expanse of screen up front. Maybe he'll go see a western with those strange landscapes so alien to Wisconsin: rusty-orange desert flatland

and jutting mesas and buttes, tumbleweed and cactus, arroyos and snakes and gunfights atop runaway trains or stagecoaches. Maybe he will fall asleep there, too, let his body go limp into that chair cushion until some kind theater attendant shakes him awake and leads him out by the guidance of a flashlight, back out into the too-bright glare of a late afternoon, the sun sliding down over the city's pair of wide rivers, the tire factory, the beer brewery, and the paper plant panting out its rotten-egg steam, its choking fumes.

NELSON CANNOT RECALL Wilbur excusing them from supper, nor does he remember rising from his table with the rest of his troop. Just the sensation of walking beside them, down that familiar path, back to their campsite, with nothing on their agenda except toasting marshmallows or reading the tales of Algernon Blackwood, with the wicked goal of trying to terrify some younger boy in the troop into having a nightmare.

Sunset is still hours away in the west when Nelson slinks out of the camp and returns to his lakeside cook fire, the coals by this point close to perfect. Now he will mix the batter, pour it into the two greased Dutch ovens, and hope for that evenly browned flawlessness Tim will be expecting. His biggest challenge, he realizes, will be carrying the Dutch ovens all the way out to the old amphitheater; no small task considering each one weighs more than ten pounds. He decides to wrap one in towels and place it into his Duluth Trading Company portage pack. The other he will have to carry in his hands; it will be largely cool by then, though he could always wrap it, too, in a towel or blanket or perhaps wear a pair of oven mitts. He doubts anyone in camp will question where he is going; the latrine incident has elevated his name, he senses, to some kind of camp legend status, the other boys now in awe of him, if not even spooked.

He sets the two Dutch ovens on the coals and then jogs quietly back to his tent, collects his needed supplies, and returns to the campfire. The cobblers will take about forty-five minutes of cooking, but already he can smell the peaches and the cakelike batter rising around the orange slices of fruit. Nelson imagines melting ice cream and a dash of fresh cinnamon, imagines sitting at the kitchen table while his mother hums a favorite melody, a cigarette smoldering in her favorite ashtray, coffee percolating on the stove, and outside, birds on the telephone wire calling out to the late afternoon neighborhood. Casually, his mom would turn from the Formica countertop where she was working a crossword puzzle, a pen balanced lightly between her teeth, and, from her apron produce three or four packs of baseball cards. *These are for you, darling. I had to stop at the hardware store today on an errand for your father. I hope you get some good ones.*

BY NOW THE LITTLE BAY SMELLS LIKE A KITCHEN, and using oven mitts and two heavy-duty pliers that Counselor Tim had included in the supply bag, Nelson moves the Dutch ovens off the coals and lets them cool near the shore. Lifting the lids, he reveals two flawless cobblers. Satisfied, he sits down and glances out over the lake, where a pair of loons are diving.

There is no guarantee that the party tonight is necessarily running afoul of Scout laws, but Nelson senses that something immoral is indeed happening. The cobblers will be his Trojan horse, the distraction he needs to bring Wilbur to the scene of the crime. He only hopes the old Scoutmaster won't congratulate him for his participation right then and there, in front of everyone; he hopes there is a subtle white lie to tell in that moment, *Well, I just happened to see Nelson carrying this heavy Dutch oven and thought to give him a hand. He refused but I just wouldn't take no as an answer. Now, what's happening here, boys? Wait a minute—*

are those cigars you're smoking? And gambling! Either way, his desire to make friends has waned. In his mind, he sees himself working as hard as can be at school so that he can leave, build a new life, a new identity, accrue new skills. He is committed to this notion. He doesn't want to be *Bugler* forever, but rather, a leader, a captain of men, a lieutenant or general, perhaps.

By eight o'clock, dusk is descending over the forest, the sun low over the western horizon, where it drapes the treetops in layers of pink, purple, and orange. Nelson removes the cobblers from the dutch oven, wraps them carefully, and stows one in the bag.

BACK AT HIS TENT HE DRESSES NEATLY, as if off to a Scouting soiree. He takes great care with his uniform, polishes his boots until they shine a dull brown. Combs his hair, cringes at the state of his eyeglasses, the cuts and scrapes still adorning his face. Leaves the cobblers inside his tent, where he'll collect them before leaving.

He walks to his father's tent, where Clete Doughty lies on his cot, snoring lightly.

"Dad?" he says, slipping through the unzipped tent flaps.

The soft snores continue.

"Dad," Nelson says a little more loudly.

His father stirs, rubs at his nose, then pushes up on one elbow. "Nelson?"

"Dad," Nelson begins again, "I promised Scoutmaster Wilbur that I'd help him carry some things to the mess hall tonight. I guess they found some old silverware in the basement of the canteen that Wilbur wants to put into circulation. I was wondering, will you be here tonight, at the campfire?"

His father stares at him with dull, tired eyes. "Why?" he asks, almost irritably.

"Just that it'd be nice," Nelson says, "to sit by the fire tonight, before we have to head back home. Our last night together and all."

His father coughs twice, itches the back of his scalp, yawns. "Thing is, Nelson, some other fathers and I might visit another troop's campsite tonight. Apparently one of the men's got a very fine old bottle of Scotch." He pauses. "It might be good for business if I went along. Do you understand?"

"Dad," Nelson says again. "Please. Stay in camp tonight. I have something I need to get off my chest."

"Go on now, Nelson, before Wilbur thinks you've forgotten. And I'll think about staying put." He clasps his hands behind his head, purses his lips. "You're a good boy," he says finally. "Now go help Wilbur."

Nelson makes one other stop before marching to Wilbur's cabin.

"Anybody in there?" he says, outside Jonathan's tent.

"Hold on," Jonathan says, "let me put on a shirt." It's a few seconds before the older boy unzips the tent and stands before Nelson. "What is it?"

"I just wanted to warn you, that, well, if you were planning on leaving camp tonight to smoke a cigarette, I would highly recommend that you don't."

"What are you talking about, Nelson?"

Nelson feels his hand reaching out to touch Jonathan's shoulder. "Please," he urges. "Just don't go out tonight. Stay in your tent. Trust me." It is possible that Jonathan is the closest thing to a friend Nelson has, and he has no interest in potentially submarining Jonathan's Boy Scout career.

"Everything okay, old chum? Are you feeling all right? You seem a little . . . odd, you know?"

"I'm fine," Nelson says. "Good night, Jonathan."

"Good night, Nelson."

He leaves the campsite quietly, and no one pays him any mind.

Holding the Dutch oven before him, he might have been taking it to a new neighbor's home, a welcoming present. Not a single Scout does he encounter on the path to the parade ground; but, then, some of the troops, he knows, are gathering around a telescope out on a dock by Bass Lake tonight for a tour of the galaxy, there to practice identifying heavenly bodies, participation required for the Astronomy merit badge. Others, no doubt, are packing up gear before their imminent departures tomorrow night or Saturday morning.

Monday, Nelson thinks, *seems so, so long ago.*

16

✕

WILBUR SITS AT A SMALL TABLE INSIDE HIS CABIN, and from the relative darkness outside Nelson watches him a moment, through the screen door. The inside of the cabin is spartan: a few framed photographs, some fly-fishing rods and wicker creels hanging from the wall, a wide bookshelf. A lantern glows on the table beside Wilbur, and Nelson is quietly pleased to see it is a forest-green Coleman, same as his. The old Scoutmaster appears to be writing a letter.

"Come in," he says, without turning.

Startled, Nelson opens the door. The back wall of the cabin is two large picture windows that look out over the lake. In the middle of the cabin is a great fieldstone fireplace. Nelson cannot see Wilbur's sleeping chamber.

"How'd you know I—"

"I could *smell* you coming, Nelson, for one thing. Do you normally sneak up on people carrying peach cobbler? You would make a terrible spy. A soldier, perhaps. A good soldier, I reckon."

The boy squeaks out a laugh. It feels about the first time he has smiled in a week, and it almost hurts, feels like the laughter could spill right over into tears, a total collapse. He fixes his eyes down at the floor of the cabin.

"So you brought me dessert. That was kind of you." The old man is looking at him now, doling out his words evenly, calmly.

"No," Nelson says quietly. *This is the moment. After this, he may never want to return to camp, may never again be welcome here.* "Scoutmaster Wilbur, I have to tell you . . . I was invited by one of the counselors to take these cobblers to a party tonight." He swallows his budding Adam's apple, re-grips the Dutch oven in his sweaty hands.

"Yes?"

A clock ticks in another room.

"It's a secret, the party. Out in the old amphitheater."

Wilbur sighs, sets his pencil on the table beside a pocketknife and a small pile of shavings. "Sit down," he says.

"I'm supposed to be there at nine," Nelson explains.

"Sit down," Wilbur says more firmly. He moves a chair away from the table with the toe of his boot so that the seat faces the boy. "And set those cobblers down by the door, why don't you."

Nelson does as he is asked, sits down, clears his throat, laces his fingers above his lap, shuffles his feet, as if about to suffer through what may be a lengthy sermon. He feels Wilbur's eyes on him.

"You have two choices now, Nelson," Wilbur says. "You can come with me to this, this *party*, and everyone will know what you've done. You won't make any new friends, I can assure you of that. You may even suffer unforeseen consequences when you return home, tribulations that I cannot protect you from."

Nelson thinks of his father, the belt. Were he to rat out several dozen campers, it certainly wouldn't do his father any favors in drawing new clients. He thinks of his mother, and how she might be punished, too, for simply trying to intercept his father's inevitable assault. They will both be beaten, and after he's been finished with, he'll have to listen to her cries from behind his parents' locked bedroom door.

"Or," Wilbur continues, "you can simply go back to your tent, and tomorrow morning, the whole camp will be different, and while it may be that boys will suspect that you were the informant, I will deny it. I will tell the guilty parties that I saw you walking down the path with those cobblers and when I asked you where you were going, you would not tell me and I grew suspicious, and it was only when I threatened to punish your entire troop, to send you all back home and inform all your parents, that you volunteered to take the blame. I will paint you as a martyr, in fact. It may be that the Scouts at this party are released without punishment. But any participating counselors and camp employees will then of course be summarily fired.

"In any case, and no matter your decision, I'm indebted to you, Nelson, for this gesture. I just can't *believe* I was so blind. Scouts do bad things every summer, without fail. But it was the counselors that I could not believe, wouldn't believe were mixed up in something abhorrent. Oh, Nelson. Thank you, son, for this. I hope you will feel comfortable in asking me for whatever recommendations you need. I know the headmasters at many fine preparatory schools around the nation, and not a few politicians and businessmen in high places as well."

Wilbur shakes his head.

"Those boys, they gave me such smiles each time I departed their company. I thought their hearts were really into it, the work. But I was deceived, I suppose, like some senile old grandfather."

Now even the sun's afterglow has blued to dark. The smoke of a dozen campfires hangs in the air over the lake.

"What will we find out there?" Nelson asks. "I mean, what do you think they're doing?"

"I don't know, son. Ascribing to a code isn't convenient. What we should be trying to impart upon you boys is a lifelong commitment to a set of virtues that will guide you throughout your days. The teenage years are difficult, there is no doubt. But they're certainly no more difficult than being a father, or a husband, or leading men into war . . . no more difficult than being responsible for hundreds of employees.

"What is happening out there tonight, I can assure you, is not congruent with the Scout oath or laws. I don't need to tell you that."

Nelson nods his head slowly.

"What's your decision, then?" Wilbur asks.

"Can we hope we're mistaken?"

"It is good of you, to want to believe the best of your peers," Wilbur says, rising from the table. "And I wouldn't want you to lose that optimism, either. But don't allow yourself to be made a fool, Nelson. Now, what is your decision?"

"I'll come," the boy says, stepping into the current.

THEY SPEAK NOT A WORD to each other as they walk deep into the woods, Wilbur moving effortlessly along the old path, no need for any maps, no need even to check for the old blazes painted or scarred onto tree trunks. Nelson struggles to keep up, one Dutch oven heavy and still warm in his hands, the other borne upon his back, like some iron baby in a strange papoose.

Even from five hundred yards, they can hear laughter, can make out the dance of flames. And there is something else. Something seems to flicker out there, in a steady click of beats, some softly mechanical cricket-whisper Nelson half-recognizes but cannot quite place . . .

"Hold on," says Wilbur quietly. "Stay right here. I want to have a look around before barging in there. Some of these folks are likely to skedaddle, and I'll want to see their faces before I accuse them of something—before I have to fire them." And, like that, he is off again, disappearing into the underbrush, quiet as a deer. Nelson kneels down on the trail, closes his eyes, concentrates on *that* sound. *What is it?*

This kind of focus is crucial in ornithology, when, waking early in the morning, a person cannot see the birds they are so eager to catalog. And so, to learn everything he can, Nelson has stood in a forest more than once before the break of dawn, joined by a group of older women and older men, binoculars resting on all their chests, who advised him to listen, strain his ears, and isolate the songs filtering down out of the tree-tops. Patterns, that is what they are, after all, patterns of sound and song, certain notes repeated, certain pitches, imitations, rifts, calls and repeats.

A Mrs. Patton it was who kindly leaned down beside him and enu-merated the invisible birds he was hungry to identify. "Anyone can identify a bird with a guide and a pair of binoculars," she said. "*We're* teaching you to identify something in the dark, you see.

"There," she whispered, then, a moment or two later, "hear that? A good place to start. That's *Carduelis tristis*, the American goldfinch." They listened. "Boy, long-winded this morning, isn't she? Still, a beauti-ful bird, and of course, they're everywhere. Some folks call them wild canaries. I don't know which I like better, goldfinch or canary—both magnificent names."

She paused, and they listened again.

"Now listen carefully. Hear that? *Whata-cheer-cheer-cheer* . . . It's a good one to know, and you'll never forget it. Easy-to-remember Latin name, too, *Cardinalis cardinalis*." She smiled sweetly. "We take them for granted, because they're common enough in Wisconsin, but you bring a European into your backyard and they'll be amazed at the color of our birds. Cardinals and blue jays, and orioles, indigo buntings and scarlet tanagers and pileated woodpeckers . . ."

And suddenly it comes to Nelson, the sound—from all the dozens and dozens of matinees he's sat through in Eau Claire, at that old movie house, *that* sound over and behind his shoulder, sputtering but steady;

just faintly filtered through the forest the sound of a reel-to-reel movie projector is impossible to mistake as it trickles toward him. The ferns shake and then part and Wilbur is back beside him again, slightly out of breath, wiping his brow with an extra bandanna he keeps in a back pocket. Nelson can't recall ever seeing Wilbur sweat before.

"They're watching a movie," the boy says quietly.

Wilbur purses his lips. Scratches at the trail with a pointed finger. "You're going to see something," he whispers, "that I suspect you've never seen before, and I apologize for that. What is happening over yonder, is, well, not in keeping with any Scouting law. It is an abomination, Nelson, and . . . Well, I'm ashamed to have you here right now." He pauses. "Anyway, you were right. Counselor Tim is amongst them, as are many of my finest counselors. There are many Scouts out there as well, many so-called fine boys, not a few of them appearing to be quite drunk. I just don't understand . . ."

Nelson says nothing.

Through the darkness comes Wilbur's hand, reaching out for the boy's shoulder. "I'm sorry, son. Just know you've done well. In fact, perhaps you *would* make a good spy."

"I wish," Nelson tries, "I wish . . . I'm sorry, sir."

"You were *loyal* to me, Nelson, and you were *reverent*. So, now you just need to be *brave*, all right? Keep your chin up, look into their eyes, and forget about what you see. Look without seeing, if you can manage it. I hope you never have to go to war, but if you do, then . . . that is what will perhaps keep you sane, *looking without seeing*."

He draws the boy up, dusts off his knees and elbows. "You go first, now," Wilbur advises. "I'll be behind you in a bit. Perhaps they'll believe I followed you here, and not fault you. All right. Go now."

NELSON WALKS THE PATH through the darkness holding the Dutch oven ahead of him, moving toward the sound of the movie projector, the peals of laughter, the increasing pungency of cigar, pipe, and cigarette smoke. There are other strange fragrances in the air, too, scents of skunk or pine. Tin cups kissing in toast, backslapping, hearty guffaws. It sounds like fellowship, fraternity, the very kind of male community and camaraderie Nelson has so often sought during his days, years, at this camp. And then, thirteen-year-old Nelson Doughty, carrying his perfectly baked peach cobblers, emerges from the forest.

Emerges to what seems like sincere welcome! Cheers! Every face turns to smile at him; nor are the smiles contrived, that much is plain to see. Boys who have never spoken to him, boys from his own troop, turn from their conversations to wave at Nelson, *wave* at him! And there is Jack Lovell, Jack-the-Ginger among them, gesturing him over as he removes an improbable cigar from his mouth and yells, "Nelson! There's our boy!" Jack reaches into his breast pocket and holds up a fistful of cigars for Nelson to see, as if a proud new celebratory father looking to spread the mirth.

A set of hands take the Dutch oven from him now, slide the back-pack off, and suddenly, a cold steel can is in his hands, all the colder for the warm dish he's been clutching for how long—twenty minutes? He brings the can to his lips, as he's seen his father do at barbecues, and family reunions. The smell is interesting enough, sweetly pungent . . . but the taste of the liquid itself is terrible. Rot and gym socks and old wet corn. *Beer*, he thinks, stunned slightly. *My first beer.* He glances at the movie screen, which is, in fact, a giant white sheet stretched between two white pines, or rather several bedsheets sewn or stitched together. It might be twenty feet long by twelve feet tall. Nelson gulps down an-other swig of beer, holding on to the cool sweat of that aluminum can for dear life.

There, up on the bedsheet is a young woman, the most beautiful woman he's ever seen, with dark, silky Audrey Hepburn hair and skin pale as milk—the film is black and white, but the shades of gray are so fantastically subtle, so shiny, nuanced, shadowed, inviting. And she is stark naked, reclined on a davenport, her arms moving languidly, as if part of some agonizingly slow swim-dance. Her mascaraed eyelids are exquisitely shut, and then suddenly open, staring right out at Nelson. Averting his gaze, he turns now to the audience. Where rows and rows of boys watch, mouths agape, eyes wide open, some hands digging into bowls of popcorn, or taking pulls from bottles of beer, or tin cups of what he imagines must be whiskey or brandy. Some of the boys touch contemplative fingers to their lips, as if NASA engineers, struggling with some impossible mathematical conundrum, while across their faces, infantile happiness spreads easily across shiny lips.

The young woman on-screen rearranges herself, as if she were fluffing cushions or folding some throw blanket, and now she is on all fours, laughing at the camera that films her, laughing at all those collected boys in this Wisconsin forest, so intoxicated by her beauty, so breathless. Nelson is suddenly dimly aware that someone is trying to speak to him.

"Nelson!" It is Counselor Tim. He is shaking the boy's shoulders, grinning so wide Nelson might have thought he'd just hit a home run in the bottom of the ninth inning to extinguish the New York Yankees from the World Series. He closes his eyes, tastes the beer on his palate, at the back of his throat. He feels sick, confused . . . at once happy, sad. *It will all end soon enough . . .*

"Nelson! I've been standing here for a whole minute, trying to get your attention, man! What? Never seen a girl naked before? Hey, how's your beer? Say, I've got your money, by the way, right here, just like we talked about."

Tim holds the dollar bills out for him to take, but Nelson isn't interested in touching anyone's hand. All he wants is to look up at the night sky, the gently undulating leaves of the maples, like so many sequins shuffling against each other . . . *And yet . . .* His eyes keep drawing back to the woman. Now there seems to be a man on top of her, his muscles, all of them, bulging as he sweats, thrusts. He is covered in dark hair: his buttocks, his ankles, his shoulders. The woman is shaking her head, tousling her hair, sucking at her own fingers. Nelson cannot decide if it's pain she is in, or some kind of bright ecstasy.

"Take the money!" Tim says, stuffing it into Nelson's front pockets. "Say, you want to take a seat? Get comfortable? I can find you a cigarette if you'd like to try one. Whad'ya say there, Nelson, old pal?"

"No," Nelson says. "No, it's okay, Tim, really." It occurs to him suddenly that he has not noticed Jonathan anywhere in the mix. The thought leaves him at least a little relieved.

Tim looks concerned. "All right, all right. Hey, you okay? I mean, you don't have to stay if you don't want to. Just, you can't tell anyone, understand? But you can go. Is that what you want to do?"

Nelson can't take his eyes off the screen, wants desperately to avert his gaze, but can't. It's all too much. The woman on-screen is still on her knees, her back so flat that a cup of coffee would be safe from spilling, were it not for the man pounding at her from behind.

"Scouts!" thunders a righteously indignant voice all of a sudden. "Stop this stag smut right now!"

It is Wilbur, standing on the edge of the forest, knuckles pressed into his waist, elbows at perfectly congruous angles, kneecaps bulging over high socks, mustache waxed into two tiny horns. His eyes ablaze.

The projectionist fumbles, the film either tearing or simply falling away from its spool, and now the white screen glows in the night as the rows of moviegoers fiddle and readjust, their faces telegraphing shame and dread. Some of the partygoers have already slinked off into the woods to the sound of branches breaking and boughs snapping, their hasty retreat resounding through the forest. Many of the counselors in attendance simply hang their heads, spilling drinks onto the ground. A few younger boys seem close to tears.

"A stag movie," Wilbur says indignantly. "Tobacco, alcohol, *pornog-*

raphy . . ." He is positively fuming. "Not a one of you is a true Scout, do you hear? Not a one of you, a true man." He looks down upon the Scouts who have not yet absconded, looks down upon them with such fury, such indignation, and, what is worse, with such *disappointment*, that Nelson knows all their faces are pointed, as his is, down at their boots.

"You will all be sent home tomorrow. All of you. You boys, your Scoutmasters will be notified. I will try to determine if your parents should be informed likewise. As for the counselors among you here, begin packing your effects tonight. At three P.M. tomorrow afternoon, I will inspect your cabins, and any possessions left on camp premises shall be burned. You should be ashamed of yourselves. Role models? Leaders? Citizens?" He spits at the movie projector some ten feet away. "Perverts, is what you are. Unfit. Indecent. I have half a mind to call the police, do you hear me? I am just . . . disgusted."

"Now wait just a second," one older boy says, emerging from the shadows. He is very tall, already regal-looking even, broad across the shoulders and slim at the waist. This, Nelson knows at once, is Rand Cook, a boy known across the state as the son of a paper company magnate who once ran for governor. A state track star, Rand lives with his family on the eastern side of Wisconsin along the banks of the rivers where once French trappers and Jesuit priests had come exploring America, and where now great factories burp out noxious steam and piss into those same swift-running waters. It is not uncommon to see Rand Cook standing in a back corner of the mess hall while others eat, him surrounded by a U of younger boys, holding court, gesticulating with long fingers, wide palms, and the loud, forceful delivery of a boy supremely confident and rarely interrupted or second-guessed. "I mean, listen," he says with a soft, courtly laugh, moving smoothly toward Wilbur, "there's no need to go off half-cocked here, Scoutmaster. Boys will be boys, right? And this is just—"

"I am trying to make men of you all!" Wilbur roars, turning to intercept Cook, spittle flying from his lips, past that magnificent anachronism of a mustache, his thin, veiny arms atremble. "Honorable men! Men that won't divorce their wives. That won't leave their friends on the battlefield. That will pay their taxes and vote and work hard. Do you understand me? This is an insult not just to me, but to *yourselves*. It is lewd and pernicious and you, you little twerp, should be ashamed! Truly. Shame on you!"

"Now, Mr. Whiteside, come on. Let's get a hold of ourselves, all right? I mean, you seem a bit distraught." Cook lays a condescending hand on Wilbur's quivering shoulder.

In a single movement, Wilbur swipes the youth's hand off his person, moves directly into Cook, grabbing the boy by his windpipe, pushing him against the trunk of a tree, holding him there long enough for everyone left around the amphitheater to gasp, take a step toward them, and then think better of it.

"Leave my camp," Wilbur says. "Don't come back. You hear? Call your daddy, why don't you, and tell him *why* I've given you the boot." He releases his hold. "Everyone, get back to your campsites. Pack up, now. I want you gone by lunch." He kicks at the dust. "Now!" he snaps.

NELSON HIDES IN THE UNDERBRUSH, waits for the amphitheater to empty. He watches Wilbur hang his head, kick at bottles of rum, whiskey, brandy. Watches him stoop to collect cigarette butts, stuffing them into his pockets. Wilbur struggles to pull the screen down from its mooring above the stage, and Nelson emerges from the shadows to help him, climbing up onto the stage, where he begins ripping and wrenching at the fabric.

"Thank you, son," says the old man. "I'm so tired this evening, I must say."

"Shall I walk with you," Nelson says, "back to your cabin?"

"I want you to know, Nelson, that film. You have to forget that. See, that isn't how . . . Your wife, she may not look like that. You can't expect every woman, any woman to . . . Those films warp a man's mind." Wilbur gives a strong tug on the sheet's last remaining stay, but it doesn't want to give. "It becomes like any other vice. I'm at a loss for words, son. Boys come to camp for . . . Not to see, not to be shown . . ."

And now the fabric breaks loose and flutters down, like a banner of defeat that settles all over Wilbur, over his head and shoulders, all the way down to his polished boots. The old man does not even struggle out from beneath it, just stands, and waits until Nelson pulls it off him, as if unveiling a statue from another time, his mustache now slightly askew, and drooping.

THE CAMPSITE IS ABUZZ when Nelson returns: father-son shouting matches, tents collapsing in hurried heaps, clothes rushed into bags. He watches one father spank his teenage son, a boy who might be larger than his own dad, and yet . . . General confusion has descended over the camp and already some boys are marching down the path back to the parking lot, their fathers behind them, cursing, saying, "I just can't believe . . ." or "Wait until your mother hears about . . ."

Nelson finds his father sitting beside the campfire.

"You weren't mixed up in this whole fiasco, I trust?" Clete asks, shaking his head. "I don't know what happened, but *holy shit*. Whiteside's gone crazy."

"No, Dad," he says, settling down beside him on a wooden bench. He sits close enough to his father that their arms touch, their knees, this minuscule contact so reassuring somehow, so grounding. "What happened?"

"I don't know. Can't figure it out. Reminds me of the army, though. Like a bunch of kids went AWOL or something. Hard to tell."

"Huh."

They stare at the fire for some time.

"You're a good boy, though," Clete says. "I know I've been hard on you at times, but you're a good boy."

"Thanks, Dad."

Clete yawns. "Let's talk tomorrow, all right, son? I think I'm going to turn in."

"Me, too," the boy says.

His eyelids feel so heavy. He rests his head on his father's shoulder, wishes he were small enough to be carried back to his tent and tucked into his sleeping bag.

17

NINETY MILES FROM THE ENTRANCE OF CAMP CHIP-
pewa to Nelson's driveway back in Eau Claire and the car ride is epically
silent. His father rolls down his window, hangs an elbow out into the
sun, occasionally glancing at the boy in the rearview, and smokes a rare
chain of cigarettes; he keeps a secret pack in the glove compartment for
those sporadic instances of flat tires, speeding tickets, or near-death col-
lisions. The smoke rolls back to Nelson, making him green.

He played reveille this morning before a group of campers shrunk
by fully a quarter, with very few counselors standing alongside Wilbur.
Even a few of the cooks were missing, and breakfast came slowly, the
bacon badly undercooked, the scrambled eggs runny, burning toast filling the mess hall with smoke.

Cars loaded with scared-looking kids and sullen, angry fathers left
the camp in an all-too-speedy parade of exhaust and flicked cigarette
butts. Wilbur stood motionless at the entrance of the camp. Nelson had
waved at him, but the old man just nodded—that was all.

"I can't even believe what I had to hear at breakfast," his father says finally, the first words between them in more than an hour. "That a bunch of Scouts jerry-rigged some kind of stag theater? Out in the woods? And you sniffed them out? You were the snitch?" He eyeballs Nelson in the rearview mirror. "Do I have that correct?"

Nelson lowers his head. "Yes, sir."

"And you even indicted some of the boys from your own goddamn troop?"

The boy nods.

"Well, great goddamn," Clete says under his breath, "I might be getting out of business at the right time after all . . ."

"What?"

"Nothing, Nelson." He stares at the boy in the rearview. "All right, well, you got something in return, I hope?"

"What do you mean?"

"Quid pro quo and all that," Clete says. "Wilbur scratching your back, too?"

Nelson squirms in his seat slightly. "It was just the right thing to do, Dad. I didn't . . . I mean, I didn't need a reward, if that's what you're saying."

Clete shrugs. "Well, Nelson, see, most people *would*. Because, the thing of it is, people don't like snitches, and afterward, sometimes the snitch isn't exactly treated like a real war hero, you catch my drift?"

"I'm not a *snitch*," the boy insists.

The car returns to silence and Nelson cups his chin in his hands and leans against the window, scanning out over the passing fields as they fly by.

"Where'd they get the films anyway?"

Nelson shrugs. "Someone's uncle passed away, I guess? I don't know. They didn't tell me much. They were in his basement or something."

At this, Clete Doughty begins laughing. Laughing and laughing and coughing smoke and pounding his hand against the steering wheel.

Nelson is startled, confused. "I don't understand, Dad. What's so funny?"

"It's nothing," his father says. "Just that . . . all this fuss, and they were probably just watching someone's aunt maybe. Someone's mom."

Nelson can't help feeling very sad.

DAYS LATER, Nelson, his mother, and his father sit around the kitchen table, a large casserole dish between them, along with a bowl of salad, a loaf of bread, and some butter. The days are growing infinitesimally shorter, but still there is the sound of children at play on the street before their mothers issue a stern last call from the front steps. The silence around the table ever since they returned home from camp has grown more stifling, crushing even. The loud secret inside the house is that Clete's bosses at work seem on the brink of firing him. This Nelson has gleaned from a late-night conversation between his parents; having snuck out of his bed to press an ear against the bedroom door—and eavesdrop on what was being said in the kitchen down the hall. Now he is afraid to look his father in his eyes, afraid to turn his back to him; worries that his snitching in camp may have lost his dad some clients. Certainly, it is hard to imagine his snitching having benefited his father.

"You're a good woman, Dorothy," his father mumbles uncharacteristically, scratching with a fork at a few cold peas left on his plate. "Always been a good wife to me."

"What did you say, dear?" Nelson's mother asks, quite surprised.

Now Clete swallows, wipes at his stubbled face with a red and white gingham napkin, and looks at Nelson. "I'm proud of you, too, son. You are your own person, always have been. The truth is, I haven't always understood who that *is*, but . . ."

"Clete," Dorothy says. "Clete, now what in blazes are you talking about? You're not making a lick of sense."

He rises from the table somewhat unsteadily. "I think I might just rest for a moment," he says softly.

"Sure, sure thing," says Dorothy. "Let me fix you a Manhattan, dear. You go put up your feet, go rest."

Nelson finishes his dinner, wanders into the living room, where his father is reclined in his chair, staring at the blank screen of the television. The cocktail in his hand seems precariously close to slipping right through his fingers to the carpeting. Nelson takes the glass from his father's hand, sets it on the coffee table.

"Dad, are you okay?" Nelson asks.

Clete blinks slowly, looks at his son. "Come here," he says.

The boy moves cautiously toward his father, half-afraid of being slapped.

But Clete pulls him in close, sits up in his chair, and hugs the boy, fiercely, then kisses him on the top of his head. *A kiss.*

"I'm going to bed now," Clete says. "I'm tired. Have a good day at school tomorrow, okay?"

18

THE NEXT NIGHT DOROTHY AND NELSON SIT AT THE
kitchen table for almost an hour before Clete shows up. He is drunk,
smells of alcohol and of cigarettes. His eyelids droop over angry-looking
red eyes. He rips into the roast chicken on the table in a way that makes
Dorothy gasp, as if he's a wild animal. He doesn't say a word to them.

Dorothy asks, "How was work today, dear?"

He begins laughing.

What happens next does not elapse in a single movement, the way
James Cagney did it in movies, no. Clete's legs graze the table as he
rises, the chair tips over slowly, then skids against the wall, leaving a
rip in the wallpaper. And when he tries to flip the table over, his hand
slips, and he almost falls to the floor, before finding better purchase,
and then lifting just that side of the table, causing all the food, all the
china, all the silverware to go sliding off in a single wave, right past his
wife and son. Now, the table lighter, he manages to throw it against

the kitchen counter. His glasses are crazily crooked, his forehead is so very red, and his lower jaw protrudes, the teeth visible and spittle connecting them.

"My son the snitch," Clete says. "What? The old man offered you some chocolate? Some fucking baseball cards?"

"Clete!" his mother shrieks. "Leave him *alone*!" She places her own body between Nelson and his father. She is trembling and when her hands touch her son, he feels the strength and fear in her fingers and forearms.

"I was fired!" Clete roars. "And guess what the boss mentions, after he gives me the news. He asks me about my son, the snitch. Turns out his nephew was one of the boys Nelson ratted out. So thanks, you little shit." He is upon them now, about to make his rage felt as surely as he's ever done, one broad hand raised up high, the other one pushing this woman of his aside like the nuisance she is.

"Stop it!" she screams.

"Go on, protect him! That'll make him a man! Can't go through life with a mother holding his hand. Defending him everywhere he goes." He pushes her hard enough now that she falls to the floor. Nelson's eyes widen as he registers what is about to happen.

Only Dorothy is done with this. She picks up a fork that has fallen to the floor and for a moment, seems almost to fumble it, unable to commit to a grip. Then she raises it, and screaming, rushes Clete, begins to stab him in the arm, and then she is pushing him out of the kitchen, knocking him to the floor of the living room, falling down upon him, plunging the tines of the fork right down into his face, raking his forehead and cheeks, at one point catching the fork on the helix of Clete's ear, into that delicately curved translucent flesh. His ear tears open and for a moment appears in danger of ripping off. Blood everywhere. He is screaming, too, now, as he crawls toward the front door, and with Dorothy following him every step of the way, stabbing at his back and awkwardly kicking at his butt, shouting at him to leave, never come back, good riddance.

Finally he is out the door and running toward the Chevrolet.

"Get him his keys," his mother orders her son in a strangely commanding lower register of her voice. He rushes to the coat tree, rifles through his father's pockets, finds the keys, brings them to her.

She steps out the front door now and throws the keys at the car. "Get out of here, you ugly, stupid man. Go!"

Up and down the street porch lights are blinking on, dogs barking, windows cracking, doors opening discreetly, faces peering out, and no one says a word—the jubilant cries of summertime children have been hushed, AM radios turned *way way* down, and dessert and coffee conversation shrunk to wrinkled forehead whispers, *What on earth is going on over at the Doughty house?* Meanwhile, Dorothy is shuddering violently with adrenaline, holding her own shoulders, and leaning against the door, blood on her hands.

Clete collects the keys off the ground. "I haven't been in love with you for years," he says pointing at Dorothy. "So long, you old cow."

Then he is in the car, slamming it into reverse, out onto the street, and in a scream of Firestones he is gone, just two angry red taillights receding down the block. Oh, the street is so quiet now. You can hear the streetlights flickering on, humming their nocturnal return to steady service. And how the house at 1325 Fairway Street is suddenly so much bigger for his absence, so much quieter. The screen door closes and mother and son sit silently in the living room, she sprawled across the couch, and Nelson, in shock, sliding to the carpeting beside her.

"I'm sorry," he says, taking her hand, not knowing what to do with it. He squeezes.

"For what?" she says, wearily, eyes closed.

"When I was at camp I thought, *My whole life, and you've always been my best friend.* I missed you so much, Mom."

She kisses the top of his head. "That was a beautiful letter you wrote me. Thank you."

He crawls beside her on the couch and together they sob, without a care for who might hear them, who might know what has happened. Minutes pass. It feels so good to cry, Nelson thinks.

"Thank you, Nelson," she says at last. "I love you so much, you know. You are *such* a good boy, you know that? You've always been so kind, so sensitive."

He nods, wipes away more tears, then begins laughing, little trickles of laughter.

"What?" she asks. She hits him, lightly, on the shoulder. "What is it?"

"Just that—you stabbed Dad with a *fork*."

She snorts, two or three loud snorts. And then they are both nervously laughing. Nelson loves when he can make her snort like this.

"You really got his ear. Did you see that? I mean, there was a *hole* there—in his *ear*!"

She breathes deeply, but then, hiccupping, covers her mouth.

"Oh dear," she says. Now she covers her face with her hands, talks through her fingers. "Nelson—oh Jesus. What've I done?"

"What do you mean?"

She looks up, eyes red, bleary, wild. "What will we even do? For food, I mean . . . this house?" She holds up her hands, as if indicating the ceiling, rafters, roof. "Nelson," she says, "I've never worked. We don't have another car." She shakes her head, bites her lip. She stands from the couch abruptly, walks past him, into the kitchen, begins to pick up the chaos of food, broken china, dirty silverware, the overturned table lying there, like a wooden animal, its legs rigor mortis stiff in the air. Nelson follows her.

"You don't have to worry about me," he says, surprising himself.

"What?"

"This is my fault," he says. "It's my fault Dad is gone."

"Nelson, don't say that. It's simply not true."

"I've got a friend, though, and he can help, see? So, you won't have to worry about me."

"*What?*" she says. "*Who?* Nelson, what are you talking about?"

"Scoutmaster Wilbur. He offered to help me. To find me a school."

"Nelson, stop. I don't understand. You *have* a school."

"No, but a really good one, Mom. Where I could start over. Maybe make some friends. He would help, Mom. I know he would. Maybe he could help you find a job, too."

"You would do that? You could just, leave? What would— Nelson, I don't know. Really?"

"It would be better," he says. "You wouldn't have to worry about me. And I could come back, for holidays, summers. It's just you wouldn't have to worry about me."

She sighs. "Nelson . . ."

"What?"

"The reality is . . ." She throws a pea at the window screen, where it bounces off, lands near her outstretched foot. "Nelson . . . I never went to college. I can't even type. I don't have a resumé, no nice clothes. What am I supposed to do?"

"I don't know."

"You don't know."

He is silent a moment, then asks, "You really think he's gone for good?"

She nods. Thinks about the letter from Wrigley Field. Decides to tell the boy the truth, "Nelson, your father took another job. In Chicago. He was always planning to leave, I think. Tonight was . . . his goodbye." She shakes her head.

"Oh," Nelson says. "But, why?" His little heart hurts.

"He wasn't happy here, I guess. I don't know."

"So he's not coming home again? Ever?"

"I don't know, Nelson. I don't know. You are a good, good boy. But you are still just a boy. Let's not make any rash decisions right now, okay?"

She continues picking up debris, depositing it into the garbage can. Night has spread itself evenly over the horizon.

Nelson stands, takes the telephone down, dials the operator, waits, then says, "Operator? Good evening, ma'am. Please connect me to Camp Chippewa. Haugen, Wisconsin. Yes, ma'am. I'll wait."

"What are you doing, Nelson?" his mother asks, rising from the kitchen floor, her face flushing with blood. "Nelson! Who are you calling?" Her voice is loud, sharp.

He does not acknowledge her. He has stepped into the river again, made a decision, and now feels the flow of it about him, carrying him off.

"Nelson!"

"Yes, Scoutmaster Wilbur. Sorry to disturb you at this hour, sir, but . . . I'll cut right to the chase."

Less than a minute later, he hangs up the receiver. "I'm to be ready in two hours' time. You are welcome to come along, Scoutmaster Wilbur says."

He turns, and makes for his bedroom.

"Nelson? You are my son, you can't just . . . *leave*."

"If he isn't coming back, Mom, then we have to start thinking. We have to be prepared. We have to plan for the future." His voice is confident and he realizes he is reciting his training.

"Nelson?"

"Yes, Mom."

"You are a sweet, kind boy. It's just . . ." She slumps to the kitchen floor, her back flush against the wall. She holds two halves of a broken plate.

"Please just come, Mom."

She shakes her head no.

Then his boy footsteps, disappearing up the staircase, and she is alone on the floor, amid shards of china, the already drying blood, casserole splattered everywhere. The dogs have finally slowed their barking. Porch lights along the block are blinking off. Each time a car passes down the street she turns to the window.

She stands, wipes her eyes, frees the broom from the closet, and begins cleaning up the kitchen.

Oh Lord, she thinks, *protect my child. Protect my sweet boy.*

PART II

»——→

SUMMER, 1996

STARDUST SUPPER
CLUB & LOUNGE

19

THE BICYCLES LEAN BORED ON THEIR KICKSTANDS, casually awaiting a decision.

"You should take them, honey, honestly," says Sarah Quick, arms crossed. "You've got a couple days on either end of the trip. So you don't use 'em? At least you've got them. What's your motto, 'Be Prepared'?"

"Mom," her son, Trevor, whines, "nobody actually, like, says that out loud."

"You can't say your motto out loud?"

"Never mind."

"'Be Prepared.' I like it. Soon enough you'll be off to college. Gotta be prepared there, too. Your dad and I will get you a box of condoms. Heck, a case. What else? Kleenex, deodorant, cologne, Q-tips, toilet paper, socks, underwear . . . What am I forgetting?"

"Dad, can we *please* get going?"

Jonathan Quick, forty-nine years old, president/CEO of Quick

Trucking & Transport, stands on his newly repaved driveway, studying his shadow, thinking, *Seven grand for a bunch of concrete is a helluva way to spend money.* "Your mom's right," he says distractedly, running a hand across a smoothly shaven face. "Let's take the bikes. After camp is done, who knows? Maybe we'll get bored. Want to poke around. I can think of a few paths up there."

A black tubular apparatus is hauled out of the garage, trailing its confusion of black straps, and affixed to the backside of the minivan, and the bicycles are secured to this rack with a motley collection of additional bungee cords and ropes. Sarah uses the idle moments to pull dandelions from the yard, and stands back up to assess her husband's progress, rubbing her toes against the wet morning lawn.

"Dad, your knot tying is terrible."

"Yeah, well, I never made Eagle, remember?" Jonathan says, giving a winsome smile. And to think, he had been so close to achieving that prestigious rank in an organization for boys. Then again, what good would that badge serve now? Not exactly like being a four-star general, say, or captain of the Yankees. Hell, it's not even president of the local Rotary. Being an Eagle Scout is more on par with having served as drum major of your high school marching band, secretary of the student council. Pretty useless, really.

The boy is retying his dad's knots and the truth is, everything does look more secure. He's a good kid. They've done something right, he and Sarah. They can hang their hat on this boy at least.

"Gimme a hug," Sarah says to Trevor, before pulling the boy into her. He's taller than she is, and threatening to overtake Jonathan soon, too. The embrace is awkward, one-sided, fleeting, and just as quickly Trevor promptly installs himself in the passenger side of the family minivan, pulls his seat belt across his chest, then stares blankly at the neighbor's sprinkler spritzing out its steady frond of morning irrigation.

Jonathan wonders if the boy isn't getting a little old for this Boy

Scout camp business. He's got a driver's license for chrissakes, listens to Dr. Dre and Snoop Dogg with his buddies. *Rollin down the street, smokin indo, sippin on gin and juice / Laid back (with my mind on my money and my money on my mind)* . . . The world of merit badges and trust-falls and sing-alongs is more for your twelve- and thirteen-year-old kids, no? It's like the difference in reality between a child believing in Santa Claus, or not. How do you describe that? Magic, or no magic. And isn't that what it is, Boy Scout camp? An attempt at magic. Unlike, say, getting a job at Shopko and bringing home a paycheck to help pay for auto insurance or the Smashing Pumpkins tickets the kid has been begging for all spring long—that's a teenager's reality.

"I love you," Sarah says, kissing Jonathan on the cheek. She pats his butt, as if for good luck. Or, he thinks, like spanking a horse to hasten a goodbye. Adios, amigo. Happy trails. Married now for twenty-five years and here he is, back to Boy Scout camp again, when he might be mowing the lawn or flipping a flank steak on the grill, mixing up a chimichurri sauce, lighting a fat Partagas with a strip of cedar. He wraps his arms around her, and she raises up on her toes, kisses him again more fully. "Miss me," she advises.

"I already do," he says. Then slaps her ass in return. Sarah gives one last wave goodbye to Trevor and then walks back up the driveway, a spring in her step, runs a hand lightly over her bed of impatiens, bursting with blossoms in the full morning sunlight. Jonathan hangs his head for a minute, scratches at his neck. *Boy Scout camp.*

Trevor leans across the van, honks the horn. "Come on, Dad," he groans.

Sure, son. Sure thing.

MAYBE HE COULD HAVE LEFT WISCONSIN, but what for? The family business firmly ensconced in Eau Claire. His fraternity network from college, sprinkled across the state, all across the upper Midwest. His parents still clinging to their house in Eau Claire's Third Ward, a big brick cube that is developing an odor he can't quite place, drawers filled with old greeting cards, closets chock-full of his mother's craft projects and tubes of Christmas wrapping paper, the basement a tomb of moldering *National Geographic*s, *LIFE*s, and poorly folded road maps, free from AAA. He's been to Paris, London, Cape Town, Moscow, Tokyo, Sydney. Seen the world and been away long enough to know that the trick is making enough money to skip town each winter for someplace warmer. Sarah likes Florida, has found this marine institute where she can volunteer for a week feeding the dolphins, petting manta rays, or whatever the hell it is she does. Jonathan prefers New Mexico, where the air is drier, with no traffic, and he can stare at all the Mexican women from behind his Ray-Bans. No surprise, most of the time they're in Florida and everyone just goes their separate direction. Trevor slinks off to the resort's hot tub, even in ninety-degree temperatures, or the arcade, where he pumps a small fortune into a video game called Terminator 2, complete with two Uzi-looking assault pistols that lay carnage to hordes of metallic silver, red-eyed cyborgs. Sarah plays with her dolphins or scrubs the aquarium glass clean of its endless green film of slime, while Jonathan goes to a driving range and lays into six or seven buckets of derelict Titleists before adjourning to a strip mall bar for drinks that taste of coconut or suntan lotion, the two commingled in his mind to the point he can no longer tell the difference. All afternoon he'll sit there, rubbing at the swelling blisters arrayed across his palm. Wincing at the sunburn on the slope of his nose, flirting with the bartender, and watching NASCAR highlights. It's a good life. Sometimes the bartender stands just in front of him, leaning across the rail, tying cherry stems using only her tongue, and afterward, swallowing the knots. He tips her a five-dollar bill for each one, a game they play all afternoon, and by the end of the week they may or may not rent a room in the Silver Palm on A1A a mile from the bar. One year, she insisted on a pre-fuck baby-oil wrestling match, which Jonathan successfully incorporated into his married sex life one awkward evening when Trevor was sleeping over at a buddy's house. Sarah complained that it ruined their bedsheets, which was true, but hardly the point.

Sort of a metaphor for married life, he thinks.

He and Trevor are barely two blocks from the house, slowly approaching a stop sign, when it occurs to Jonathan to ask, "Wanna drive?"

The kid looks over at him, stone-cold shocked.

"You got your license. *Do-you-want-to-drive?*"

Rare is this opportunity. Trevor only just snagged his license a matter of weeks ago, and today's journey north would mark the kid's first ever road trip—bona fide open-road, highway mileage; not just some jaunt to school, or out to the Dairy Queen for a Blizzard or something. This is a chance to *open that V6 up.*

Trevor grins, actually says, "Thanks, Dad."

The two do a little Chinese fire drill. Settling himself into the passenger seat, Jonathan ponders the origin of the phrase, fairly confident it isn't complimentary.

"Tell you what," Jonathan says. "You know that liquor store on Clairemont? The old run-down one?"

"Yeah?" The kid's tone is cautious. He's excited to hit the road now, no detours for him, with the possible exception maybe of a greasy white and blue paper sack full of Culver's butter burgers, added fuel for that teenage furnace burning inside him.

"Pull on in there. I need to pick up some rations."

"Dad . . ."

"I'll be quick, back in a jiff. Stay in the van. Hey, you bring your CDs? Maybe find us some music for the ride." Jonathan slaps the kid on the shoulder, jumps out of the vehicle. So much of parenting is

mock enthusiasm like this, little tasks, engaging their own interests—
Jedi mind tricks, if you will.

The liquor store is deliciously cool and quiet, like slipping into a
perfectly maintained swimming pool, aqua blue and shimmering. The
light feels like that, too, the fluorescent bulbs flickering just so, as sunlight does when passing through aspen leaves. And the morning light
slants into the building in an optimistic sort of way. Knowing Trevor
will be distracted by the jewel case full of CDs, Jonathan grabs a cart
and pushes it down the narrow aisles, grabbing what he needs. Gin,
tonic, vodka, some of those imported beers in green bottles, a handful
of sorry-looking limes, tequila, some shooters of brandy for his morning coffee. Several of those. Once on the "reservation"—that's actually
what camp is called these days—access to alcohol will be difficult. Not
impossible, but . . . Jonathan knows he can shake down a counselor or
two. It'll take a few days, to gauge which ones he can isolate and then
bribe, but there's always a couple of black sheep. He can begin to profile
the candidates by length of hair, footwear (the wannabe hippies prefer
Chacos or Tevas), piercings, hemp necklaces, Grateful Dead or Phish
paraphernalia, tattoos. Already, Trevor's friends have begun identifying
themselves this way. How early some of us find our tribes.

After paying, he pushes the cart outside into the humid summer
air. The pavement is wet; this shopkeeper has been out early, spraying
cigarette butts and candy wrappers off his cement and into the gutter.
Trevor shakes his head at the sight of all the booze.

"Come on, Dad—we barely have enough room. Besides, how are
you even going to get any of that into camp . . ."

"Don't be so damn responsible," Jonathan says. "Let *me* worry about
that. Christ, how old are you?"

"I just don't want you, like, drunk the whole week."

"Don't worry about that. You and your pals will hardly see me." *This
is vacation*, Jonathan thinks. *Why wouldn't I be drunk all week?*

THE BOY KNOWS HIS AUDIENCE, that's for sure, and windows cranked down, forearms and elbows browning, they drive the speed limit nodding their heads to Creedence as Jonathan sips a road pop, his bare feet up on the dusty dashboard, warm under the rising sun. Trevor white-knuckles the wheel, jaw clenched so tight it pops audibly now and again, even over the road din. This kid is so damn *conscientious.*

"Look, Trev, you gotta relax. All right? You're gonna kill yourself with that kind of tension. Everything's fine. We're in a minivan, all right? No cop in his right mind is gonna pull over a minivan. You're going fifty-five, the license plate is up to date, the insurance all paid up. So chill. In fact, what'd ya say we push that speedometer up to, oh, I don't know, *fifty-nine?* I mean, you're killing me here. We're gonna get passed by a John Deere, for chrissakes."

"An open container, Dad, really?" the kid says, his voice trembling. "If we got caught . . ."

"I want you to pull over when we get to Bloomer," Jonathan says, sipping his beer, motioning in the general direction of north with his beer can.

"Already? Is your bladder that pathetic?"

"Shut up. Just do it."

"Where?"

"I don't care. Somewhere scenic."

The kid sighs, right on schedule, shakes his head, redoubles his clench on the wheel. Jonathan never imagined himself the owner of a Chevrolet Astro minivan, but the machine is like a boxy spaceship, with a front window that has the visibility of the Millennium Falcon. He feels like Han Solo allowing a teenage Wookie to drive. The beer is ever so cold and bright, like swallowing winter sunlight carrying a memory of summer wildflowers, resting hay.

Jonathan drinks beer to remember the freedom of his high school and college days; drinks vodka to forget the reality of his present situation: almost fifty years old, upper-middle-class bourgeois, somehow less than happily married, owner of a minivan and a whole fleet of eighteen-wheelers, due for yet another colonoscopy in two years.

"They have rest stops, Dad. Geez . . ."

"Rest stops are for the Great Unwashed," Jonathan declares. "We Quicks prefer to piss on nature."

THEY EXIT THE HIGHWAY and Trevor drives east into the countryside, pulls off on a lesser county highway where the land is flat as a dinner plate, the trees young and sparse, the earth sprouting nothing but corn and marsh grasses.

"You see any cover around here?" Jonathan asks, opening his car door and flipping the empty into the ditch. He spreads his arms to indicate the vast vulnerability of their position. "There isn't even a sapling to pee on."

"Yeah, well, we could have just stopped at a restaurant, Dad."

"I know that."

Jonathan unbuckles his belt, loosens his blue jeans, then kneels in the gravel beside the front passenger wheel of the car. In a move he's copied from professional soccer players competing in long, intense matches, he pretends he's tying his shoes. His urine comes shyly, at first, then urgently, sending a small puff of pale dust into the air. He shakes, tucks himself back in, and stands, stretching deliberately for all the prairie to see.

"We're above the forty-fifth now," he announces breezily, scratching at his stomach hair, then performing some cursory stretches: the touching of toes, leg stretches, about a dozen jumping jacks.

"So? What?" Trevor asks, bored as can be, restless as a sheet of newspaper in the wind. He lays a teenage hand across his forehead in utter exasperation.

"The forty-fifth parallel. We're now more than halfway between the equator and the north pole. Isn't that something?"

"Dad, it's just an arbitrary line some, like, cartographer drew across the globe a long time ago. It means nothing. Can we go?"

"Trev, camp starts tomorrow. What's the hurry?"

"I want to check into our motel."

"Why?"

"I dunno. TV."

"You want to hurry up to watch TV?"

"Better than *this.*"

"You know why I stopped us here?"

This time, nothing. No response from the kid. Not even an exhausted sigh or embarrassed, "*Daaaaddd . . .*"

"Every time my dad, your grandpa Jasper, and I came up to camp, we would stop right about here. Sometimes a little farther up the road. And he'd say to me, the same thing, every summer—every fall, too, for hunting camp. He'd say, "Jon, *my boy*, everything that happens henceforth, from here north, that's our little secret. Between you and me.' He started me on that philosophy when I was twelve. And you're what, sixteen going on forty? Fifty? Sixty?"

"Dad."

"Seventy. I don't know. You've gotta be about the stodgiest teenager I ever met."

"Dad . . ."

"What I'm saying is, *relax.* Tonight we're going to a famous supper club. It's an institution. Theodore Roosevelt once ate there, I think. Or maybe Franklin, I dunno. Anyway, I want you to meet a friend of mine. We're going to have a very nice, civilized dinner. If you want to have a beer, or a nice glass of wine, that's fine. I won't tell your mom. If you'd like to order a cocktail, that is also fine. Order whatever you like. Heck, as long as you're acting the teetotaler, order a damn Shirley

Temple, I don't give a shit. You can remain my designated driver—the Morgan Freeman to my, ah, Jessica Tandy. What I'm *saying* is, this is vacation. Okay? All I'm saying. Just don't be so damn judgmental. All right? You're a kid. Loosen up."

"Yeah, well, someone's got to be responsible."

"What are you, Trev, a goddamn Republican? Where's your hope and excitement and irresponsibility and carefree fucking la-dee-dah?"

"Are you done?"

"Yes. I just wanted to give you that speech, which happens to be part of your family's history. Take it or leave it."

"Fine."

"I get the sense that you're leaving it, so to speak."

"*Dad . . .*"

CREEDENCE GIVES WAY TO THE DOORS. Jonathan is three beers into things by the time they pass Rice Lake on their right, fully into what is nominally dubbed the Northwoods, demarcated mostly by greasy cooking, two-lane roads, cutover forests, and a general nostalgia surrounding the heyday of the place—the 1950s—when everyone's dads and brothers and uncles were safely back from World War II and there was some spare money to spend and, hey, why the hell *not* buy a shitty little cabin or pop-up camper in the memory of wilderness and spend the summer up there, swatting mosquitoes and shuttlecocks, eating fried bluegill and crappie every night, playing euchre or trying to shoot the moon, all with roasted marshmallow and cobwebs in your hair?

"Is Bugler coming to dinner tonight?" Trevor asks, a note of earnestness in his voice.

"You shouldn't call him that," Jonathan says, for the first time all day exhibiting some trace of seriousness.

"Sorry. Mr. Doughty. Is he coming to dinner?"

"I don't know. I invited him. Sent him a letter with the date, the time of our dinner reservation, the restaurant. Haven't heard back."

"I hope he comes." A deep, sensitive, thoughtful teenage silence fills the cab of the van, a silence that Jonathan decides has about the color and density of lemon pudding. Trevor reveres Nelson, loves seeing him each year at camp; Jonathan hears all about him every summer. Nelson tying knots blindfolded and with impressive speed. Nelson hitting bull's-eyes from impossible distances. Nelson squatting three hundred and fifty pounds without shedding a bead of sweat . . . The stories are legion. "Dad, could I ask Bu— Could I ask Mr. Doughty about Vietnam?"

"I wouldn't."

"Why not?"

"Because, Trev, it's not polite. The fucking guy was nearly killed over there, and his spine is held together with shrapnel and Crazy Glue. It's just not real rosy dinner conversation, all right? The way you handle stuff like this, as an adult, is to wait patiently, until said person *wants* to offer you something of their experience, and then, boom, you're there, ready to hear it. But you can't just, you know, dive right in there, asking about the Viet Cong and fucking bouncing betties and pongee sticks and whatever other fucking shit he saw. Not over shrimp cocktail and popovers."

And like that, the sincere teenage curiosity suddenly dissolves, turns to poisonous silence, leaving Jonathan to half-regret his delivery. Not *what* he said, not the content. But goddamn, the kid's sensitive. Boom, he's shut out, Trev looking fully forward, straight ahead at the road like some presidential chauffeur, eyes totally blank, save for the edge of anger constantly rippling through that teenage body. *Jesus.*

"Sorry, Trev. But, come on, you know what I mean, right?"

"I'm just wondering, is all, okay? Geez, Dad. Not like I'm going to ask him how many gooks he fucking shot."

Jonathan exhales. "Watch the language, all right? Vietnamese, please. Or possibly Cambodian, uh, you know, depending on . . . Never mind—look, maybe you get a pass if you actually fought in the war and lost your buddies, but you're a sixteen-year-old kid from Eau Claire, Wisconsin. So, chill out, all right? I won't sanction a bunch of ethnic slurs." So exhausting, this parenting gig—how fast the tables can turn.

Fields and fields of waist-high Cargill corn and knee-high Pioneer soybeans, muddy barnyards of shit-splattered Guernseys and Holsteins, sun-bleached and woebegone trailer parks, falling-down barns begging for a splash of gasoline and a match, cemeteries ringed in browning arbor vitae and chain-link fences, derelict stone silos, small to middling northern rivers, forests of maple and oak and red pine sliding by at fifty-five miles per hour.

At last, the kid breaks the silence. "Sorry, Dad."

Jonathan cracks his heavy eyelids, stirs. That's another parenting tip: Try to remain silent, however long it takes. Most of the time, parenting is like a contractual negotiation. Let them spill their guts. Let them come to you. *Don't go chasing waterfalls*, as the FM radio is right now so prone to preaching.

"It's okay." *He's still just a kid. Just imitates what he hears, like a fucking toucan or something. A parrot.*

"Just—so, did he, like, kill anyone, over there?"

Jonathan looks out the window, away from his son, and thinks about Bugler, the years and years in which he and Bugler did not speak, exchanging letters no more than two, three times a year, especially when Bugler was in Vietnam, and then years of total silence, until, improbably, the news that Bugler had been hired to replace Wilbur Whiteside, Camp Chippewa's legendary Scoutmaster. The newspaper said Wilbur had gone out for his regular morning swim and returned to his cabin, but never made it out for the flag ceremony, and when he was late, everyone knew something was horribly wrong. Though, it is difficult to feel too much sorrow for a man who lived such a good long life, survived a world war even, and manages to leave in excess of three million dollars to the camp that now bears his name, the Whiteside Scout Reservation.

"I think," Jonathan says carefully, "that Mr. Doughty killed a lot of people, over there, and I'm not sure he needs to be reminded of it, either."

"Oh."

"Green Berets, Trev. Mr. Doughty is a bad mamma jamma."

"Oh."

Jonathan decides to reorient the conversation in an unexpected direction. He clears his throat.

"So, how's that, ah, your girlfriend of yours?" he asks, stumbling a bit. "Sorry, is it Robin, Raquel, Rose . . . Help me out here." He's always teasing Trevor about her name, partly because he's never actually taken the time to memorize it, assuming this girl his son is dating won't last. That she's just a phase he's going through.

"Rachel," the kid corrects flatly. "Rachel Gunderson. Jesus, Dad. We've been dating for, like, six months."

"That so? Terrific, Trev. Really great." Jonathan doesn't think much of Trevor's girlfriend. To start with, they're sixteen years old, for chrissakes. This is the time for casual backseat explorations. *Heavy petting*, as Jimmy Carter called it. Oh, Rachel is cute enough. Big, big brown eyes with a dumb kind of gleam. Slender about the hips, and maybe a little lacking across the chest, but still, cute. He can really only imagine her in the capacity of a babysitter, though, or maybe working at a McDonald's drive-through. She hardly seems edgy enough for seriously rewarding teenage sexual shenanigans. Always refers to him as *Mr. Quick* (even after his dogged encouragements to call him Jon), is stingy with her eye contact, and troublingly, cites as her favorite book *Misty of Chincoteague*.

Jonathan sips his beer with eyes closed. Listens to Ray Manzarek's fingers float over the Vox Continental organ.

"Dad?"

"I'm still here."

"I think I'm in love with Rachel."

The car fills with lemon pudding, heavy citrus air, like a fucking cloud nine bursting with buttery shafts of sunflower light or something. It's a little embarrassing how happy this lovestruck boy is right now.

"That's great, Trev."

"She's like, so amazing, Dad. You know? So talented. I guess some colleges are going to scout her next year for their softball teams, you believe that? And she turned me on to this amazing book, *The Celestine Prophecy*? Dad, it's totally changing the way I see the world."

"I am delighted for you, Trevor. Love like that—a wonderful feeling, yessir."

Jonathan scans his memory banks in search of that teenage sensation, *being in love*. And how about now? Is he *in love* with Deanna? No, he's pretty sure he isn't *in love* with her. Not exactly. Well, maybe. Is he *in love* with his wife, Sarah? No. That ship sailed a long time ago, he thinks. Christ, decades ago . . . But why? How? He *was* in love with her once, he recalls that much. Their honeymoon in Hawaii . . .

How pale her skin was beneath her bikini, the billowy fabric of her dress at dinner one night, the sound of surf in the background, thinking, *We're adults. We're starting our life together.* They rented a little Jeep and rode around the island, stopping along the road to slip into the jungle and make love, then running back to the vehicle laughing like two bank robbers with bags of cash in their fists. Marching up the slope of a volcano and standing within spitting distance of a lava flow; following it down to the ocean where the newest ground on the planet had just cooled black and steaming, *right there before them*, the newest thing in the world. At night they ate beneath tiki torches, big feasts of barbecued pork and fresh exotic fruits and grilled fish. She wore a tropical flower in her hair, each day, and how sunburnt she became—sun poisoned, actually, the night before their flight home. How painful that long flight must have been for her, nowhere to lie down comfortably, no way to groan or weep or complain without drawing attention to herself. So she simply laid her head against his shoulder and shivered with pain, snoring lightly.

"What?" Trevor asks, actually glancing away from the road for a second to look at his dad's lax face. "You don't like her, do you?"

Jonathan sighs, scooches up in his seat, finishes the can of beer, and chucks it out the window. He turns the Doors down, just as "The End" is coming on. Not exactly midmorning, summer highway tuneage.

"Look, Trev. Here's the thing. You're sixteen, okay? Why do you want to commit to anything as heavy as *love* right now? I mean, you can go to Baskin-Robbins and try all the flavors. *All thirty-one flavors.* Don't get me wrong, you like one flavor, by all means. Get two, three scoops. But why, oh, *why* would a sixteen-year-old boy lock into vanilla for the rest of his life? I don't get it. *I* didn't do it. Neither did your mom, I don't think." He seems to recall that as a high school exchange student in Venice, she fell in love with a boy named Gianmario, remembers feeling seriously jealous of this Italian phantom, even five years into their marriage. Imagining his wife making love to some dark-haired, olive-skinned stud muffin as gondolas navigated the romantic waters below their fourteenth-century rococo sex den.

"Rachel is *not* vanilla, Dad."

"Well, Trev. She ain't piña colada either. Or blue moon. Or mint chocolate chip. She's a sixteen-year-old girl who likes playing softball and reading pseudo-religious self-help books. I mean, don't you want to join the Peace Corps? Fall in love with some girl from fucking—I don't know—Colombia or something? Nepal? Ethiopia? Iran? Iranian girls are hot."

"I don't want other girls, Dad. I love Rachel."

"All right, then. What about college, huh? Right? You've got college ahead. What are you gonna do—go to the same school? That's kind of immature, don't you think? Don't you want to meet new people, branch out, party, have some good, old-fashioned anonymous sex?"

"Dad, that sounds terrible. That's how people get HIV."

This kid!

"Are you Mormon?" Jonathan asks.

"What?"

"Never mind."

"Anyway, I thought you would like to know. You're always asking about, like, my life, and stuff."

"When I ask about your life, Trev, mostly I'm just trying to determine if you're on drugs, or hanging out with the wrong kids, or need help procuring rubbers—which, I guess, is actually an opportune time to ask you about that . . . I assume you're taking precautions to protect yourself from sexually transmitted diseases, and or the possibility of an unwanted pregnancy?"

"Dad . . . Jesus."

"Well, you brought up your undying love of Rachel, and now you don't want to talk about brass tacks. Brother, love at the major-league level, like marriage, is *all* brass tacks. Fucking jobs and mortgages and health care and taxes and wall sconces and wallpaper and Roth IRAs and *honey, we're-out-of-baking-powder-can-you-go-get-some?* and oil changes and driving your kid to soccer practice and a million nameless other drudgeries. *Capisce?* So let's talk brass tacks. You guys using a condom?"

Trevor grips the steering wheel with what seems enough force to snap it off the column. "We haven't gotten that far."

"That's too bad. Well, do you *want* some condoms? You could practice with them, on your own time, or whatever."

"Dad!"

Jonathan raises his hands up—don't shoot. "What happens if she gets pregnant?"

"I *just* told you, we haven't had sex!"

"Oh, right. But it's totally *not* a slippery slope, is it? Right now, you're probably getting a few hand jobs, maybe getting proficient at unclasping her bra. But, mark my words: a month from now, you'll be playing Just-the-Tip, and let me tell you something—after that, watch out. Baby-making time."

"You're gross, you know that, don't you? You're, like, a dirty old man. A lech."

Jonathan ignores that. "So, where does she stand? She gets pregnant tomorrow, right? To keep, or not to keep?"

"I don't know."

"Do you want to be a dad, right now, at sixteen?"

Trevor squirms behind the wheel. "I don't think so."

"Good answer because I don't want to be a grandpa yet, either. What about her?"

"Well, I'm pretty sure neither of us wants a kid right now . . ."

"But *what if* it happened? Would she consider an abortion? Have you guys talked about that kind of thing?"

"I don't think so. Her family's pretty conservative."

"All right, then. That's fine. But you guys should be on the same page. Think about it. I'm serious now, Trevor. That's what I'm talking about, brass tacks."

THEY DRIVE WELL NORTH OF CAMP, past Haugen, through Trego, tiny Seeley, through Hayward, Drummond, to Cable, little Cable—not much more than a gas station, grocery store, café, bar, and library. Outside Cable is their motel, the Bel-Aire, a relic of the 1950s, with molded plastic chairs standing vigil outside exterior doors numbered 1–8. Out front is a small pool and a Coke machine, and beyond that, a derelict nine-hole miniature golf course with threadbare Astro-Turf, the windmill on hole number 3 missing two of its half-sailed arms.

The Bel Aire has valiantly hung on through the years and Jonathan finds this slightly moving. What's more, the proprietors know him, accept cash without question, and the rates are low enough to snag three rooms. (Trevor asked no questions about this multi-room setup: Jonathan snores like a grizzly bear [he is told]. And Trevor no doubt enjoys the privacy for purposes of telephoning Rachel.) One is for Trevor, and one for himself—and one, hopefully, for his lady friend, Deanna, a woman Jonathan met two years ago, almost to the day, when he took Trevor to camp, back in 1994.

There had been the typical camp paperwork rigmarole of getting your kid signed up and registered. A lot of legalese in duplicate carbon copy and releases should young Trevor drown after spilling out of his canoe, say, or end up taking an errant arrow to the eye socket, contract the Hanta virus from an abundance of mouse droppings in his cabin, or perhaps fall upon a porcupine. Blah, blah, blah. Yes, yes, autograph every last damn form and then the long sentimental slog from mess hall and camp HQ to that year's particular site and all the parents and all the Scouts, carrying bags with varying levels of wilderness practicality and inevitably stuffed with Starburst, Oreos, gummy bears, Swedish Fish, Skittles, and a hundred kinds of miniature chocolate bars, all guaranteed to melt into goop before the second day was through. Then, settle your kid into his new cabin—for gone now were the canvas tents of old—and hope like hell he was popular enough to attract a few decent roommates, or suffer the indignity of a sobbing preteen/teenage boy, a backpack strapped to swollen shoulders, simply in search of two or three other boys who will nonviolently suffer his company. Luckily, Trev always seemed to have friends.

That moment, though, of establishing Trev into a cabin of other boys always reminded Jonathan so keenly of Bugler. Poor Bugler. His wet canvas tent maliciously collapsed upon its occupant. Or his wrecked eyeglasses. His bugle. The latrine . . .

After Trevor had chosen a cot, stowed away his clothing, and un-packed his sleeping bag, Jonathan administered a hug goodbye, and then a "thank you" to Trev's scoutmasters and the other chaperoning fathers before hustling back to the Stardust Supper Club & Lounge for a vodka martini, a nice steak, a baked potato, and perhaps an enchant-ing conversation with a wayward woman his own age or younger, before driving back to Eau Claire—or not—that evening.

Which is how he met Deanna, who, ironically enough, was also in the area, dropping off her son at camp, though a different one, and had decided on a whim to visit the Stardust, a venerable supper club she, too, had perennially visited, as a girl, when her parents were en route to the family cottage outside the bustling tourist town of Hayward, Wisconsin, home to a giant muskellunge statue and the Lumberjack Olympics.

Deanna, who looked eerily like Sarah: same hair color, eyes, height, weight, body. Her husband was a litigator in Milwaukee whom she sus-pected of cheating on her with his secretary, a much younger "chickee" with fake boobs, no stretch marks, no C-section scar, no children to watch . . .

"So," she asked him, "what about you? Where's *your* better half?"

He could be pretty sure that Sarah was at their home, no doubt beautifying the grounds, or perhaps simply sitting on their front stoop, as she liked to do, where she read her John Grisham books and sipped lemonade and talked easily to the neighbors as they passed by.

"I want to hear more about *you*," Jonathan said cannily, touching her forearm with his right index finger. "Care for another cocktail?"

ONE GENERALLY HOPES, in taking a lover on the sly, there is an improvement in the bedroom department; otherwise, what's the point? And while it would be incorrect to say that Deanna was a *bad* lover, or, for that matter, that Jonathan was himself some American Adonis, that first coupling at least was . . . awkward. Deanna had two torn medial collateral ligaments stemming from her days as a college volleyball player that were painful, so positioning herself on all fours was a no-no. Also, Sarah had delivered Trevor vaginally, and Jonathan was unprepared for Deanna's C-section scar, which seemed to smile at him as he spread her legs and began to lick.

"Yeah, I don't like that, either," she said with a sad chuckle. "No one ever seems to do it right."

That *almost* sapped Jonathan of his desire, but there was the notion that if they'd come this far, it was already pretty much infidelity, and why not just go the distance. So they did it, missionary, which was about as fine as a bowl of vanilla pudding, though as she lay in his arms, he noticed for the first time her perfume, the skin of her throat, the way her feet rubbed at his calves, her ears and earrings, and there was something about her company that was . . . a comfort and took him away from the stresses at home. His throat felt thickened inside, he realized, his heart as jittery as a baby rabbit's.

In the two years since that first meeting, he and Deanna have slept together only a handful of times, chanced some desperate phone calls, the distance between them only fanning the flames of his desire. Perhaps, he supposes, because he is a man accustomed to getting more or less what he wants; Deanna is that dessert that has kept him waiting and waiting, tapping his shoes under the table until the sole wears out.

"Here's your key," Jonathan says, handing Trevor a six-inch-long slab of oak painted baby blue with a key attached by way of a three-inch loop of steel.

The kid laughs. "Is that a motel key in your pocket, or are you just happy to see me?"

Jonathan snickers, "Good one."

"Seriously, what's up with the keys?"

"You know these mom-and-pop places. Probably costs 'em an arm and leg to get the rooms rekeyed if one gets lost. Over the years, the owners get bitter, and the room keys get bigger and bigger. By the time you're my age, that room key will be attached to a piece of driftwood or a canoe paddle. A spare tire maybe."

"I might call Rachel. That okay?"

"Sure, just try to keep it under twenty minutes. Let's not break the bank with our lovesick long-distance calls, huh?"

"Okay," says the kid, shutting his door.

Jonathan enters his room. A queen-size bed, television resting on a set of drawers, a table and two chairs near the window, a nightstand, small closet, bathroom. The wall hangings are all prints depicting mountain men stalking their prey, in some cases cougars or grizzly bears, in other cases gangs of American Indians wielding bloody tomahawks. It reminds him of a night, several weeks ago, when Trevor complained about some friends teasing him, calling him a "White Indian," a term here meaning "a lame white guy badly imitating Native American culture." Jonathan had to laugh at that one; it was, after all, largely, sadly true.

The Boy Scouts of America were never known for their subtlety, or, for that matter, their sensitivity. A Scout is: *trustworthy, loyal, helpful, friendly, courteous, kind, obedient, thrifty, brave, clean, and reverent.* But not gay, for instance, or female or atheist, either, apparently. Jonathan was grimly pessimistic about the world, but not dogmatic. Scouting, as an organization, it seemed to Jonathan, was a dogged fraternity of paramilitary Young Republicans desperately clinging to some nineteenth-century notion of goodness in a modern world filled with intercontinental ballistic missiles, Jerry Springer, the Unabomber, and now, of all things, a cloned sheep named Dolly.

He calls Deanna, who is staying in room 1 of the same motel. The phone rings five times before she picks up.

"What took so long?" he says, annoyed at himself as soon as the words leave his lips.

"Oh, I just stepped out of the shower."

"*Did* you?"

"I did."

Flirting, Jonathan thinks. *I'm—we're—*flirting.

"Too bad," he says.

"Why?"

"I was just about to get into the shower myself."

"Well then," Deanna drawls. "It's possible I missed a few spots."

"Hard-to-reach areas," Jonathan says, nodding, licking his chapped lips.

"Exactly. Care to visit my room?"

"Possibly."

"I'll leave the door unlocked."

"Wouldn't matter," he says. "My penis is so hard right now I could use it as a battering ram." He immediately regrets this. Also, it's not quite as true as he'd like, not for the past five years or so.

Silence, then, "Boy, you sure know how to seduce a girl, don't you?" She giggles a little.

"I'll be right there," he says.

THEY LIE IN BED TOGETHER, watching *Oprah* on a battered TV set.

"Nervous?" Deanna asks him.

"About what?"

"About me. About, you know, introducing me to your son, and vice versa."

Jonathan yawns. "Trevor? He's so genteel, so proper. I wouldn't worry. I'm just trying to prepare him for the real world. Right now he's infatuated with his girl, this sixteen-year-old girl, and I keep trying to tell him not to take it so seriously."

"He's in love," Deanna says sweetly.

"He is," Jonathan agrees, "yes. Can I fix you a glass of brandy?"

"Oh, I don't know, Jonathan. I'm afraid I might fall asleep. When's dinner, anyway?"

Jonathan fills a plastic motel cup with Korbel, parts the curtains with two fingers, and looks out at the pool. One of the owners, a woman about the age of Jonathan's own mother, is right now guiding a large net gracefully through the pool, collecting pine needles and leaves. She is wearing a rainbow-colored tank top, longish yellow boy shorts, and a pair of extremely purple flip-flops. Occasionally she peers at his window. He offers a guilty wave back.

"Jonathan?"

"Sorry—five o'clock. We're to meet Bu— ah, my friend Nelson in the bar at five. It's a bit of a drive for him, and he doesn't dine out much, apparently." The drudgery of it: to be cooped up at a Boy Scout camp as an almost fifty-year-old man. Jonathan can't imagine. Might as well be a monastery; and, at least at a monastery there are no children, just dozens of world-weary men who want to be quiet, be left alone to read, chant, eat bland food, and tend their bee colonies, brew beer . . . Not so bad, really, come to think of it . . . No bills, no responsibilities, three squares, a bed . . .

"Your friend Nelson, he's really a Boy Scout camp director?"

"Yep."

"Is he married?"

Jonathan shakes his head. "Never married. He came back from Vietnam pretty rattled. Spent about a decade living out west, working on ranches, guiding rafts down the Grand Canyon, doing some monkeywrenching, and then the old director died, Wilbur Whiteside. Bu— Nelson was sort of his protégé."

"Does he have some kind of nickname? You keep correcting yourself."

"Well, we used to call him 'Bugler,' but now . . . you know. Well, he's a grown man. I don't suppose he'd appreciate that."

"No," she says, "I wouldn't think so." She has rolled onto her stomach, and peers at him over her shoulder.

"What?" he asks.

"There's still time, you know . . ."

He dives back on top of her, mindful of her knees, the positioning of her legs. Once unsure of this new lover, he has come to revel in his hard-won understanding of her limitations, her preferences—delights in accommodating her, rising to the challenge of learning someone new.

20

AT FOUR THIRTY JONATHAN KNOCKS ON TREVOR'S door. The boy comes to the door holding the telephone base in one hand, the handset linked by a spiral umbilical cord pressed tight to his ear. He is dressed already, his hair parted and wet. Jonathan sits on the bed, picks up a hardcover book with a black-and-white jacket, an old school bus overgrown by a Northwoods jungle and buried in snow. *Into the Wild*, it's called. He has no idea where the boy even finds these books, where or how he buys them. This whole world Trevor dwells in, where true love is still a reality, where people say NO! to drugs (instead of, you know, THANK YOU!), where mothers and fathers love one another, and Boy Scout camp is something to be excited about.

"... I gotta go, baby. Yeah. I'm sorry. My dad's here and we're ... Oh, okay." Trevor turns to Jonathan and says, "Rachel says, 'Hello, Mr. Quick!'"

"Hello, Rachel," Jonathan says, deadpan.

Trevor turns his back to his father, lowers his voice in both volume and tone, and whispers, "I miss you so much, baby. I love you. Okay. I love you, too. I'll write you every day. Okay. I love you. Bye." And finally he hangs up, letting out a deep, tortured sigh of teenage melancholy.

"Well," says Jonathan helpfully, "everything copacetic?"

"I miss her, Dad."

"Ah. You'll get over it," Jonathan says. "Anyway, you look about ready to go."

The kid nods. He's frowning, actually frowning at the floor, water welling against his eyes.

"Christ," Jonathan mumbles. He stands, wraps his arms around this teenager, not quite six feet tall, but close enough. *His baby*, this Goliath with armpit hair, a smattering of soft whiskers, body odor, a small constellation of whiteheads on his chin, size thirteen feet, and a bleeding-itself-raw-heart for Rachel Gunderson. He pats this oaf on the back and says, "Come on, there's someone I'd like you to meet."

"Okay," the boy mutters, still clinging to him.

"You need my handkerchief?"

"No," the boy sniffs.

DEANNA IS STANDING BESIDE THE VAN ALREADY, looking, Jonathan thinks, beautiful. White Capri pants, a white jacket, a tastefully cut pink tank top, and white sandals. She seems to favor gold in jewelry, he notes—a difference from Sarah, who, thankfully (to his way of thinking), has never worn much jewelry of any kind, really, with the exception of the narrow silver band and tiny diamond he bought from a rock shop when they were first engaged, all those years ago.

"Hello," says Deanna, shuffling toward Trevor in her sandals. "It is such a pleasure to meet you. In fact, I feel like I already know you. Your dad gloats about you constantly, and now I see why. You're handsome, like him."

Trevor shakes her hand politely, blushing so completely Jonathan is concerned there may not be enough blood to go around. *Maybe this will be a piece of cake*, Jonathan thinks. *Maybe the kid is more cosmopolitan than I give him credit for.*

IT'S A SUNDAY NIGHT IN LATE JULY, and the bar of the supper club is quiet, though hardly abandoned. The old pine floors, the knotty pine wall paneling, the taxidermy, the gleaming brass beer taps at the bar, the neon backlit liquor bottles—it all glows a buttery gold, the ceiling low and warm, and walking toward the bar, Deanna subtly at his arm, Trevor walking on ahead of them, Jonathan feels the timelessness of this place. It is known that Al Capone and John Dillinger once haunted many such Wisconsin establishments. A person could imagine that: a dozen men in pin-striped suits, each packing two or three pistols, and deployed across the bar, tommy guns, wads of dough, whiskey flowing freely as the jazz pushing the cigarette smoke in spirals and dips through the heavy air of the place.

The three of them at the bar now and Deanna orders rosé. The bartender shakes his head in the negative, slinging a towel over one shoulder, inventories, "Chardonnay, pinot grigio, champagne."

Deanna claps her hands excitedly. "Oh, champagne, then."

"And for you, sir?"

"Vodka martini, real dry, with a twist of lemon, up."

"Very well. And you?" The bartender raises an eyebrow at Trevor.

"I'll just have a Coke," the kid says.

"You got it," says the barkeep, pivoting down below the bar in search of the champagne.

"Or, no—wait a minute," Trevor yelps, leaning over the rail. His voice has just cracked something awful. Jonathan winces.

The bartender turns back to them, rises up. "Yeah?"

"Maybe a strawberry daiquiri, actually. Please."

"A strawberry daiquiri?" the bartender squints.

"Yep," says Trevor.

Jonathan leans in close to his son's ear. "You don't want maybe a beer or a glass of wine or a gin and tonic or a screwdriver—you'd probably *really* like a screwdriver . . ."

Deanna slaps Jonathan on the arm. "Let him order what he wants." Then, placing a hand lightly on the boy's shoulder: "I think it's a perfect choice. Light, refreshing, easy to drink."

"Thanks," he mumbles.

Moments later the drinks arrive and are divvied up. Jonathan raises his glass. "A toast. To another summer."

"Another summer," Deanna and Trevor repeat, clinking their glasses.

"Where's Nelson, Dad?"

"I dunno, Trev. Like I said, he doesn't get out much."

"Do you suppose he'll come in full uniform?" Deanna asks, chortling, covering her mouth with a hand.

Jonathan begins to echo her laughter only to stop short. He remembers the latrine and the nickel; thinks of Vietnam, of this man, who has spent his entire life in one uniform or another, living up to impossible codes and laws, mottoes and slogans that can only be seen as outdated, arcane, antique.

"How's that daiquiri, guy?" Jonathan asks, swiveling over to this son of his, and away from any gloomy, guilty thoughts.

The kid, sucking away at his punch bowl glass with a steady PSI eagerness, nods his head, cheeks flushed.

"I'm going to have to carry you home, aren't I?"

"Dad . . ."

FIVE O'CLOCK SHARP they watch Nelson bang through the front door dressed quite nattily in a three-piece linen suit with shoes the color of some exotic tropical wood and matching the skin of his face, neck, forehead, and hands. He seems to bowl methodically forward with the grit and determination of a man whose body has suffered through the insults and injuries of war. He's not tall, not an inch over five-five, but his suit coat, though tailored, seems distressed, clings to a formidable set of forearms, biceps, and a perfectly wide chest. He's built like an aged fullback. Above his lip, a perfectly well-kempt mustache, waxed at the corners, much like old Whiteside's, Jonathan realizes. He walks directly toward Deanna.

"Very pleased to meet you," he says, bowing slightly, and then taking her hand, which he kisses delicately. When his face rises again to preside over those well-yoked shoulders, it is centered by two sadly observant eyes, the look of a man quite bored with most of what passes for the world's business.

"Likewise," she says.

He slips sideways and presents a thick hand to Trevor. "Good to see you, Mr. Quick. Though, I see, you're already imbibing . . ." Their handshake takes on a new intensity, with Nelson resting his left hand on Trevor's shoulder. "I hope I don't need to worry about your partaking at camp, do I?"

"Absolutely not, sir. I'm sorry."

"Don't apologize, Trevor. You want to drink like a man, act like it, too. Simply accept the consequences."

"Awful hard, though, Nelson," Jonathan laughs, "to act like a man, when holding twenty-four ounces of strawberry daiquiri."

Releasing his grip on Trevor, Nelson now slides to his left and faces Jonathan.

"Thank you, Jon, for inviting me this evening," Nelson says, extending his hand.

Jonathan accepts the solid handshake offered him. "It's good to see you, Nelson. That's a fine suit, too. Very dapper. Can I get you a drink?"

"Laphroaig. And if there's no Laphroaig, Lagavulin."

"Smoke bombs, uh," Jonathan drawls, inching closer to the bar, and ordering their drinks. He likes this. The prospect of drinking single malt with Bugler, this man so unlike the boy in his childhood memories: so corded in muscle now, broad as a wildebeest, so utterly lacking in the sort of phony bonhomie that makes the country club go round. Sliding a twenty across the bar, Jonathan glances back to spy Nelson leaning into Deanna, speaking in a volume so low Jonathan hears nothing. And then: a rose blossom of delight flushes across Deanna's face. *What did he say?* And Trevor moving closer to Bugler, listening in, an absurdly rare teenage smile stretching below his greasy nose.

Jonathan scoops both Scotches and delivers one to Nelson, toasting, "To old friends," as he raises his glass.

Nelson offers a little nod, readying his lowball for the toss back.

"To friends," says Deanna, raising her champagne, and then turning to Trevor, "So nice to meet *both* of you. How lucky am I? Eating dinner with three such handsome men."

And then Trevor, moments behind everyone else, breaks from really slurping that daiquiri. "Sorry," he says, touching her flute with his oversize glass goblet.

"So," Deanna begins, "your father tells me you have a girlfriend?"

"Yeah," Trevor admits, suddenly shy, examining his shoelaces as if they are in desperate need of retying.

"How long have you been seeing each other?"

"Six months," he stammers, "about a hundred and ninety-one days, actually."

Deanna laughs, touches his arm.

"What?" he asks defensively.

"Nothing," she says sweetly. "You're just in love is all. It's quite charming."

"Are you married, Mrs. . . . I'm sorry. Dad never told me your last name."

"Tolbert," she says flatly, as if the name were a badge she wore with chagrin, an aged garment or brooch she once inherited and has never particularly liked. "And yes. I am married. Twenty-five years in September."

"Where's your husband?" Then, "I'm sorry. Is that rude? I'm just— Dad said you were a friend, but . . . until a few days ago, I'd never even heard him mention your name."

Nelson holds his glass, face implacable, eyes turning subtly to Jonathan as Deanna clears her throat, sips at her champagne, and then from the kitchen, to the rescue, a loaded serving tray hits the deck to a cacophony of broken glass and dropped silverware.

"Lemme go check on our reservation," Jonathan says, giving Trevor's shoulder a light squeeze.

THEIR TABLE SITS immediately beside a bank of expansive windows looking out onto a lake lined by majestic white and red pines, and out on the water, the occasional pontoon boat motors lethargically past, its skipper and passengers waving contentedly from the deck, an American flag mounted off the stern, hardly undulating as the craft duffs along at perhaps a knot or two.

There is almost nothing Jonathan loves more than a supper club. The warm woods, low ceiling, ample bar, more-than-competent kitchen . . . Sitting at a four-top, Deanna and Nelson at his sides, Trevor across the white-linen tablecloth with a single votive candle to mark the center, Jonathan finds the evening about as perfect as he could have hoped. *There* is his boy, Trevor, almost a man now, sipping a daiquiri as he studies the menu, mouth moving slightly as he reads. And Deanna, her readers perched on her nose, a single finger raised to her lips. Nelson, his menu resting on the table, his right index finger circulating the ice around his Scotch, eyes downcast, the candle's light now and again drawing shadows from his sharp nose and mustache, the wrinkles cracked around those sad old eyes of his.

Jonathan is glad now for Trevor's daiquiri. *Let the boy drink*, he thinks. No need to have the kid sleuthing around his sex life. Then again, wasn't that the idea? He had intended to introduce Deanna and Trevor, and *Shit, I don't know. Maybe if the kid approves, a divorce might not be so traumatic. Maybe he'll understand, take it all in stride . . .*

The waiter arrives, takes their orders, and resolutely collects menus before moving off. Nelson sips his Scotch, and Deanna clears her throat, rearranging a napkin across her lap. Trevor sucks loudly at what remains of his daiquiri through a straw that must be over a foot long; it reminds Jonathan of a pole vault.

"Thirsty, huh?" Jonathan says. "Better go easy on that second one, tiger. We don't need any hungover Scouts tomorrow, now do we, Nelson?"

"Wouldn't be the first time, I'm afraid," Nelson says. "Or likely the last."

"Oh," Deanna trills, "I'm sure it doesn't happen very often though, does it, Nelson? That kind of behavior?" *Beneath the table, her hand lands as lightly as a butterfly on Jonathan's knee, her index finger rubbing a figure eight there . . . and then another . . .*

"Every summer," Nelson says, grinning sadly. "In the final analysis, Deanna, Boy Scout camp is fairly similar to a juvenile detention facility, really, or, taken a step further, maybe prison. I've got a population of kids that I'm in charge of. The camp counselors are my guards, and I'm counting on the troop leaders and adult chaperones to act as tribal leaders, keeping things in check in each campsite."

He takes another sip of Scotch. "Nobody's being punished, of course. And we're not trying to rehabilitate anyone exactly . . . But, for better or worse, they're captive for a week, their day regimented, and of course, they're asked to wear their uniforms." He shrugs his shoulders. "I've got kids coming to camp every year with contraband. Been that way for decades. Beer, vodka, whiskey, schnapps—whatever they can procure from dad's liquor cabinet. Cigarettes, cigars. Hell, a year ago, I caught a counselor who planted about an acre of marijuana deep in the woods. Genius idea, really."

Deanna's fingers inching forward in the darkness, Jonathan takes another rip of Scotch, woozy with anticipation . . . And the old joystick in his pants, still in good working order, he is pleased to report . . .

"What happened to the weed?" Trevor blurts out.

"Naturally, I confiscated it," Nelson says, twirling his ice cubes again.

"I'm sure you did," Deanna giggles, lifting her champagne glass to take a sip.

"Yeah, but *then* what'd you do with it?" Trevor presses on.

"After the Scouts left that summer, I had a big bonfire. Torched it all."

"Too bad," sighs Jonathan. "An acre of grass? You could've retired down in Cabo. Set up a new Scout camp on some deluxe Mexican stretch of beach." *Her hand fully massaging his crotch now, the Scotch taking effect, the warmth of the room, bread and butter aromas, and off in the distance, the evening's last waterskier, carving up the flat mirror of the lake and sending a distant curtain of sliced water toward their shore as he vanishes, leaving behind only the softening drone of an outboard motor, and the dining room's sound track: silverware touching, laughter, voices rising in disagreement, a radio on somewhere back in the kitchen . . .*

"Dad?" Trevor asks. "Are you okay?" His voice is so sincere.

"Yeah, Dad," Deanna says, "you all right, there?" Her hand has fluttered away; now it's just her toes at his ankles, and blessedly holding their position. He realizes he must have closed his eyes for a blissed-out moment at the dinner table.

"How about you, Jon?" Nelson asks calmly, peering over the table as if this is all some very cordial interrogation, no hurry, they've got all night. "How's the trucking business?"

"Business is good," Jonathan says, nodding his head. "Real good, actually." It's true, business has never been better. Quick Trucking & Transport has grown from a dozen drivers working a Chicago–Minneapolis Highway 94 route to more than six dozen employees spread all over the country. He can't say how it even happened. One day, he's twenty-six years old, freshly back home after some cushy Reserves deployment over in Germany, working a desk his father assigned him to in Receiving. And now, he's forty-nine years old, president of the same company, with revenues expected to exceed six million dollars next year. He can't even call what he does "work" anymore. He has other people to do the actual "work." And him? He sits on a half-dozen boards, plays golf whenever the weather allows (his secretary schedules it on his calendar as "client development"), swims thirty laps a day at the YMCA, and plays racquetball twice a week with a retired trial attorney whom he has never beaten—not even close.

And now, here he sits, with Deanna, a woman whose role in his own life is yet to be defined. Is she, as he told Trevor, "a friend"? Or is she a "girlfriend"? His mistress? His future wife? Suddenly he isn't so sure about this dinner, about having invited her along . . . Putting a label on their fun has somewhat dampened his enthusiasm. There is a searing flash of realization, for one thing, that to marry Deanna means divorcing Sarah, and *that* will be a costly thing indeed. He might just have to return to work.

He moves his leg, away from Deanna's toying foot.

"Business is good," he repeats for a third time, nodding. *He's a trucking magnate, or something. How did this happen? Where did those twenty-five years go? One afternoon, you're drinking kolsch in a German bier-garden with two nineteen-year-old backpackers from Colombia, and the next you're operating a trucking empire from Eau Claire, Wisconsin?*

"You must be very proud," Nelson continues. "Great family, great son, great business. I'm truly happy for you, Jonathan."

Deanna looks down at her plate.

Perhaps because his daiquiri has run dry or perhaps because the relish tray and bread still haven't arrived, Trevor decides to plunge back into the conversation, with little to distract him but the banter swirling around the table.

"I'm sorry, Deanna," he says gingerly. "How did you and Dad meet?"

"Well," she begins, rearranging her silverware. "I, uh . . . I guess I would have thought, that, uh, your father would have told you before now."

"We actually met here," Jonathan says dryly, adding no superfluous details. "A few years back. Deanna was dropping her son off at camp, too."

"Oh, do you know my mom?" Trevor continues. "I mean, are you friends with her, too?"

Deanna coughs into her fist, not so accidentally knocking a soup spoon to the floor.

"No," Jonathan says, "Deanna and Mom haven't met." He pauses. "Not yet anyway."

"It's just that"—Trevor rubs his forehead—"I'm confused. I mean, I've never heard you tell Mom about Deanna, Dad. Do you, like, call each other sometimes? Why are you friends, exactly?" He giggles to himself. "I just can't imagine my dad making friends like that, you know? Like, what do you do together? Just eat dinner once a year?" He laughs again, peers around for the waiter, his empty daiquiri glass held searchingly aloft.

"Look, Trevor," Jonathan says, exhaling deeply, "Deanna's my girlfriend." He has stepped into the river, and the current has taken him. There's no swimming back to shore now. He feels at once stupid relief and gripping fear. And until they return home, Trevor is now an accomplice to this secret. Jonathan wonders what exactly the boy will do with this newfound knowledge, realizes he's begun sweating.

Nelson coughs into his napkin and shifts in his chair as the waiter delivers a basket of bread, a plate of butter, and a bountiful relish tray laden with radishes, celery, carrots, cheeses, charcuterie, dips . . .

Trevor stares at his father. "Excuse me?" he says.

"She's my girlfriend," Jonathan repeats, clumsily reaching for her hand.

"But, you said . . . Dad, you said she was your *friend*, not your *girlfriend*. I mean . . ." Trevor runs his hand all the way back through his longish, wavy brown hair. He's been growing it for months now, and Jonathan regularly tousles it, compliments the kid, telling him it reminds him of the Beatles, of mop-tops, of when he grew his own hair out and how much it annoyed his own father. But Trevor's not that kind of kid. Jonathan can't remember a single incidence of Trevor ever knowingly trying to annoy him, let alone undermine his power. This is a *good boy*. Well on the path to Eagle Scout.

"Jesus!" Trevor suddenly shouts, the dining room stilling to the very barest register of white noise.

"Trevor," Jonathan says calmly, leaning toward his son. "Chill out. All right? Here—do you want another drink?"

"I *do*, yes!" he shouts, and then, "I mean, goddamnit, Dad. *Goddamn* you."

"Your father should have told you," Deanna says, moving her chair closer to Trevor, reaching out a hand to rub his shoulder. "I'm sorry. This is something that should have happened back home, I suppose. Are you okay?"

"Don't *touch* me," the kid says. "Jesus, where's your shame, lady?"

"Beg your pardon?" she asks, leaning back. Though no moralist, Deanna is a woman with a backbone. She always gets a laugh when tabloids focus on the men in cheating scandals, those aging silver foxes on the downhill slide of a midlife crisis. How the affairs are always *their* fault, the men clearly pigs. The irony, of course, is that they're sleeping with women, oftentimes, married women. Two to tango, and all that jazz. Her own father married four different women before he died, and left her mother to raise three girls in a one-bedroom shotgun bunga-low in Milwaukee. So she's tired of the self-righteousness of men, the righteousness of anyone for that matter, and the sanctimony of this boy in particular. In a way, she already regrets her last comment to the kid. *No*—better he learn before the divorce. *Give him a burden to carry. Let him grow up already.*

"Well, just that—" Trevor begins again. "You're married, aren't you?"

She nods, squeezes Jonathan's hand, thinks back to earlier this same day, their tryst in her motel room, the tenderness with which he handles her body, the compliments he offers her, better than any chocolates or flowers, saying these, these, *sweet nothings*, these unnecessary kindnesses that had become so foreign to her. *God, I love your toes*, he says to her. *Your ass . . . your lips . . . your hair. God, you're beautiful. And the way you smell.*

The waiter is suddenly standing at attention beside Nelson. He is an older gentleman, with the rather regal and severe look of an Austrian butler, his back ramrod straight in a black uniform, utterly without stain or wrinkle, his eyebrows two hedgerows merged together and gone without pruning for years under a great dome of a bald pate. Jonathan notices Nelson appraising the waiter, perhaps admiring the man's clear attention to detail.

"Another drink?" the waiter asks.

"Christ yes," says Jonathan. "We've been dry here for eons."

"The same, then?" the waiter asks.

"You wanna slow down there, Trev? Or is it damn the torpedoes?" Jonathan reclines in his chair a bit. Their canoe is already headed straight for the falls. Why the fuck not?

"Sure," says Trevor, "Yep. I'm game."

"Very well," the waiter nods before moving off.

Nelson rests a heavy hand on Trevor's shoulder, whispers, "I'm sorry, son."

"What are *you* sorry for?" Trevor blurts out. "You're not my dad! You didn't ambush me with this . . ." He stutters for a moment, hesitant to curse before Nelson. " . . . bullshit. You know? This fucking *bullshit*."

"Hang tough, all right?" Nelson continues. "Look, if you want to head back to the motel, or even come to camp a night early, I can give you a ride."

"Now hold on there, Nelson," Jonathan says. "This is my son. All right? He's *my* son, damnit. And this was my decision." Jonathan has straightened his posture, risen up in his chair, laid a hand on the table close to Nelson's almost-empty Scotch glass; his fingertips are within five inches of Nelson's cuff link, and his voice is cold and authoritative, a tone he rarely needs to employ these days, but is perfectly able to. How many times has he had to strike fear in the hearts of local politicians, Teamsters, shift supervisors, and so on?

Nelson, looking nonplussed, holds his hands up in mock surrender, then brings one arm to rest behind Trevor's shoulders, like a most favored uncle.

Jonathan now unleashes the speech he's been clandestinely preparing since the night he first slept with Deanna, and realized with a start, that perhaps his life was moving in a separate direction from that of his wife and only son.

"The thing is, Trevor, your mom drives me crazy, okay? She's insane. She isn't the woman I married. And, hell, I don't know. I suppose this is all news to you, but the thing is, the woman I married, she was a spunky little thing, and it was the beginning of disco, and we'd go out every night," he says, stabbing down at the table, suddenly impassioned, "*every single fucking night*, and we'd go dancing. And nights we weren't dancing, we were *still* going out. Still having drinks or having dinner or going to see a show or a concert.

"And then, somewhere along the way, all of that . . . stopped. The travel, the culture, the food, the dancing, the sex . . . It just dribbled away into nothing. And that wasn't *my* decision, okay? There was no dialogue about all that."

He's pointing at his chest now, feeling his blood rise, the alcohol in his bloodstream. "I love you," he says to Trevor. "You're the best thing your mother and I ever did together. And nothing that happens on a move-forward has anything to do with that. Nothing will change that. I'll always love you. And, in a way, I will always love your mom. But our job is done now. I mean, look at you." He reaches across, takes—seizes Trevor by a tensed-up shoulder. "You're a man now. Right? Well on your way to Eagle, no less." He laughs. "My work is done."

The table is silent, just dining room din now. Outside the window, evening shadows have collected in darkened pools beneath the pines, and the moon is low over the horizon, just a skinny little crescent.

Trevor's head is in his hands.

"What is it, son? Tell me what you're thinking."

"It's just that," the boy begins . . . His voice trails off, disappears. He cannot look at these adults, this father of his, leaning back just slightly in his chair, with the repose of a poker player holding a straight flush. Or this woman, her arms crossed, eyes aimed away from him. She stands suddenly, white napkin falling to the floor, and marches toward the bathroom, sandals sliding beneath forceful calves, purse clutched tight in her right hand.

Nelson gazes after her, then back at the dinner table, docilely scratching at the back of his skull. He removes a plastic toothpick from his Swiss Army knife and scratches at his gum line . . .

"I don't understand why you're doing this to me," mutters Trevor.

"I'll tell you why," his father says, leaning forward. "Because you're naïve, Trev. Because you're dating this girl and—I can see it— you're going to get your heart broken. You're what the shrinks call codependent. So . . . Why wait? Would it have been better to do this at home? During the school year? What? You think that's how it works? You think we have a family powwow and your mom and I just amicably explain that our marriage sucks, that it's sucked for years? Come on, Trev. Grow up."

"What does this have to do with Rachel?" Trevor pipes up now, no longer sad, but defensive, angry, ready to pounce.

His father shrugs. "What? You want me to outline the whole thing for you? You want me to map it out? What do you want? Best-case scenario or worst? Okay, let's go worst first, get that out of the way. So: You two go to the same college. Lovey-dovey all the way. Everything's copacetic. For about a year, maybe eighteen months. Then she real- izes she's in love with somebody else. Nobody's fault, but . . . there's another boy. Lives in the same dorm as you, in fact. Talks to her in the hallways when she's on her way to class. He's more handsome than you, more forceful, more exciting, too. She can't break it to you, that's she's no longer interested, so she starts messing around with this other guy behind your back. Now she's a little distant from you, a little, you know, aloof. You're twenty years old and for some reason you're not having sex. So you pour on the adoration, the affection. You're buying flowers for her every week, and then, every couple of days. Only, the more you do, the harder you try, the less attractive you seem to appear to her. So now she's listening to different music, music that's unfamiliar to you. It might as well be a foreign language, and she's pontificating about this music, about specific lyrics that you can't even understand. Until one day, you pour your guts out—the old hara kiri kind of emo- tional confession. And she just tells you, 'Trevor, I'm not in love with you anymore.' And now what? All those years. All those opportunities that you shunned just to preserve some kind of romantic notion about young love? *Why?*"

The boy's face is red and he exhales deeply, worrying his hands through thick brown hair. "I don't understand," he continues. "I just don't understand why you're telling me this stuff."

"Because," his father says, "this is the real world."

"So you don't want me to believe in love? What? You don't want me to become good or decent . . . Is that it? Jesus, Dad."

"I just want you to take those fucking blinders off, is all."

"But, I mean, if I can't be good now, if I can't believe in love now, when I am supposed to? You don't, obviously. Deanna doesn't. Mr. Doughty isn't married. I mean, what the hell? What's the moral here? Don't get married? Or, get married, but then feel free to cheat on your wife? Why did you even put me in Boy Scouts, then? What the hell am I doing here?"

"You are a good boy, and you're going to become an even better man. Better than me by a country mile," Jonathan says. "I just want you to get the most out of your life. I just don't want to see your heart get broken."

"So . . . You thought you'd insult my relationship with Rachel, *and* admit that you're not in love with Mom, all in the same night, and, like, *that* wouldn't break my heart? What the hell, Dad?"

Nelson reaches for a wicker basket where a burgundy napkin loosely embraces a half-dozen warms rolls, their steam quickly dissipating into the dining room as he selects one and replaces the napkin, then spreads a pat of butter onto the bread and chews dispassionately, staring out the window at the night calm of the lake.

"What do you think, Nelson?" Jonathan asks. "Would you advise a sixteen-year-old boy to go all-in on a high school relationship? You think that's a prudent decision?"

Nelson reaches into the relish tray, gathers some baby carrots, some celery, some radishes, and spoons some creamy dill dip onto a small plate. He eats slowly, patiently, sipping his Scotch, clearly in no hurry to answer his old friend.

"I think," he says at last, "that I have no great understanding of why one person falls in love with another. And in my experience, trying to talk sense to a man or woman in love is useless. But then again," he adds, chewing his roll, "love doesn't make sense. Love is an emotion."

21

WILBUR WHITESIDE ARRIVED AT NELSON'S HOUSE late that evening, long after the sun had gone down, the streetlights humming to life, illuminating the day's bicycles and baseballs left helter-skelter on front lawns, dew already beginning to glisten on still spokes.

He knocked gently on the screen door and it was Nelson who came to the entryway and found him, bathed in the yellowish porch light, moths flying erratically about his white-haired head. He held his hat in his hands, spun the brim between his fingers.

"Nelson," he said sadly. Then, after a moment, "May I come in?"

Nelson opened the door and led Wilbur into the sitting room, where his mother sat in her rocking chair, wiping the edges of her eyes with her thumb and index finger, first the right side, then the left.

Wilbur sat on the couch, his hat held low between his knees. He was quiet a long time. Then he said, "My father died before I ever met him."

Nelson's mother began to tear up again.

Wilbur looked down at his shoes as he continued. "He was a coal miner in Ohio, and the way it was told to me, a tunnel collapsed and a great piece of rock hit him in the back of the skull and killed him. My mother was eight months pregnant with me at the time.

"I suppose we were poor, but I don't remember it that way. I remember helping my mother make sauerkraut, and how she stored it in this great barrel beneath our basement stairs, that smell. I remember collecting coal that fell off the trains, which was technically stealing, but then, the coal mine had stolen my father, so to be honest, I didn't give a damn what anyone thought."

Nelson's mother laughed sadly into her kerchief.

"I remember my mother's blackberry preserves and her fresh rye bread. I remember her parents, my grandparents, speaking German. I remember a day where we ate a picnic beside a little stream and my mother gave me a bit of chocolate. I remember hearing about the flood in Johnstown and remembering from my Bible studies all about Noah, and being afraid that water was coming for us. I remember moving to Wisconsin. Remember seeing Lake Michigan for the first time.

"But I have no memory of my father, nor did I ever once wish I had a father, and I want to tell you why. There were many boys in my neighborhood, see, who were beaten every night by their fathers. And it wasn't just them. The mothers were beaten, too, and I do remember that. These sweet women who fed me apples and grapes and their homemade cheeses, and then, one day they might smile at me but when their lips parted it was to reveal that they had lost two or three teeth, or one eye might never open all the way again, and it was those fathers, I knew, come up out of the mine and drunk on whiskey, and how they would destroy everything in their sight, and, ma'am, I am not lying to you when I say that there were many, many nights when I went to bed and thanked the stars above that I had no father, because my home was a happy one, and a warm one, and it was just my mother and me.

"I don't mean to whitewash what you and Nelson are going through right now, and I don't mean to suggest that your lives will be easy without your husband in the house, but I do want to assure you that it can be done, and not only that, but it just might make you and your boy both stronger.

"I am also here this evening because I would like to offer to send Nelson to St. John's Military Academy, near Milwaukee. I will pay the cost of his tuition and lodging. Nelson is a good boy—I can see that—and I believe in his future. This gesture would bring me great pleasure, ma'am, and it is my hope that you will see not only the wisdom in it, but the latitude it would give you, as well, to operate in the world without the stress of feeding or caring for Nelson without a father in the house. Oh, and I'd also like to give you this, if you'll take it." He handed her an envelope, thick with what looked to Nelson like a neat stack of bills.

Nelson's mother covered her mouth now with both hands, tears falling freely from her eyes. Her shoulders began to heave. The living room was dark, with just the light from the front porch to illuminate the floor of the entryway and, on the other side of the living room, a glow from the kitchen laying a rhombus of secondhand light over the couch. Dorothy rocked back and forth, Wilbur perched on the edge of the couch, and Nelson stood to one side, listening to it all.

"What if he wants his son? What if he disagrees?" Nelson's mother asked. "I can't just send a man's son off like this, without his say-so? Without so much as a conversation, now, can I? He could come back tonight for all we know. After he's had time to . . . cool off."

Wilbur set his hat on a kneecap and tugged at the ends of his mustache. "I've thought about that, ma'am. Which is why, with your permission, I'd like to bivouac in your backyard, at least overnight. Look, this could have been an act of passion, and perhaps your husband will return tonight after he's had a chance to cool down. Maybe he's at a local watering hole right now, blowing off steam. And if that's the case, I'd still like to talk to him, about St. John's, I mean."

Dorothy stared at the old man a moment before saying, "Bivouac?"

Nelson stayed up for hours that night, lying in bed, his face aimed at the window, half-wishing never to see his father ever again, half-willing their family station wagon to rumble right back down the street. Once, long after midnight, a throaty old engine did wheeze down the street, but it just rattled past, didn't even slow down. And, fleetingly, from the backyard, Nelson thought he heard Wilbur's snoring, a gentle rippling sound that was almost comforting, like an insignificant wind ruffling an untidy sail.

And then it was morning. From his bed Nelson heard his mother and Wilbur talking in low voices, though there was light laughter, too, and the percolating of coffee, the sizzle and buzz of cooking bacon, and outside, birdsong and the vague sounds of an awakening world: car doors slamming shut, garage doors opening and closing, dogs barking to be let out or let in, a garbage truck's steadily interrupted route and the heave, throw, and crash of big aluminum cans flying through morning air and back down onto grassy boulevard. He dressed quickly and entered the kitchen.

They were sitting together at the kitchen table, Wilbur and his mother. Wilbur was already immaculately uniformed, while his mother very uncharacteristically sat in one of her better church dresses, hair and makeup done. Their faces turned to meet him.

HE RETURNED TO CAMP with Wilbur that day, and a few short weeks later, in September, matriculated at St. John's Military Academy, where his first year of schooling was a cold, cruel, agonizing period of intermittent hazing that bordered on torture. A favorite game the older boys liked to play was to force a group of, say, five or six younger students to clench a single maraschino cherry between their butt cheeks and race down the slippery granite hallway. A racer who "dropped" his cherry was forced to eat it. The older boys loved to bet on this game.

But the following summer and fall, Nelson's body began to stretch itself out, as if in adaptation to the many threats of his new circumstances. He would never rise over six feet, but neither would he remain a five-foot shrimp. And each summer he endeavored to make himself stronger, bigger, more capable. By the time he returned for a second year at St. John's in September, Nelson looked like a badger or a wolverine: a low center of gravity, all armored in muscle and sunburned, hair cut close to the scalp, and eyes that no longer radiated warmth or compassion or apology, but simply a wary patience, or was it not in fact a latent anger waiting to detonate?

A week after that second fall term began, an older boy slapped Nelson's glasses off his face in the steamy locker room. Three seconds later, Nelson had pinned him to the slippery ceramic tile, and pulled his arm behind his back until he heard a series of unnatural pops accompanied by screaming. There were three more attacks after that, but each ended similarly until finally he was left alone. And then, mysteriously, he began making friends. At first it was just a couple of other loners and misfits, but later, it became boys Nelson respected for their smarts, their kindness, their quiet inner strength. By the time he graduated, Nelson had been voted Most Likely to Succeed.

Years later, after graduating from West Point, he was earmarked for Vietnam, his Boy Scout experience considered a boon by his superiors, and later, it was his relatively short stature that made him an excellent tunnel rat, able to be sent down into the Viet Cong's subterranean tunnel system, the poor son of bitch, with only a flashlight and pistol.

22

DEANNA RETURNS TO THE TABLE UTTERLY COMPOSED and there is Nelson, already standing to pull her chair out for her and slide it beneath her as she resettles a napkin across her lap. Jonathan guzzles down his Scotch, sinking into the half darkness of the dining room, the cozy shadows, the golden light, the familiar smell of freshly baked rolls and popovers and melted butter. He seems not to even realize Deanna has returned until she rests her hand on his forearm and he is brought back to the table. He appreciates her gentle touch, this tiny act of solidarity. Across the table, Trevor is obviously still fuming.

"I want to say something to you, Trevor," Deanna says now, taking a sip of her champagne. "It's not quite an apology, because, well, I'm sincerely happy to be here with you, to have met you, and I think you know that. I hope, though, that you can also find it within yourself to . . . relax, you know? And just have a nice evening. Recognize the moment for what it is—time with your father, and Mr. Doughty, two men who clearly love you . . . What your father's trying to say to you—and, look, I know it's a difficult thing to hear—but the reality is, he most likely is right—you and Rachel won't last. And that's *okay;* it's nobody's fault. It's part of growing up, you know? Part of becoming an adult."

Trevor leans back on his chair's rear two legs with the disconsolate posture of a teenager whose ear is close to overflowing.

"But, the thing about love, Trevor, is that a person should foster it, foster that feeling as long as they can. And if you're in love right now, then, you should ride that feeling for all its worth. And I wish you the best of luck. Still, you're a Boy Scout, you have to be prepared— prepared to understand reality, too. I won't say another thing to you this evening to deter you or to make you feel bad, because you're obviously a good boy with a good heart. Your parents, I can see, have done a terrific job in raising you." Deanna settles back in her chair, now apparently finished. Outside the restaurant, night has consumed the landscape, leaving only a pale necklace of lights glowing around the far shore of the lake. The moon, it seems, is lost in the trees.

"Yeah? What do *you* know about my parents?" Trevor asks. "What do you even know about my mom? Geez . . . I mean, honestly. She's back home, probably—shit, I don't know, folding our laundry, making sure Dad's company runs right. Who do you think was his first bookkeeper? Who do you think laid off Dad's workers when they first started, huh? What? Dad didn't tell you that part? How he wasn't man enough to fire someone? Had to send my mom in to do his dirty work? And what for? So Dad can meet up with his girlfriend while we're up here, ostensibly learning how to become better men, better Scouts? What a fucking load of horseshit."

"And that's exactly what I mean," Deanna continues calmly. "I would hope that *my* son defended *me* the way you're defending your mom right now."

But Trevor isn't finished. "Did you know she lost both her parents before she was twenty years old? Both of them. Cancer. They died about a year apart." Trevor grips his fork, aims his eyes at the table. "Did you know that? Did you know that she had three miscarriages before she was able to have me? Three. I just want you to know, ma'am. You think you're in love with my dad, or maybe, I don't know, you guys are just having a . . . Jesus, an affair, or whatever . . . But we're all my mom has. We're her family. And I never even thought about that before, you know? It never dawned on me until now, but . . ." He points the tines of his fork at his father. "She would never do this to you, that's for goddamn sure."

Two waiters approach their table, dishes in hand, and proceed to settle the meal over the table, all four diners sitting more or less motionless, slowly tilting glasses toward their lips, until finally, the waiters gone again, Nelson reaches for Trevor's shoulder and, leaning into the boy, says gently, "Come on now, you have to eat something. It'll make you feel better. Something to sop up that daiquiri sloshing around inside you."

Famished and heartbroken, the boy takes up his utensils and begins to devour the meal in front of him, as Jonathan, Deanna, and Nelson look on, astonished at how quickly he vanishes the food. In a corner of the supper club, a jazz trio starts in on a cover of Dave Brubeck's "Take Five," even as the volume of the diners' voices rises to a crescendo, the dining room now truly packed, the bar elbow to elbow and two deep in places, dinner service cranking, and most of the patrons well sauced.

"Tell you what," Jonathan says, leaning toward his son, "let's make a bet."

"Oh, come on, Jon," Deanna says. "Don't be cruel."

"What? The kid is confident. So what? It'll be easy money for him, then."

Nelson crosses his arms.

"I bet a hundred bucks you and Racquel won't last through high school."

"Her name's Rachel, Dad. Rachel. You knew that."

Jonathan reaches for his back pocket, produces a bulging wallet, licks his fingers, and picks out a single hundred-dollar bill, setting it on the white linen, so close to the candle that the light passes easily through the thin paper. "A hundred bucks."

"You're betting that my heart will be broken, is that it?" Trevor asks. "You're actually betting that we're going to break up? God, why does this *matter* so much to you?"

Jonathan leans into the center of the table, two spears of asparagus on his fork. "Because I don't want you to miss out, Trev. All right? I want you to experience everything. I don't want you committing yourself to something because you're this goddamn throwback, this paragon of goodness. Right now, you're just seeing the world in right and wrong, black and white, but you get to be our age, it ain't that simple, see. Everybody's fucked up. Everybody's nailing each other's wives, stealing from work, cheating on their taxes. It's like, if you're not trying to cheat, you're a moron, a cretin. And what am I supposed to do, send you into that world unarmed? Like we're waltzing through Disney World, and it's all cotton candy and Mickey Mouse? All cartoons and Sunday school, and happily ever after? Look at me, Trevor."

But Trevor's eyes will not budge from his empty plate.

"Look at me, damnit!" Jonathan snaps—loudly enough to still the conversations at four nearby tables, loudly enough that Deanna places her hand on his forearm.

Trevor looks at his father.

"You're a good young man, Trev, but, look, kiddo, the world will eat you up if you don't open your eyes. Christ, you remind me of Bu— you got a little of Nelson's spirit in you."

"What's wrong with that?" asks Trevor. "Huh? People look up to Mr. Doughty. He's a war hero. He gets to live year-round at a Boy Scout camp."

"Gets?" laughs Jonathan. "Gets? Trev, most grown men would hardly see . . . Look, it's great and all that, but . . ."

"I'm sitting right here, Jonathan," Nelson says quietly, his voice a low growl beneath the din of the cacophonous room.

"Oh, I know where you're at, Nelson," Jonathan says, cutting loose from any last shreds of propriety. "Care to elaborate on your status as 'war hero,' 'cause I'm sure young Trevor here would love to be regaled with tales of your time in 'The Shit.'"

Nelson reaches out for the dying votive candle, this tiny light in his hand now, like he's carrying some small white spark for a bonfire waiting to be ignited.

"I'm sorry to disappoint you, old friend," he says, staring at the candle, "but I don't have any war stories to tell."

"Aww, you don't have any stories?" Jonathan guffaws, hoisting his Scotch glass up in the air for the waiter to see. "I don't buy that for a second. How many tours did you do, two, three?"

"Three," Nelson says quietly.

"He doesn't want to talk about it, Dad," says Trevor. "Geez."

"Weren't you the one asking me questions this morning about Bugler's Vietnam days? Well—here's your chance. Come on, Nelson, regale us. Something slightly sanitary, though. Polite war talk, now. No severed ears or, you know, napalmed grandmas."

"Jesus, Jonathan," says Deanna, "*easy.*"

"Or, you know what, don't hold back, Bugler. On second thought, hell, give it to him straight. You don't want the kid volunteering for another idiotic American war, now do you?"

"No. No, I don't."

23

⤬

THERE WAS NELSON, TWENTY-FIVE YEARS OLD, STAND-
ing on the crumbling cement stoop of his mother's postage-stamp Cape
Cod in Eau Claire's East Hill neighborhood. It was May, the air sweet
and heavy with the perfume of lilacs and, discordantly, the stench of
rubber and fire emanating from the Uniroyal plant across the river, the
world positively vibrating with twenty-four-hour industry and labor:
forklifts exhausting propane fumes, trains slinking slowly by, eighteen-
wheelers idling at loading docks, and the steady hum of hundreds of
pairs of hands toiling in that enormous brick building.

Nelson was slightly drunk. A reddish brown beard covering the
lower half of his face, an olive green rucksack balanced on his shoulder.
He had hitchhiked all the way back to Wisconsin from Fort Bragg,
in North Carolina, a three-day journey fueled in part by some potent
hash, cheap American beer, and heavy diner food at every stop along
the way: corned beef hash, bacon, biscuits and gravy, fried eggs, toast,

cheeseburgers, pork chops, Swiss steak, fried chicken, ice cream, banana cream pie . . . His best ride had come in the form of a busload of softball players making their way north from their homes in Rockford, Illinois, up to a tournament in Duluth, Minnesota. The bus was crammed with coolers of cold Schlitz beer and some of the younger men on the team had even served in Vietnam, too. Noshing cold Oscar Mayer wieners as they sipped their beers, they asked polite yet precise questions about where Nelson had served, for how long, and whether he'd seen casualties.

The bus dropped him off along Highway 53, near the Catholic high school and a bustling McDonald's. Just before he shrugged on his bag to disembark, one of the older men on the team handed him a wad of five- and ten-dollar bills held tight with a rubber band.

"You ever need a place to crash," the man said, "you got friends in Illinois. We're the Rockford Redbirds of the Northern Independent Softball League. Sponsored by Rockford Engine and Transmission. You ask around, you'll find one of us." Nelson shook his hand, and the older man nodded curtly. The bus passed on north then, but not before all the softball players stood at attention inside the bus, saluting Nelson all the way up the road until they disappeared.

First the porch light flickered on, and then his mother opened the front door, and stared out at her son, this man she had seen so very little of since his thirteenth birthday, when he had essentially moved out of her house.

"Hey, Mom," Nelson said, with more or less the same intonation, the same chagrined happiness that might have colored his voice as a twelve-year-old. "I'm home."

In an instant, she'd collapsed in tears, falling to her knees and sobbing, her hands shielding her eyes.

"Mom," Nelson said, dropping his rucksack and opening the door, bending down beside this woman, his mother, now more than fifty years old somehow, so much more gray, so much paler than she had been on that morning when Wilbur spirited him away, that first morning his father was no longer a presence in their lives.

He picked her up in his arms, and it made him happy to do so, after so many years of dragging his maimed and dismembered and deceased friends through rice paddies or clearings of elephant grass. Her body was familiar to him and her smell, that same dull, cheap, drugstore perfume she'd been wearing for decades, her thin arms and thin legs, the entirety of her body shuddering with the relief of seeing him, at last.

He carried her into the tiny sunken living room, a ceiling fan turning steadily above them, and laid her down on the couch, still sobbing. She turned away from him, as if ashamed. He sat down in the overstuffed chair his father had once favored, sank into its cushions, rested his arms on those of the chair, and felt his breathing ease.

"I thought you were never coming home," she said. "So often, I worried you were dead."

His eyelids closed, and instinctively he listened for sounds that might indicate danger. Tried to visualize the entire room—its corners, blind spots, potential sources of cover. He reached one hand toward the floor of the living room for the M16 he knew would not be there, fingers brushing only against that tired old turf of shag carpeting. He felt suddenly that his body was just so much still-wet cement, a bag of skin containing almost a hundred and seventy-five pounds of wet cement. And then, despite himself, he drifted off into sleep, his mother's voice occasionally there, asking him questions he could not understand, or, from time to time sobbing again and then snoring. At one point he woke to the steady chatter of cicadas outside the house, the wall of sound sifting through the screened windows, and reminding him of the jungle he'd slept in these past three years, never once thinking of it as "home," but where he nonetheless happened to reside, in a hammock above a forest floor crawling with millions upon millions of unseen insects and snakes, and his platoon arrayed all about him, aslumber, some snoring just as loudly as his mother was right now, others whimpering for girlfriends back home in Marion, Iowa; or Iron River, Michigan; or for some last-second fiancée in Hoboken, New Jersey; or Tempe, Arizona. Nelson had taken to a nightly exercise wherein very softly, in a whisper that was almost not his voice, he recited the Vietnamese alphabet—first forward, then backward, as if stepping in his own footsteps: A, Ă, Â, B, C, D, Đ, E, Ê, G, H, I, K, L, M, N, O, Ô, Ơ, P, Q, R, S, T, U, Ư, V, X, Y . . . —his voice becoming his own lullaby and sometimes he might overlap this ritual with the memory of lying in bed in a remote Cambodian whorehouse, a prostitute running her short fingers through his oily hair and humming some anonymous song to him while he recited the alphabet. She had one sleepy eye, this woman, and must have delivered a child recently. This would not have been evident save for the fact that when he pressed his mouth to her breasts, they issued forth a sweet milk that he drank, unabashed, throughout the night, until he and his comrades left in the early morning without so much as a word, just a collective gathering of bandoliers, machine guns, and packs shouldered again. Then they disappeared back in the direction of the border, into the certain danger of an endless jungle.

He woke the next morning with a start, nearly pouncing out of the chair. His mother was in the kitchen, he could hear her, the sound of her orthopedic shoe soles on the linoleum, squeaking at every turn of her heel. Rubbing his eyes, he stood and stretched, then walked in to join her.

"Good morning," he said.

It had been more than ten years since they lived together in the same house, falling asleep and waking under the same roof, sharing breakfast. He had come back, of course, for holidays, but every summer between his thirteenth birthday and his admission to West Point, he had worked as either a cook or counselor at Camp Chippewa, his connection to his mother growing more and more obscure, defined by little more than the infrequent letters they exchanged, or the monthly visits she paid to the camp between June and September, when Wilbur would drive them to a local restaurant or supper club and treat them to dinner, describing Nelson's accomplishments in the kind of golden adjectives reserved only for adoring grandparents, mentors, or coaches in awe of a person so much younger than themselves.

"What impresses me about Nelson, ma'am, is not just the boy's skill with a rope or a compass, or the fact that he's become the camp's strongest swimmer and best shot with a twenty-two rifle. To be honest, I expect those kinds of accomplishments from every boy, and to my discredit, find myself disappointed when boys *don't* excel at such pursuits. No, the thing that impresses me so much about Nelson is that I've seen him become a leader. The other boys, they look to him, almost by default. And there's a toughness in him, ma'am—a toughness uncommon in boys his age, in most men even. He is righteous; he knows right and wrong and he won't tolerate bullying or cruelty. I've seen it, and heard about his deeds from other counselors and troop leaders. Why, just a week ago, Nelson observed an older boy, a big boy, who thought he'd get some kicks by holding another boy's head underwater in the lake. I don't believe he meant the other boy grievous harm, ma'am, but just the same, this was un-Scout-like behavior and entirely unbecoming. In fact, it was torture. The lifeguard on duty couldn't see what was happening, because the lake water was frothing with activity, boys swimming and splashing, but Nelson saw it right away. Well, ma'am. I'm happy to report that older boy was subdued by Nelson and subsequently dismissed from the camp. And the younger boy's parents, it won't surprise you, wrote me a letter commending Nelson's efforts."

He reached into a wool suit pocket and produced an envelope folded once across its middle. "Here is that letter, ma'am. They describe your son as a hero."

Nelson watched as his mother reached across to take the warm envelope from Wilbur, her wrist very close to the flame of a candle. She unfolded the letter and began reading, her lips bouncing as her eyes moved left to right and back again. She read slowly, almost as if the act were a struggle for her. Then she folded the letter back into the envelope, slipped it into her purse, and said, "You've done a fine job mentoring my son, Mr. Whiteside, and I . . . I'm indebted to you. Truly."

"*You* are the one who should be proud, Mrs. Doughty," Wilbur said. "You've made some difficult decisions to ensure your son's success, ma'am, his future. That was very brave, indeed."

Nelson's mother's hand shook as she raised a water glass to her lips, the ice cubes clinking first against her teeth, and the perspiring glass. "Was it?" she mumbled after a moment, reaching into her purse for a handkerchief to blow her nose into.

"THERE'S COFFEE IN THE THERMOS, if you'd like," said Dorothy. "I have to go to work." She was dressed in a uniform of sorts: white stockings, a light gray-blue skirt and blouse, her graying hair tied tightly into a bun, two circles of rouge on her cheeks below bagged eyes and eyebrows etched tight with sadness.

"Where, uh, where do you work?" Nelson coughed. He realized, quite suddenly, that he knew next to nothing about this aged woman his mother had become.

"Becker's Dry Cleaning, on Barstow."

"Oh," he said. "Uh, when do you get done?"

She held her purse against her chest, stood very straight. "Depends. Five thirty, six."

"Maybe I could prepare dinner?" he offered, studying his toes, only then at a loss as to what dish he was even capable of making, after so much time eating out of brown plastic MREs, the cold contents of little tin cans. Suddenly he remembered her chow mein.

"Do you know *how* to cook?" she asked.

"A little," he lied.

"Well," she reached into her purse, producing a five-dollar bill, and set it on the counter to the left of the sink. "Here's some grocery money, then. If you don't feel up to it, though, or if you're exhausted, just buy some steaks and I'll fix them when . . ." Then, her voice trailing off, she held a hand over her mouth, closed her eyes.

"Mom," he began, and thought to go to her, only did not know how.

She waved a hand, as if indicating it was all so much nothing, a trifle next to everything else. She waved it all away and said, "I'll see you tonight."

"Mom . . ."

But she was already pushing her way through the front door, the screen door slapping open and then banging shut again. He stood in the doorway, watching her stride purposefully down the sidewalk, away from him, and he could hear her blowing her nose, see her shoulders still shaking slightly.

Once, he had been her boy, and then something more like a ghost. Now who was he to her? This man, this bearded man, almost twenty-five years old, with the tang of hash perhaps embedded in the fiber of his clothing and in his unkempt whiskers, a permanent glaze over his eyes, and now this history of secrets he could never share with her: the coffin-black tunnels burrowed through, the dozens of killings (how many *were* there?), the countless ways in which he had witnessed his friends, his comrades, killed? Even the things he was only slightly unashamed of: the opium dens, the whorehouses, the blue-eyed babies he might have left behind—how to explain any of those things? Better left a matter of discretion. Of silence. That, at least, could stand in for some kind of virtue.

24

✗

THE CANDLE SPUTTERS OUT FINALLY, DROWNED IN its own whitish wax.

"I still want to make a wager," Jonathan says, leaning jauntily back in his chair. "Deanna? You going to bet with me? How 'bout you, Nelson? Or is that against the Scout code? I can't fucking recollect all those goddamn laws and rules and what have you."

"Dad . . . ," Trevor moans. "You're drunk. Can we go back to the motel, please?"

"No," Jonathan says forcefully. "This night's just warming up, isn't that right, Nelson? We're above the forty-fifth now, Trev. There's no going to bed early. No school in the morning, no girlfriend to report back to. No, we're going to have some goddamn *fun* tonight." He scooches his chair closer to Deanna, swoops an arm around the shoulder of her chair. She winces at his touch at first, swipes at something in her lap, and then glances up at Trevor, and smiles.

"You're always drunk," Trevor says. "Do you even know that? Do you know the difference anymore?"

Jonathan raises one finger in the air, burps gently, and leans toward the center of the table. "I have to take a leak," he says very slowly, "and then I'm going to take a step outside to have a cigarette and talk to the stars." He pushes his chair back and it falls over, slowly, and there is a moment as Jonathan stands, when it seems entirely possible that he, too, may also fall over and become entangled with the chair, like two barroom brawlers embracing awkwardly, but he steadies himself to rise almost regally as a waiter hurries over, righting the chair and then sweeping away the empty glasses. "Just have to powder my nose," Jonathan says with a wink as he teeters toward the bathroom. With his silver hair, his khaki pants, a baby-blue button-down shirt, and Sperry topsiders, he might be a yachtsman accounting for the pitch and roll of the sea beneath him.

Trevor's arms are crossed over his chest and he glowers down at the white linen of the table. Nelson seems to be fixing his gaze at the same remarkable point on the tabletop. All around them, the dining room is abuzz with laughter, the promise of romance, the comfortable two-top silence of long-married couples, the low-toned voices of political debate or business negotiations, the optimistic toasts, and one table blearily singing the easy refrain of "Piano Man."

"I'm just so happy to meet you," Deanna says at last, clapping her hands together and holding them near her heart, the way, Trevor imagines, a missionary might before raising their face toward God in prayer. "I know this dinner has been, well, a bit of a shit show, but . . . You're exactly how your father described you."

"Oh yeah?" Trevor asks sullenly, staring back at her now, unyielding. "How's that?"

She looks down, lets her hands fall. "Handsome," she says quietly. "And good."

"*Good?*" He snorts with mock amusement. "Good? You heard him. He thinks I'm simple."

"No, he doesn't. He thinks you're incredibly intelligent. I just think . . . I think he's worried that you're maybe a little . . . naïve, is all."

"Naïve? Naïve! Of course I'm naïve! I'm sixteen fucking years old! I don't understand. Does he want me to be a *bad man*? Is that what this is about? Soured on life before I even get to college? Is it about finding some kind of coconspirator or something?" The boy places the heels of his palms on his eyes and emits a deep teenage sigh. "Like, I just don't understand. I don't think I was raised to disrespect my mother. I mean, what the hell is happening here? What does he even want from me? Some seal of approval?"

"Maybe," she says, "or maybe—"

"Well screw that!" Trevor snaps. "And screw him!"

The waiter is suddenly stationed at Deanna's shoulder, standing at attention like any good soldier, an array of menus in his hands, and a look of polite concern on his face.

"Would you all be interested in dessert?" he asks.

"Give us a moment, please," Nelson says, leaning into the center of the table from the shadows where he's been biding his time. He coughs into the white flower of his napkin. "Deanna, perhaps you'd kindly give me a few minutes with Trevor, here?" He winks at her, inches his chair closer to Trevor, who could hardly look more uncomfortable.

"Of course," she says, pushing away from the table and after grabbing her purse, moving toward the bathrooms. When she is out of sight, Nelson places a heavy hand on Trevor's back, and the boy stares down at the linen of the table, making little indentations in the cloth with his fingernails.

"So, my parents are getting divorced?" Trevor asks. "Is that what this means?"

"I don't know, bud. But I'm afraid it's looking that way."

"I don't understand," Trevor says, looking up at Nelson. "I mean, she's not even that good looking. It's not like he's leaving Mom for some twenty-something bikini model. You know? Not that it would make it *okay*, but, I mean, at least I could understand. Some kind of midlife crisis, or whatever they're called. But I don't know, geez . . ." He laces his fingers behind his head. "Why'd he go and organize all this? Do *you* understand?"

Nelson leans back in his chair, glances out the window. There are Jonathan and Deanna, standing on a narrow walkway in the glow of the restaurant, sharing a cigarette. They look natural together. He's leaning on a wooden rail and she's standing to his right, her left hand on his back. In her right hand, she holds their cigarette. They might be standing on the deck of a transatlantic ocean liner, this debonair couple, comfortable in their silence, their little throwaway gestures.

"I don't know either, bud," Nelson says, "but, listen, I want you to know something."

The kid peers intently down at the table.

"Are you listening to me?"

Trevor nods.

"You're a fine young man."

Trevor laughs, dismissively. Nelson reaches for the boy's wrist, holds it, with some pressure, and says, "I mean what I said."

"Okay—I *heard* you," the kid scoffs, "I'm a fine young man. Great. My dad's banging another woman, he hates my girlfriend, and I'm totally fucking confused, but you think I'm fine. Great."

"Trevor," Nelson intones, "I've had the great misfortune to watch dozens and dozens of my friends die." His voice is low now, and it cuts right through the haze of the restaurant. "Many of them were fine young men, too. Many of them, I suppose, weren't as bright as you are now, maybe, or as sensitive. They really were more like boys. And I watched them be blown to bits. Do you understand?"

Trevor almost shakes his head in the negative.

Nelson places his hand on the boy's heart. Leaves it there, warm and heavy, and though Trevor's first impulse is to retreat from this touch, he doesn't, and the hand feels like a quilt, a comfort. Nelson's eyes are unflinching, strong, haunted. "I've known cowards and I've known heroes," he says. "The heroes were always ruled by their hearts; the cowards, by their brains. Don't forget that. Heroes don't calculate or calibrate. They do what is right."

Jonathan and Deanna weave back through the restaurant now, trailing a bouquet of cigarette smoke and fresh, piney air. Jonathan sits down happily, heavily, places a hand on Trevor's shoulder.

"You order us some dessert?" he asks.

"No," says the boy.

"Well, now's your chance. We're going to drop Deanna off at the motel and then I'm going to take you someplace real special, but they ain't gonna have any dessert, I can guarantee you that."

"Dad, I don't know . . . Can I go back to the motel, too? I'm kind of bushed."

Jonathan reaches into his wallet, produces a hundred-dollar bill, holds it before his son. "The thing is, it's a bit of a drive. So I really do think we'd be best served by ordering some coffee, having a little dessert, and collecting ourselves before we go. I'll pay you a hundred dollars if you come."

"Dad . . . I mean, look, I just want to go back to the motel, okay? It's not about money or anything."

Jonathan pulls another hundred-dollar bill from his pocket, holds one in each hand, like winning lottery tickets.

"How about two hundred dollars, then?" he asks. He raises his eyebrows and purses his lips like some crazed TV game show host trying to make a deal.

"Dad . . ."

Jonathan laughs, looks at Deanna, and raises an eyebrow. "Kid drives a hard bargain." He sits up off his chair a bit, reaches for his wallet, examines its contents, before licking his fingers and extracting another hundred-dollar bill. "Three hundred dollars. How about it?"

"Looks like Trevor has the basics of negotiation down," Nelson says, crossing his arms. "Stay quiet, seem disinterested. He's also created a little immediacy by claiming he wants to call it a night. Must have a smart mother."

Deanna glances at Nelson, nibbles benignly at her fingertips. The restaurant seems to have downshifted into another speed, a slower speed. The music taking on a less buoyant tone, yielding now to those sad-sack, tear-in-your-martini dirges Sinatra might've crooned if it were just him at the bar, him and Set-em-Up-Joe, *I could tell you a lot, but you've got to be true to your code . . .*

And now another hundred-dollar bill comes out, two for each hand. "Imagine the date you could take what's-her-face out on, huh?" says Jonathan, grinning. "For four hundred dollars you could hire a limousine, have dinner in Minneapolis, or hell, get a hotel room down in Milwaukee or Chicago, give each other hand jobs or whatever it is you guys do these days."

Trevor's arms are crossed and he's frowning deeply. "Rachel," he mutters.

"Also," Jonathan says, "we still have that matter of the bet. I'm going to get Nelson to pony up later tonight."

"He's coming, too?" Trevor asks hopefully. "To the next place?"

Nelson leans toward the center of the table. "Somebody's got to keep your dad honest."

"Last call," Jonathan says. "What'll it be? Four hundred dollars and some unknown fun, or back to the motel to watch a shitty little TV and hope your Rochelle is home? For what it's worth, I kinda think you'll like where we're headed. Hell, if I can't educate you here, maybe some-body else can."

"Rachel, Dad. Rachel. And if we're going to do this nonsense, I want five hundred," Trevor blurts. "Five hundred. Cash on the barrelhead."

Jonathan smiles in the golden light, his teeth shining.

25

NELSON LIVED WITH HIS MOTHER FOR TWO MONTHS, the tedium of everyday life beginning to drown him almost immediately. Nowhere to go, nothing to do, no one who understood precisely where he'd come from, what he had seen, the things he had done. The first month he contented himself by sleeping sixteen hours a day, rising only to eat ice cream and then walk into downtown and drink with the enthusiasm and urgency of someone desperately trying to black out into an eternal velveteen Johnnie Walker night. Most times, he couldn't even find someone to fight; every insult he flung, every chest he pushed, every beer he tossed into an unsuspecting face—they all went ignored. He daydreamed about his adolescence, when boys used to mob him, their fists churning at his body, their feet kicking him like a ball in the middle of a scrum.

His favorite part of the day came either when a bartender or bouncer smacked him with a blackjack, or their thick hand found his yellowed crumpled collar or a tangle of hair and dragged him into the soft blue evening's humid embrace or onto the sidewalk halo of a sentinel streetlight. How many times had he lain on the cement, laughing, thinking, *I'm alive, I'm fucking alive, this is life, I am alive and drunk in Wisconsin.* Lay there, on the cement, smoking a crooked Marlboro, and fingering the nickel he kept on a chain necklace.

On the first day of August, early in the morning, he entered his mother's bedroom, sat gently on her bed, and said quietly, "Mom, wake up. Wake up, Mom."

She startled awake, sat upright, looking so very old.

"No, I mean, it's okay," he said, "lie back down. It's okay. Sorry to wake you. It's just . . ."

She held the hem of her blankets below her chin, studied him with a look of fear and confusion. The lace curtains framing her window twirled with the wind; they were no longer white, but the stained yellow of a cigarette filter—the color, really, of just . . . time.

"I'm leaving, Mom," he said. "I'm sorry."

"*Why?*" she croaked.

"I don't know," he said, "I'm afraid . . . I'm afraid something bad will happen if I stay here."

His favorite fantasy, his favorite dream involved a bar fight in which he did not stop punching his opponent's face, kept throwing haymakers until it was little more than hamburger, that face, a mess of spaghetti and meat sauce. It was a dream he experienced often, and not even with horror, either—just a splendid sense of relief, more relief than he could get swallowing any kind of downer. He dreaded the thought of his mother visiting him in the county jail, sitting in a courtroom, with Nelson having nothing to say for himself except perhaps that he was going exactly where he belonged, to prison. He had, after all, killed so many human beings in Vietnam. Wasn't he, in fact, a murderer?

"Well, you have to do what you think is right, Nelson," she managed.

They were silent a moment before he spoke again.

"Did you ever see him again?" Nelson asked. "Did he ever call?"

She shook her head, covered her mouth, began crying as she seemed to do so easily, weeping with that same sense of resignation.

"There's a box down in the basement. Letters, I suppose, he sent you after you left St. John's. They seemed to come around your birthday."

"He's down in Chicago, isn't he?"

"Yes, well . . . I don't know. Does it matter, Nelson? Would it matter so much? Don't you see? You leaving now . . . Oh, please—just—*go*. Go already!" She swatted at him, rather feebly.

"Do you have his address?"

"No," she sniffled, "I don't care, either. I would have burned those letters if they weren't addressed to you."

"Why Chicago?"

"He would talk about living there sometimes, about the lake and the trains, I guess he had a cousin who was a bus driver or something. Anyway, he wasn't happy here. I don't have to remind you of that." She turned away from him. "Where will you go?" she asked after a moment.

"West," he said. "Somewhere out west."

"Will you do me one favor?" she asked.

"I'll try."

"Two favors, actually. Send me a postcard, if you would, so at least I know you're alive. And come back for Christmas, will you? Take me to church. Is that too much to ask?"

"No," he said, "it isn't too much to ask. I can do that."

"And take that box of letters. I want them out of my house."

He leaned down and kissed the top of her head. There was something inside him, in fact, that wished nothing more than to crawl into bed beside her and watch the day brighten. But instead, he rose, collected a small backpack, found the box in the basement, emptied its contents into his bag, and walked downtown to the bus station beside the Eau Claire River, and bought a westbound ticket for Albuquerque,

New Mexico, a destination attractive to him for several reasons, not the least of which was he knew not a soul in that city.

He took work on ranches, mucking out horse stalls, fixing fence lines—all the dude duties of a greenhorn farmhand. Nelson relished the labor; he woke early, ate quietly, and the other hands left him pretty much alone. At night he went to bed tired, and on some evenings he walked out to a campfire where some of the men sat on stumps laughing and telling stories and over time they asked him about where he'd come from, and it was these men he first told about Vietnam.

He sent his mother a postcard in early October that read: *Dear Mom, Working on a ranch north of Santa Fe. Please don't worry about me. See you soon. Love, Nelson.*

He did not come home for Christmas that year, or any year, for that matter. Did not return to Wisconsin until the fall of his thirtieth birthday when he received a call at the ranch from Sacred Heart Hospital in Eau Claire. He'd been in the horse barn talking to the farrier, passing him tools and shoes, when the owner of the ranch, an elderly woman named Maria, hurried through the barn's open doors and spoke his name with a note of concern in her voice. "Phone's for you," she said, with a hand covering her heart.

He buried her on a cold day in October with low, gray bristly clouds sweeping through the sky. Fourteen people attended her funeral; he'd had to pointedly ask her neighbors if they would come, unsure they would even have enough coffin bearers otherwise.

The minister, after reading his liturgy and leading the grieving through a graveside prayer, lingered a polite amount of time, shook hands with the attendees, and then, before passing Nelson en route to his car, said quietly, "I want you to know she didn't suffer, if that helps. I was there at the end. It was some kind of stroke. But I don't believe she was ever in any kind of pain."

Nelson stared at her graveside coffin, the one he had hastily picked out at the funeral home, its shiny wood now beaded with rain. The funeral home director's wife herself had come out to Nelson's mother's home, to pick out her eternal ensemble. His relatives were now crossing themselves and retreating to their cars, most without so much as shaking his hand or bothering to mumble their condolences. Fifty feet away he saw a man sitting inside a small Bobcat tractor, a cigarette smoldering between his lips, a mound of dark soil next to the machine.

26

$$\times$$

JONATHAN AND DEANNA IN THE VAN, TREVOR WITH
Nelson in his cool old beater of a Land Rover.

"You got any notion where Dad's taking us?" Trevor asks, as they
pull into the parking lot of the motel, Deanna, at the wheel of the Astro van, guiding the vehicle to a spot just in front of Jonathan's room.
Trevor watches as his dad leans from the passenger seat across the
center console to kiss Deanna, her hands on his face, the headlights
backlighting their heads. The kiss is excruciatingly slow and real, and
after a moment Trevor turns to look instead toward the sickly glow of
the pool.

Nelson nods dispassionately. "If I were you, I'd just remember that
five hundred dollars. Focus on your girlfriend, focus on your feelings for
her. Your dad seems hell-bent on some kind of juvenile antics, but that
doesn't mean you need to engage in it. And, Trevor—"

"What?" the kid asks.

"You might not understand now, or even in a few years, but . . . try to give your Dad a break, if you can, you know? Cut him some slack."

"Are you kidding me?" Trevor says. "Of all people, I thought you'd be, like, outraged! Now you're, what, colluding with him or something? I mean, are you seriously condoning this bullshit? Look at them! Look at them over there!" He points to the lovebirds, necking in plain sight. "That's my fucking dad! Who is *married*, by the way. Married!"

"I'm sorry, Trevor. Truly. I'm sorry about your parents."

The boy shakes his head resolutely. "This is just so fucked up."

"All you can do is try to be a better man, you know? You take moments like this, and you learn from them. You think to yourself, *This isn't the dad I want to be. This isn't the husband I want to be.* And you hold that inside you, like a memory, but bigger, too. Like a code."

Trevor is focused on the pool.

Sliding the Land Rover into park, Nelson kills the engine. "Look, Trevor, do you think I'm a good man? Right now, do you think I'm a better man than your father? Do you think I'm a better man, some sort of paragon? Is that how you think of me?"

Trevor turns to look at him. "I don't know. Yeah, I guess. I mean, you're not a married guy making out with some married woman in clear view of his son, so . . . you've got that going for you. Yeah, I think you're better than him."

Deanna gets out of the van and very elegantly walks over to Nelson's aged vehicle, parked just a few spots away. Trevor quickly reclines his chair, turns his head, and feigns sleep, even as she raps her knuckles lightly on the window, her left ring finger making a different-sounding tap. Nelson leans over the teenager and rolls down the window for him.

"Oh," she says, taking in Trevor, the light snoring he affects. "Well, Nelson, it was a pleasure meeting you this evening. I hope we'll have another opportunity to see each other."

"Let me get out and say a proper goodbye," he says, opening his door and walking around the Land Rover to give her a polite kiss on the cheek, and a gentle hug.

She holds him by both elbows, leans in close to his face. "Please tell Trevor how much I enjoyed meeting him, too. I'm sorry tonight, you know, turned out so awkward for us all."

"He's a good kid, isn't he?" Nelson says. "I'm sure he'll take things very maturely. These things are difficult to understand, I think, no matter what a person's age."

"We're in love," Deanna says with a shrug. "What can I say?"

"It shows," Nelson says, smiling.

Over her shoulder Nelson has been watching Jonathan struggle with his room key, the lock on his motel room door some sort of moving target. Finally, and with two hands, the key finds its bull's-eye and he shoulders the door open, only to emerge moments later, belt unbuckled, shirt untucked. It can be so difficult, Nelson thinks, to look dignified when drunk.

"When do you head home?" Nelson asks, filling time.

"Tomorrow morning. Wish me luck."

"Good luck, Deanna."

"And you take care of these two," she advises, pointing her chin at Trevor, and then, reaching through the open window to caress the boy's shoulder. He startles as soon as her hand touches him, surely betraying his ruse. "Good night, Trevor," she says, each of her words soft as a petal falling from a flower. "It really was so nice to meet you. Maybe sometime soon you can meet my son."

Jonathan, finally having weaved his way across the parking lot, stands beside Deanna. "Walk you to your room?" he slurs.

"No, that's all right," she says, laying a hand on his chest. "Don't misbehave too much tonight." She pecks him on the cheek.

"Oh," he says, "we wouldn't think of it." He winks at Nelson, a slow, one-eyed wink that quickly degrades into just shutting his eyes.

They kiss once more, and then she walks to her room.

"The kid asleep?" Jonathan asks. "Did they say goodbye?"

"Get in the back and shut up," Nelson says, returning to the driver's seat. "My rig, my rules."

"In that case, let's take my van. Look at it this way, the cops are a helluva lot less likely to finger a minivan for drunk driving, don't you think?" Jonathan hands Nelson the keys.

Nelson smirks, nods. Shakes the kid's shoulder. "Wake up," he orders. They pile into the van. Trevor immediately pretends he's sleeping again.

"You know the way?" Jonathan says, slumping down across the backseat and lying down, closing his eyes.

"I think I can get us there," Nelson says, aiming the Astro north and east toward Hurley, a town of about 1,100 with six strip clubs lining the main street and not much else to speak of.

ABOUT FIVE MINUTES down the road from the motel and with Jonathan dozing resoundingly on the backseat, Nelson growls, "You can quit pretending to be asleep now."

Trevor sits up and says, "Why, so you can tell me about how the world isn't black and white, that we're all doomed to some kind of moral mediocrity, that sort of thing? Maybe I'd be safer asleep."

Nelson chuckles, glances in the rearview at the backseat. "Hey, Jon!" he calls out. "Got any smokes?"

"Check the glove box," Jonathan murmurs.

"Whad'ya say, Trevor? Pass me one of those cancer sticks, would you?"

"I didn't know you smoked," Trevor says, obliging.

Nelson rolls his window down, hangs an elbow out into the night. They're off the main highways now, deep in some forest that is truly emblematic of the Northwoods: close, dark tamarack forests and bogs, tall white and red pines, not a trace of civilization in sight. The stars are uninterrupted, a perfect circuitry, pulsing, and steadily, gently, twirling, like the lighted gears of the grandest machine. Nelson lights a cigarette, takes a deep drag, rubs his middle and index finger against his temple, and exhales.

"Your dad was the only friend I ever had," he begins, "and—though this may not be especially evident this evening—he happens to be one of the kindest people I've ever met. I'm not sure I'd be alive today without him." He turns his attention away from the road, stares directly at Trevor until the boy looks down into his own lap.

He tells Trevor about his childhood, about the bullying, the alienation; about his own father, his abandonment; the depression and desperation that began to overtake his mother; the years in military school, away from home. In this narrative, Nelson's only friend is Jonathan, which isn't exactly true; for there were others, especially at St. John's, and then, of course, in the Green Berets. But that isn't important tonight. Tonight, Nelson thinks, the kid needs to know that his dad saved a boy from the horrors of an outhouse hell, that his dad wrote letters addressed to Vietnam, that his dad was the only kid at that birthday party . . .

He makes up other legends, other heroic tall tales, nothing so dramatic that Jonathan will deny it out of hand if ever interrogated about the details. But Nelson knows enough. He removes the chain necklace and passes it to Trevor; the old buffalo nickel with a little hole drilled into it to accept a necklace—his lucky charm through Vietnam. He tells Trevor about how while traveling through Spain back in college, Jonathan had been running with the bulls in Pamplona and saved another runner from being gored (all this from those infrequent epistles during Nelson's days in Vietnam). Nelson exaggerates the details: how the runner Jonathan saved was an old man who'd broken his ankle on an uneven cobblestone, how Jonathan hoisted the man off the street with superhuman strength;

and how the man's family gave a party for Jonathan, a party where the beautiful young niece of the man promised herself to Jonathan . . . Other stories, too, each meant to obliquely explain Jonathan's behavior this evening: his own big vulnerable romantic heart, his disdain for money, his uncommon charity, his pride in Trevor and love of the boy.

The Jonathan that Nelson constructs is an impossibly good and decent man, flawed only in ways all grown men are—susceptible to the wiles of women, ever lonely, always sacrificing, forever vigilant of their child's future. If Jonathan has fallen out of love with Trevor's mom, then, well, surely this is as natural as a coastline collapsing into the ocean, almost an inevitability, and who knows? Who knows whose fault it was?

Nelson is careful not to portray Sarah Quick in any sort of villainous light. Not least as he is sensitive to the fact that Jonathan is very likely responsible for this marital schism, such as it is. Nor does he care to fabricate some notion that Trevor's mother won't be sideswiped, dumbstruck, heartbroken. But the truth is this: Jonathan is not a *bad* man; he won't abandon this boy, and he'll likely support Sarah financially in a more than generous manner—they'll both be cared for. And anyway, isn't this the reality of today's America? No one's marriage lasts; no one is innocent; and the Boy Scouts, like every other code of morality, is just an antiquated set of stone tablets, the words melting into obscurity, acid-washed by rain and returning stone to sand, until it is all just so much tiny particulate, forever shifting beneath our feet.

Trevor's posture seems to straighten as the road goes on and Nelson continues his chain-smoking. Rolling down his own window, the boy peers out at the stars.

"I thought you were going to tell me about yourself," Trevor says, after a time. "I thought you were going to tell me about how bad *you* are. All the *bad* things you've done." He leans his chin into a cupped hand, breathes in the cool, wet air. "As if."

And so, for the first time since he worked at that ranch in New Mexico, Nelson talks about his time in Vietnam. Tells the boy about the horrifying hum of flies on open-eyed children, the napalm scars on the legs of young girls; the whorehouses and their opium pipes and acid nightmares; tells him about the long, long deaths of his friends, their chest wounds sucking and wheezing; the letters they received from girlfriends and wives who had taken new lovers, the parents who passed away, the altar boys who forgot God, the former Boy Scouts who were soon practicing only nooses; the men they killed who were not men, but boys, like Trevor—just boys.

He tells Trevor about his own father and his mother, too. And as loose as he was with the facts of Jonathan's life, he is brutally specific with his own autobiography, utterly truthful. He tells the boy about the closet he discovered in his mother's house, before the place was sold, this closet that held all those Christmas presents she'd bought him, while he lived in New Mexico, happy to forget her, forget that house. New cowboy boots, bolo ties, books, calfskin gloves, a watch, and for each year that he was away: a set of Topps baseball cards, wrapped in cellophane, untouched.

THEY PULL INTO HURLEY, to the single set of stoplights and the corner gas station where four bikers huddle in a loose circle, smoking cigarettes, tugging at their beards.

"So this is it," Nelson says with a flourish. "*Hurley*."

The light turns green and Nelson slowly turns left.

"Strip clubs," Trevor says. "All I see is a bunch of strip clubs."

From the backseat they hear Jonathan lurch up. He leans between their seats, wipes his mouth, and from a back pocket extracts a comb, begins to work it through his thick head of hair.

"A bit of advice," Jonathan says, his hand on the back of Trevor's seat. "You got five hundred dollars in your pocket. Spend it however you please. But I'll say this, you may get a little more bang for your buck back home with Rachel. So . . . gird your loins. We'll just stay for a beer or two. Continue your miseducation before I relinquish"—a word that takes a painfully long time to pronounce—"you to the morality police tomorrow."

"Wait a minute, Dad—I'm sixteen," he practically giggles. "There's no *way* they're going to let me in there. I can't even smoke yet."

"Oh yeah?" Jonathan says. "Nelson, kindly hand me one of those smokes, eh?"

Passing the box over his right shoulder, Nelson parks the van on an otherwise abandoned street slick with a recent cloudburst off nearby Lake Superior. The neon lights reflect garishly off the asphalt, like a circus kaleidoscope.

27

THE DOORMAN WOULD SEEM A GOOD DEAL LESS AD-
ept at negotiating than Trevor, because the boy is waved into the club on
the strength of a twenty-dollar handshake and a cursory glance up and
down Main for the presence of any cop cars, of which there are none.

Inside the club it's a pounding pandemonium of AC/DC, strobing
colors, an intense low-hanging cloud of cigarette smoke, and, of course,
skin, skin, skin. Women at the bar, long legs crisscrossed, impossibly
high heels dangling off the floor like daggers, big hair ponderously per-
fumed and sprayed into place for ease of movement in every other part
of the body. There might be ten or twelve patrons in the place, arrayed
about the long, narrow room, some scattered at the bar, a few others sitting at high tables on the margins, staring intently at the stage,
where an upside-down woman is languidly sliding down a brass pole
scissor-clenched between her legs as five men closer to the stage clap
their hands approvingly with cigarettes pursed beneath mustaches, inside yellow-stained goatees.

All Trevor can manage is a feeble, dazed, "Wow."

Jonathan stands beside his son, slapping him on the back, and taking a final drag from the cigarette before letting it fall to the floor and rubbing at it with the toe of his shoe. "Yessirree—in my experience, sin rarely registers until the next morning. So, for now, I'd advise you to thoroughly enjoy this cultural epicenter of the great Northwoods."

"What?" the kid asks, still staring and stunned.

"Well, there ain't any ballet in town, but that looks curiously akin to modern dance, if you ask me."

Nelson joins them, with three bottles of cold Leinenkugel's. "Let's find a table," he growls agreeably enough.

AC/DC gives way to Whitesnake: *Here I am again on my own . . .* The dancer is sweating now and Trevor is really looking at her, really scrutinizing her. He realizes he's never seen Rachel naked before, though he can feel her body, even from two hundred miles away: her smallish breasts, the soft, nearly invisible hair on her thighs, the pads of her feet, the fingernails she chews to nubs mostly while sitting in the classroom, or on the bench during a softball game. *This*, however, is a woman and her body looks . . . so much different; it is astonishing, a miracle.

These raw, raw gymnastics she's performing, and her breasts, no, these can only be called tits—her tits are big and appear to be peppered by some kind of glitter. She's the glossiest, most shimmering thing he's ever seen and he sort of feels in love with everything about her: the piercings in her belly button and wide, dark nipples, the places where the folds of her meet and sweat collects to roll to the floor below where dollar bills go flying like paper planes, little green balls. And when she lies on her back, raises her long legs, and peels her panties off the way you might peel a price tag off the cover of a book you intended for a present . . . she hides herself with both hands for a period of five seconds before unfolding her legs and it's like the mystery of the cosmos has opened for Trevor: her vagina, no: *pussy.*

He feels a lump in his throat, suddenly can't remember what Rachel looks like at all.

"I'm going to sit by the stage," he tells his father and Nelson, carrying his bottle of Leinie's like he's done this a hundred times before.

"All right," Jonathan says, drowsily, his chair leaned up against the wall. Then he thinks to sit upright, reaches for his wallet, and peels off about ten one-dollar bills, handing them to Trevor. "Please don't give her one of those hundreds, okay? You want to tip these dancers, you give them singles. This is Hurley, Wisconsin. Not Las Vegas. *Capisce?*"

"So, what do I do?" Trevor asks. "Just throw it on the stage?"

Jonathan closes his eyes, yawns. "She'll help you, I promise."

The kid finds a seat near the stage, is uncertain how to sit, whether to lean forward like an eager pupil (he *is* eager) or to slouch back, cool as can be, like this is all very stale news. Also, there is a noticeable stiffening in his pants that he would prefer to camouflage. As he fidgets, readjusts, and tries to establish where to store his ten singles, he knocks the bottle of Leinie's over and some of it spills on his crotch, quickly extinguishing that problem. Only there are no paper napkins and the only waitress he sees is snapping her gum near the bar, talking to Nelson—*Nelson?!?*

"Ummm, looks like you've made a mess of yourself," coos a voice just above him.

It's her. She's on all fours, her face a scant six inches from Trevor's and her perfume is the most intoxicating thing he's ever smelled. Rachel doesn't wear perfume; she usually smells like Dove or Irish Spring, or sometimes the horses she rides on Sunday afternoons, after church.

"I'm sorry," Trevor squeaks. It is the best he can manage. His hands smell like beer and his head is as fuzzy as a poorly tuned radio, this new frequency buzzing within him.

She moves forward, her chest and head and arms out over the lip of the stage and now she's pressing Trevor back into his chair, her hair arrayed all around him. Her breath, he thinks, smells like tequila and lime, and possibly Doritos. Her tongue looks shiny as a honey dipper and he so wants to taste her, has never wanted to kiss anyone as desperately as this glistening stranger. She breathes in his ears—Rachel has never done that—runs her hands down his chest, and his body tightens like a coil as she draws closer and closer to his increasingly erect penis, which feels like a secret he needs to simultaneously defend and release into the world. His body's supply of blood is rushing away from his heart to flood his face with a blush so intense he feels his ears will blow off; meanwhile, an awful lot of blood also seems to be careening south as well—he has literally lost control of himself. It feels wonderful: like here beneath this woman he is the most immovable object in the universe, and yet, every cell in his body is as light and effervescent as a vagabond bubble.

Then, just as quickly, the music is gone and she is sitting on her knees, onstage, like they were just playing a game of marbles. She is staring at him.

"Wow," he says. "You're . . . amazing."

"Ummm, how amazing, exactly?" She raises a pierced eyebrow, looks pointedly at his left pant pocket, from which the corners of at least four dollar bills poke out, like magazines fanned out at the dentist's office.

"Oh, right," he says, "sorry about that."

"You're cute," she smirks. "How old are you anyway?"

"Uh, tonight's my twenty-first birthday." He is a terrible liar, tries to take a sip of his beer, but it is, of course, empty.

"Not much of a poker player, are ya?" she giggles.

"I like cribbage," he says with one hundred percent genuine earnestness, as if maybe they could play a game now that she's done dancing.

She laughs so hard that for a moment it is the loudest sound in the bar, turning heads in their direction; she has a belly laugh that truly snags his heart. She covers her mouth. "So, you're sixteen, right? Maybe seventeen? You're *way* too nice to be twenty-one, that's for sure." She blinks slowly, her eyelashes two exquisite onyx curtains.

He hands her two dollar bills as if he were buying a milk shake or a Coke, and she stands somewhat awkwardly on her heels, begins retrieving the other money onstage, crumpled like so many discarded cocktail napkins or paper flowers. Someone has actually thrown onstage what appears to be a Hallmark greeting card, a deep purple envelope that she now collects like dropped mail.

"I'll look for you," she says over her shoulder. "Maybe you'd like a private dance later."

"All right," he says. "It was nice to meet you."

This time she turns and comes back to him, kisses him on the cheek.

He watches her walk off the stage, disappear into some side room. He is entranced, wants to follow her to the ends of the earth, but just stands instead, readjusts himself through some pocket finagling, and wobbles back to his father and Nelson, who actually do happen to be playing cribbage, oblivious, it would seem, to their surroundings.

"Make a friend?" Jonathan asks.

"Yeah," Trevor says, touching his cheek. *She didn't kiss anyone else in the bar—that has to mean something, doesn't it?* The kid slumps into a chair.

"Well, what do you think?" Jonathan asks. "Ready to head back to the motel? Or do you want another beer?"

Trevor sighs, looks to the stage. Guns N' Roses' "Paradise City" is blaring as a new dancer storms onto the stage wearing what appears to be Slash's signature black hat and strumming furiously at an air guitar strategically held over her hunter-orange thong panties.

"Uh, I guess I'll take another beer. Thanks, Dad."

Nelson shakes his head, rises from the table, and says, "I got this."

28

THERE IS A WIDOW WHO LIVES IN A SMALL RANCH house outside the town of Haugen, Wisconsin, not far from the southernmost boundary of the Whiteside Scout Reservation. Her name is Lorraine, and she works as a receptionist at the nearby pool cue factory, fielding phone calls from around the world; customers placing orders, confirming shipments, lodging complaints, purchasing supplies such as chalk, talcum powder, cue tips.

She lives on a five-acre parcel of meadow surrounded by cornfields. Her husband died in a drunk-driving accident, at age forty-eight. Every day she feels fortunate for his death, for the poetic justice that the passengers in the other vehicle, a family of four, driving south from a vacation in Bayfield, were all spared; the daughter who broke only her clavicle, the father whose left eye socket was irreparably caved in, the mother and son who escaped unharmed, a few scratches. At her late husband's funeral she remembers standing by his grave thinking, *Stupid selfish sonuvabitch.*

In summertime she tends to an elaborate garden of tomatoes, peas, beans, broccoli, cauliflower, kale, squash, pumpkins, peppers. From June until October her fingers smell like tomato plants, her toenails are crescented with dirt, her neck, arms, and legs burnt a deep chestnut. She likes to wear tank tops; imagines each freckle speckling her chest as representing a long summer day toiling beneath the punishing but beneficent sun. On the southern edge of her garden is a flimsy aluminum camping chair with a plastic woven seat where she sits beneath a huge faded Corona beach umbrella, there to sip a glass of sun tea, a lemonade, perhaps a light beer, and when she closes her eyes and flexes her toes in the dirt, she hears the hum of passing bees, feels the occasional butterfly or moth alight on her forearms.

She lives to garden. And for her two-week vacation every winter to Costa Rica, when she packs a suitcase full of paperback mysteries and romances, two swimsuits, three sundresses, plenty of underwear, and two pairs of nice flip-flops. She plays on a volleyball league with some folks from work, goes to the same bar most every Friday for a fish fry and a brandy old-fashioned, and then heads home, where she watches TV and crochets blankets for the local church charity sale each December.

And this: two or three times a week he rings her doorbell. In summertime, always after nightfall, sometimes holding a VHS movie in his hands, or a bottle of lukewarm white wine. September through May, he might visit a little more frequently, often before dusk. She'll watch him, walking down Whiteside Road, then taking a shortcut path that he has grooved through the field grasses to her backyard, and then to her front door, always her front door, where he waits as patiently as a little boy, never just allowing himself in, no matter how many times she's invited him, *implored* him to. She's even given him a key.

They eat supper together and after he always washes and dries their dishes. Most evenings they watch TV together, or play cards. Sometimes he fixes her toilet, mends a patch of leaky roof, changes her car's oil. And then she takes his hand and guides him into her bedroom.

The first time, she was afraid of his body. The myriad scars, each one a brutally crude pucker. But he was so kind, so kind to *her* body. To her breasts, her nipples, her backbone, her shoulders. He smelled of lake water and cigarettes, burnt coffee and the cologne of open fields, northern bogs. It was the first time in her life that she considered clothing as a method of camouflaging our scars, the traumas of our lives. She'd seen him around Haugen before: filling up the gas tank on an old blue International pickup truck or an aged Land Rover, picking up the ditch trash along Highway 53, and once, outside the Lutheran church on Christmas Eve, with a somewhat melancholy look on his face as he inspected the snowflakes falling through the glow of a streetlight.

She is a secret, she supposes, though this is foolishness, of course; there is no need for secrets. He could take a wife if he liked, a girlfriend. She could live with him at the camp, in his little cabin, a building she has only twice visited, in the camp's off-season. It has the atmosphere of an old-men's working club—everything in its place, the floor perfectly swept, even the clutter bearing a certain utility: old fishing rods and creels, snowshoes, two rifles clearly unfired in decades. She remembers staring at the wool blanket on his bed, how perfect and tidy it was, the flat surface smooth as the felt of a billiard table.

When his nightmares come, as they do most nights, she holds him tighter than she ever gripped her husband, because the sounds he makes are the whimpers of a scared little boy so far away from home, so terrified of the dark and the secrets kept there, so sad for the bad things he must have done.

One dream, more than the rest, seems to haunt him. He talks about it some mornings, at her kitchen table, a cup of coffee before him.

They discover a tunnel outside a village and when they pull back the bamboo hatch covering its opening out plumes a smell like death. This is not unusual. The men of his platoon help him shed his backpack, his M16, and they hand him two extra pistols, four extra clips. There's not enough room to enter the tunnel feetfirst, so he must slither into the darkness like a snake. He crawls and crawls, feels hairy roots brush his face and ears, dry slick insects scuttle past his forearms, over his hands. He crawls for minutes, hours, days, and the air is a noxious fume he chokes on.

And then he feels a presence, another life-form in the tunnel, ahead of him. It is not a small thing, not a rodent or a snake. It is a person. There is a ragged breathing. It may or may not be his own, though, he can't be sure. There is no light ahead and the entrance is ages behind him. He carries a penlight on a cord looped around his neck, the same cord that holds his lucky nickel, but this other person in the dream is invariably a VC. It is the first time he's encountered someone alive inside a tunnel—if they *are* alive, that is; if his senses haven't failed him, his mind, his imagination. Always these tunnels lead to chambers, to caches of weapons or ammunition, maps, intelligence, or food. Sometimes the tunnels lead to other tunnels or to villages. Sometimes the tunnels are not even completed, dead-ending in nothing more than a wall of damp soil—the last, worst place on the planet.

Only this is not a dead end. He reaches a hand into the gloom, and, touching a face, screams, even as the other man does. Without hesitating, he aims his pistol in front of him and pulls the trigger, feeling the man's face and brains wash over his own face as the deafening report of the gun rings in his shattered eardrums. He is weeping and the planet is trying to crush him.

It is his platoon that pulls him out. Hruska, a big Polish kid from Vermont, no doubt too tall for the tunnel but the bravest of the bunch, clambers right in and seizes hold of Nelson's ankles, wrenches him backward until—an eternity later—both men are free of the tunnel and holding each other as hot rain falls from the sky above them, washing the mud and blood off Nelson's face.

"Poor baby," she'll shush, "poor, poor baby." She'll pet his hair, rub at his earlobes, while he sobs and sobs, this damaged little boy. Sometimes in his sleep, during his dreams, he calls out for his mother.

29

TREVOR IS SCANNING THE BAR WITH THE EAGERNESS
of a birder but without the aid of binoculars. He's seen three other dancers take the stage since her, but none of them *are* her—none of them
half as beautiful as she is. Two of the women looked to be about his
mother's age and when he asked his father if this was normal, his dad just
shrugged. "This is northern Wisconsin, Trev. Not exactly Wall Street.
They've probably got kids to feed. People do what they have to do."

This was a revelation. That there were mothers in the world without husbands. Trevor thought of his own orderly neighborhood: the
jade-green lawns, the fathers out washing new cars on Saturday mornings, the weekend backyard campfires where dads passed around flasks
of whiskey and mothers sat on Adirondack chairs, legs folded beneath
their butts, chic Hudson Bay blankets spread across their laps. He could
not quite visualize any of those women living up here, this neon intersection of a hardscrabble neighborhood in Hurley, Wisconsin.

"Hey, there."

Out of nowhere. It's her. *Sweet Jesus holy shit.* Trevor turns, manages a clumsy, "Oh, hey."

"I'm Aspen," she says, standing right there in front of his dad, *in front of his Scoutmaster*, producing a hand for him to shake.

He takes it. *Jesus.* "I'm Trevor. Trevor Quick."

"Yeah, last names really aren't that useful in places like this," says Jonathan, extending an eager hand. "I'm Jonathan. Trev's old man. And this here is Nelson, chieftain of the northern wilderness clan of Scouts."

Nelson nods at Aspen, gives her a tiny salute.

"Oh, we've met," says Aspen, giggling.

Jonathan leans away from his old friend, whistles. "You old dog."

Nelson shrugs, takes a long pull off his beer. Trevor stares at him, his ears burning with jealousy, envy, disbelief.

Aspen wraps an arm around Trevor's elbow, asks, "You want a private dance?"

"Um, sure," the kid manages, as she pulls him away from the bar.

"Don't forget what I said!" Jonathan yells into the Aerosmith din of "Sweet Emotion." "She'll take you for all you're worth!"

Trevor shakes his head, and Aspen laughs, turning to give the two men a long, perfectly manicured middle finger.

NEAR THE BACK OF THE BAR they approach another bouncer, a big man perched on a very small, fragile-looking stool. He appears to be reading *Guns & Ammo.* "Twenty-five bucks," the man mutters, not looking up as he holds out his thick pork chop of a well-callused hand.

"Uh . . . ," Trevor stutters.

"It's for the dance," Aspen explains, pressing her body against Trevor's. All those soft curves, her smell. In her heels, they are of about the same height and now she rests her head onto his shoulder, against his neck. He can't remember Rachel ever doing that.

He reaches for his wallet, peers into it through the gloom, sees only hundred-dollar bills.

"If you want," she presses, "you could pay for two dances . . . or more. So we won't be interrupted . . ."

That sounds good to Trevor. He finds a hundred-dollar bill, lays it into the man's huge palm.

"How long is each dance?" he asks. He imagines prom, hopes that his hundred dollars might ensure that they have hours of something more than slow-dancing below the glittering of a disco ball.

"'Bout three songs," the man grunts. "Enjoy."

Trevor does the math. About twelve, maybe thirteen, fourteen minutes. "Can I pick the songs?" he blurts. *The most bang for the buck, he thinks quickly: Don McLean's "American Pie," The Allman Brothers Band's "Mountain Jam," and CCR's version of "I Heard It Through the Grapevine"—true jukebox values.*

But she is already leading him through a set of velvet curtains into a deeper, close-hanging darkness. The music is more diffuse here and there are five or six wooden booths with the kind of swinging doors you see in spaghetti westerns. She guides him into one.

"The deejay handles all that," she says. "You just sit down. And relax."

She begins slowly removing her clothing.

"Do you know the rules?" she asks huskily.

"No," he gulps. He feels himself sinking into a very warm, languid sea. The darkness seems to swirl. She swings her legs over his thighs and sits lightly down upon him, runs her fingers through his hair. He touches her hips, gently.

"That's rule number one," she whispers. "*You* don't touch me. *I* touch you. And no kissing. Or licking." She licks at his earlobe.

He looks at her breasts, a single-incision scar, like a small bowed-out U just visible beneath the slope of each one.

"How did you hurt yourself?" he asks.

She sits back. "What?"

"Your . . . uh, your . . ." He points.

"My tits?" She slaps at him playfully. "I had a boob job."

"Oh," he says.

Her chest sparkles with that glitter, reminds him of a cliff of quartz or the alleyway by the State Theatre in downtown Eau Claire, always awash with broken glass glimmering beneath the midnight moon, bouncing headlights, the furtive orange of throwaway cigarettes.

He looks at her wrists.

"What about there?" He touches them very lightly, with the pressure of smoothing a stamp, the flap of an envelope.

She shakes her head.

"How 'bout we just be quiet?" she asks.

"Okay," he agrees. "I'm sorry."

"You're sweet," she whispers. "Nobody ever apologizes to me."

"You're beautiful," he says, even as he notices her heavy makeup, the tiny bumps of acne on her chin, the wrinkles on her forehead. He can't say whether she's twenty-five or thirty-five. Older than he is, that's for sure, and certainly younger than his parents.

"Do you have kids?" he ventures.

She smiles, breaking for a moment from the act. "I have a son."

"I bet you're a good mom."

She closes her eyes and moves in the darkness above him, but says nothing at all, and he watches like the supplicant he's become—worshipper of this backroom goddess.

Armies of warm, frothy waves wash over his head, break on his shoulders, and he thinks of nothing but this woman, Aspen, the specific weight and smell of her. The maddeningly sweet ticking clock that is this heavy metal music, and outside, still audible, the laughter and beer-bottle clatter of grown men, the distant revving of Harley-Davidsons, the rattle and cough of bad mufflers—all of it the insulated crash of the sea deep within a conch shell that is pressed right to his ear.

"Is Aspen your real name?" he manages after a while.

"Shhhh," she says, "it's really better if we don't talk."

She moves against him with a rhythm quite apart from the new song that's come on, Night Ranger's "Sister Christian," and he is glad for that.

"How old are you?" he persists, something like hope rising in his throat.

"How old are *you*?" she breathes into his neck, holds his arms up over his head.

"I told you," he says, and then, with the bravery of several daiquiris and a couple of beers, "twenty-five."

She laughs, "*Now* you're getting the hang of it. And what do you do for a living, my twenty-five-year-old boy toy?"

His voice catches, but he thinks he can play this game if it means hearing her laugh, prolonging this moment, "I'm a war correspondent, actually. For the BBC."

She sits back and there are her breasts. Like, right there. "I've never heard that one before."

"It's true," he continues heavily, speaking slowly with the fabrication of it all. "Iraq, Rwanda, Algeria, Afghanistan . . . You may have seen my work in *National Geographic*, too? Or do you get the *Times*?"

"Absolutely," she drawls. "You must be wise beyond your years." She tugs a little at her nipples.

He delves forward. "Yeah, but . . . you could probably teach me a few things . . ."

"The trouble is," she says, now touching her lower lip with a finger, her eyes playfully sad in the darkness, "we're out of time."

He reaches into his pocket and produces a hundred-dollar bill, as if this was as commonplace as a quarter.

"Maybe you could get us some beers," he suggests, "or daiquiris? I often drink daiquiris when I'm"—he stumbles for a moment then rights himself—"abroad."

She takes his money, stands, re-dresses, and says, "I'll be right back." And then she leans back into him and runs her hand across the back of his neck, his hair, and kisses him on the lips in a way no one has ever kissed him before.

30

WHEN THE LIGHTS COME UP, EVEN IN THE MOST RE-
mote corners of the bar, Trevor's lips are red with lipstick and he is
wearing her perfume. She leads him back toward the bar, where a few
die-hard bikers lean against the rail while the bartender stares at them
with derision, washing glasses. The dancers seem a jagged mixture of
newfound energy and complete exhaustion as they sip coffee topped
with whipped cream, or pound shots of Jameson and Jägermeister.

Aspen gives Trevor the long hug of two ultimately ill-fated potential
lovers, then stands with her hands on her hips and looks at him, all
devil-may-care, and slightly glistening. He notices that she no longer
wears her high heels, and is now significantly shorter than him, seemingly more frail. He looks at her, tries to imagine how old her son is,
what his name is, where he is sleeping at that moment, *Her dressing
room? A friend's place? Or maybe she's actually married . . .* Then he peers
around the bar for his father, nowhere to be seen.

He leans toward Aspen. "Uh, have you seen my dad?"

"Twenty-five, huh?" she says, glancing around and shrugging her shoulders.

"Check outside," the barkeep barks. "Took off about fifteen, twenty minutes ago."

Trevor touches Aspen on the elbow, then leans down, and, taking the biggest chance of his young life, kisses her on the cheek. "Thanks," he says.

"Stay safe," she advises, blowing him a halfhearted kiss even as she rubs her feet against the dirty floorboards strewn with cigarette butts, spent matchbooks, and scratched-off and worthless lottery tickets. The music has quit and now toward the front of the bar someone is extinguishing each of the neon lights in turn.

Outside, the bars are all emptying, men teetering on broken-concrete sidewalks, fumbling with lighters and smokes, while above them, moths and June bugs still orbit the streetlights. Farther down Main, two pugilists are dizzily swinging at each other and one man wobbles over and falls off the curb into the street. The other fighter begins kicking his ribs like a hated soccer ball and around the two a small crowd gathers to seal the violence into a huddle of cheering fists, jeering insults, a growing pool of blood.

The cops come at last, scattering the mob, though the one fighter kicks on. The beaten man lies still. Trevor's heart rattles. He is ready to be home; not here in Hurley, not at the motel, not at camp. He wants his own house, the bed he seems to have outgrown, the soft threadbare Green Bay Packers sheets Rachel teases him about, the Brett Favre posters tacked and taped to his walls, his Mom's buckwheat pancakes waiting for him in the morning, her hands on a steaming mug of coffee, asking him about his tenuous plans for college, asking him about Rachel though he suspects she does not really approve of her either, though in a different way from his father; and his dad coming down the creaking stairs in his khaki shorts, pink Polo golf shirt, and black visor, smelling of cologne, ready for a weekend round at the country club. Trevor recently noticed that his dad's ankles were oddly bare of hair and he wondered if that was some hallmark of getting old, of being a father; that eventually all those years of wearing socks and winter boots would rub away at you, and that maybe this was what happened to men's heads as well, their hair just worn away with worry.

He looks down the street to their van. The bikes are missing.

"Ah, crap," Trevor mumbles, quickening his step. The rack still juts from a trailer hitch off the back of the van and nothing else seems awry—no windows broken, no doors left ajar. Trevor sits on the curb, his chin in his hands. He smells like Aspen and that at least makes him happy. Maybe he'll wait a few days before showering at camp.

Another police cruiser and an ambulance have pulled toward the scene of the fight and the winning combatant has been tossed into the back of a squad car by two cops while the defeated man lies on a gurney, motionless, red, white, and blue lights strobing across his bloody face, a stethoscope pressed to his chest.

"On three," a paramedic says, and the man disappears into the closed-door ambulance, quick to wail its sirens, abruptly U-turn in the wide street, and peel off into the night for whatever regional infirmary they even have this far north.

One last cop stands jauntily on the sidewalk, thumbs crooked into his belt, and that is enough to disperse most of the remaining gawkers, though two or three bikers stay on to stare right back at the police through their dark sunglasses, until that last cruiser flashes its lights once, hiccups a timid siren, and slides away into the night. Five minutes later, the bikers mount up and roar off, satisfied in their way.

Trevor stands, walks up the street, and peers down at the gutter puddle of blood coagulating dark on the pavement. He's never seen a fight before, except on television. A little pushing and shoving in the hallways at school, sure, but not like this. He leans down and picks up a tooth lying on the pavement, then four more, one of them golden. For some reason, he pockets the teeth, all of them.

It is foggy and the night air has turned cool. He turns back toward the van. Sits down. Closes his eyes. Then he hears his name, repeated, high-pitched and merry, like a tease, "*Treevv-orrr!*" And how he wishes it might be Aspen, idling her car on Main Street, speaking to him through the open passenger window, inviting him to go make out in that steamy-windowed late-model Camaro, off some long-abandoned logging road.

But, of course, it is his father's voice, far off but coming closer, and opening his barroom smoke-crusty eyes, he watches the wobbly eighteen-speed approach of two older men drunkenly pedaling and coasting, cigarettes dangled precariously between their lips. They ride right past him, waving like participants in some tragic fools' parade, and he watches them teeter along, through the early morning fog, standing up on the pedals now and belting out what seems to be, what sounds like, what might have been . . . "Wonderwall"?

Trevor stands, the evening's binge having reduced the world to a rush and blur, and then sits back down heavily, empties his stomach between his shoes, very thankful indeed that Aspen is not idling her car in front of him just now. His father's voice is vectoring back toward him, and then he hears both bicycles crash onto the pavement, the dull spill of two grown men falling in more or less slow motion. Now they are laughing, sprawled flat out on the pavement.

"Toss your cookies?" Jonathan asks in the aftershocks of laughter.

"*No*," Trevor lies, wiping the corners of his mouth with his shirt.

"Probably for the best," Jonathan says. "You'll wake up good and sober for Scout camp tomorrow."

"Jesus," Nelson groans.

"He can't help us now," Jonathan says.

"A Scout is *reverent*," Nelson reminds him. "Reverent, I'll have you know."

"Got any money left?" Jonathan asks his son.

Trevor hangs his head, then decides to move to another stretch of curb. He spits into the street.

"And this is why I'm going to win that bet," Jonathan says.

"Yeah, well, I'm still in love with Rachel," Trevor protests, though without perhaps the same resolve he felt earlier in the evening. He smells like another woman's perfume, can even taste her lipstick, knows that one of her breasts is slightly larger than the other. That when she tans, most likely in some dirty Hurley salon, she does not, apparently, wear bikini bottoms. Somehow all this knowledge makes him feel at once worldly and tainted.

"You think I'm a jerk for tonight, don't you?" asks Jonathan. "That I'm the devil?"

At the beginning of the evening, Trevor might have said yes; now he's simply confused, frazzled. "I just don't understand," Trevor says. "I don't get it. Why do you want me to fail, too? Why don't you want me to be my best person? The best I can be? Why am I even in Scouts? What's the point of all this if we're just going to end up embracing this badness?" Not that he is convinced that congress with a beautiful woman necessarily equates to *badness*, but . . . The world is such a very confusing place.

Jonathan rises wearily, lights a cigarette bent slightly askew at its filter. "Because, Trevor. I don't want you judging me. That's all. You just got a taste of it—how easy it is, falling down. Happens every day. Like being born, or dying. People fall in love. People fall out of love. It's no one's fault. Look, I knew what would happen tonight if we took you here. You didn't do anything any other guy, or hell, gal, wouldn't've done."

"But what about Mom?" Trevor asks.

Jonathan lowers himself to the curb beside him; Trevor isn't accustomed to seeing his father smoke. "She'll be all right, Trev. Hell, she might be better off without me, you know?" Jonathan rubs his son's head.

"Did she cheat on you, too? I mean, is everybody cheating on every-one?" Trevor asks, picking up a pebble from the gutter, throwing it at a manhole about ten feet off.

"I don't think so," Jonathan says. "Though she'd certainly be en-titled. And if you want me to be candid—"

"Dad," Trevor says, "actually, I just want to go to sleep, I think. If that's okay. I just . . . I don't really need to hear any more confessions tonight."

"Fair enough," Jonathan says.

"*I* still believe in the kid," Nelson says from the pavement. "He can learn from this, from you."

"I hope so," Jonathan says. "I believe in him, too. He'll be better than me someday, I'm sure of it." *And that's all there is,* Jonathan thinks, *raising a better man than yourself, on into the future forever and ever.* It is the second time today he's considered the possibility that someday, he might be a grandfather.

NELSON, APPOINTED THE LEAST DRUNK DRIVER, shuttles them back to their motel. The drive is quiet, somber, as the van plows through banks of low-hanging fog past armies of lightning bugs in the bogs. From the ditch, a pure white deer stares into the headlights, then saunters off. Nelson hits the brakes, hoping to catch sight of it again, but the deer is gone. No question, though, it was one of old Wilbur's. Only, so far from camp. He hopes it is safe.

IN THE PARKING LOT, Nelson stands beside the minivan, shakes both of their hands. "I'll see you tomorrow." He stands at rigid atten-tion, gives them a salute, then wheels, finds his Land Rover and climbs in, revving up the big engine before finally pulling away.

"Good night, kiddo," Jonathan says.

"Good night, Dad," Trevor says.

In his motel room, Trevor dials Rachel's number, hoping against hope that she'll be awake, too, restless beside the telephone, waiting for his voice. But the phone rings and rings and just as he decides that his late-night call may be obnoxious and poorly timed (it is past three o'clock in the morning), Rachel's father answers.

"Hello?" he grumbles. "Who is this?"

"Uh, hey, Mr. Gunderson, it's Trevor. Trev—"

"It's three o' clock in the morning, Trevor. Is everything all right? Are you in jail? Hurt? Are you in trouble?" Mr. Gunderson's questions are surprisingly fast. Staccato, like gunfire.

"Uh, no, I'm just . . . Do you think I could talk to Rachel?" The Gundersons have only three telephones, Trevor knows, one in the kitchen, one in their family room, and one in the basement laundry room. The family room phone is cordless, and he was banking on Rachel perhaps having brought that up to her bedroom.

"No, Trevor. She's sleeping. *I* was sleeping, too, until you called, actually. And now I'm going back to sleep. Good night, then," and with that, Mr. Gunderson hangs up.

Trevor sits up in his bed, sighs deeply. He is lonely, lonely enough almost to talk to his dad, but no doubt his father will already have tiptoed down to Deanna's room, Pink Panther–style, and that's not something he wishes to witness, interrupt, or frankly, even think about. He turns on the TV, but most of the stations have retired for the night, so sighing again, he turns it back off. The room is so very quiet now, not even a set of headlights to split the night. He thinks about Aspen, places his forearm by his nose and inhales. She is still a little there.

31

IN THE MORNING, SUNLIGHT PARTS THE CURTAINS like a white sword and he wakes, cotton-mouthed. A maid is pushing her cart outside the window, listening to a boom box. Crosby, Stills & Nash's "Suite: Judy Blue Eyes." He swings his legs out of bed, leans his head into his hands. It doesn't hurt half as much as he feared; in fact, he isn't really hungover at all. Standing, he scratches the small patch of hair on his belly and stretches. Many mornings back home, this is when his mother will tackle him onto a couch to tickle him. It is one of the things she does that both annoy him and fill him with an unaccountable happiness. Though smaller than he is, she always manages to surprise him with these tackles, careful to time her attacks so that she won't end up toppling coffee tables, vases, lamps in the process—impediments that only a mother's vigilant radar would detect, even in the heat of a fight.

He decides to call her. She answers after the second ring.

"Hello?" she says, cheerfully. He imagines her in their kitchen, her reading glasses on, as she leans against a kitchen counter with her hip, one foot balanced on the other, a mug of coffee within easy reach.

"Hey, Mom," he says. He feels old, calling her. Like this is what he might do as a college freshman on Mother's Day, or as a thirty-year-old, or further off yet, when perhaps she'll be living in a nursing home. The thought that his parents will very likely divorce in the not-too-distant future makes him instantly morose; he doesn't like the idea of her spending her final years alone.

"Trevor?" she says, clearly surprised. "Are you okay up there? Is Dad okay?"

He shifts the receiver to the other ear, carries the ancient phone to the window, separates the drapes. His father is standing beside Deanna's car. Her arms encircle his trim waist and her face is upturned, toward his. They're kissing now, like sweethearts, like new love—even Trevor can see it. He lets the drapes fall.

"No, we're okay," he says, slumping onto the bed.

She is silent a moment. "Are you sure? Trevor?"

He feels like crying. He feels very far from home, very far from the young man he supposed he was. He misses Rachel, the odd smell of her family's laundry, that off-brand detergent. He wants to be in his family's kitchen, with his mom, waiting for her to place a tall stack of pancakes before him.

"We're fine," he says. "We're all just fine."

32

NELSON KEEPS HIS COLLECTION IN A CABINET HE
once bought at an estate sale. The prior owner was a rock hound who
filled the case with hundreds of geological specimens from however many
trips around the world, and these specimens came in handy for instructing the Geology merit badge. Handy enough that Nelson had a small
cabinet built to house the collection so it wouldn't be hidden in these
dusty old drawers. With his own money, he even bought a largish piece
of fulgurite—fossilized lightning—which is a favorite among the boys.

Now, each drawer of the old maple cabinet, liberated of its rocks
and minerals, holds dozens and dozens of Nelson's most valuable, most
treasured baseball cards, collected over the years, ever since he was eight
years old, squirreling away nickels and dimes he found like treasure in
the seat cushions of the couch, the shag of the living room, the shadowed crannies of the family's station wagon, or pilfered from atop his
father's dresser drawers. Mickey Mantle, Willie Mays, Satchel Paige,

Larry Doby, Yogi Berra, Phil Rizzuto, Bob Gibson, Jackie Robinson, Frank Robinson, Harmon Killebrew, and even a Lou Gehrig card his grandfather had once casually bequeathed to him, saying, "Not much good for anything other than a bookmark."

In a separate cabinet, once utilized by a now-defunct small-town Carnegie library's Dewey Decimal System, Nelson stores another collection of cards, a collection he hasn't had to curate, but which had come to him mysteriously, through the United States mail, without fail, every year on his birthday: one baseball card, carefully protected between two pieces of thick, rigid cardboard, taped so that no edge of the card ever kisses the adhesive binding it in place. These envelopes were first mailed to St. John's, then West Point, then his mother's house, and the last few to the Whiteside Scout Reservation.

And each year, the card is that of a Chicago Cub, autographed, "To Nelson, Happy Birthday, 19__."

Through the years: Ernie Banks, Ron Santo, Shawon Dunston, Jose Cardenal, Rick Sutcliffe, Bill Madlock, Rick Reuschel, Bruce Sutter, Lee Smith, Andre Dawson, Mark Grace, Greg Maddux, Ryne Sandberg, Fergie Jenkins, Billy Williams, Dwight Smith, Jerome Walton . . .

The same inscription, *To Nelson, Happy Birthday, 1962, 1963, 1964 . . . 1975, 1976, 1977* . . . Every year until 1994, the year of baseball's strike, when the cards finally stopped coming.

The Chicago Cubs have never even been his favorite team; that honor would belong first to the Milwaukee Braves, and then, later, the Milwaukee Brewers, that team within radio earshot, whose box-score triumphs and tribulations can be found in the *Eau Claire Leader-Telegram* or the *Rice Lake Chronotype*.

And so, after the drive back to the Whiteside Scout Reservation, after parking his Land Rover in the far lot near the mess hall, and making his way back to his cabin in the darkest of night, he goes to the filing cabinet, removes the first five cards he received in the mail, all those years back, and turning on a floor lamp, slumps into an old leather chair that accepts his weight so easily, so generously.

The first card is signed by Ken Hubbs, who in 1962 was the starting second baseman for the Cubs at the age of twenty. It was a monumental year for Hubbs, the first rookie to ever win a Golden Glove for his play in the infield and also be awarded the Rookie of the Year Award, despite leading the National League in strikeouts.

Hubbs's rookie card is part of the seminal 1962 Topps set, a design that mimics many basement living rooms of that time with its faux wood panel framing a youthful portrait of the second baseman on a pumpkin-colored background that seems to peel upward from its bottom right hand corner. Above and to the left of Hubbs's face is a yellow star that reads: "1962 ROOKIE."

The corners have long since been rounded on that first card Nelson received on his birthday, so many years ago now; Hubbs's left ear appears to have been almost buffed off, worn away with time. So, too, is part of his inscription: the word *birthday* is barely legible. All those nights when a much younger Nelson, lying in his bed, would rub this card between his thumb and forefinger, staring at this strange memento that arrived in his mailbox with no return address, his name typewritten on the envelope, as if by a secretary.

Ken Hubbs, whom Nelson followed with an almost religious fanaticism, even pestering old Whiteside to purchase a shortwave radio so that he could tune into the Cub's games late into the summer of 1963 from his cabin. This scrappy second baseman who was terrified of flying in airplanes, but who resolved to overcome his fear, took up flying lessons. This smooth-fielding epitome of happiness and health, who was lauded for his generosity and kindness. This young Cub, who, in the winter preceding the '64 season, died in an airplane crash in his native Utah. This young Cub, whose pallbearers included Ernie Banks, Don Elston, Glen Hobbie, and Ron Santo—consummate Cubs, all.

Hubbs's death was reported on February 15, 1964. Nelson cried himself to sleep that night, clutching the card that was one of two keepsakes he brought to St. John's from his mother's house in Eau Claire, the other being a card signed by the great Cubs first baseman inscribed with: *To Nelson, Happy Birthday, 1963—Ernie Banks.*

That card is nearly in pristine condition, despite the years it was stored in his mother's attic while he studied at West Point, or was off in Vietnam, or New Mexico.

For over thirty years, Nelson has imagined his father attending games at Wrigley Field. Perhaps with his new family, perhaps sitting over the first base or third base dugouts, or standing near the guardrails, calling down to the players during batting practice or between innings, asking, "Hey, mister, you mind signing a card for my boy? It's his birthday. His name's Nelson."

For more than thirty years, on and off, Nelson has been falling asleep, in beds or, as he grew older, in chairs, his boots still tied, with this thin little rectangle of cardboard between his fingers, tucked into his hand, imagining that great emerald field with its brick and ivy walls, its crowded Budweiser bleachers, its encroaching brownstones crowned with roofs full of businesswomen and businessmen looking on, cheering, and surrounded by miles and miles of metropolis, spilling out in every direction save east, where the great Lake Michigan shines on and on, every rolling wave a sparkling phalanx of freshwater foam hustling on to crash against the shore.

PART III

SUMMER, 2019
ORIENTEERING

33

THESE DAYS THEY COMMUNICATE SOLELY THROUGH their telephones and tablets in a language so broken that a hundred years ago it might have been identified as idiot pidgin, though the phones do wonders, damn near anticipating thought itself. Their communications float between each other inside this old house via bubbles. Indeed, without his phone texts she would know next to nothing about her son's life, except what she can glean by rifling through his closet, his dresser drawers, the pockets of his pants as she does their laundry.

> Where are you? It's getting late.

> Sleeping at Jim's. See you tomorrow for dinner.

She wishes she could take one of her long knitting needles and pop these bubbles from the air—*pop pop pop*—so that instead of reading his thoughts, she could actually hear his voice, fill this house of silence with conversation, sound. In two years he'll be off to college and she honestly wonders if she'll ever hear from him again.

> We're going to camp tomorrow, remember?

Fuck, for real?

> Are you packed? I don't see a bag . . .

Do I have to go? I'm 16. Camp is moronic.

This is the only time he communicates in complete, intelligent thoughts: when he is arguing. Suddenly his contrarian teenage intellect is honed to a stake-sharp point, and sometimes, yes, he does skewer her, pierce her right in the heart.

> I'm not arguing. You're eight merit badges away from Eagle. I don't ask much. Do this for me.

Or, what she might just as easily have said: *Do this for your father.*

Can you pack for me? I'll be home before lunch.

> I love you. Be safe.

There is no need these days to hide a stash of *Playboy*s in a closet, some racy photos of a girlfriend—all of that safe now behind a password on the smartphone. Still, his room holds its attempted secrets: a Ziploc bag of pot, a pipe, a bracelet from a concert in Minneapolis she never knew he attended, a rainbow selection of condoms, a receipt from a café in Milwaukee . . . Perhaps someday they'll find a way to digitize drugs, but for now, she's glad that pot still seems analog. She finds this as she packs his bag for camp. Men's underwear, socks, shorts, pants, shirts, his Boy Scout uniform. All these things she throws into a bag. His deodorant, toothbrush, toothpaste. He'll be pissed, she knows, but she intentionally leaves his tablet behind. It's not what camp is about.

She flops onto his bed and stares at the ceiling where a poster of some actress she can't identify stares back down at her, leeringly. The bed smells of teenage boy: sweaty feet, fast-food farts, overscented deodorant, stale masturbation. Not like crawling into bed with him when he was five or six years old and staring at the stars he'd asked her to affix to the bedroom ceiling—*I gave him the stars*—smelling his little-boy hair, all fresh air, sunshine, and shampoo. She thinks better of the nostalgia, sits up, carries the bag downstairs, and begins packing her own bag.

She's always enjoyed taking Thomas to camp. As a little girl, she was first a Brownie, then a Girl Scout—and hated every minute of it—envying the boys she knew who journeyed on semidangerous back-packing treks and canoe trips. *Their* camps were wilderness outposts where sometimes gruesome injuries were suffered and returning back to school those boys had tall tales of encounters with bears, wolves, coyotes. They learned to shoot guns, manufacture rope bridges, administer tourniquets, and fly-fish. Rachel did not want to sell cookies, or have lame sleepovers and gossip about boys. And so for almost ten years she's made up for lost time by chaperoning these trips to the Whiteside Scout Reservation. Some years there have been other female leaders at camp: a mother or two, a youthful grandma, a favorite aunt. Other years she's been the sole woman in attendance, an odd feeling, to be sure; sur-rounded by hundreds of teenage boys wrestling with their pubescent hormones, and, let's face it, dozens of grown men no doubt fantasizing about sneaking out into the woods with her. She's still pretty attractive, has never let herself go, even when Lord knows there were times it would have been the easy thing to do.

From Trevor's closet she removes his old Boy Scout shirt and tries it on. It fits her well enough, not very flatteringly, of course. The fabric lies flat over her chest and the sleeves are a bit too wide and long, but she doesn't much see the point in purchasing a uniform that adheres to her any more snugly; she does not chaperone these trips to put her body on display, to attract a new lover or husband. No, at thirty-nine, having been married three times already, she has sworn that institution off as the curse it seems to be. Trevor, she thinks, might have been the last good man; or, at the very least, the last good man for her.

No, it is for other reasons that Rachel chaperones these trips. She relishes the Northwoods morning air, the serene lake water for her daily swims, the access to beautiful old wooden rowboats and canoes, the time she spends sitting in the back of merit-badge sessions, practicing her knot-tying or first-aid skills. And, of course, the evenings in Nelson's cabin, playing chess or cribbage, and drinking from his cabinet of good Scotch: Laphroaig, Talisker, Lagavulin . . .

He's almost seventy years old now, and time hasn't been especially kind to him. Despite his years in the Green Berets, he has begun to slouch forward, his backbone bowed and stooped, and in recent years he has suffered some falls and the subsequent setbacks that accompany broken hips. His hair is white but he keeps it shorn tight on the skull. And though he won't admit to it, he must have suffered a stroke, because his left eye seems a little dull, a little saggy, and he no longer swims beside her in the mornings; instead, he'll take to an Adirondack chair and watch her from shore with a cup of coffee.

She tries to pack light, smart, filling a single large Duluth pack with enough clothes for the six-day trip, a swimsuit, a beach blanket, two bedsheets, a small camera, some toiletries, a few novels and some poetry. She sets aside two hours of every day to lie beside a lake and read the books that always seem to Jenga up on her bedside table without her managing to actually read them. She carries their two bags to the front door, where their sleeping bags wait.

It's just past nine in the evening, and the western horizon is smeared in pinks and purples, like hastily applied makeup. The house is too big for just the two of them. It is the house she and Trevor bought together before he was killed, when the world still held forth some bright promise, when there was hope of creating a family, of traveling the world together, of attending PTA meetings, family reunions, growing old together . . .

How exciting, that day out of days, not long after they'd decided together to buy a home, to start a life, to raise a family together in this old farmhouse outside Menomonie. That was a conscious decision, too, to stay in Wisconsin. With Trevor deployed so frequently, he insisted she have help from their parents. She refused to live in Eau Claire itself, though; just a little farther afield, enough so that her mother couldn't simply drop in without first calling.

Less than a year after they'd bought the house, Trevor was killed. Her last very clear memory of him was the weekend they had in Paris, when at some point over the course of two days, making love almost constantly, breaking only to walk the city, to eat and drink, hold hands, they conceived their boy. Trevor looking *so* out of place with his long beard, long hair, sunburned skin—the men in his Special Forces unit took a certain pride in that mountain man look, in their beards. It had surprised her, that aspect of him, thrilled her even. That this man she had known more than a decade had become an elite soldier, this bear of a human being, so wide and thick at the chest, so quiet and strong—in some ways just a truer, more intense version of who he'd been at sixteen or seventeen, and yet, so much of that earlier softness just completely melted away, even the frequency of his smiles, too, his laughter and jokes. He was a different man.

She lay against his chest in that hotel bed in Paris, his hairy forearm holding her, a big technical watch circling his wrist.

"You want to understand war?" he said, apropos of *what* she can no longer even remember. "Politics? Check out a book on thermodynamics. All the rules apply. What you're talking about is essentially energy, or the absence of energy. Because in most cases, political power is totally congruent with energy, with heat. For over a hundred years Afghanistan looks like a very erratic weather pattern, right? The only constant is the Afghanis themselves. Otherwise, you've got the British, the Russians, the Taliban, and now us—chaos and colonialism. And someday we'll be gone, and that vacuum opens up again, with someone to fill it."

He had told her, vehemently, that he did not wish to be buried at Fort Snelling, outside of Minneapolis and underneath the flight paths of the hundreds of airliners taking off and landing at MSP. Not Arlington, either. It was strange, really, how ever since joining the Special Forces, he had become, almost at once, completely disenchanted with the military, foreign policy, politics. Strange, too, how he'd come to accept his own fate, or at the very least, foresee it, a reality, she supposed, of that unknowable life he led, so close to extreme violence.

She never said, *Let's make a baby*, but that's what it felt like they were doing—something desperate, something ecstatic, some transference of, yes, energy. His thick hands running through her hair, holding her hair, while they kissed eagerly, roughly . . . After Thomas was born, she began to feel guilty, as if she'd somehow sapped Trevor of his light, his power, made him vulnerable somehow.

THOMAS RETURNS HOME just before lunch, his eyes bloodshot and his clothes stinking of cigarette smoke.

"I was just about to text you," she says. "We have to head out. We're supposed to check in at three."

"Sure," he says. "We got any orange juice?"

He rifles through the refrigerator.

"Are you high, Thomas?" she asks.

"Mom," he sighs, "we were smoking cigarettes."

"Oh, like *that's* okay?" she says, already exasperated. "I mean, I know you're a smart kid. So, when I tell you those things will kill you, this hopefully isn't news to you. And where are you getting money for those, anyway? I mean, what do they cost now, twenty bucks a pack?"

He crooks a finger around the handle of the plastic container and drinks, like some thirsty peasant farmer, orange juice leaking out of the corner of his mouth, down his chin, onto the floor. Sometimes she feels that he is in cahoots with the ants and mice that every day seem to threaten to overtake their household. She wets a paper towel, bends down, and wipes up his mess.

"Go take a shower," she orders.

"Ten-four, *capitan*," he says, burping.

"And we really do need to leave soon."

"You know, we don't have to do this," he says, stopping at the staircase. "I mean, nobody's in Scouts anymore. It's, like, pointless. Just this stupid paramilitary Christian fraternity or something. Bunch of paranoid Republicans shooting guns and preparing for the damn apocalypse. Jesus."

They've had this argument, and every time it breaks her heart. Not because of the words falling out of his teenage mouth—no, she expects that sort of pyrotechnics. What crushes her is that this young man has no memory of his father, just pictures of a stranger. He does not understand, for example, that his father collected more than eighty merit badges, that by the age of eighteen, Trevor could have been dropped into any wilderness on any continent and survived on his wits alone. That he always credited his time in the Boy Scouts for helping him later in basic training, Special Forces training, and beyond. She imagines him standing in their kitchen now, this hirsute, imposing man, dwarfing the coffee mug in his hands. Imagines Thomas's enthusiasm as the two of them head off for camp, Trevor later on surrounded by a group of young boys, showing them how to take a compass bearing, explaining why orienteering is one of the very most practical skills a person can master.

But all she can say is, "Get upstairs," in a tone that will suggest she is on the verge of either crying or throwing something at him—both of which happen to be true right now.

Within an hour they are in the Cherokee, headed north up Highway 53, driving in complete and resounding silence, and all that she can think about is asking, *Did you bring any of those cigarettes with you?* She doesn't smoke cigarettes often, but sometimes it is a welcome release valve. Thomas thumbs away at his telephone in the backseat of the Jeep. He can't even sit beside her. So she rolls down the window, the air rifling up her left sleeve, and feels like the saddest taxi driver in all of northern Wisconsin.

TROOP #42 HAS RESERVED THE SAME CAMPSITE at Whiteside ever since Thomas's grandfather, Jonathan, was a boy. And so after parking the Jeep in the lot, Rachel and Thomas shoulder their belongings to begin the one-mile trek through the parade ground, past the counselors' campsite, and all the way down the shady two-track path that leads to their site, Arrowhead.

Rachel slaps at her legs, her arms, her head. "The flies are *terrible* this year."

"Could've stayed home," Thomas says flatly. "It's not too late, either."

Chagrinned, she does her best to ignore the mosquitoes and flies burrowing through her hair to bite into her scalp. "Oh well—a little discomfort's good for a person, right?" she says, gritting her teeth. "We've probably gotten too soft, all of us. I mean, how many people are doing what we're doing right now? Hiking into a remote campsite—no tablets, no laptops, no social media, none of the modern distractions."

"What did you just say?" Thomas has stopped walking and stares daggers at her; she can feel it.

Wincing, she presses on: "I was just talking about how soft we've grown, you know? About how fortunate we are to be up here . . ." Her voice trails off.

"You're telling me you *forgot to pack* my iPad?" Thomas shouts.

She shrugs her pack up higher on her shoulders, swats a hand at her forehead. "Actually, Thomas, I didn't forget."

He stares at her, aghast.

"You fucking left my shit at home—what, to just, like, get under my skin?" Thomas hollers, "To rub this whole fucking thing in? Making me come up here like some kinda kid! And all because Trevor was an Eagle Scout or whatever? *Jesus*, Mom!"

She rushes at him now, and though he is taller and stronger than her, she is his mother, and she does not fear him, will *never* fear him. Because she made him, *this kid*, and cared for him, and more than any emotion, no matter how disrespectful he is, how crude or nasty, what she feels for him overwhelmingly is love.

Raising her hand as if to slap him, Rachel instead takes his hot face between her hands and says, "He was your father. And I'm sorry that I haven't been a better mother, that you've grown up without a dad. I'm sorry about some of my choices, too, those men . . ."

She shakes her head, as if to clear her thoughts, to collect herself. "But none of that is your father's fault. He did the best he could. But—" She begins to cry. It's been months since she fell apart like this, but now her emotions are bubbling up, burning her cheeks, making her head heavy with pressure, spilling tears. "And I know he's watching you, right now. I *know* that he is." She wants to say, *Just make him proud.*

He hugs her now, the heavy, gawky hug of a teenage boy saddled with a backpack and unaccustomed to even these brief moments of affection with his mother.

"I'm sorry, Mom," he says, his cigarette breath near her ear. "Okay? Just . . . Please stop crying, all right? I'm really sorry."

She wipes her nose with a Kleenex and pats him on the chest, backs slowly away, then points a finger at him.

"I don't like it when you disrespect me," she says quietly, firmly. "But I will never, *ever* tolerate you disparaging your father. *Do-you-understand-me?*"

He nods his head, murmurs, "Can we go now?"

34

THERE ARE CERTAIN PERKS TO BEING THE ONLY woman in a camp full of men. For one, she has a small cabin to herself. Oh, they aren't "real" cabins, certainly not. The walls are aluminum mesh screens framed in by old two-by-fours, and the floors are sheets of plywood. The roof is corrugated plastic, the screen door loose at the hinge and riddled with holes, some "patched" by nothing better than purple, green, or pink bubble gum. The door has all the security of a hook-and-eye lock, the walls nothing more than rolls of moldering olive green canvas a camper can unfurl to create some semblance of privacy.

But she loves her cabin, the sounds of boys outside, all around, only with none of the expectations that she must constantly mother, parent, supervise, discipline. The cabin has four single bed frames, each outfitted with a very abused mattress. The air inside is close, tight. A slight breeze goes unnoticed; only strong winds seem to pass through the somewhat rusty screens.

Rachel lays out her effects, careful not to leave her bras and panties out in open sight; those will remain secure in her bag. She pushes two bunks together and, utilizing one of the few luxuries she packed, wraps both mattresses in a queen-size pad and bedsheet, then unrolls her sleeping bag and lies down, closes her eyes.

Her world sounds like this: mosquitoes, screen doors slamming, the wild running of boys, an ax splitting wood, the wind rustling the copse of aspens outside.

THE ONLY RESPONSIBILITIES on this first Monday are dinner in the mess hall and an early evening *charge*—a kind of challenge Nelson traditionally levels at the boys: What kind of men do they want to become? How will they achieve their goals—this week, this year, and beyond? Normally the entire camp meets at an amphitheater adjacent to Bass Lake and a film or PowerPoint is presented before the boys are dismissed. This first night, their candy supplies will seem unlimited, the fresh air invigorating, each campsite ringing with laughter and tomfoolery into the early, early hours of the morning.

At dinner in the mess hall, the father of one of the boys in Thomas's troop sits down the table from Rachel. He is a big man, well over six feet tall. The molded plastic tray in his hands looks very small, like he's holding some dainty dessert plate, a coffee saucer maybe. It takes him some time to swing a leg over the table's bench, then the other leg, and after he is sitting, his gut so exceeds the bounds of this tight space that he needs to scooch the bench back a couple of inches to even get at his food.

"Christ, Bill," snickers one of the other fathers at the table, "that bench is made for hundred-pound boys, not a lummox like you." The table titters with a laughter that is clearly little more than nerves, social awkwardness, the desire to settle in. She notices that not just one, but as many as two silver flasks are rotating about the table, the fathers pouring what smells like brandy into their mugs of coffee; some of the men, she realizes, are already drunk, their eyes beneath sunburnt foreheads marked by that glazed, dazed look of the well soused.

The big man across from her, Bill, looks at Rachel and without so much as blinking says, "Maybe when they changed this place to a Girl Scout camp they brought in some more feminine benches, too."

Rachel tends to consider herself a strong woman; still, she can't hold this ugly man's stare, and looks down at the food she no longer hungers for.

A couple of men at the table guffaw, raise coffee mugs to their mouths. Most of the fathers at the table say nothing.

"I mean," Bill continues, "seems like every goddamn institution in this country is broken. Everywhere you go. Gays in the military. Gays in Scouts. Gays getting married. These tranny freaks, or whatever they call themselves . . ." He disappears a dinner roll in a single bite without removing his eyes from Rachel. "Half the time, I don't recognize this country anymore. Ain't *my* country—that's for sure. Land of the free, but"—his great big hands fly up before his face in mock horror—"don't say what you think, what you *feel*. Don't hurt anyone's feelings. Don't *offend* anyone. We can fly a goddamn Chinese flag at the UN but we can't fly the Stars and Bars? Don't make sense to me."

This is a moment, Rachel thinks, when a person should say something, stand up, leave, fight . . . But she can't think of anything to say, can't even seem to move. Pinned where she is by his gaze, by his sheer size, and seemingly without a sympathetic mind in the bunch. He is a particular kind of Wisconsinite, she understands. The world is a bullet train that has passed him by so quickly, it's as if he's standing on the side of the tracks spinning like a weather vane.

"Listen," she finally manages, "women have been coming to Scout camps for a generation or more, leading troops, working in the front office . . ." It's a lame rebuttal, she knows, but in such moments her brain has never fired as quickly as she'd like, and she already knows that tonight she won't sleep, thinking about every plank of her argument that went unsaid, undefended. Somehow, this nimrod has left her tongue-tied, unable to claim the intellectual high ground she knows is hers, if she can only locate it. She peers up at him, *the intellectual high ground, sweet Lord.*

He is spooning corn into his mouth, kernels dropping onto his chest, his lap, like poorly broadcast seed. He wipes his face with a paper napkin, points a fat finger at her, says, "And are there more Scouts now than there were thirty years ago? Hell, no. Scouting's dying. And it's because of women, 'cause of gays, 'cause we've thrown the doors open to every religion under the sun. Hell, we got Muslim Boy Scouts out there, prob'ly. That make sense to you? Christ, it's like training al-Qaeda, ISIS, right here at home."

Now she is incensed, notices that her fists are clenched. *Why isn't anyone else saying something?*

"If Scouting is dying," she says, her voice tremulous, "maybe it's because we waited so long to welcome those people in." *You stupid bastard,* she would dearly like to add, but it is only the first day of camp. "This isn't 1950. Heck, you were born when? The early eighties? Exactly what country is it *you think* you remember?" Her face is hot and red but she is proud of herself, proud of standing up to this ignorance.

"I'm with Bill on this one," another man says.

Rachel looks down the table at him. He has thickly flowing red hair, designer glasses, thin fingers that spin a green apple by its stem. He is finely featured, not a big man—the opposite of Bill. She dimly recognizes him as the father of a boy named Ulysses. This man, the father, is a surgeon in Eau Claire, Dr. Platz, if memory serves.

"I think we're all a little too sensitive these days," he says, breezily. "How does that prepare these boys for the world? How does that pre-

pare them for the evil out there? The competition, hell, the brutality?"
He takes a pull from a flask, as casually as if it were a canteen, right out
there in the open. No one seems to take note.

She thinks, *This is another argument . . .*

But the doctor leans into the table now, looks at the men around
him, almost as if intentionally avoiding her eyes. "The thing is," he
says, "in the real world, you're not invited to every party. Right? You
can't join every club. Not everyone wants to be your friend. And I'll be
honest with you, there are people I don't want my son going to school
with. There are people I don't want to have to see on my weekends, at
dinner."

What is he even talking about?

"But," she says, determined to redirect this conversation, "we were
just talking about women in Scouting. Surely you believe that women
belong in Scouting." She pauses. "Right?"

"Well," the doctor says, "isn't there Girl Scouts?"

"But my son," she says, "I have a son. What about parents like me."
Widows, she would like to say. And, *Where is the cavalry? Where are the
gentlemen? Other mothers, wives?*

"Doesn't he have a father? Or a grandfather? An uncle? Some family friend?" the doctor presses on, a cruel sort of kindness to his tone.
He has removed his glasses, rubs at the bridge of his nose, and looks at
her now with the condescension of someone with a small but certain
amount of power in the world. This is the air of someone manning a
backwater security checkpoint, a jaded receptionist, a disgruntled ca-
shier or tollbooth operator—their power at once minuscule and ultimately final.

His tone and delivery, so reasonable, seem to lend some credence
to his argument, and for a moment, she wonders, *Is this all about me?
Is this my problem? Thomas doesn't even want to be here . . . Or perhaps
Jonathan could . . .*

But Jonathan Quick is now something like a recluse, a hermit with means. He lives in a cabin on a small lake in northern Wisconsin, where he spends his days drinking Baileys with coffee, his nights eating frozen pizzas and fish sticks and drinking bourbon. He putters around a woodshop, ostensibly building furniture, but mostly, she thinks, smoking cigarettes and reading spy novels. He is now divorced a second time, and she doesn't see him much, on Thanksgiving perhaps, when he'll venture down to Menomonie with a bottle of expensive Bordeaux and some eccentric gift for Thomas: a hand-woven basket, a French pocketknife, an Italian bicycle, a small stock stake in some upstart tech company . . . Jonathan's first wife, Sarah, remarried a man she met online, and eventually moved to Hawaii. Every couple of years she pays for plane tickets for Rachel and Thomas and they ride a zip-line through the rainforest, surf the constant Pacific swells, and for a week Thomas eats nothing but shrimp.

Her own father, a retired Lutheran minister, has battled cancer on and off for a decade. He is so weak these days, so frail, so tired. Her mother is his constant caretaker. There are no uncles, no cousins. She and Trevor were both only children. Inventorying her family and Trevor's right now makes her desolate, clarifies her own aloneness in the world, how much Thomas means to her, how gaping Trevor's absence is. She lowers her head for a second, thinks, *Some of these men must know about Trevor.* She scans their faces, fairly confident she and Trevor went to high school with at least one or two of them.

"No," she says, "there isn't anyone else. Thomas's dad died. It's just us." Standing up from the table, she collects her tray, says, "Excuse me."

On her way out of the mess hall she spots Nelson, sitting at the edge of a table, near a boy in a wheelchair, who is talking excitedly to the old man, gesticulating as if reenacting some epic battle. It's the first time she's seen him since arriving, and, boy, can she use a welcoming face right about now. Rachel makes her way to this old friend, where he listens intently to the boy, a terribly gangly fellow, suffering that awkward intersection of baby fat, glasses, and acne. He is clearly thrilled to have Nelson's ear.

"Excuse me," Rachel says kindly to the boy, and then, "Scoutmaster Doughty." She lays a soft hand on the old man's shoulder and he jumps, as if gently shocked, before turning his head to look at her.

"Rachel," he says and begins to stand, ever so slowly. His feet seem tangled, knotted beneath the table, and he accidentally topples a glass of water. "Hellfire," he mutters.

"Please," she urges, "you sit down." She quickly cleans the spill with a handful of paper napkins, then gives him a hug and instantly her body feels warmed, soothed, like slipping a foot into a warm sock, a slipper. He has always been so very kind to her, always. She never knew her own grandfather, but allows herself to imagine him a man like Nelson Doughty, smelling of tobacco, wood shavings, pine-tar soap, and some old-man pomade that he employs to curl his white mustache up.

"You'll come by my cabin tonight?" he asks with an eager, quavering voice. He leans toward her, places a shaky hand on her shoulder, whispers, "Got a bottle of your favorite."

"Oban?" she asks, smiling, then remembers the fathers at her table, their own drinking. She waves their behavior away as unsanctioned public drinking, irresponsible, like a group of Aqualung hobos daydrinking at the school playground.

He nods, blinks his eyes, holding her hands in his, as if she were his daughter, come for a long-awaited visit.

"Maybe not tonight." She frowns. "I'm afraid I might not be too much fun."

"Nonsense," he insists, tightening his grip. "It is *especially* on such nights that a person should not be left alone." He lets go of her hands, holds out one finger in the air. "One drink. With an old man."

She smiles. "Okay, one drink."

He adds another finger, winks. "Or maybe two."

35

BEFORE LEAVING HER CABIN TO WALK TO NELSON'S, she visits Thomas's cabin, knocks on the door. No one answers. She peers through the screened wall. No one around.

She punches into her phone.

> Where are you?

> Camp, Mom. Chillax.

> I'm going to visit Mr. Doughty.
> Have a great night, sweetie!

No reply. Typical. He seems to respond only to threats, real or perceived. Or offers of food. This has the effect of making her feel like a prison guard. She often wonders what it would have been like to parent before the advent of cell phones, texting, Facebook, Twitter, Snapchat, and all the other technology and social media that parents now seem to depend on.

The night carries a chill and she grabs a light sweatshirt from the cabin. Sets out on the path back to the parade ground.

Dinner has left her unnerved, really rattled. Never before has the camp felt to her an unwelcoming or hostile place, and surely Nelson has certainly always embraced her presence. But, then, it's not just this small place, she thinks—there seems an atmosphere everywhere these days in America, a malevolent vibration in the air, every citizen so quick to righteous rage, some tribal defensiveness, seeing the fault in each other's arguments, rather than some larger common field of compromise, if not agreement.

From across the parade ground, she sees Nelson's cabin aglow; her pace quickens, like a girl visiting a beloved grandparent or uncle. How right he was. She is suddenly aware of her need for adult interaction, a good honest conversation. At the door she knocks lightly, hears a distant, "Come in."

The cabin is like a diorama of early-twentieth-century America, softly backlit by old, dust-encrusted lightbulbs, every stick of furniture the softest, oldest wicker or leather, no book on any given shelf published after about 1970, it seems, the walls festooned with bone-dry, fragile snowshoes, fishing nets and poles, lacrosse sticks, cross-country skis, and old, old taxidermy. A lynx whose charismatic ears seem rubbed to nubbins, a huge lunging northern pike minus several sharp teeth, a massive sixteen-point buck less one shining, marble-like eye.

Nelson is back in the tiny galley kitchen, little more than a wall where the refrigerator, stove, and sink reside. He's lifting a kettle of boiling water off a burner. The air smells of moldering paper, leather, and dust, commingled with the zest of the freshly sliced lemon on the counter. All at once, she feels heavy; her bones and all her muscles, lead.

She wants nothing more than to flop into one of Nelson's chairs and close her eyes. Nelson's got his old Grundig switched on, and she recognizes a deejay's voice from the nearby radio station, WOJB, operated by the Lac Courte Oreilles band of Lake Superior Anishinaabe. Soon, one voice is replaced by another—George Jones.

"How was your day?" Nelson asks lightly, puttering about the kitchen.

She exhales. "Other than the fact that Thomas hates me, resents being here, and the other parents are a bunch of friggin' fascists . . ."

He frowns at her. "Fascists?"

She thinks, *No, right-wing nutjobs is probably more accurate*, waves a hand in the air as if to dismiss her own complaints. "I'm just . . . happy to see you."

"Me too, kiddo," he says, smiling. "Me too."

THEY LISTEN TO CLASSIC COUNTRY—Merle Haggard, Johnny Paycheck, Patsy Cline, Johnny Cash, Hank Williams—drink their Scotch, and stare out into the night, at bats swooping over the lake for insects, the stars reflected perfectly in the water below them.

"Strange—I don't hear any kids," she says, swirling the ice cubes around in her Scotch; she pulls her feet up and sits on them for warmth. It feels like she's having some very sophisticated sleepover with her spiritual sensei or guru. She has always avoided the term *life coach*, finding it utterly pathetic: You need a coach to live? To help you live? Get up in the morning?

"Kids keep you young," Nelson says. "I believe that." He takes a sip of Oban. "But Christ, they make you feel old, too."

"How long you plan to keep doing this?" she asks.

"This'll be my last summer," he says, looking at the floor. "I haven't told anyone yet. You're the first. I ain't gonna' die here, though, like

Wilbur. I love Scouts, Scouting, but . . . I ain't gonna die at a Boy Scout camp. I got a lady friend and we're thinking about buying a place down in Costa Rica, Belize, maybe. To hell with winter. I want to croak with a cold *cerveza* in my hand."

Startled by this news, saddened even, she gives him a smile of encouragement, summons a toast.

"To cold drinks and warm beaches," she says, her glass raised up to meet his.

"I'll drink to that," Nelson says.

The notion of the Whiteside Reservation without Nelson Doughty is jarring to her, and she can't banish a profound sense, even now, of abandonment. Who will she have left? Thomas? Jonathan?

"I'll miss you," she says, careful to aim her eyes away.

"It's time," he says. "Time for some young blood. New ideas, new energy." He takes another sip of his Scotch.

THE BOYS THESE DAYS come to camp with their laptops and tablets, their telephones, their gaming systems, their earbuds, and it is a *miracle* if they ever hear the cry of a loon, or watch a star fall to earth. He's walked by their cabins after dusk and seen their tablets illuminated with fake fire while four separate boys lie in their cots thumbing away at their phones. In some campgrounds, the fire rings are mossy and perennially cold, the fishing line on certain rods grown brittle with age. Dry rot eats at the beautiful wooden canoes, like some infection. He's even heard some kids insist that burning wood is *bad.*

"*Why?*" he'll ask.

"*Because it's killing trees, for one thing. And, plus, putting more crap in the atmosphere,*" they smugly reply.

"*What about dead trees?*" he'll ask.

To which, they shrug their shoulders. Few of them make eye contact anymore, so trained are they to monitor their phones for the constant updates to their world. Many of them, he expects, have never touched an ax, a hatchet, or a chain saw, let alone a pocketknife.

For the past five years not one Scout has signed up for the Orienteering merit badge. It took him a while to understand why before he realized that kids these days of course carry their compasses with them everywhere, right inside their telephones, along with their cameras, televisions, movies, music, watches, maps, notebooks, calculators . . . Not such a bad thing, he supposes, unless it rains. Unless there is no electricity handy. Or you're fighting a war, and don't want to broadcast your position to the enemy. Likewise, no one has taken: Coin Collecting (Everyone uses plastic, or their phones to buy things, why carry a pocket of metal? Why bother collecting it?), Collections, Radio, Signaling, Stamp Collecting (What kind of fossil buys stamps anymore?) . . .

For years, Nelson fought the onslaught of technology the only way he knew how—banishing it—watching his camp's attendance plummet as other camps installed Wi-Fi, Internet-connected canteens, and movie theaters. Finally he acquiesced to a cell phone tower on the far side of the camp, over a ridge. In camp, the signal is surprisingly weak. He was advised, after all, to install it in the center of the parade ground, where interference would be minimal—no forest or hills to interrupt the signals. But he prefers this solution: the boys can still log on to the Internet, but at frustratingly slow speeds, and the tower blinks off to the northeast so that looking out at the lake from his cabin, his view isn't the least bit disturbed. Campers are charged twenty-five dollars for access, and this drives them bonkers, not to mention their parents, who are frequently, if anything, more addicted to their technology than the boys. He really doesn't give a shit. That money makes up for the steadily sliding numbers in attendance. Let the next Scoutmaster move Whiteside all the way into the twenty-first century.

He has grown so weary of the world. To the south and west the stars are becoming increasingly crowded out by the light spilling out of ever-sprawling Minneapolis and St. Paul and even Eau Claire and Rice Lake. There are too many deer, many of them diseased. Fewer birds every year. The lake water more and more acidic. Last year he found the carcass of a dead wolf on the margins of the camp; he found its DNR radio collar in the ditch on a walk over to Lorraine's. The animal was probably killed by a neighboring farmer or some yahoo out shining—cowardly gut shot. He only hopes it wasn't a Scout, or the parent of a Scout, or even a counselor. Nelson has always had an affection for wolves, for predators. In his earlier years, after all, he was one.

"Are you, uh, I'm not sure how to ask this politely . . . ," Nelson says, adjusting himself in the chair.

"Refill my glass," she orders, "then ask your question."

He laughs, retrieves the bottle, pours her an inch.

"Are you dating anyone these days?" he asks now, settling back into his chair.

She shakes her head. Though a more accurate answer might be, *maybe*. There is always Spencer, waiting patiently in the shadows. If he owned a top hat he'd probably be clutching the rim 24/7 and frowning, like some staunchly patient Victorian suitor.

"Why not?" Nelson says, leaning forward. "You're beautiful. Smart. A good mother. I'm telling you, if I was thirty years younger—hell, *ten* years younger." He pours himself another finger or so of Oban.

"You're sweet," she says.

"You're evading my question."

"I don't know. I've been married three times, Nelson," she says. "Maybe that's a sign, you know? That I'm actually kind of a horrible wife." She laughs, sips her Scotch.

"Not your fault," Nelson argues. "You know that, don't you? Tell me you know that."

She is shaking her head again, then sets her glass down on the coffee table and covers her eyes, bites her lower lip.

He sets his own glass down, stands slowly, walks to her, bends down, and kneeling before her, wraps his arms around her. She hugs him so fiercely.

"He was a good boy," Nelson says. "Such a good boy. He loved you more than anything."

"I miss him every day," she sobs. "Oh God, I miss him every fucking day."

They stay that way for a while, for many minutes, until Rachel sits up, wipes her eyes again with Nelson's handkerchief, then loudly blows her nose.

"Could I have some tea," she asks.

"Of course," he says, rising slowly from his old knees. "I take mine with a little bourbon. You?"

She laughs. "No, I think I'm done for the night, thank you."

CLUTCHING A MUG OF TEA, blowing at the lemony-honey steam, she says, "Maybe I never should have remarried, you know? But I thought that just seemed kind of hokey." She sips her tea. "No. Honestly, I wondered about other people, too. Other men. I'd been with Trevor since we were sixteen. Well, you know, of course. Am I a horrible person for thinking that? For being curious?"

"Of course not," Nelson says. A dim, long-undisturbed memory rises, and he recollects a night in Hurley, years ago, watching Trevor disappear into the nether regions of a certain bar, holding the hand of a woman not named Rachel.

"But the reality was," she continues, "no one could ever stack up to Trevor. No one. These other men, they were okay, but the truth is, most of them were pussies. They weren't—I don't know, they weren't *real men*. They wouldn't hold open doors or buy dinner; they weren't kind, they certainly weren't tough or strong. And after a while I'd just get disgusted. Goddamn golf shirts and gym memberships and fake muscles and tans and cell phones and new cars. Trevor didn't care about any of that garbage. All he wanted was a garden. Isn't that funny?

"I don't even give a fuck about chivalry," she continues, pausing to sip deeply from the tea, considering. "I care about strength. Thoughtfulness. Kindness. All these other guys seem to have confused strength with, I don't know . . . muscles? Authority. Power. *Meanness*. That's the worst. Trevor was never like that. And definitely never to me. He worshipped me. Maybe too much at times."

She sips her tea again.

"This is just the sentiment of an old, unmarried man," Nelson says finally, "but it seems to me we ought to worship our spouses, our partners." They are silent a moment, both of them. "Isn't that the idea?"

She shakes her head. "I just wish I'd known. I wish I'd known where it was all going, but of course . . . we can't; I couldn't."

36

WHEN SHE WAS TWENTY-ONE YEARS OLD, A JUNIOR IN college, she was awarded a scholarship, traveled to Botswana, and fell in love with an Afrikaner, a huge, sunburnt man who'd played semi-professional rugby, bench-pressed four hundred pounds, could speak four languages. He sported a massive scar on his forearm from a bar fight and could drink a case of beer in a long, dry veldt evening. Willem was his name, though people called him Sundown—a preposterous nickname if there ever was one.

Trevor was back home in Wisconsin, studying in Madison, working two part-time jobs to avoid the strings that came attached to his father's money. He lived in a ratty old house on St. James Court, where the bats migrated from the belfry of the street's namesake church into the house's attic and came crawling literally through the woodwork. It was not uncommon for Trevor to walk around the house armed with a frying pan or a tennis racket.

He wrote her the most beautiful heartsick love letters, pages long. Letters written late at night from the hotel where he worked as the night auditor. Letters written in the early morning from the kitchen of Mickey's Dairy Bar, where he bused tables, arriving early to drink coffee with the cooks. She could imagine everything, that little old café, staring out at Camp Randall Stadium, how quiet Madison was on those weekend mornings as the students nursed crushing hangovers or walked home shamefully, clutching their high heels, holding their shoulders against the cold—jackets lost in some new lover's room. She could imagine the garbage trucks moving slowly through the morning, a few cabs, the capitol building lit up like a white citadel, early-bird joggers pounding the sidewalks, the Greenbush Bakery, its trays of doughnuts tantalizing the insomniac drunks and stoners and homeless . . .

The letters came twice a week, sometimes more frequently. And they were intense, even profound at times; Trevor had always been like that. The way he loved was almost like a vise, a weight; at times she felt it verged on codependence—that his identity, his value system, all of it very much hinged on her. And who was she? A twenty-one-year-old girl from Eau Claire, Wisconsin, who had seen so little of the world, who had known exactly one lover, whose favorite book until college had been basically a kid's book about horses?

God, how embarrassing! To land in college never having read Kerouac. Steinbeck. Flannery O' Connor. Even Ayn Rand. To have only ever traveled to Cancún? Never eaten sushi!

Willem's family was unfathomably wealthy. They owned wineries in Stellenbosch, vacationed in Monaco. Occasionally his mother took her shopping in Cape Town, where they were doted upon by storekeepers. Once, she made the mistake of asking how much a dress cost. "Ten thousand rand," the storekeeper replied. "About a thousand of your American dollars."

Rachel wilted with embarrassment.

"It's a good lesson, child," the mother had said with friendly amusement, sipping a glass of Veuve as she appraised Rachel's body outside the dressing room. "If you have to ask . . . well, there you are, aren't you?"

She had met Willem in one of Gaborone's expat bars, she talking to a group of wildlife biologists about the black rhino, and he, leaning against the bar, staring at her, just staring.

Late in the evening, drunk, he walked across the barroom and said to her, "You ever *seen* a black rhino, sweetheart?"

She was dumbfounded, curious, and her body vibrated with an excitement she wasn't sure she'd ever felt before. No one had ever approached her like this, talked to her in this manner.

"I'm sorry," she said. "Uh, did you just call me sweetheart?"

He grinned at her, standing there, sipping his bottle of Tusker.

"Come on," he said.

"No way," she protested. "I'm here with my friends—I mean, I just got here."

He set his bottle down, reached out a hand. "Please, come with me," he said. "I want to show you something."

And for some reason, she went.

They drove through the darkest night, under a southern sky totally unfamiliar to her. He drove an open-roofed Range Rover, took her thigh in his hand, and then pushed his fingers farther up her leg. She felt her eyes closing, the vehicle slowing, her breathing became a frenzy, her shoes on the floor of the Rover, her bare feet against the dashboard, and then his lips on hers, his tongue. Her hips smashed into his hand.

She did not see a black rhinoceros that night, or the next week, for that matter. She did not check her mailbox for post, or monitor her email. She did not answer her telephone. She did not eat until late at night, when they went to restaurants, eager for the meal to end so they could return to his flat. She did not feel happy or sad or homesick or guilty. She felt free, alive, revived, new.

This went on for weeks, and if anything, Trevor's communications became more frantic, more dutiful. She watched as his letters stacked up on her bed; the postman had begun to rubber-band them together, the only mail she ever received. Her voice mail box filled to full, until she could accept no more messages.

And then one night, alone in her apartment, there only to pick up some books, toiletries, and take a quick shower, her phone rang. Trevor. She decided to answer. Maybe this wouldn't be so painful for her after all. After the standard lame litany of sweet nothings and what seemed like an endless cavalcade of "what's it like?" and "how are you?" she simply said it.

"I'm not in love with you anymore. I'm sorry, Trevor."

Even his name sounded ridiculous to her now, this very midwestern-sounding American name. Trevor. Like the name you'd give to a kitchen tool: trivet, baster, cleaver, trevor . . . And frankly, she was not sorry, not in the least. She was having more fun than she could remember. Even his upbeat voice, familiar accent (her own long gone, missing somewhere around the first two weeks in Africa), and reportage from the home front could not forestall this breakup.

"What?" he said.

"I'm not in love with you," she repeated. "So, *please*, Trev, can you stop sending me these stupid love letters? I don't even have time to read them."

"Oh," he lamely offered. "Because you're, like, having an affair or something. With another dude."

Had she cared to listen closely, she might have heard his heart breaking just then. Only this wasn't exactly how she had imagined it; she'd imagined him screaming at her, asking juvenile questions about her new lover: his penis size, blow jobs, how many times they'd had sex. But he just seemed . . . stunned. Stunned and somehow . . . accepting of it all.

"Well, Trevor," she said, "I'm not sure it really constitutes an affair if you and I aren't even engaged, let alone married. And he's actually Afrikaner, more of a man, you know, than a 'dude.'"

The sound of a phone receiver juggled between sweaty hands, of a face wiped clear of tears . . . How powerful she felt. To live here, in Africa. To sleep with whomever she wanted. To study one of the last wild places on the continent . . .

"Um, well," he stuttered.

She sighed with exasperation. He was snuffling and sniffling like such a little boy. She began to jam books into a duffel bag.

"Well, um, you probably don't really care anymore, but I want you to know that I'm going to volunteer for the Marines," he said. "I tried to call you before, and I wrote to you, but . . . Geez, Rachel, this is really shitty."

"What? Come on, Trevor, don't be so fucking dramatic!" She slumped down on her bed, held her hair in her hands, away from her face.

Now his tone was different. "You really haven't read my letters, have you? I mean, not for, like, weeks."

"No," she said, "I haven't. I've been living . . ." *My life.* ". . . I've been busy."

"Did you get that copy of *A Sand County Almanac*? I sent it about a month ago."

This was her favorite book, a discovery during her first year in college, and Aldo Leopold had since become her favorite writer, one of the reasons she had pursued a degree in biology. But Leopold was a Wisconsinite, and she didn't want to think about Wisconsin right now.

"Maybe. I don't know, Trevor. Jesus. Who cares?"

"Wow, maybe my fucking dad was right," he said. *A long pause.* "Maybe you really are a bitch."

That gave her some level of satisfaction, to be called a name. Trevor wasn't exactly the name-calling type. Though she didn't much care for the mention of Jonathan, the notion of Trevor's smirkingly omniscient father seeing this coming like some slow-moving storm front.

"Your dad *what?*" she said, rising to the bait.

"It doesn't matter now," Trevor said, "but he warned me—God, like four, five years ago—*told* me this would happen. Told me it'd be pretty much just like this."

"Your dad never liked me," she said. "He never even learned my name. Not until, like, last year. He used to call me 'Racquel,' or 'Rochelle.' How do you think that made me feel, huh?"

"I'd say it doesn't really matter anymore, does it?" he said.

"So you're—wait, you're gonna join the Marines? Trevor, that's just stupid."

"I don't think so," he said calmly. "I've really thought about it."

"Thought about what?"

"After nine-eleven," he continued, "I just couldn't see not volunteering. I couldn't see standing on the sidelines. I've always wanted to be something more than what I am."

"It's so strange," she murmured, "because nobody really talks about nine-eleven here. They talk about Bush this, or Cheney that, sometimes it's about Halliburton, or oil, of course . . . but I don't think it's the same thing. People aren't as connected."

She felt a pang of guiltiness for her ignorance of what was happening back home, but it was true, she liked not being upset about Bush, liked feeling distant from the still smoldering World Trade Center site. She thought of the night sky, the limitless flat of Botswana, the sand dunes of Namibia and sleeping with Willem in a hostel there, of the Canadian flag she'd stitched to her backpack.

"I suppose not," he said.

"Have you already signed the papers?" she asked.

"Yep, I head down to Fort Benning this summer, after school's done."

"Oh, Trevor."

She could hear him, blowing his nose quietly, could picture him, shaking his head.

"I don't fault you," he said, with some effort. "I think I'll always love you, but I don't fault you for this."

"I have to go," she said.

"Okay," he said.

And she hung up. Without saying "good luck" or "stay in touch" or anything. For all she knew, he could be dead before she returned to America. There was something sobering in that thought, that she was now traveling down a completely separate path from him, and he her.

Her bed was strewn with envelopes, small packages. She opened several before finding the copy of *A Sand County Almanac*. From its pages fell several leaves: oak, maple, aspen, ash, birch, catalpa, cherry, hackberry, walnut, ironwood . . .

SIX MONTHS LATER, she was living in Willem's flat, vacuuming his floors, washing his dishes, and spending most of her time waiting for him to return from the bush, a bar, some other trip. Her research had stalled, she had no friends, and she was now fully in love with him.

"Why can't I come with you?" she asked. "Why can't I come out to the bush, too? Tell me it's not lonely out there, all alone, in your tent. I mean, don't you miss me?"

Their conversations by now had become rote: She appealed; while he, stoic, aloof, frequently drunk, endured those appeals until he no longer felt like it, at which point he would simply excuse himself for a jog, or to hit the weights in his garage.

"It doesn't work like that," he said. "People pay thousands of dollars for these safaris, babe. You can't just bum along. If every guide did that, the camps would be overflowing with girlfriends and wives and who-knows-what sort of tag-alongs. Wouldn't work."

"Couldn't you get me some kind of job?" she asked. "As a cook, or something? Maybe in the office? That way I could visit your camps, maybe even work on my research. I can pull my own weight." She grasped for any kind of hold. "Doesn't your family have any sway? Couldn't they help—"

"*Don't* presume to know about my family!" he shouted. "And just chill out, all right? Look, we're not married. We started this thing as two people with two separate lives. I don't tell *you* what to do. I don't ask to follow *you* around, like some lost little American puppy."

"What did you say?" she snapped.

"I'm going out for a smoke," he muttered. And then, mostly to himself, "Fucking bitch."

"*You* were the one who chased me, you fucking asshole!" she shouted after him. "You were the one who promised me rhinos and lions and elephants. You were the one who stuck your fucking hands down my pants!"

He looked over his shoulder at her, blew a jet of smoke in her direction, and said, "Yeah, well—we all make mistakes, right, love? So, maybe you should just leave, then."

"What?"

"Get out, all right? How clear do you want me to be? Or I'll bloody throw your shit out of here myself."

So she moved back to her old flat, where her three roommates now treated her as a stranger, where many of her belongings had gone missing, and where her bed looked not just slept in, but fucked in.

"Yeah, we didn't really think you were coming back," one of her flatmates said, "so one of my buddies crashed here for two months." Then he turned, and walked into the kitchen, there to share a conspiratorial laugh with his own girlfriend. Soon enough they were kissing.

37

SHE AWAKES WITH A START AND GLANCES AT HER watch. It is almost one o'clock in the morning. She must have fallen asleep. They both must have. WOJB seems stuck on a rather hypnotic drum circle, complete with tribal singers. She rises stiffly from the chair, stretches, carries their two mugs to the sink, and stands there, running the tap. She washes her face and her hands, then takes a long drink of cold, cold water, listening to the frogs chiming and croaking outside. She peers out the little kitchen window. Between the trees here and there, a few lightning bugs still strobe on and off.

There used to be so many, many more of them, she thinks.

She checks her phone. Even with less than reliable service, here they are, four successive messages from Thomas:

We're having a campfire. Other
dads wondering where you are . . .

???

Hello McFly???

That one makes her grin. When Thomas was just a boy they had watched *Back to the Future* repeatedly. It gives her some amount of pleasure, even now, reminding him that Steven Spielberg himself, the genius who produced that film, was an Eagle Scout. Also David Lynch, though that one didn't seem to resonate yet.

We're working on our Meth Manufacturing Merit Badge. See you tomorrow. Camp boyfriend?

On some level, Thomas is perhaps right to chide her. Drinking Scotch with the camp Scoutmaster at an hour past midnight probably doesn't look right; the so-called *optics* of a single woman inside his cabin. And yet, *what the hell?* Nelson has been like family to her since Trevor's death. Surely, they are entitled to a few adult beverages and some conversation.

The old man snores loudly from his chair. She lays a blanket over top of him, and then, quite without thinking about it, kisses his forehead, and runs a finger over his fine, short white hair.

"Good night," she says.

He continues snoring.

THE GRASS IS WET WITH DEW as she walks over the parade ground to the path that leads through the forest. The camp is quiet. She hugs her shoulders, knows that those glasses of Scotch will haunt her in the morning. Entering the forest the night sky disappears to just the slenderest pockets that open and close with the barely perceptible sway of the canopy. She can barely make out the white bark of the densely

clustered poplars, and the loop-de-loop shadows of the little bats working the darkness as if on trapezes, guide wires.

She is close to the camp when she sees the figure ahead, smoking a
cigarette in the gloom, an orange bead of light throbbing and glowing,
only to be flicked out away into the ferns as she closes the gap between
them.

"Hello?" she calls out pleasantly, firmly.

The figure does not answer. No matter, she thinks; these boys all
wear damn earbuds. Every one of them will be deaf by fifty.

"Hello?" she calls again.

"A little late to be out, don't you think?" It is Bill, the man from
dinner.

She laughs it off, though already her skin is crawling, the fine hairs
on her arms and neck standing at attention. "*I'm* sorry," she says with a
jovially exaggerated politeness. "I don't know that we were introduced
at dinner. My name is Rachel." She extends a hand into the darkness.

"Bill," he says, his huge hand at first seeking, but not finding hers.
Then, after clumsily touching fingers, his hand swallows hers. His skin
is rough, his arm hairy. It's as if she's touching some huge circus animal,
and she can smell him through the clean night air: a staleness, like a
damp basement, or a closet that hasn't been opened in years. She can't tell
whether or not it is his breath, or his body, but she instantly regrets not
walking right past him. Nor does he relinquish his grip of her; in fact,
his fingers seem to scuttle slowly up her wrist. She pulls her hand away.

"I was just catching up with Scoutmaster Doughty," she says, em-
ploying that name, that authority, for whatever it's worth to this man.
The camp is so far from a real police department, after all, if anything
were to happen.

"Didn't think the old man had it in him," Bill grunts.

"Anyway, good night," she says, ignoring the crude barb.

"Hey," he calls out, seemingly unconcerned about waking their
nearby campsite.

She turns quickly. "Bill, I'm pretty tired, okay? I want to get to bed."

"I just wanted to say," he continues, "that I'm sorry about your husband. I still don't believe that this is a place for women, but, just the same . . ."

She is stunned; he might as well have struck her in the forehead with a stone.

"Thank you," she says. "I . . . appreciate that. Good night, then."

She can hear his lighter behind her: the scrape of the sparkwheel, the suck of gas, a little light in the night, and his cigarette burning, the cloud of smoke drifting toward her, and then, his big feet, plodding on, down the gravel path in the other direction, a deep, phlegmy cough.

Reaching Arrowhead, she gropes through the dark at tree trunks, picnic tables, makeshift laundry lines. The campfire is all but burnt out, and only a very few flashlights blur light across the cabin's thick canvas siding and heavy plastic ceilings. Finding her cabin, she locks the screen door and crawls onto her bed, no longer even exhausted so much as simply gratified to have reached the sanctuary of this space. Her breathing is frenzied. She does not sleep at all well and then, too soon, it is morning already.

38

THOMAS POUNDS ON THE SCREEN DOOR OF HER CABIN. The camp is lively, loud. Boys scampering like loosed dogs, fathers barking orders, the splash of water, even music playing.

"Mom," he says, "the door's locked."

Her head pounding, she rises from the bed, unlatches the door, and flops back down on her double cot.

"Are you hungover, Mom?" he asks. Then, with real amusement, poking a finger at her shoulder, "Mommmmm . . . are you, like, seriously hungover? Were you out drinking last night?"

Little pokes jabbing her armpits, her belly, her neck. She could kill him, but, of course, this is her fault. She sits up.

"What do you want?" she asks, suddenly remembering the gallon jug of water that she cached under one of the bunks. She leans over to fill a large tin camp cup and begins slugging back water as if she's just returned from an epic jog.

"I was looking for you last night," he says.

"Why's that?"

"Needed money for the canteen," he explains easily, this sixteen-year-old who is looking more and more like a young man.

"You don't have any money?" she asks.

"It's just that, if you're the one dragging me to camp, I figure you can finance it, too," he says. "By the way, flag is in ten minutes."

He bounds out of the cabin, and the screen door slamming might as well be an atomic bomb for the throbbing pain reverberating through her temples, her poor skull. She groans, then collects herself and begins to dress for the day. She'll have to shower later. No need to impress anyone here, anyway.

NO LONGER IS reveille played by an actual bugler, some boy who plays trumpet in his high school marching band. A number of years ago the camp could not find a bugler, and Nelson simply erected a series of sirens throughout the camp that double as an emergency alert system, and so it is that while Rachel walks briskly down the forest path to the parade ground, she is suddenly greeted with the triumphant recorded sound of an early morning bugle, echoing through the glades of maples, armies of oak.

She stops in her place, closes her eyes, relaxes her breathing. *It is good to be here*, she thinks. *Good to be here with my son. To see Nelson, too.* Unexpectedly, she drops into a down dog, feels chips of bark, tiny stones, and dirt on the palms of her hands, brushing her kneecaps. There, alone in the forest, as Nelson prattles through the morning announcements, his voice warbling and far off, she practices five minutes of yoga. When he calls the boys to breakfast, she feels renewed, and imagines for a second that she is at some expensive retreat where wealthy alcoholics, sex addicts, and pill poppers pay a couple thousand a day to dry out and what not.

"Namaste," she whispers to the forest.

IT WOULD BE IMPOSSIBLE TO REMAIN A CYNIC, she thinks, eating breakfast with these boys every morning in this mess hall. She is thoughtful, totally at ease, and there is something deeply comforting in simply standing outside the cafeteria, listening to the laughter and boy conversation within. No phones bleating, no text alerts, just chatter, rising in volume occasionally, but mainly a cheerful cacophony. She enters the mess hall, sits down beside the fathers of her boy's troop.

"Good morning," she says, swinging one leg over the bench seat, and then the other.

"Coffee?" one of the fathers asks, and she nods, gratefully, as they pass a mug in her direction. There isn't much discussion among the men, and she has the sense that perhaps they've been talking about her, is slightly embarrassed to realize, *Of course they've been talking about me.*

One of them leans down the table and says, "Excuse me, Miss Quick. This is probably rude, but I wondered where your husband served. In the Marines, was it?"

She blows on her coffee, nods thoughtfully. It's a common enough question, even posed in this manner, not exactly rude, if perhaps a bit forward. "The SEALs," she explains. "He did two tours in Afghanistan, but he was involved in other specific missions in other countries. I'll be honest, I didn't ask a lot of questions because he couldn't tell me, even if he wanted to." She smiles grimly at the questioner. "Of course I was curious, but . . . I was also just happy to have him home."

"Top-secret stuff, uh?" the man says.

"Yes." She presses a finger against her wedding band, pushes it around the flesh of her finger. "He was elite."

The table is quiet again. She is passed a tray of pancakes, then a dish of margarine, some Aunt Jemima syrup. She hates this fake stuff—*corn syrup, more like diabetes in a bottle.* She sighs. Between the men at her table and the two dry pancakes on her plate, she allows herself to dream of a weekend campout with Thomas in Michigan's Upper Peninsula, maybe the Porcupine Mountains. She imagines them waking up, grilling flapjacks on an old iron skillet; apple butter and *real* maple syrup, blueberries and bacon. Coffee strong enough to eat the enamel right off her teeth. Thick flannel shirts and the sound of the nearest public radio station emanating from the radio of the Cherokee. Or is this just the fantasy time she dreams of with the husband she lost? She has to take care not to commingle her responsibilities for Thomas with her unfulfilled desires for his father. It is not the boy's fault she was widowed.

"Well, look," says the good doctor Platz, scratching at the scarred wood of the table, "the guys and I were talking a bit last night, and we want to just reiterate that, you know, *we* can keep an eye on Thomas, if you'd like, you know—if you'd feel more comfortable heading back home. Relax, you know, or get some chores done." He motions around the table. "The troop's got plenty of chaperones this year, so, he'll be well watched."

"I'm sorry, I don't think I understand," she says, setting her knife and fork down.

"It's just that," the doctor continues, "well, we're all sort of in agreement that this is sort of a sacred time for us, between father and son. It's the only place a lot of us have to get away from everything, you know? To be *alone*."

"Get away?" she asks.

The doctor pushes his glasses up his nose, smiles condescendingly. "That's right. It's an escape."

"From what, exactly? Who?" She wants to call him out, ask, *Do you mean women?*

He pushes back from the table, crosses his arms, "All right, we realize that perhaps you've taken vacation time of your own, which is why we're all happy to pitch in and rent you a cabin at Roger's Island. I've got friends over there, you know. Very exclusive resort, but we could manage it. Probably be real nice for you there. Quiet. They pamper you, too. Great food." He laughs, motions to his plate. "Not *this* garbage." The other men at the table give nervous laughs behind hands covering cowardly poker faces.

The only thing she can think to say is, "Wow."

The doctor gives a hearty laugh. "Well, we knew this probably wasn't your first choice, to be here. I mean, what woman wants to come to a Boy Scout camp for a week, sleep in some dingy little cabin, and hang out with a bunch of stinky teenage kids, right?" He reaches for her shoulder, gives it a series of squeezes. "It's the least we can do."

She shrugs his hand away. "You're kidding me, right?"

He shakes his head. "I'm afraid I don't understand."

"You actually want me to go? This isn't just, some kind of bad joke?"

He stutters out a laugh somewhere between nervous and cocky. "Well, it's not that we necessarily want you to *go*; it's that, well, we thought you might be more comfortable somewhere else. Relaxing and what have you. Roger's Island has a massage therapist on-staff. Probably a nail technician, too. Like I said, happy to cover the cost."

"Oh, how *very* kind of you. You do know that I'm a *field biologist* for the DNR? So, I might actually enjoy spending time in the outdoors."

She stands from the table without having taken as much as a bite from the pancakes.

"Excuse me," she says, "I think maybe I'll go for a little swim. Work out some of this anger I'm presently feeling."

"So, should we make a reservation for you?" the doctor says, quite satisfied with the negotiation.

She lays a hand very softly on his shoulder, leans in close to his ear. "You're too sweet, really," she says. "But I think I'll stay right here, thank you so much."

She leaves the mess hall furious, speed-walking and in desperate need of a door to slam—slam hard enough to punish the hinges.

Ten years—*ten years* she's been coming to Camp Whiteside, and it feels like longer, frankly, given all she'd heard about the camp from Trevor dating back to their late teens, long before they were even married, to say nothing of his old photo albums, Scout paraphernalia, and all the mementoes and equipment stretching back into her father-in-law's childhood. She's come here in every season. Slept in a tent in subzero temperatures when their troop's campfire melted down some two feet through ice and snow, creating its own wintry crater. Walked the forest floors in spring when trilliums blanket the recently thawed ground with their white blossoms; hunted fiddleheads and morel mushrooms. And in autumn, staying up late to watch the aurora borealis, or collecting fallen leaves with Thomas, assembling a string of yellow or orange like the photographs of Andy Goldsworthy's work she saw once in a coffee table book.

"Assholes," she says aloud. And it feels good, to call them that. What they so clearly are.

The day is already warming, the haze over the forest's canopy beginning to burn off. She decides to take a swim while the rest of the camp is still eating their breakfast. This, too, is one of the pleasures of this camp, her time here: swimming in a freshwater lake without fear of motor boats or jet-skis, drunken pontoonists or waterskiers slaloming behind some speedboat.

Inside her cabin she changes into a navy-blue one-piece suit, which always has the effect of making her feel like a "mom." Even her mother and her mother-in-law, Sarah, still wear bikinis, both of them crowing that they are "in better shape now than I was at forty-five." Or, "Who am I trying to impress?"

Her telephone vibrates where she set it down on one of the unused mattresses.

I feel like a parent . . .

She smiles.

Why is that?

Because I never see you. I'm the one checking in on you! No breakfast? Where are you?

Going for a swim. Wanna join me?

She stands in the cabin while minutes tick by. Finally the phone vibrates again.

Ha. You made a funny.

She stretches on the reedy shores of Bass Lake, bends to touch the pebbles between her toes, reaches up into the blue sky to caress the clouds. She breathes deeply, wades slowly into the cool, cool water, and finally plunges forward.

After holding her breath for half a minute as she pushes herself surely through the water, so much cooler even a couple of inches below the surface, she rises, perhaps twenty yards away from shore. Treading water, she wipes at her eyes. The tremulous mist clings to the shoreline. She hears the rising sound of boy noise, laughter. Diving down again, she swims in the direction of a tiny island, five hundred yards out into the lake.

What relief she feels, standing up, some ten yards off the island, and wading ashore, her feet now and then slipping on algae-slimed rocks, on sunken logs smooth as soapstone. Finally, she sets herself down on a large flat granite slab, wringing her hair of water. The sun is well above the forest canopy now, the morning fog burnt away, and far off, she can see boys running through the forest.

She'll never marry again. Why would she? And it isn't that she even desires another husband, or even, for that matter, a man, a lover. Men bore her, frankly. If only it weren't so lonely, fighting the single-parent fight. Wouldn't it be nice, she thinks, to simply have someone to confide in? Who had dinner ready when she came home from work? To occasionally help discipline Thomas, so she isn't the sole villain, the dreaded Voice of Authority. To help pay bills, carry the garbage out, remove a dead mouse from the basement. Someone to call on the phone and say, *Can you believe these assholes? It's the twenty-first century! Of course a woman can come to Boy Scout camp!*

There is a man at work and they've gone on three dates. Spencer. He's ten years younger than she is. He's also a field biologist, and twenty years ago she would have found him irresistible: six foot three, narrow at the hip, longish wavy black hair, perennially sunburnt (except around the eyes, where his temple-hugging sunglasses keep the skin always paper-white). His feet are flipper-long and he wears Chacos in the office; his cologne seems a mixture of insect repellent and pine sap.

On their first date they canoed the Chippewa River, beginning their journey in downtown Eau Claire, where the Chippewa and Eau Claire converge near the new Farmer's Market building and the Haymarket Landing. He portaged the canoe single-handedly a short distance from a nearby parking lot, his shoulder and bicep muscles bulging, which might have been the idea all along—displaying the goods, so to speak.

"I can help you carry that, you know," she offered.

"And I'd let you," he said, "but someone's got to carry the picnic basket and cooler."

She laughed. "If you think I packed a picnic basket, you're going to be totally disappointed. I'm really not that kind of woman." It was eight in the morning on a Saturday and downtown was bustling with shoppers milling about the market. Rachel had barely woken up in time to meet him. She prized her Saturday mornings, savored them, usually lingering in her bed until ten or ten thirty, then rising to make coffee and listen to public radio. Thomas rarely woke before noon.

Spencer smiled. "Got it covered."

"Oh," she breathed.

So they paddled the morning away, the conversation easy. It was nice, talking to Spencer. About work, Thomas, her old farmhouse and its myriad maintenance issues.

"I'm not a carpenter," he said from the stern, "but if you need some help, my dad and I could maybe come out. He's pretty handy with a hammer."

She turned around. "Should I be dating your dad, then?"

He smiled. "I dunno . . . You *are* quite a bit older than I am . . ."

She splashed him with her paddle; a good one, water drenching his face and shirt.

"Is this some kind of ploy to get my shirt off?" he asked.

She turned back around, denying him her grin, the obvious flush on her face from their flirtation. "No, I'm still thinking about your dad and that hammer of his."

But in truth, she was frankly more attracted to the kind of man who was handy, practical, and no-nonsense. Much more so than she was to the sort of guy who spent any amount of time grooming his body hair or what not, sculpting his six-pack. At thirty-nine, Rachel's primary interest in men seemed to align with their interests in camping, NPR, books, the ability to make a strong pot of coffee, the willingness to keep quiet, and a genuine concern for Thomas's welfare. She glanced at her watch, deciding she'd test Spencer's aptitude for silence.

The river flowed on.

Under the Water Street Bridge, and then University of Wisconsin–Eau Claire's pedestrian bridge, beside Water Street's shopping and bar district, under the Clairemont Bridge, past Shawtown, under the Highway 94 bridge where swallows dive-bombed them and traffic screamed overhead . . . Finally, they were away from the city. So far, her canoeing partner had been silent for almost a half hour.

"*Lycaeides melissa samuelis,*" Spencer said at last. "I think." He pointed his paddle toward a break in the shore's forest, what seemed to be a patch of remnant prairie perhaps.

Their canoe had drifted close to shore, but she squinted into the vegetation.

"If memory serves," she began, "that's Latin for, *you're fucking with me.*"

He laughed, "No. I was pretty sure I saw it, a Karner blue butterfly, up there on top of that escarpment. Just a flash of blue." He pointed again with his paddle. "Wait—there!"

She couldn't see anything. Another sign of her age. A month prior she'd had her eyes checked and her prescription updated. There had even been a trip to Walmart for a pair of reading glasses, which seemed to cement in her mind the notion of mortality as an actual reality.

"I don't see it," she admitted. "The sun's too bright."

"Or your eyes are too old," he joked, splashing her with a polite volume of river water.

She made a show of exhaling. "All right, the age jokes? Getting a little stale. We're on a date, remember?"

"Sorry," he allowed, paddling quietly.

"It's okay. The sad thing is, it's true. Ughhh . . . With birds, I find it doesn't much matter. I can still get by because of a college ornithology class. Their songs. But something like a butterfly . . ."

"For what it's worth," he said softly, "you look great."

She turned. "Thanks."

She allowed herself to enjoy this a moment. It felt good. Then, a minute or so later, "I didn't think we had many of those butterflies left."

"I know," he agreed. "I'll be honest with you, I'm sorta freaking out back here about it. Mind if we stopped for a second? I'd like to try and photograph that sucker if we can find it."

"Let's do it," she said, paddling forward.

THEY SCRAMBLED UP a steep talus slope, Spencer first, offering her a hand when he reached the top. Just a simple gesture, but the kind of thing Trevor would have done. Nothing patronizing, nothing sexist—just a slightly outdated politeness, and the general regard it might suggest.

"You have a camera?" she asked Spencer.

He held up his phone, said, "Boy, you *are* old."

She shook her head.

They wandered the grasses and shrubs looking for the bright-winged insect.

"There can't be too many of those butterflies left," Rachel said, offhandedly, letting bee balm and milkweed tickle her palms.

"Probably not," Spencer admitted, shrugging his shoulders. "But it sure would be cool if we had a lot more."

"You think anything will be left?" she asks. "In say, a hundred years or so?"

"Oh, I don't know. Of course there will be something left. The question is, what? If you're asking me about lions and orangutans and Karner blue butterflies, my answer's probably no. But I don't think we have to worry about crows, say, or deer or coyotes."

"Can you imagine?" she continued. "Growing up as a kid in a world without elephants? Or whales? Even monarch butterflies?"

They'd reached the edge of the pasture, where an ancient knee-high stone wall separated them from a sea of gently undulating corn. The leaves made a most pleasant sound in the wind; so stiff and glossy, those elongated olive-green leaves.

"When I was sixteen," Spencer said, peering out at the corn, "my parents took us on a trip to Alaska. I'd always hated family trips before then. Just the usual classic teenage sulking around. All I ever wanted to do was watch TV, play video games. But my dad and I went fishing one day, and I'll never forget, this sow grizzly and her two cubs came down to the river, and at first, I was terrified. I've never been so scared. But my dad settled me down. This was during the salmon run, and the bears were pretty content, fairly docile. So we reeled in our lines and just sat there, by the river, watching them fish and play. And, I think . . ." His voice trailed off.

"What?" Rachel prodded.

"It's just that . . . I know this sounds mushy, but, for me at least it's true. It was the first time I ever remember feeling *alive*. Exhilarated, you know."

"And that's why you became a biologist?"

He nodded, turned to look at her. "And to get chicks."

She snorted with laughter. "Right, chicks."

"I tell you what," he said, stretching his arms up to the sky. "Corn might be the epidemic that kills us, but I've always loved staring at a big field of it, perfectly planted."

"Better than soybeans, I guess," she agreed, though without much excitement.

"You get a nice field of corn planted on a rolling landscape, it's like a topographic map."

"'Course, it's also the reason we're searching for one butterfly," she says, "rather than seeing, you know, hundreds of them," she says.

"No doubt, no doubt," he conceded. "Corn is king."

THEY WALKED BACK toward the river, and standing on top of the shore's slope, he noticed a small blue butterfly on one of the canoe's gunwales. They did not say a word, but slowly sat down, feet dangling over the lip of the scarp, to watch the creature's wings fold up and then out, as it rested.

She whispered in his ear, "Aren't you going to take a picture?"

He turned his head, and the short, dark whiskers of his chin brushed her exposed, sun-browned shoulder. "I thought maybe I'd kiss you instead."

She looked down at the light dappling off the river. At the symmetry of the canoe. At the butterfly. Shook her head no.

"Not yet," she whispered.

Moments passed before Spencer reached slowly into his pocket for his phone, and in doing so, disturbed a small stone, which rolled down the bank, plinking off the fiberglass of the canoe and sending the butterfly wobbling away across the water.

"Shit," he said. "I'm sorry." He waved his hands in the air now, quite like the escaping butterfly. "I'm such a—just—sorry about that. Sorry about, I don't know, everything."

"Don't be," she replied, already climbing down the scree. "Let's keep going."

FARTHER DOWN THE RIVER he spoke up again. "I don't know how to ask this."

She knew what was coming. One of two things. "It's okay," she told him. "I don't mind."

"You don't even know what I'm going to ask." He laughed.

She squinted into the sun, sweat trickling down her backbone, off her forehead. "I bet I do."

He was quiet again for a moment. "Yes," he said, "I suppose you do. Still, I'm curious. You've been married before?"

She rested her paddle across her knees, turned back to him. "I've been married three times, actually," she said. "My first husband died when he was twenty-four. The second two husbands were . . . well, complete mistakes. Let's put it that way. One of them had a gambling problem. Thought he was clairvoyant or something when it came to betting on college basketball. Took all our money and moved to Phoenix. The third one was just a drunk. A bad drunk, too. Liked to throw things so he could really hear 'em smash. Punched drywall and doors. That kind of thing. One day after the Packers lost a playoff game, I watched him take all my coffee mugs and walk outside with a baseball bat. Then he just tossed them into the air and swung at them like they were balls. I locked the door and called the police before he could get to my grandma's china."

"How did your first husband die?"

She sighed deeply. "He was on leave, back home in Eau Claire. A younger boy, one of his old neighbors, was excited that Trevor was back in town and they went out to the movies. The kid was in Trevor's Boy Scout troop. This is back in 2003.

"It was one of the Matrix movies. A Friday. The theater was packed, and at first a little rowdy. I think people were geared up to see something revolutionary, something incendiary, you know? This was during the Bush years, you know? Everyone was angry, right and left.

"Apparently there was a drunk guy sitting in the row behind them, catcalling the movie, making a big scene. He was drunk, pretended like he was shooting the screen, made his hands into pistols and was all *boomboomboomboom*. A lot of people were scared, but they didn't know what to do. This drunk, he was a big man, almost six foot six, I guess, long scraggly hair. Everybody in the theater just froze. Nobody did a goddamn thing. Finally Trevor had enough, warned the guy, and then went to complain to security. The theater manager and a cop came and got the guy and escorted him out. After the film was done, people actually applauded Trevor. The neighbor kid told me that he was mobbed by folks trying to shake his hand.

"Anyway, they get out of the theater and they're almost at the car when this crazy man, he uh . . ."

She covered her mouth, closed her eyes, breathed deeply.

"Um, the guy shot Trevor in the head. Killed him. In front of this kid. I mean, right there. One shot." She motioned to the back of her head, then blossomed her fingers out to imitate the subsequent explosion. "Dead."

"Look, Rachel . . . ," Spencer began, "I'm—I'm so sorry. I didn't . . . I didn't mean to . . ."

Neither of them paddled. Spencer leaned forward, placed a warm hand on her shoulder.

"The thing is," she said, pulling away from his light, sincere touch, "Trevor was just like that. He was a hero, in the truest sense of the word. And I hate that word, I fucking *hate* it. But . . . he was. He really was. I don't know how else to say it. He was righteous. He had a sense of duty, of what was right and wrong in the world, and I don't mean that in some evangelical sense of the word. And I don't mean that his world was just black and white. He just had a code, you know? He used to talk about that, about how few people had *codes* anymore. It was his thing. He was always reading books about the samurai, about Japanese culture."

The river conveyed them south and west, all the time toward the Mississippi, that great American jugular coursing all the way south to the Gulf of Mexico.

"He sounds like an amazing man," Spencer said.

"He was."

"I'd like to see a photo of him sometime."

"He looked like a bear, by the end. Had a huge beard." She laughed, motioning to her own face. "That was the other thing about the day he was killed. He'd just shaved his beard off. I remember that, going into the bathroom that morning where he'd left all his whiskers in the sink, like this crazy bird's nest.

"Can you imagine? He served all that time in the most dangerous places on the planet, fighting terrorists, parachuting into war zones, climbing mountains, carrying his buddies on his back for miles at a time. And he gets killed in a parking lot of a movie theater in Eau Claire fucking Wisconsin. Some drunk asshole who'd lost a softball game earlier in the day. Kills my beautiful husband."

Just then the canoe slid to a stop against a sandbar and they simply rested there, beneath the white banking light of the midday sun. She stared at the shallow shore, the tiny tracks of water birds, reeds bent with the wind.

"And you were pregnant at the time?" Spencer asked.

She nodded.

"Jesus, I'm sorry," he said. "I'm so sorry."

She placed her hands on the gunwales, looked up at the passing clouds, some jetliner soaring away from Wisconsin.

"I don't mean to be a bitch," she said. "Actually, you know, I'm *not* a bitch, and I know that. But when you wanted to kiss me, you have to understand: Trevor is my gold standard. He just is. Maybe that's why my other marriages didn't work out. Who knows? Maybe that's why I'm single. So the question, really, I guess is: do you want to date a woman who's as haunted as I am, by this bright and shining ghost—you know—this unattainable ideal? Because most of the time, I honestly don't even know why I'm out on a date; I actually forget. Forget what I'm even doing, what I'm looking for. Does that make any sense at all to you?"

He lifted one leg out of the canoe, then the other, stood ankle deep in the river. "Maybe," he said, "the best thing I can offer you, then, is my friendship. So let me apologize for that—you know, for trying to kiss you. I'm sorry about that." His shoulders slumped, and standing beside the canoe he looked like a voyageur after a day's paddle with a very long portage ahead.

Rachel climbed out of the canoe, pulled the boat out of the water, up onto the shore. She stretched, said, "Don't apologize, Spencer. No doubt it was just due to your raging teenage hormones."

"Hey," he said, brightening a bit, "I'll be thirty in like, four months."

She patted his chest, let her hand linger awhile on his left pec; it bulged impressively, perhaps from the morning's paddling. "I'm going to find us a patch of shade. Whad'ya say you grab our picnic basket. I'm hoping there's some chilled rosé in there."

He blanched, shoulders slumped again. "Four bottles of Leinie's okay?"

"Rookie mistake," she lied, eminently impressed he'd packed a picnic basket in the first place. She kissed him lightly on the cheek.

WHEN SHE WADES BACK INTO THE LAKE, a loon is drifting off the shore—one of her favorite birds. It seems to watch her before diving down into the water and disappearing; she does not see it resurface. The lake is calm and she swims lazily back to camp, occasionally rolling onto her back to feel the sunlight on her closed eyelids. About thirty feet from shore, she stops swimming, lets her feet touch the bottom, silty and soft. Standing up, she pulls her hair back, adjusts the straps of her suit, and rubbing the water from her eyes, looks ahead.

Dr. Platz stands onshore, one hand raised in greeting. He is nonchalantly smoking a cigarette, like a rather bored coach assessing a particularly lackluster swim meet.

"Hello again," he calls out boldly, his eyes never leaving her body.

Suddenly aware of the tightness of her nipples, she covers her chest with her arms, thinks momentarily about simply staying in the water, or swimming to some other part of the lake, but really, how childish, to run from this little man. And yet, what is he doing there? It doesn't feel right.

Her towel is draped over a shrub, and he rather daintily picks it up, steps forward, and hands it to her. She quickly wraps it around her shoulders like a cape, moves past him, and stops near the trail, regretting her decision not to bring along a change of clothing, a can of Mace, some bear spray. *What a creep.*

"How was the water?" he asks, dropping his cigarette and rubbing it into the moist shore soil. "Still a little cold?"

"Nope," she says, "water's fine." Then, before she turns to go, "What are you doing down here?"

He shrugs. "Saw something swimming and couldn't figure out what it was. Came down for a closer look." His eyes seem to search her body. "Look who it turned out to be, huh?"

Peeping Tom, she thinks, and begins to walk away, back toward Arrowhead. She doesn't like this man one bit, and his strange presence here, on this abandoned shore, it unnerves her. She wants very desperately to be near her son, other campers, Nelson—anyone. If he *was* peeping—and she's pretty sure that is the case—there is nothing in his body language to suggest he feels any shame about it.

"Maybe I was wrong," he says. "I don't know. Maybe you're on to something here. Maybe men and women going to camp together— maybe it's kind of a perfect idea." He smirks, moves closer to her, a slither almost.

Slowly she backpedals her way up the trail; it takes a good deal of self-control simply not to run away from him, but they are, after all, adults, and he has yet to do anything really wrong. Just the kind of garden-variety male come-on a woman endures all the time until, of course, her body ages into simple invisibility.

"Aren't you married?" she asks, trying to be a good sport about it, despite the repulsion she feels.

"Well, here we are. Alone, beside a lake, in this beautiful forest. You've got no husband . . . My wife would never have to know." He smiles, singing under his breath, "Summer lovin', happened so fast . . ."

"Remember yourself," she says, in a tone not nearly fierce enough, a volume much too muted. She backs up, feeling so vulnerable now, without so much as a telephone, a pocketknife, a goddamned whistle.

"You're so beautiful," he says, coming toward her, almost close enough now to seize her wrist, his light green eyes focused on her. "I didn't see it at first, but you really *are*. You've got an amazing body."

"Fuck off," she seethes.

"Come on, I'm just complimenting you. Seriously, though . . . Wow. I mean, what do you *expect* me to say, after seeing you in a swimsuit?"

"I expect you to be an adult, to treat me like every other parent here."

"Ah, but you're not like every other parent here. That's the thing. And I *am* treating you like an adult."

"I'll tell Nelson," she says finally, firmly. "Take one step closer and I'll fucking get you booted right outta here. You hear me?"

This seems to startle Platz, as if he were spellbound before. He holds up both hands. "All right," he purrs, "let's just chill out, huh? Let's just . . . calm down. Why don't you just take this as a compliment or something? All right, I admit it, I think you're really sexy. I'm guilty. But I mean, I haven't *done* anything, right—what did I do? I haven't even touched you. Have I touched you?"

"You're a fucking pig," she spits. "Your poor wife."

Hands still casually raised in a way that lets him win even as he loses, he shrugs. "I'm just a guy," he says. As if that were pardon enough.

She wheels and quickly moves toward her cabin, suddenly atremble, and very close to nausea.

39

INSIDE HER CABIN SHE DROPS THE CANVAS PANELS
before peeling off her swimsuit, painfully aware of her nakedness. She
suddenly thinks to lock the door, too, for good measure. *What should
she do? Leave? Go to Nelson? With what? News that Platz is a pervert? Is she
in true danger? Doubtful.*

She startles when the door shudders loudly with an insistent knock,
the flimsy hook-and-eye lock bouncing under the stress, and then
Thomas's voice—bless him—"Mom? You in there?"

"Hold on, a minute," she says, her voice quavering, hands aflutter.
She dresses quickly, unlocks the door.

"Jesus," Thomas says. "I've been trying to text you, like, all morning. I mean, I haven't seen you in two *days*."

She sits down on a cot, covers her face with her hands, tries to stabi-
lize the world, to focus her breathing. She reaches for her phone, then
covers her face again. Her hands feel like hummingbirds, vibrating with
adrenaline, desperate to fly away.

"Mom, are you okay?"

She nods vigorously, but she isn't. She isn't okay.

Thomas takes a step toward her, as if a part of him would like to sit down beside her, perhaps wrap an arm around her—but he doesn't, just stands in the doorway, hugging his own shoulders, looking so concerned. *He is just a teenage boy*, she thinks. *These aren't his problems to solve, or even things he needs to be aware of.*

She breathes deeply, claps her hands and looks up at him.

"Sorry about that," she says happily enough. "Weird morning, that's all."

He hesitates, fingering the door's eye hook. "Are you sure?"

"Absolutely. I'm fine, Thomas." Brightly, there, yes, that's right. "So. What's up?"

"Ummm, I was headed to Shotgun merit badge and wondered if you'd want to come watch." He is still staring at her with genuine concern. "Mom? You sure you're okay?"

She shakes her head, trying to recenter herself. "Yes, I'm just, I'm sorry. I think my blood sugar's low or something. Shouldn't have skipped breakfast this morning. Anyhow, yes, I'll come with you, thanks for asking." She nods with further newfound excitement. *Give me something to do . . . Someone other than Platz to worry about . . .*

"We kind of have to get hiking, though, Mom—like, pretty much pronto."

"All right," she sighs. "Lemme get a bag."

She collects her phone, a book (she's rereading *East of Eden* for the third time), suntan lotion, a bottle of water, a baseball cap, and a bag of gorp—*good old raisins and peanuts.*

SO SELDOM does she take walks with her son, that at first she is shocked he's chosen not to run along ahead, or lower his face to ogle his phone or wristwatch or some other gadget. Or even maintain a safe ten-pace buffer zone off to her right or left on the margin of the trail. No, here he is, loping right alongside her, long arms swinging cheerfully enough. His uniform is a fright, all rumpled and stained, and he insists on wearing Chuck Taylors rather than boots or even sandals. His hair is greasy and floppy and his skin shines with enough oil to polish a saddle.

"Mom?" he asks.

She looks at him.

"Uh, do you think I have to come to camp next year? I mean, like, if I work hard all year and get my Eagle done, or really close to done, it wouldn't like, make sense to come back, would it?"

She smiles grimly.

Her job as a parent is in some ways winding down, though she knows that she'll always be his mother, this lanky teenager striding beside her, bobbing his head to some unknowable beat, some inner music utterly foreign to her. She peers over at him, wonders what secret mysteries might reside in his heart and brain. What girls he's surreptitiously in love with. What drugs he's experimenting with. What books he might be discovering. What music. What colleges he's researching.

This human being she has parented largely alone—this organism— once so small he weighed less than a large watermelon. And how she carried him everywhere in those early years: to the grocery store, on hikes, around airports, to the farmer's market, the library. He went everywhere, wrapped to her chest, his eyes staring up at her, or out at the world. How they were companions. Closer than spouses, closer than lovers, or friends. This little boy, falling asleep at her breast, petting her face, his fragile little fingers near her lips, her ears, clutching her hair. Her whole life, this boy.

"Thomas," she says.

He looks over at her. "What?"

"I'm proud of you."

"Mom . . ."

"No, I'm serious. I mean, you can be a total asshole, of course, and are there plenty of times you disappoint me, yes. Frequently. But . . . I'm just really very proud of you." *You are the only thing I have in this world,* she wants to say.

"So . . . What about camp, though? Do I have to come next year?"

The answer comes to her lips more easily than she might have thought. "No," she says, "you don't have to come back here. Not if you don't want to."

The only people in the world who might notice his absence are Nelson and her, possibly Jonathan, who occasionally asks about Thomas's progress toward Eagle. The world, it seems, does not much care anymore if you are an Eagle Scout, or even a Tenderfoot. It's all about how many "followers" you have, the perfection of your spray-tanned abs; whether you had the genius to sell a start-up company that hasn't produced a single viable product.

Maybe she won't miss it, either, with Nelson retiring and goons like Platz lurking around. No, she'd be better off at home, she knows, tending to her garden or chipping paint off the house, maybe getting it ready to be put on the market. It is, after all, a house meant for a family, not a soon-to-be empty-nester.

"Mom?" Thomas asks.

"Yes?"

"Look, I know this is sort of weird and everything, but would it be okay if you didn't go to Scoutmaster Doughty's cabin anymore? Some of the guys were talking about it and . . . I know you're just friends, but still . . ."

She stops on the trail, confounded by these boys, their fathers. "Thomas," she says, "Mr. Doughty is seventy years old. Do you really think I'm interested in him *romantically*?"

The kid shrugs. "Someone said you left his cabin at like, five in the morning. That's, like, Walk-of-Shame type stuff, Mom."

She's not about to argue the correct sequence of time or the legitimacy of her visit. Easier just to acquiesce, agree to his demands, which she is about to do, when she remembers that this is also *her* vacation, her time, her camp. She cares about this place, too. She cares about Nelson, and this might be her final year coming here. No—she won't be treated as some kind of pariah simply because she's a woman. How would that make it easier for the moms, aunts, and grandmothers who may come after her?

"No, Thomas. No. Look, if I want to visit Mr. Doughty, that's my business and his. We are two adults and we happen to be old friends. I know this is a difficult concept for you, because you're a teenage boy, but, believe it not, men and women *can* be friends without desiring some kind of sexual escapade." Rachel's voice has risen during this, she realizes. "I mean, Jesus."

"Sorry, Mom," Thomas mumbles, then glances up at her. "Still, wouldn't you be pretty pissed at me for coming home at like, five, after being at a girl's house?"

Hypothetically, the kid is right, of course. The difference is, Thomas didn't have any girlfriends that he *wasn't* interested in necking with, whereas she couldn't possibly imagine Nelson in a romantic light without collapsing into giggles.

"Tell you what," she says. "If I pay Mr. Doughty another visit, I'll be back at camp by midnight. That seems reasonable. Most of you boys won't even be asleep by then—still looking at your phones or pads or whatever." She does not care to think about what precisely they may be looking at on those phones or pads, blotting out the natural world.

"Fine," he says.

THE GUN RANGE is not much more than an open-air pavilion with some picnic tables, and a clearing where shooters take aim on the clay pigeons "thrown" out of a bunker carved into the rocky soil. Rachel takes her book and sits on a bench, casually listening as the counselor takes roll call. Then the class of boys begins discussing gun safety and etiquette, a shotgun laid out on the table before them, the instructor (himself not quite twenty-one years of age) pointing at the stock, the barrel, the magazine . . .

She opens her book, but remains distracted by the instruction, though the boys are paying rapt attention, not a one of them reaching for his phone, or taking pictures, and all of them silent. One reason why she and Trevor settled on a house in the country was his affection for firearms, something that stupefied Rachel at first, and in fact made her fairly uncomfortable. To see him sitting at the dining room table in winter, disassembling one of his shotguns, and cleaning the components, or walking outside with one of his assault rifles, ready to take target practice. This was not something she grew up with; her own father had never been a gun owner, had not, that she knew of, ever even been hunting.

But she never said anything to Trevor because, after all, guns were his tools. And as long as he was active duty, she wanted him to be the world's best gun expert, the sharpest shooter.

He would invite her out to the shooting range he had established on the southern part of their property, though it was a while before she ever took him up on it. The range was really just a small ridge covered in sumac and away from the road, beyond which there was nothing but fields of corn and some raggedy patches of forest, but the houses were few and far between, the traffic scant. He'd built a shooting table out of plywood and lengths of throwaway two-by-fours, onto which he set his ammunition and guns not presently in use. From the second story of their farmhouse, earplugs jammed in, she'd watch him: this bearded man five hundred yards away, breathing the cool autumn, winter, and spring air, making beer bottles shatter or blasting apart at the rotten fruit he picked up at grocery stores for free. Watermelons exploding to reveal the pink fruit inside, black seeds and chunks flying out into the white snow. Cantaloupe, honeydews, pineapples. Trevor, out there, a thermos of coffee behind him maybe and spitting his Skoal every now and then, but mostly, she knew, just gutting the brown juices.

The first pineapple he'd set perhaps fifty yards away. Then he'd walk another one twice that far, brushing its crew-cut leaves before walking back to his gun. By the time he was satisfied that a gun was properly sighted in, he would set an orange on a fence post and pace off a hundred and fifty yards. She would hold her breath, up in that drafty bedroom, the curtains occasionally fluttering beside her even with the windows tightly shut, and without fail, the orange detonated, staining the snow, sometimes sending a crow flapping up out of the crown of a nearby white pine. The very panes of glass shivered from the report.

He would practice for hours, stopping only to eat lunch in the kitchen, or to visit the bathroom, and always he would invite her to come shoot, too.

"Look," he would say, "I understand that you don't feel comfortable around guns. And, in a way, I think that's a good thing. It would be a better world, of course, if there were no guns at all."

He would lean against the kitchen counter, forearms bulging beneath a flannel shirt with the sleeves rolled up. Five separate times, he gave her this speech, she remembers. Never once breaking eye contact, never once raising the tone of his voice, or making the speech less serious than what he thought it merited.

"But that's not the way it is," he continued. "Guns are everywhere. A person should know how to use them. In case of emergency."

Sometimes she'd stare at him blankly during this speech, sometimes she'd just nod attentively as she spread butter or marmalade on a piece of toast.

"Look, Rachel. The world is not composed of good people and bad people. The world is composed of people who are hungry, and those who are not hungry. It goes back to energy, to entropy. If you are hungry for food, you will be hungry for God, too. Or politics, or some kind of love. The people who are hungry have holes in them that can't be filled. Don't get me wrong. I've seen starving people at peace with the world. I've been in villages where starving people gave me their supper. Food doesn't have anything to do with it; it's about the deeper kind of hunger, those holes.

"So, if I want you to learn how to shoot a gun, it is not because I want us to share some kind of 'hobby.' It is not because I think this is *fun*. It's because I want you to be prepared."

The first two times she heard this speech, she laughed. "The ol' Boy Scout motto," she said, giving him a light push before turning back to whatever it was she was in the middle of.

"That's right," he'd say, solemnly.

"Be prepared for what?" she asked him the first time.

"For anything."

"No, but seriously. For what?" she pressed him.

He pointed a finger at her belly, then looked her clearly in the eyes, without any expression at all, and said, "Someone possessed with hunger, with a thought, with a craving, with a perversion, someone who needs their drug, someone who comes to your door in the middle of the night—they won't have any light in their eyes. And that's how you know. That's what I look for. I don't look at their mouths. People lie with their mouths. I look at their eyes."

It was the only time in their entire relationship when she feared him, had some sense, suddenly, of what he understood about the earth, politics, war. About evil.

"Imagine I'm gone," he said to her, pulling his finger back. "What would you do? What would you do if you went to the front door and that face was staring back at you from the dark. And the only thing separating you from that darkness is a plank of wood. A little window."

"Trev," she said, nervously, "you're actually scaring me." She meant it, too. She'd spent many dozens and dozens of solitary nights, and knew of the hundreds or maybe even thousands she could expect in the future. The nights she'd woken in fear at the sound of a tree branch scratching at their shingles, a set of headlights turning around in their driveway, the sparrow banging around in their attic.

"Would you be prepared?"

"Stop it."

"Would you be prepared, Rachel, for that kind of hunger. That kind of darkness?"

Outside their kitchen window, it was a dark, gray November morning, crows black-winging over the stubbled cornfields.

She did not yet know she was pregnant. "Quit it!" she said, "Okay? Just . . . *stop* it!"

He walked to the back porch door, then just stood there a moment, looking at his boots. He was neither upset nor excited. What he had said, she could see, was something he'd spent hours, perhaps days, thinking about—and not just here, in this, their house; in their bed or out walking the gravel roads together, hand in hand; but also in the field, with or without his comrades, walking mountaintops and steep ravines, entering village after village, building after building, in search of that same darkness, that same dread hunger.

He looked at her now, and she stared back into his eyes and they might have stood that way for minutes, she could not tell. His eyes were not happy, no. But they were not full of darkness, either. Just a deep well of sadness; that is what she would think of later, long after his funeral. And that his sadness was the knowledge of this absence of light, this hunger, so at odds with his own early optimism and kindness, so foreign to the letters he once sent her, that teenage boy she'd fallen in love with so many years before.

"The world is full of bad men," he said finally, "but if you are pre-pared, and if you are *strong*, then you cannot be taken off guard, and you will not be scared. And when they *do* come to your door in the middle of the night and you are there to greet them with all the light there is inside you, all the strength, they are the ones who will run for the shadows. And I've *seen* it.

"You have to make your light into a fire," he said.

She realized she was trembling now. "I'm sorry, Trevor. I'm sorry for what you've seen. I'm sorry for what you've had to do."

"Don't apologize to me," he said, kindly. "If you want to be nice to me, just know that when I'm talking to you about this stuff, about preparation, I'm doing it because I love you more than anything. And *I know* you're tough. But I still worry. I worry about not coming back to you and—"

"Please don't say that!" she said. "Jesus, please don't say that!"

"I'm sorry."

He knelt down to tie his boot laces and she walked right past him into their mudroom. Gathered up her Wellingtons, a barn jacket, a watch cap, and then stood beside the back door, peering down at him.

"What?" he asked.

"Fine, then," she said. "Teach me how to shoot."

IT BECAME ONE of her favorite things to do, something they shared together, on Saturday or Sunday mornings, walking into that southern pasture, the topography of the land slipping away beneath them, draw-ing them gently downhill. Occasionally startling a pheasant or grouse, a cote of doves. Trevor, carrying a shotgun with his right hand, a backpack of ammunition over that same shoulder, and Rachel lugging another bag with a thermos of hot coffee and four small bacon sandwiches, per-haps a banana, too, or a bar of chocolate. It was like that, whenever he was back home; they always held hands.

"All this talk about Second Amendment rights, assault rifles, high-capacity magazines," Trevor would say, exhaling a plume of morning air, "that's all bullshit. A bunch of ignoramuses playing soldier and acting tough. A regulated militia means nothing against a drone or a missile strike, or a Special Forces unit. But I'll tell you this: there ain't any substitute for a good, old-fashioned double-barreled shotgun. The toughest bad dude in the world is going to hit the floor if you shoot him with a twelve-gauge slug. Guaranteed. "

She nodded her head, smiled at him. "When exactly did you become, you know, such a badass?"

He shrugged his shoulders, sipped at the coffee. "Probably about the time you broke my heart."

She slapped him across the butt. "You always said you were joining because of nine-eleven. Asshole."

"Well, sure. Although, when you were in Africa," he said, "and I began to understand what was happening, that maybe you weren't in love with me anymore, it was, like, I don't know—a rip in the sky or something. All the colors of the rainbow draining away. I didn't know what else to do with myself. And the doors weren't exactly flying open for me and my cum laude in English."

"I'm sorry," Rachel said, rubbing his back now, pulling him close, hugging him, feeling his chin stubble through her hair, on her scalp. The dewy morning air, a hint of woodsmoke, the spice of prairie grasses.

"It was for the best," he said. "I was probably a pretty big pussy before. Just a little boy."

"You were sweet. Always sweet to me. I miss those letters you used to write me."

"How'd you even fall back into love with me? I mean, how does a person do that?" He pushed away from her playfully. "Maybe you're an impostor. A phony. A spy. A goddamn Taliban she-mole."

"I don't know," she admitted, though there were memories of him—visiting him at Fort Bragg, in North Carolina, after driving more than eighteen hours straight, and then meeting him at a Holiday Inn, touching his face, now chiseled, his newfound physique, even those gruesome yellowish calluses of his feet, the palms of his hands. She remembers lying on that hotel bed, fucking him, feeling him come inside her, the release of years of anger and affection, loss and love, wrapping her legs around the small of his back, and hooking her feet together, closing her eyes, flexing her whole body against him.

And the next memory, breakfast the following day, rain sweeping across the parking lot as they ran into a Perkins. Tucked into a booth together, the Naugahyde benches sagging with neglect, Trevor stacking containers of jelly and jam into wobbly cairns, balancing small plastic cups of creamer into trembling towers that inevitably toppled over. They drank mug after mug of cheap, hot coffee, devoured plates of pancakes and sausages and scrambled eggs, and afterward, when the rain finally quit, they returned to the hotel room and took a nap together, the room dark and pleasantly deodorized, though also detectable, the smell of sex hanging in the close air of that little room.

Before they ate dinner that night, they made love again, and later, as she brushed her hair while perched on the edge of the bed, she asked, "Did you ever, you know, date anyone while we were broken up?"

He laughed, leaned against a wall while he brushed his teeth. "What, we're not still broken up?"

Involuntarily, she scrunched her nose. "I might want to reconcile our situation."

He nodded, continued brushing, stretched a leg. "You would."

"I might."

"But I'm a free agent now. I've got a woman in every port from here to Kabul. Why'd I want to settle down with the *one* person on this planet capable of destroying me in a way nobody else ever has? Hmm?"

She stopped brushing her hair. "First of all, I hope like hell you don't have a woman in every port from here to there because we just had sex, like, fifteen times." She laughed nervously, and then, after a moment, more serious now said, "I'm sorry. It was a mistake, okay?" She shuddered, just thinking about Willem. *Fucking asshole.* "I'm sorry, Trev. What else can I say?"

He spits into the sink, washes his face, leans against the wall again, crosses his arms, a smallish hotel towel wrapped around his narrow waist, trim hips. "Seriously, Rach. Why would I ever trust you again?"

Suddenly, she feels desperate for him. "I don't know, to be honest. Maybe it's too late. Maybe I can never make it right again." Her hands fly into the air and she flops on the bed.

"I didn't do anything wrong," he said. "I never mistreated you, never stepped out on you. Looking back, I'm sure I smothered you, and I know I could be childish about how I expressed myself. But I never would have hurt you, never."

"I know that."

"And, you really screwed me, Rachel." The cool chuckle he gave right then, shaking his head, just about broke her heart.

She nodded, wiped her nose with the back of her hand.

"And now," he said, shaking his head slowly, "I mean, I've got commitments. I can't just up and quit on the U.S. military. My brothers. And I don't want to, to be honest. I *like* what I'm doing. So if we're together, what it really means is that we're going to be apart most of the time. Right? I mean, are you okay with that? Or are you going to flake out on me again? Because I can't go out into the shit and be thinking about you with some other dude, or having a bunch of really sad phone calls and emails while I'm trying to focus on a mission. I see my friends going through that, the married guys, and it takes a toll. To be honest, I don't think it's sustainable. To be totally fucking honest, I think it may have cost one or two of them their lives."

This new reality, this new Trevor, was paradigm shattering, surreal. "Really?"

"Yes," he said, "really."

"I'd like to try," she said gently, looking straight at him. "I want to try."

"Try? That's not good enough. It has to be commitment."

"Okay. I understand."

"Why? Why now?"

"Because I love you. I've always loved you."

"You sure didn't in Africa."

"Oh, fuck Africa, okay? I made a mistake. I'm sorry. What, you never make mistakes? You're always so confident?"

He studied his feet. "No. I've made mistakes."

"Like what?"

He sighed. "I don't want to tell you."

"You have to. Otherwise, I won't believe you. You'll still be this scary archetype of goodness and morality. You'll still be untouchable."

"Okay," he said. "Sit down."

She smiled at him from the bed.

"Good," he said. "Maybe I should sit down, too. I have to remember everything." He rubbed his forehead.

40

⤤⤢

A MAN DRESSED AS AN AFGHAN POLICE OFFICER EN-
tered their barracks, which was unusual, though not out of the realm of
possibility, and it was somehow Otter, the youngest among them, the
most likely to be plugged into his Xbox or thrashing away to some hid-
eously loud metal, who intercepted him at the door, only to be blown
away, no longer identifiable even as a man, but as a hot, wet, red shrapnel of flesh, blood, and bone exploded across their bunks and faces.
For the remainder of his life, no day passed in which Trevor did not
recall with revulsion and horror that moment, the blood on his face, his
friend. Even looking in the mirror afterward became a difficulty.

The bomber, Trevor would always remember, had the exact same
look on his face as an NFL free safety preparing to tackle the bejeezus
out of an unsuspecting wide receiver, the target's rib cage stretched taut
and totally unprotected. His eyes were wide, wild, and somehow glee-
ful. Ahead, no doubt, was paradise and some absurd sum of virgins,

which the older guys in Trevor's unit always chuckled about, claiming that virgins, after all, were notoriously boring lays, not exactly the ideal partners for an eternity in heaven. The married men in the unit said Valhalla would be populated by thirty- and forty-something single mothers with all the experience in the world and plenty of lonely, exhausted nights to plan their next foray. Now *that* would be a paradise.

Because Otter met the intruder at the door, instead of allowing him into the center of the room, where most likely the entire unit would have created a monkey-pile scrum on top of the attacker, the bomb detonated just inside the doorway and was somewhat contained. Thus, there were only two deaths that day, rather than ten or twenty, or more. This is more or less the definition of the Congressional Medal of Honor, which Otter's fiancée was too nervous to accept on his behalf. Nor would his mother or father, who were far too furious at the government, at Halliburton, at the Saudis, at God, to be trusted at any such ceremony. The so-called honor was left to Otter's younger brother, a thirteen-year-old kid named Mickey, after his dad's boyhood idol, Mantle, who'd spent time during spring training fishing off the coast of Florida, his giant, blond-haired home-run-cracking forearms flexing in the hot sun.

Otter was to be married within the next month, while on home leave, to a Florida girl he talked about incessantly, a twenty-year-old knockout named Brittany. He claimed her hair smelled like tangerines and her skin of strawberries and vanilla. Said she liked to go tanning back in Tallahassee, and described her reclining in the back of his truck, resting on a mattress, a little Playboy decal just above her pelvic bone, that she'd peel off when her sunbathing was concluded. He liked to kiss her there. Said it reminded him of the sun going down over the ocean, that star kiss of light and endless azure sea; her Hawaiian Tropic–smelling skin and the triangle of her bikini bottom. That was about the extent of Otter's poetics.

Most of them had bought tickets to their wedding down in Florida a month and a half later, and so it was that they held a celebration of sorts anyway, even after he was laid to rest in a cemetery. The "reception" was held in the courtyard of Brittany's apartment complex, a slightly claustrophobic rectangle with a few rusty barbecues, a small pool heated to what must have been a hundred degrees, and one mangy palm that in the close, damp air barely rustled out a sound. Brittany wore her wedding dress, pink flip-flops, glitter sprinkled across her face, her hair all done up with about a thousand pins and two aerosol cans of hair spray holding it in place. The guys there stood around in full dress uniform drinking Bud Light from red Solo cups, big dips of Skoal pooching their lower lips, swaying listlessly in dress shoes, getting drunk quickly in the near-tropical air. Neither Brittany's family nor Otter's attended; across the board they dubbed the event "morbid, macabre, and tragic." Perhaps they were right, but then again, they weren't fighting for their lives in Afghanistan.

The "catering" consisted of Pizza Hut galore, cold beers, wine coolers, and about eight rotating bottles of Jack Daniel's. No one seemed to mind. This was less a marriage, after all, than the funeral of a brother. There was no deejay and no band. About a dozen of Brittany's closest friends and cousins were there and someone plugged an iPod into a set of overmatched speakers. Food was snatched from a folding table, buffet style. Trevor had been Otter's closest friend, at least within their unit, if for no other reason than the fact that they were the youngest. Otter forever ballyhooing Gator football while Trev rolled his eyes and tried to read a book.

Throughout the evening, Brittany hung close to Trevor, brushing against his elbows, or sweeping her hair in a manner that brushed his chin or ears. She updated him regularly on her drunkenness, whispering, "I'm so hammered. I'm so sad."

Then someone starting playing Outkast and the girls were twerking up against the men, and the men looking around for any sign of authority, wanting desperately to peel their formals off, and a few girls were jumping into the pool, and then rising up, like mermaids, their sundresses and cocktail dresses clinging to their Florida brown skin, their nipples the most beautiful thing the men had seen in months, the married men staring, their wives swatting them less and less good-naturedly, and then everyone was kissing, tongues slipping over tongues, all Bartles & Jaymes, Bud Light and lime, all Tennessee fuckin' whiskey.

At some point in all this, Brittany leaned in close to Trevor and said, "I'll be in my apartment. Door's unlocked." Then she handed him something very soft and his first thought was that it was a silk hand-kerchief. But examining his hand more closely, he registered it as her underwear, bright white, lacy, soft . . .

"Jesus," he murmured, scratching his face.

"You know," said one of the older men in their unit, Barnes, a mar-ried father of five young kids, "you only ever regret the things you didn't do. And by 'things,' I mean women." His hand on Trevor's shoulder, he leaned all his weight onto the younger man, his eyes wide open in ap-parent seriousness and exaggerated sobriety, as if talking to a cop.

"Really? That's the extent of your fatherly wisdom?" Trevor asked. "You wouldn't have any qualms about this?"

"All part of the mourning process," chimed in Chowda. "She's obvi-ously trying to forget how sad she is," he explained with unimpeachably Bostonian street smarts. "You would absolutely be doin' Otta' a huge fayva. Trust me." He smiled a wide, gap-toothed grin.

"You don't git yo' self in there, I sure as shit will," said Wiggins. "C'mon, man."

THE APARTMENT WAS DARK, lit sparingly by an array of candles, curtains drawn against the music pumping outside, muffling it only slightly. A television, an Xbox, a Tupperware container of video games, a card table likely purchased from Walmart, two chairs, a white pleather couch with a faux tiger-skin throw. A small kitchen: microwave, some cheap pans, a roll of paper towels.

He moved slowly forward through air smelling of sweet perfume and hair spray. "Brittany?" he called out.

"In here," she said, in a low, husky voice.

HE STEPPED GINGERLY into her, their bedroom. She was still in her wedding dress, the spaghetti straps pulled down over her shoulders, though, the candlelight throwing sweet, mysterious shadows on her clavicles, her throat, her breasts. Nice shadows. His breath caught. He hadn't been with a woman since before Rachel left for Botswana. Sure, there had been some innocent fumblings, some heavy petting after bar time. But those incidents always ended the same: his walking the girl home, or to a cab, or holding her hair as she puked into his toilet. But now there were two doors behind him, and he felt something in his chest snag, felt his face flush so hot, his blood surging, veins coursing with blood.

Pulling her dress up a bit, she parted her legs and he almost felt himself faint. The apartment was so hot and his uniform stifling.

He began unbuttoning, fingers growing more confident as they went. Soon he was naked before her, and standing at the foot of the bed. He realized he was covering his crotch with his hands, like there was about to be a well-struck penalty kick.

She giggled.

"You're beautiful," he said.

"Come here," she said.

"I'm nervous."

"Don't be."

"I'm sorry about—"

She slapped him, lightly, across the face. "No," she said sternly. "*No.*"

And then they kissed, his arms full of the frills, folds, and delicate fabric of her dress, never quite removing the garment. Her legs were scissored behind him, while outside, the men of his unit were now singing along to what sounded like Bon Jovi, with every so often the wet crash of someone cannonballing into the pool. *Take my hand, we'll make it I swear . . .*

41

"WOW," RACHEL SAID. "SO, YOU'VE HAD A WEDDING night already."

He stymied a laugh, rubbed his nose. "I guess. Kind of."

"Just that once?"

He shook his head. "No, we sort of dated for a few months. She's a little bit crazy, turns out."

"Turns out?"

"Yeah."

"Hmm, so you fucked your dead friend's wife; that's your mortal sin, huh?"

"They weren't married."

"Right."

"But pretty much, yes."

"That's kind of shitty."

"I know."

"So there is a chance, then, that you're *not* actually the spokesperson of cosmic decency, some Knight of the Round Table. You might be more or less human."

"I'm not proud of . . . of what I did there that night, no. After a while though, we became more than just that one thing, though. She was definitely crazy, but she was a good woman, too. I still think about her, in fact. Maybe you don't want to hear that, but it's true. When I was back on leave, we'd drive around Otter's hometown down there in Florida, this place on the panhandle called Apalachicola. His folks didn't even know that Brittany and I were, you know, together. Or hell, maybe they didn't care, really. I remember, they invited me into his bedroom, you know, his old childhood bedroom. And it turned out he was a Boy Scout, too, an Eagle Scout, actually. Otter never talked about that. He talked a lot about football, but never said shit about the Scouts.

"But then I remembered, we used to lie in our cots at night and we'd have these competitions to see who could tie the most arcane knots. The cleat hitch. The bowline. The sheepshank. The Karash. And that sonuvabitch, he knew most of 'em, too. Then it became a game to see who could tie what knot the fastest . . .

"He was the goofiest kid, you know? And I think about that. That really, he was just a kid. A fucking kid. His whole life out there. Just about to be married. And his favorite thing in the world was playing video games and talking SEC football. Doing these stupid Steve Spurrier impersonations."

He went quiet here. She waited for him to go on, but he just sighed out a long, sad breath.

"I'm sorry," Rachel murmured. She reached for his hand.

"So you asked me if I ever did anything wrong, if I ever slept with anyone else." He looked her in the eye. "The truth is, I don't regret sleeping with Brittany. I think of her as my friend. Maybe I was even in love with her. Because if I'm being honest, she was *there* for me, you know? When I needed someone. She seemed to understand what I was going through. Almost every part of it. Including losing my buddy. My fucking friend."

42

THERE ARE FIVE SHOOTING STATIONS ARRAYED BE-
fore the bunker, and behind the stations is an elevated chair where the
counselor sits, much like a judge, keeping score. Each Scout will shoot
twenty-five clay pigeons. The boys wear belts around their narrow waists
with pouches to carry both spent and live ammunition.

"Puller ready?" the counselor calls out. "Shooters ready? All right,
let's have one."

A junior counselor hidden in the bunker activates the throwing machine and a clay pigeon goes sailing out ahead of the shooters before
falling into the grasses, some fifty yards out. Now the boy on the far left
readies his shotgun against his sweaty armpit, calls, "Pull!"

A clay pigeon soars out, rising up on a current of warm summer air,
only to be very nearly vaporized by the boy's ensuing blast.

Rachel looks up from her book, realizing even with earplugs at
the ready that reading is going to be futile. So she sits in the shade
and watches them shoot. Trevor would have made an excellent coach

or counselor, she thinks to herself. He was always so patient with her, teaching her how to use a gun, his voice moving into a slightly smoother, lower register, and when he needed to move his body near hers, to demonstrate how she might track a target with her shotgun, its barrel, he never turned it into something cheesy, never pressed himself against her, childishly, and when *she* did, when she ground her hips or butt back against him, he would say, "Rachel, come on. This is serious."

So when Thomas shoots twenty of twenty-five clay pigeons and turns to grin at her because he is one of the finer shots, certainly in his troop, and perhaps in the whole camp, it is with a winsome wave and smile that she acknowledges his feat. Because with all the shooting, all the exploding clay pigeons, all the young boys, she is seized with the fear that her son will eschew college altogether and follow his father's ghost into the military, there to fight some derivation of the same enemy Trevor fought.

She peers under the picnic table. A caterpillar is slinking steadily along over the cracked cement and blotches of dried bubble gum.

Twenty years, she thinks, *and we're fighting the same people in the same countries. Twenty years.*

43

SOMETIMES POSSESSING THE KNOWLEDGE THAT A person is a potential enemy is more effective than gaining a distance away from that enemy, and that is exactly how Rachel feels about Platz. *Keep your friends close and your enemies closer.* As long as she can see him, or anticipate him, she feels basically safe. Unfortunately, this has meant abandoning her dawn swims to the island, but she has quickly replaced that time by joining both a morning and late afternoon free swim and while it's sad to see such a pristine northern lake largely ignored by hundreds of boys more intent on playing video games in cabins stinking of toe jam, junk food, and patchouli incense, she is happy to be left mostly to her own devices, save for the leering if harmless stares of the boy lifeguards behind their knockoff Ray-Bans.

She's taken to joining Nelson at meals, which is a delight. She never realized that he intentionally spent time with boys whose parents might be going through a divorce, or boys from low-income families. It was one of the counselors who told her he regularly gifted such boys with new Boy Scout handbooks; nor was it unusual for such a child to crack this new book and find within a fifty-dollar bill and some ancient baseball card, dutifully protected behind two layers of plastic.

"The baseball card thing is new," the counselor told Rachel, "but he's been giving away handbooks and money for ages, I guess. I've heard stories of him driving into Rice Lake to buy new backpacks, school supplies, clothes, even shoes."

"I guess that doesn't surprise me," Rachel said, feeling a flood of warmth in her chest.

"To be honest with you," the counselor said, "we were all a little confused about the baseball card thing. Especially at first. A lot of the kids didn't understand what they *were*. Some even threw the cards away, or into their campfires." He leaned close to Rachel. "You can't tell Scoutmaster Doughty that, though, please. It might break his heart."

"I won't," she assured him.

"But then, some kid investigated the card he'd gotten from Doughty on his computer or something. Turned out the card was worth like, a hundred and fifty bucks or maybe more. We think he's like, trying to give us an investment or something? Or maybe it's like, we're supposed to start collecting cards. Nobody is sure about it because Mr. Doughty doesn't talk about his gifts. Kids just find packages outside their cabins. Tends to happen to the boys that are really well-behaved. Or someone that's been bullied. Apparently he hates bullying."

Rachel looks at the counselor.

"Funny, isn't it?" the kid continues. "A man like Scoutmaster Doughty, a war hero. I heard he used to get bullied, too, but it's hard to imagine, isn't it?"

Rachel nods her head. "We all start out as little kids."

THREE NIGHTS IN A ROW, she has returned to the campsite after dinner, climbed into her sleeping bag, and with the light of a lantern beside her, happily read *East of Eden* while outside her little cabin, a small campfire burned and there was the sound of men laughing low and in a tight circle. And each night, just as she enters her cabin, she is careful to lock the hook-and-eye bolt on her door, so that when she finally drifts off to sleep, it is free of the fear that Platz might come creeping beside her bed while she's dreaming.

She is ready to return home now. Has been since that walk with Thomas, since perhaps her first night in camp, she realized, hearing that Nelson would be retiring. An epoch seems to be coming to a bittersweet end, and she does not care to stand on the shores of these lakes she has so loved, weeping. No, when the week is just about over, she will take a good long walk around the camp, explore every building, buy a Coca-Cola from the canteen, and when it is time to climb back into the Jeep on Saturday morning, she will be ready to say goodbye to the Whiteside Scout Reservation and return to her shambling home, the stack of bills on her kitchen table, the gutters sprouting volunteer trees, and the myriad wasps' nests beneath her wraparound porch. *Maybe*, she thinks, *Thomas and I can visit Trevor's grave. Plant some new flowers.* She never intended these trips to the cemetery as chores, but there have been times, she knows, when the moping teenager in the passenger seat thought of them as such.

So, on Friday night, after taking a shower after dinner, lying in her sleeping bag, her things all policed and packed up, Rachel is surprised when there is a knock at the door of her cabin. She hesitates for a moment in her sleeping bag, decides to stay put. "Thomas," she calls out, "that you?"

There is a sardonic laugh in the darkness outside. "Sorry to disappoint you," Platz says.

"What *is* it, Mr. Platz?" she asks sternly, setting her head back down on the pillow, her book splayed open across her chest. Takes a certain satisfaction in refusing him the honorific of "Doctor" before his last name, which she knows perfectly well drives some physicians crazy. Besides, he is not *her* doctor, a disturbing thought, indeed.

"Well, look . . ." He pauses. "Can I please come inside? I feel sort of foolish talking to you through this screen door."

"Yeah, I don't think that would be appropriate at all," she replies coolly. "I can hear you just fine. How can I help you?" She does not care in the least if her tone is icy, less than inviting. This may be her final year in Scouting anyway, and this man is no friend of hers. She is exhausted and right now wants only to return to her book.

She hears him sigh, slap at a mosquito on his neck. "I just wanted to say that I was sorry about the other day by the lake. It was incorrect of me to approach you that way, and I apologize."

She listens for more.

"Do you accept my apology?"

She thinks about that for a moment before saying, "Yes."

"Good," he says, his voice rising in volume. "In that case, some of the other dads and I are going to build up a big bonfire, we've got the makings for s'mores, and we were planning on getting these lazy goddamn teenagers out of their bunks for at least one night of ghost stories, some jokes, and maybe some old-fashioned fun."

Her phone buzzes and she reaches for it:

> You going to the campfire BS?

She sits up in her sleeping bag, aware of the flimsy, threadbare T-shirt she is wearing over one of her most tired bras.

"I think that's a wonderful idea," she says sincerely. "I'll be there in a moment."

"Great," Platz says, slapping his hands together in triumph.

> Yep, you better, too! Last year of camp, you lazoid!

F

At least, she thinks, he hasn't added the *U*. Plausible deniability. She giggles, remembering reading such a message several years back. Initially, she hadn't understood and texted back, *FU what?* And then, even more embarrassing: *University of Florida? Gainesville is a nice place! Your dad had friends who loved Florida!*

She climbs out of the sleeping bag and quickly slips out of her gym shorts and into a pair of blue jeans; then socks, a pair of boots, one of Trevor's old flannel shirts, so old and well worn it won't be too warm on a summer night like this. She is excited. Even if Platz is the world's biggest asshole, she agrees that the boys should be by the fire tonight, that this is what Scouting is all about: camaraderie and fresh air and wholesome fun.

Several of the fathers nod their heads at her, smile, and tip their baseball caps or say quietly, "Evenin'." She nods back. One of them, she can't remember his name, asks, "Coffee?"

"Sounds good," she says, "thanks." Then, "Geez, this is so nice. Why haven't I been out here all week long."

The men laugh at that, and one of them says, "You didn't miss a thing. Just a bunch of lummoxes out here farting and being juvenile."

"But the coffee's fresh!" the first man says. He wipes out a blue tin cup with his shirt. "Sorry about the cup, though. We packed most of the troop gear up already."

"No worries," she says, sipping at the coffee. Truly terrible.

"The coffee no good?" the man asks, a look on his face of what appears genuine hurt.

"No," she manages, "it's great. Put some hair on my chest."

They all get a chuckle from that one.

Now the boys are leaving their cabins, screen doors slamming behind them. A few fathers emerge from the forest, hatchets in hand, dragging yet more firewood. The big lout, Bill, is down on hands and knees by the fire pit, blowing at an infant flame just now rising from a pile of kindling and tinder. His pants have fallen down off his ass a bit, so that in the dark, his butt cheeks seem to be smiling.

"Jesus Christ, Bill," someone says. "Should have taken leather-working when you were a Scout. Made yourself a damn belt to hold that shit up."

The laughter around the fire pit is steady now, jocular. She is again reminded that this was what she so desired as a little girl—not a bunch of catty gossiping and pretending to be so afraid of salamanders or snakes, not some demeaning skill development like: *Baton Twirling, Hostess, Housekeeper (actual Brownie badges up until 1995)* . . .

Bill hikes his pants up, rises to his full height; out of breath, his face red even in the gloom, but for the first time, Rachel sees him smile. She studies his eyes and sees none of the darkness Trevor warned her of. Just a childlike spark; he's having fun.

Platz elbows Rachel gently, a flask in his hands. "Care for a little bump in your coffee?"

"No thanks," she says. "I don't need it."

"Well, I'm no salesman," he says, "but this is some pretty damn fine bourbon. Pappy van Winkle, twenty year. I shouldn't even be sharing it."

"I'm more of a Scotch drinker, myself," she says, which is, in fact, true.

"No pressure," Platz says, restoring the silver flask to his back pants pocket. She notices another flask in a separate pocket, a brass-colored one.

"You actually have two flasks?" she can't help herself from remarking. "Jesus, no wonder you guys are so gung ho on Scouting tonight. You're all loaded."

"Now, now," he says. "That's not fair. Besides, you've been holed up in your cabin for the past three nights. It's not exactly like you're being the world's best chaperone or role model. Least we've been out here, keeping the fire burning."

The fire has caught by now, and there is a pile of wood growing beyond the camp chairs and benches to keep it going. One of the fathers sits on a tree stump, a guitar strapped over his shoulder and a harmonica hanging around his neck. He strums out some practice notes and she can hear the kids chattering with embarrassment and derision. Then he breaks into a fairly impressive cover of "All Apologies," and the kids quiet, which surprises her, because it seems as if they recognize the song, one of her own favorites, though she was totally oblivious to Nirvana back in the day, only discovering them while Trevor was deployed, when she was culling through his CD collection.

"Come on," said Platz, again at her elbow. "This might just be the best bourbon a person can get. Once the Chinese and Japanese developed the palates and pocketbooks to begin collecting bourbon, this shit disappeared. It's something like two hundred and fifty bucks a bottle. But it seems fitting, right? As an apology. I really am sincerely sorry."

She looks up at him. There is an impishness about his face: the thick red hair, fair Irish-American skin, fashionable glasses. Under different circumstances she might have mistaken him for being attractive, in an intellectual sort of way.

"So if I cave in here, and accept your bourbon and apologies, you'll stop talking to me?" she asks, turning her rude into charming.

He bobs his head as if considering her question, like some unrequited suitor at a bar. "Deal," he says finally. "Accept my bourbon and I'm gone."

"Deal, then," she says.

He removes the silver flask from the seat of his pants with a secretive flourish and she watches as two long glugs pour into her coffee mug.

"I tasted that coffee," he says, leaning close to her ear. "This should, ah, vastly improve your situation. You can thank me later." He pats her on the shoulder lightly, and then, just as he'd promised, quits her side.

Toasting the darkness he's slinked off into, she raises the tin cup to her lips and sips. The coffee is indeed much enhanced and through the burnt-rope and gym socks of this wretched cowboy coffee other flavor notes rise through the discord to blossom in her belly like flowers: caramel and vanilla brown sugar sweetness.

One of the boys has thrown an entire bar of magnesium fire starter into the flames and now the circle of rocks and teepee of logs glow with a white-hot brilliance. The kids group around the fire pit, oohing and aahing for all they're worth and it is better than anything they've seem on the Web in days, utterly enthralling. She is enjoying herself. This is everything Girl Scouts failed to be during her youth. The camp, the fire, the parents behaving poorly, some cool father strumming away on his guitar . . .

"Any requests?" the guitar dad calls out.

"'In-A-Gadda-Da-Vida'!" a father says and all the old heads laugh, even though she suspects most of them have no idea who Iron Butterfly was, or is.

"'Oops! I Did It Again!'" someone shouts.

"'Call Me Maybe'?"

"'Freebird'!"

The guitar dad smiles sadly. "Fucking 'Freebird,'" he gripes.

So Rachel decides to put one out there. "How about 'Heart of Gold'?"

He nods his head appreciatively and frowns at his guitar as he tunes the strings. "We can do that." He adjusts his harmonica and blows some test notes, strums out some practices chords, takes a sip of coffee, and then begins.

She drinks her coffee and watches him play and wonders why she hasn't noticed this man before, with his tired Chaco sandals and sun-tanned, dirty toes, his blue jeans in appealingly bad repair, a flimsy cardigan over a paint-splattered gray T-shirt, and closely cropped silver-black hair that shines in the firelight like a quartz stone. Maybe there is still time for love after all, her heart allows for a moment.

For hours, it seems, he plays almost every song she or anyone else might want to hear, and when one of the smartass boys requests "The Wreck of the Edmund Fitzgerald," he knows all the words of course, and leads them in the Lightfootian dirge. She finishes her cup of coffee and when Platz swings around again, she aggressively signals for more bourbon, and he obliges and disappears again. The fire is fed and fed and the coals in the center of the ring glow like some alien element and the boys run to the cabins and back with aluminum cans and throw them at the fire, watch the flimsy metal melt in minutes. Larger and larger chunks of metal are sought, until, at last, some boy throws the coffeepot into the inferno, and they all watch, rapt, as the metal deforms, then, like wax, slumps into nothing, and drips back into the earth.

How full her heart is with happiness. She peers around the fire for Thomas, but as always with teenagers, they're never close at hand when you need them. When you desire to share your love with them. She reaches for her phone, types:

> I love you so much. Your father loves you too. He is watching us, you know, right now.

She slumps back in the camp chair she must have requisitioned at some point. Overhead, the stars are like germinating seeds budding light. The branches of the trees dendritic veins, black and beautiful. She shakes her head. *Must have been too much bourbon.* Closes her eyes, feels the earth flying through outer space beneath her, stars rushing past, the moon forever in chase, streaking meteorites, exhausted satellites . . .

Rachel holds the telephone in her hands with some effort, afraid to fumble it. The fire feels so hot, her face, her hair. The voices she hears begin to garble and meld, conversations become impossible to separate. Even the flames of the fire blur into a wash of orange. She feels ill.

She hopes her fingers aren't too clumsy, or spell-check too aggressive:

Don't feel well. Please.

Drops the phone into her lap. Voices swirling around her like smoke. The chair beneath her seems to pitch and heave as if the steady ground were an angry ocean. She picks up the phone once more and tries to type one word, this time feeling confident spell-check may be her ally.

Help

She tries to form the word with her mouth, as well, *one four-letter word,* but her lips are numb as if with novocaine, the world steadily slipping away from her, a black hole that has swallowed her ability to think, to speak, to exist.

"You okay?" It was Bill, that giant galoot whose deep, unrefined voice she remembers, "Hey—"

And then his huge hand, *like Andre the Giant's,* on her shoulder, shaking her, before another voice, this one much higher in pitch, more authoritative, saying, "She's taken ill. Here, help me carry her to her cabin. I'm a doctor."

I'm a doctor I'm a doctor I'm a doctor help me help me help me I'm a help me . . .

44

THOMAS HAS CRAWLED NEARLY TO THE CROWN OF A
white pine on the shore of Bass Lake, where he straddles a stout branch,
under the big night sky, smokes a cigarette. His friend Dax is there, too,
and the moonlight is bright, reflected on every needle of the tree as if it
were a great hairy thing, every green fiber shining silver-gray and far off
in the distance, their troop's campfire still visible, if tiny now, through
the trees.

Thomas has taken to smoking unfiltered Lucky Strikes, in homage
to the Beat writers he's reading on the sly, stealing their novels from his
mom's office in their house and longing to be on the road like Kerouac,
miles and miles spooled up from the asphalt and concrete to be recorded on an old odometer. The tall buildings and big cities he's never
seen: San Francisco and New York and Los Angeles and Nashville and
Seattle and New Orleans . . . Girls he hasn't met yet, and women even.
Boys, maybe . . . How should he know? And isn't that just it? The mys-

tery over every mountain, in every stranger, their story, and those Beat writers, recording everything, *right there and living it, totally unabashed.*

How he's come to resent these weeks in camp, pretending like he's interested in this antiquated code, these *White Indians* in their phony military uniforms and made-up ranks. What if he doesn't even want to *be* an Eagle? Maybe he should have remained a Tenderfoot, because that's what he is, really, not some crazy soldier like his father, and what good had that been for anyone? To fight and survive *years in Afghanistan and Iraq*, only to come home and take a bullet from some psycho outside a movie theater. His dad's old neighbor, Kyle, was with him that day. Still visits a counselor once to week, trying to recover from that horror.

His phone jiggles an incoming message and for an instant he fears it falling from the top of the tree, what must be five stories up, feels the phone shaking out of his pocket and he struggles with what to do with the cigarette, how not to fall out of an ancient white pine. In the end he simply flicks the Lucky away, sends it arcing out through the night, this tiny orange dot, falling and falling . . . Cigarettes are hard to come by. He can't afford to keep throwing them away, half-smoked. Kerouac used to collect old butts and recycle the tobacco, he remembers.

It's just a stupid text.

> I love you so much. Your father loves you too.
> He is watching us, you know, right now.

His goddamn spooky mom. The only woman in camp. Visiting Doughty like some . . . He doesn't even want to think about it.

His mom with yet another man, though—that would be a departure, he thinks. Not another loser that's just going to abandon her, after wiping out their savings, emptying the pantry, stealing their car. Not some jackass pretending to be his dad, trying to act like an enforcer, some kind of disciplinarian. Or worse yet, acting like his "friend." Yeah, right. As if this grown-ass man would want to be his friend if he didn't happen to be tapping his mom . . . Ugh.

He still remembers the one creep's midnight escape.

Thomas must have been, what, six, seven? He'd just woken up for a glass of milk and padded down the old farmhouse stairs. He remembers his own hand on the rail as his feet navigated down in the darkness, once kicking a toy that landed in the kitchen with a clatter.

That had startled the loser, whom Thomas found packing cans of soup and boxes of macaroni and cheese into a cardboard box.

"Go back to sleep," the man growled.

Without a word to the man, Thomas went to the refrigerator, retrieved the gallon of milk, then a small cup, and sat at the kitchen table, drinking, watching him.

"What? You're just gonna sit there? Just gonna watch me?"

Thomas nodded, licked at the white of his temporary mustache.

"Weirdest kid I ever met," the man said, standing, pressing his fists into the small of his own back. He reached up into a cabinet, and there was the crinkling of plastic packaging, and then they were sitting together at the table, eating Oreos, not talking at all, moonlight spilling in through one of the old windows over all the wilting houseplants, the shelves of knickknacks and curios, shining down on his mom's collection of skeleton keys and tiny mirrors.

When they had finished two columns of Oreos and Thomas's milk was finished, the man poured him another glass, stood, tussled the kid's hair, and said, "Nobody'll ever be good enough for your mom, Thomas. Must've really been something, your dad. Lotta good it did him."

"You're leaving, too?"

"Shut up about it and I'll leave you five bucks."

So Thomas nodded, watched him load the cardboard box into the back of his mom's car, a few bags of clothing, a gun from their basement, and then the car growled to life, its taillights shone red, and the man was gone, easing away into the early morning fog that so often clung to their pastures and fields.

The next morning, his mom didn't even notice the car was gone until they were standing on the driveway where it should have been, Thomas holding the straps of his school backpack as she scratched her head and surveyed their property.

"Where's the car?" she asked Thomas, her keys in one hand, purse balanced on a wrist, and a steaming travel mug of coffee in the other hand.

"He took it," Thomas said matter-of-factly.

"When?" she asked.

"Last night."

She dropped the coffee mug and ran inside. Her screams spilled out the front door with the sounds of dishes breaking.

He began crying, his backpack so heavy a burden for his little shoulders to carry. He sat in the dewy grass and pulled clover until she stumbled back outside.

"When, Thomas? When did he leave?"

Thomas shrugged.

She was crying, too, her makeup beginning to run.

"You *saw* him leave?"

Thomas nodded.

"And you just let him go? Just like that? Watched him drive away with our fucking car?"

Now he started to seriously sob. "He left me this." Held up the five-dollar bill.

She fell into the grass beside him now, hugged the little boy to her chest.

"Should we call the police?" he sniffled.

But she just rocked him, holding his little body tight. Back and forth, back and forth.

HE'S JUST LIGHTED ANOTHER CIGARETTE when the phone vibrates again.

"Fuck, Mom! Really?"

"What is it, dude?" Dax asks.

Thomas shoves the phone deeper into his pocket.

"My fucking mom. Keeps sending me these goddamn texts."

"Maybe she needs you," Dax says. "Why'd she keep messaging you this late?"

"Nah, man," Thomas says, scraping another match into flame. "You should've seen the last one. Touchy-feely bullshit."

"Well, send her a message back," Dax says, shaking his head. "Get her off your back. Moms love that. Trust me."

The cigarette between his lips, toasty and becoming more appetizing by the second, with the spill of moonlight everywhere, on the lake, like a wedding day cake glaze, and his phone, incessantly vibrating. Dax is right. Placate her. Something nice. Tomorrow—in a matter of hours—they'll be back home. He glances at the phone.

Help

The screen glows bluish white in his palm, like a square little moon with that single awkward spur, and he stares at the message, and then the real moon, then back at the message. "I think something's wrong, Dax." He drops the cigarette.

"What do you mean?"

But Thomas is already crawling down the tree, pine sap adhering to the hair of his forearms, to his clothes, his ears burning, and Dax calling down to him, "I'll get Doughty!" And bark raining down on his head from Dax's scrambling feet, as they both wind their way down the wide trunk, leaping from bough to bough, fingers holding fast to the thick bark, fingers sticky with pitch.

45

HE COULD NOT HAVE CARRIED HER, THOUGH SHE WAS hardly a heavy thing. But between Bill and two other dads, they hurried her to her cabin and laid her out on a cot. She was not speaking.

"Should we call 911?"

"I could get Doughty. You want me to get Doughty?"

They are all looking at him with concern, as if he is the authority. It's not unlike the hospital, that thrill of controlling a room. But these are men. Grown men. And not other doctors or nurses, not paramedics or even his colleagues from medical school. These are big, dumb, Wisconsin hicks. Mouth-breathers totally unprepared for any kind of medical emergency—hell, even some minor mishap. And this is no emergency, Platz could tell them. This is a covertly administered drug—the dust of several sleeping pills. He ought to know.

"No, no," he says evenly, without a hint of concern in his voice. He runs a hand along her forehead, then smooths her hair away from her face. Sits down on the bed beside her, takes her wrist in his hands, feels for a pulse. Touches her neck in much the same way. *So beautiful . . .*

"Platz?" Bill asks. "Is she okay?"

The oaf looks genuinely concerned. This Neanderthal, this piece-of-shit Wisconsin hillbilly that Platz has had to endure all week long. His regurgitated Rush Limbaugh talking points and rants: walls along Mexico, walls along Canada for crying out loud, guns and guns and guns, and stamp out the gays . . . Jesus.

"She's fine, Bill. Just drunk is all. Passed out. Like a high school cheerleader who's overshot it a bit." He turns to the other fathers. "You remember your prom nights. Pretty much like that. They all think they can drink like champions and then, *boom*. Facedown and blacked out. I see this *way too much* at the hospital." He casually pats her arm.

"Well, is there anything we can do?" someone asks.

"Actually, yes," Platz says coolly. "Look, boys, I'll stay here with her. You know, make sure she doesn't choke on her own vomit. Somebody get me a pail for the puke. Maybe a gallon of water for when she wakes up? And some aspirin. I got it from here. There's no need to call Doughty. It would only serve to embarrass her, and unfortunately"—he clicks his tongue—"*I* was the one who served her the whiskey. So, I'm responsible, too, I suppose . . ."

They nod and dutifully charge off back into the night, ordering the boys back to their tents and then dousing the fire with water, causing a huge cloud of steam to rise hissing into the darkness and yet, the flames come right back, half as tall as before, but still raging. "*Never seen a fire like that . . .*" Platz can distantly hear. And, " *. . . Some hangover in the morning . . .*"

He inches his fingers from her shoulder, down her breast, pinches her nipples, and turns quickly to see if her face responds, but she is *out*. He smiles. Runs his hands along the flat of her stomach to where her blue jeans terminate below the belly button. Once, he can see, she must have had a piercing there, back in her teens or maybe during college. God, he is so hot to undo those pants.

Bill bursts into the cabin just then with an empty aluminum pail and a canteen. "Got these," he says proudly and utterly out of breath. The big man's eyes momentarily fall on Platz's hand, but nothing seems to register.

"Perfect," Platz almost whispers. "You did great."

"Sure she'll be okay?" Bill pesters. The man seems some sort of sympathetic ogre: big of heart, if small of brain.

Platz stands now, reaches up to pat him on the shoulder, and then holds the screen door open for him, walking him out into the night, where beneath the tight forest canopy no light falls on their faces, where Bill cannot possibly see the contempt blazing in Platz's eyes. And still: *That goddamn fire persists!*

"You've done all you could," Platz commends him. "Now, let a doctor take over. All right? Get some sleep."

Bill shakes his hand like a man overjoyed to be on the wrong end of a business transaction, as if thankful to have been duped. "Always good to have a doctor around, huh?" he says. "Fact, when I was a boy, that's what I thought I wanted to be, you know? A doctor."

Platz almost laughs, catches himself. "Now, you probably told me already, Bill, but what is it you do for work?"

"Construction," Bill says, "mostly roads. It's good work. Not fixing people, like you, but . . . Fixin' somethin' at least."

Platz *does* laugh at that one, can picture Bill leaning on a shovel, listening to AM radio with a bunch of other dropouts, convicts, and deadbeats.

"Well, Bill, if you see the other guys, tell 'em I've got it. Everything is under control. She'll be good as new, come morning."

They walk toward the fire, where he shakes Bill's hand again and wishes him good night. Then, basking in its heat, colors brassing his face, he unzips his fly and pisses down into the flames before turning back to her cabin, his belt still flopping freely. Inside the cabin, he latches the door securely shut, slowly lets the canvas walls fall loose, and then, sitting next to her body, he lights the lantern, taking some pleasure in the quality of that antiquated light, how golden it is, how the shadows of the room offer so much more promise, how her skin seems like a precious metal extravagantly spilled into this most pleasing form—every mole, every rib his fingers brushes, a lavish luxury.

He undresses.

46

HE WAS DREAMING OF VIETNAM. A STRANGE BIFUR-
cated dream, all episodic, like a poorly edited film, a home video that
jumps and skips through time. Elephant grasses spinning like der-
vishes beneath their helicopter blades. A full blue-and-red can of Pepsi
in the middle of the jungle, not even booby-trapped, not a footprint
in sight. The yellow cross on a chaplain's army-green poncho. The
head of a very old man—just the head, his beard some six inches long
and dirty with mud. Laboring through a rice paddy, the sky perfectly
reflected. A dead tiger.

And then the tunnel.

He is crawling and crawling through the tunnel, calling out his
mother's name. Calling for her. He is a little boy inside the cold, muddy
tunnel and the roots of the plants all feel like fingers. He is so afraid. Of
being buried alive. Of being trapped for ages and ages. Of never finding
her. He calls her name out through his own sobs but the tunnel is so

dense, the ground so soft and residually wet that his voice is nothing, all of it swallowed by this long throat of earth.

Just as he touches that other face, he awakens with a scream to find a boy he does not recognize standing over him, one hand on his chest. The boy is panting, sweating, and he smells like the cigarettes they were issued in Vietnam. This boy has huge jug ears and his eyes are full of the concern and fear only children are bold enough to display in such bright earnest.

"What's the matter?" Nelson asks, instantly alert.

"Thomas's mom," the kid spits out, as Nelson sits up, his face bathed in moonlight. "She sent him a text, asking for help. He thinks something is wrong."

Already Nelson is scrambling for his clothing, reaches into his night-stand for a pistol, chambers a bullet, and tightening his belt, secures the gun against the small of his back. He is practically running for the door. "Arrowhead campground, isn't it?"

The boy nods, struggles to keep up with Nelson's pace, his head down, his chest heaving for air.

Nelson stops, kneels into the dewy grass, and, clasping the boy by the face, says, "Son, I'm going to need you to grab a hold of yourself now. Can you do that for me?"

The boy nods.

"Go now to the counselors' camp," Nelson says, "Wake them up. I don't care if you're scared to. I don't care what they say. Do what you have to do. Start their cabins on fire for all I care. But do it. Tell them we may have an emergency on our hands. I want you to send one of the older counselors out to your campsite. You tell that counselor he must be prepared to call the police and an ambulance. Wake them all up. Make sure they listen to you. Do you understand me?"

The boy's eyes are wide; he has stopped breathing.

"Do you understand me, boy?"

The boy nods.

"All right then, son, go," he says, and watches the boy move through the night, fast as a frightened colt.

Now Nelson begins to move over the parade ground, walking as fast as he can, and then breaking into a jog, his old legs popping and so unsteady. Now he is running. He hasn't run in decades. The night unnaturally quiet. No boy noise. No owls. Even the frogs have gone mute. There is no wind. He is flying through the forest.

TWO HUNDRED YARDS from the camp, he hears voices, moves toward the sounds. Thomas is standing beside a campfire and two men are talking to him in hushed voices, both of their hands out, as if trying to mellow this young man. Thomas backs away from them, swats at their outstretched fingers.

Nelson is out of breath when he reaches them.

"What's the problem?" he manages, smoothing his shirt. "What's the meaning of all this? Thomas, where is your mother?"

"They won't let me see her," the kid says. "I think something's wrong. I just want to see my mom and they keep making up these excuses."

"Look, calm yourself down, Thomas," says one of the men, a smaller man, drenched in sweat, with expensive-looking glasses, and rusty-red hair. "With all due respect, Scoutmaster Doughty, if I could just talk to you privately . . ." He leads the older man away from the fire, toward the shadows of the forest.

Nelson turns to see the other man, a huge hand on Thomas's shoulder, trying to coax the kid into relaxing, pushing the boy toward a picnic table and bench.

"The thing of it is, Scoutmaster Doughty," the man begins, "and, oh, by the way, I'm Doctor Phillip Platz—we met at orientation? I practice down in Eau Claire . . . Now, I've been monitoring Ms. Quick's situation from the get-go and I think we've got everything all squared away—"

"Her *situation*? Where is she? Take me to her now!" Nelson says, ready to move through this Platz. "I've got reports she messaged her son asking for help, now—"

"See, I don't know anything about that," Platz says, laughing, "and I've been with her the whole time, as I said, monitoring her vitals and what have you—"

"I don't like this one bit," Nelson says, moving around Platz in the direction of her cabin.

"If you'll just, sir, kindly allow me a minute to give you a review of the circumstances, I think you'll agree that I've secured the situation and perhaps"—here this doctor runs his smallish hands through thick hair, nudges his glasses up, and then continues—"saved Ms. Quick's son some embarrassment. Really. Please, sir. Will you just allow me to speak." The doctor raises his hands in gentle submission as he once again maneuvers in front of Nelson. "Please?"

Nelson nods, *so exhausted, so bloody exhausted.* He blinks his eyes. He can still smell the tunnel in his dreams: the wet soil, the rot, the minerality of stone . . .

"Ms. Quick had a little too much bourbon this evening around the campfire, all right?" the doctor begins. "And she passed out. We got her back into her cabin and she's *fine.* I've been monitoring her blood pressure and pulse and, really, she's *fine.* She's going to wake up in the morning with a doozy of a hangover, sure, but she'll survive. We didn't want Thomas in there, because we thought he might be unnecessarily concerned. She's passed out, see, and it might seem *to him* that she's seriously unwell. Which she most certainly is not.

"I mean"—the doctor collapses the distance between the two men, now speaking into Nelson's ear—"would *you* want to see your mother drunk, passed out on her bed?" He steps away from Nelson. "Also, as a physician, I have to raise the very real possibility of her being an alcoholic. This behavior, I mean, it simply isn't normal."

The old man studies him. Something is not right, though he can't put his fingers on it. Rachel had also more or less passed out in his cabin . . . But would she drink so heavily, in the company of these men? In front of her son? In their camp, in front of other boys and parents? Then again, how well does he know her, really? Is she a drunk?

No, no. That's nonsense. No, there's something else. She had, after all, messaged for help. That was why he was there. She was clearly in distress.

"Fine. Then let me see her at least," Nelson says evenly. "She's my friend, and I want to see for myself that she's being well taken care of." He casually waves a hand in the air, as if to shoo away his earlier intensity. "That's all. And, if need be, I can arrange for any further medical treatment. It's my *responsibility*, you understand. This is my camp, after all."

"Tell you what," the doctor says, hands on his hips, "you give that boy some peace of mind, you get him settled, and then we'll go see her together. I need to check on her anyway."

Nelson walks back to the fire, to where Thomas is now sitting, seemingly under the observation of one of the fathers, and says, "Come on, son. Let me walk you to your cabin."

"So she's okay?" he presses. "My mom's *okay*?" He rises from the wood bench, clearly shaken, suspicious even, looking from one adult face to the next, searching for some assurance that this is not the disaster it appears it might be. "But then why did she text me looking for help? I don't understand."

"She's fine," Nelson lies in a voice loud enough for Platz to plainly hear. "Come on. Let's get you settled. Too late for so much drama."

"But she sent me a text," the kid blurts. "I've got it right here! Mr. Doughty! Why can't we just go see her?"

Nelson takes the boy by his elbow and bends toward his ear: "Keep walking now, okay? Go." He rests an arm on Thomas's shoulders and they move into the night, away from the two watching men, the curling red-orange flames of the campfire.

When they are twenty paces away, he whispers to Thomas, "You've done good, son. Okay? Now something *is* wrong, I think." They stand in front of Thomas's cabin, where two boys' faces are pressed close to the metal screen windows, flashlights dancing all over the camp, and the low buzzing of voices whispering. Looking around him now, Nelson says, "You stay inside this building for two minutes." He pushes Thomas into the cabin, then reaches behind him, and taking the pistol, places it in the boy's hand. Thomas's cabin mates titter with excitement and confusion. "If I don't come back for my pistol in two minutes, you'll know something is definitely wrong. All right? You stay here. You hear me? And if anyone comes for you, you fire a warning shot. The first one in the air. The second at their feet. And if they keep coming . . ." He kisses Thomas on the forehead. "Tell me you understand me? Help is on the way."

The boy nods. The heavy pistol in his soft young hands smells of gun oil. He can't stop looking at it, the blued metal, the carved wooden handle.

Nelson slaps him lightly across the face, holds a finger in front of his nose. "*Focus*," he says. "Steady now. Concentrate. *You're* the good guy. You're the one who is prepared. Who is smart and courageous. All right? I'll be right back."

He eases the door shut and walks back toward the fire with the flickering hope that Rachel is just as the doctor said. But if there is one emotion that he understands, it is fear, and the night right now is thick with it. If Rachel were merely drunk, no one would be afraid. If there were nothing to hide, she would have been seen by someone other than Platz by now. *No,* he thinks, *something is awry. Pray that she is safe.*

HER CABIN IS STIFLINGLY HOT, and instantly Nelson smells the telltale tang of sex in the close canvas air. He says nothing, kneels beside her bunk, his old knees on the pebble and pine-needle-scattered floor. She is facedown in a flimsy T-shirt. He pulls a thin bedsheet away from her body. She wears only underwear. He sees a stain on them.

"Awful hot in here," he mumbles, pulling the bedsheet back up and wiping strands of her hair away from her face. She does not flinch at his touch, no response at all, though she is breathing faintly, her chest rising and falling regularly.

"I wanted to save her any embarrassment," the doctor says, "so we shut her curtains. I suppose we could open those now." He crosses his arms and rubs at his nose. "I tell you, these women—"

"Dr. Platz," Nelson says in a voice almost as low as a whisper, "I'm gonna need you to start telling me the truth."

"I don't understand, I don't understand what you're talking about," Platz stutters out. "I've been trying to help her."

"She passed out?"

"Yeah, like I said, we carried her in here and—"

"And undressed her like this?"

"Like you say, it was so hot."

"Dr. Platz, I am gonna leave this cabin right now and call the sheriff unless you start making some sense."

"Look, I've only tried to help her," Platz says. "I'm a doctor. I don't need to stand here and take this from you."

Nelson turns back to Rachel, and without looking at Platz, says, "Then you've left me no choice. But I'll say this—if you're the one who hurt this woman, I am going to skin you alive."

But before the old man can rise from his knees, Platz brings the heavy lantern down hard on his head, sending him to the dirty plywood floor of the building, where he lies groaning, his feet sliding to find purchase. Kerosene spills everywhere, fumes thick. Platz drops the lantern, bends down beside the old man. "Oh my God," Platz whines, "oh my God. I didn't mean . . . *Jesus Christ, Jesus Christ, Jesus Christ*. What have I done?"

"Everything all right in there?" Bill calls through the canvased doorway.

Kneeling next to the old man now, Platz roughly takes his pulse. Still alive. "No!" he shouts. "Doughty fell. Go get help, quick!"

Bill bursts through the door, but the cabin is all darkness now, the brightest thing visible now the white of Rachel's underwear.

Platz rises, pushes him back out into the night. "Go on now! Get me some help!" He projects a roaring voice over the campground. "Go on, man! Get a goddamn ambulance!"

Boys standing outside their cabins, holding their elbows, terrified, looking from their phones to Platz, pointing: *Is that blood?* And Bill, his chest now painted red with Nelson's blood, too, backpedaling quick before moving off into the forest. Other fathers, banging out of cabins, donning eyeglasses, lanterns and flashlights in hands, approaching Platz with squinted eyes, phones held to their ears, mumbling . . . *Think we've got an emergency* . . . Scratching their heads, yawning, others more alert, holding boys back, ordering them back to their cabins.

"Don't come any closer!" Platz screams. "For chrissakes! We've got spilled kerosene here, stay away!" He ducks back into the cabin, digs quickly into a pocket for a box of matches, strikes one, and immediately the cabin huffs on fire. He bursts back out. "This thing's going up, goddamnit—get water, get water! *Fire!*"

But Thomas is walking toward him now, pistol drawn, and from a distance of perhaps ten yards, shoots two rounds over the doctor's head. The gunshots sound like the universe splitting open, thunder separating reality into crooked shards. Platz startles, raises his hands in the air, and in doing so, knocks his own glasses off so that they fall to the darkness near his shoes. The boy walks closer, brandishes the pistol confidently, looks very much as if he is about to fire a bullet between Platz's eyes.

But then one of the fathers rushes out of the darkness, and commandeering the pistol from Thomas, says, "Go get your mom, Thomas, go!"

The father holds the gun on Platz, who seems dazed now, kneeling in the dust like a stunned hostage, searching for his glasses.

Thomas runs to his mother's cabin and pulls the door open wide, to be met by flames spilling out at him. She is lying on her bed, surrounded by fire on three sides, with only the wide window screen beside her offering a possible route. He goes around the cabin, punches right through the metal screen by the bed, grabs her arms, and roughly pulls her out.

Her body falls limply to the ground, but other men are gathering, and they help him, help him drag her to safety. Now several of the men rip the cabin's door off and reach through blue kerosene flames and dripping molten plastic for Nelson's pant legs, which are on fire. They grab his shoes, which slip off. They peel off his socks, burning, too. Finally, the old man is pulled free. They begin to administer mouth-to-mouth resuscitation.

Grown men, their arms covered in burnt skin, hair singed off, sit away from the flames and weep. Their sons come to them and cry, too. The little cabin is utterly engulfed. The flames reach the treetops, where green leaves reluctantly burn. So much fire. So many men, so many boys weeping before the fire. Or stone-faced with the sheer shock of it.

Thomas holds his mother in his lap. Her lips are moving, but he cannot understand what she is saying. She is so dirty, and some of her hair is burnt away. Her arms are utterly limp, and as he holds her, it is with the sudden certainty that someday, decades from now, she will die and he will be holding her just like this then.

Now her cabin collapses entirely and the flames rush up further yet. He watches more Scouts yet emerge from the darkness, carrying buckets of water that they hand to their fathers who douse the inferno, bucket after bucket, but the flames roar on, and in the treetops fire burns like a broken matrix of frayed wires.

He holds her tight as he can.

47

RACHEL IS WATCHING A MORNING TALK SHOW, SOME-
thing she would never do in her everyday life, would never do were she
not lying in a hospital bed, when there is a knock at the door.

"May I come in?" a voice asks, and she assumes if it is not a doctor
or nurse, it will be a policeman, come to ask her yet more questions.

"Yes," she croaks. Her voice is dry and raw. An IV runs into her arm;
her veins feel cold.

Jonathan, as he steps into the room now, looks so much older than
her memories; he *is* so much older. There is a gentle stoop to his shoulders and backbone, and the skin of his face seems to be drooping down,
collecting beneath his chin. He has shaved this morning, she sees. He
carries in one hand a vase of flowers, and in the other, a thermos of
coffee. He still favors Sperry topsiders, but now shuffles his feet, rather
than strutting like a senator.

Tears slip from her eyes, unbidden, and she hurriedly wipes them
away, manages to collect herself. This unexpected ghost.

He stops, notices the wetness on her face. "Oh, dear. Darling, I can go, if you'd like. I didn't mean to disturb you. I know it's been some time." He turns away from her, seeks an unoccupied surface on which to set the vase, but there are flowers everywhere.

Fool flowers. She's always wished people would just spend their money on preserving wildlife, wildlands, other people, rather than buying flowers flown to America from Africa or South America. All that jet fuel, water, heat, labor—for what? So they can clutter funeral parlors and hospital rooms, so they can droop and wilt, finally leaving a halo of petals to sweep up and convey into the garbage?

"No, no—please stay," she says, wiping her cheeks with a bedsheet. "I'm happy to see you." And she is happy to see Jonathan. Considers that this is what Trevor might have looked like, as an old man.

He sets the vase down on a narrow windowsill finally, and draws a chair closer to her bed.

"How you feelin', kiddo?" he asks, busying himself by pouring coffee from the thermos into a paper cup and handing it to her. "I know I'm a rich old asshole, but . . . I insist on good coffee. So, there's that. I'm sure that hospital coffee is garbage." He pats her arm.

His eyes are wet, too, she sees, as they flutter over her. "Oh, darling," he says.

When she was just a girl, a teenager, *how desperately* she had sought this man's approval. Always handsome, always debonair, always armed with a barbed joke, so worldly, utterly confident. And he'd always been such a terrible prick to her, calling her by the wrong name or teasing her about her love of horses or softball. But now, all that he seems to have left in the world is a big pile of money and a thick head of silver-white hair, a lonely cabin in northern Wisconsin, and a cupboard full of bourbon.

"I'm not as bad as I probably look," she says. "They're letting me out of here tomorrow, I guess."

"I heard about what happened, Rachel. I'm so sorry."

"It's okay," she says quietly. "I don't even remember anything." She is thankful for this, at least.

"They got him, though, I guess. Got 'em in jail in Rice Lake. They're saying this isn't the first time, either. I heard it was sleeping pills, all ground-up like. But he's used other stuff on other women . . ."

"I don't want to talk about it, Jon, okay? I just—don't want to talk about that man."

He nods. "No, I suppose not."

They drink their coffee. Far off: the sound of a helicopter's rotors, and then fading.

Jonathan turns his head to the TV. "Goddamn phonies. I've always been suspicious of morning people."

She reaches for the remote and switches the TV off.

"Where's Thomas?" she asks.

"He's with your parents. Poor guy's pretty shook up. Handled himself like a hero, though."

Just like his father.

"How's Nelson?" she asks.

Jonathan shakes his head. "Not too good. Took a pretty good hit to the head. And he's got some real bad burns, I guess. Have you seen him yet?"

She shakes her head.

"Me either. He's in the ICU, I guess. After I leave you, that's where I'm headed."

A quiet settles between them. She looks past him, out the window. Decides that she'll wait for him to break the silence.

"Rachel," he says finally, "I want to apologize to you. You've been a fantastic mother to Thomas, all these years, and, well, you've had to do it by yourself." He shakes his head. "Honestly, I don't know how you've done it. You . . . you amaze me, frankly." He lays a hand on the rail of her bed, near her arm. "You're a wonderful woman, just a wonderful person. Trevor was so in love with you. He always was. Maybe that's the best compliment of all. I don't know. Funny, really. I loved him more than anything else, in all my years, and he loved *you* more than anything. So . . . I'm sorry. I'm just so goddamned sorry about everything."

In the hallway: the laughter of nurses, the squeak of rubber shoes against wet linoleum, the plaintive wheel of a mop bucket.

He reaches for her hand and now, looks her directly in the eyes.

"I'm sorry," he says again.

"Thank you."

"I'm so, so sorry."

"Jonathan . . ."

"Rachel, I just want you to know that if you and Thomas need anything, *anything* at all . . ."

She pats his hand patiently, with a kind of grace that suddenly makes her feel very old, indeed. She realizes he has come to the hospital not entirely for her exactly, but also for himself. To absolve himself, somehow, of all his years of shitty behavior. He isn't a bad man. She is reminded, all of a sudden, of that line Carly Simon sings, "*You had one eye in the mirror as you watched yourself gavotte.*"

"Thank you, Jonathan. I appreciate that. We'll get by. We will. Go, be with Nelson. I think I'd like to close my eyes."

"All right, sweetheart," he says, leaning down to kiss her forehead. "You get some rest now."

She nods, pulls the sheets up to her chin, and closes her eyes, listening for the sounds of his retreat. Wishes she could reach out and hold Trevor's hand.

NELSON IS IN AND OUT OF CONSCIOUSNESS by the time Jonathan enters the ICU. The nurses are hesitant to even let him enter the room; their first reaction is to shoo him away, but he is still an imposing man. He holds his ground, explains that Nelson was his childhood friend.

Childhood friend—is that even so? What were they to one another? Connected by such tenuous bonds: summer days, college letters, and those occasional drinks or dinners that some people might coldly deem *networking*. Still, in some way, he loves this man. Loves him for his improbable life, his semirigid moral code, and the fierce old compass that has always dwelt in his chest, pointing always the right way—true north.

Jonathan pulls up a chair beside Nelson's bed. The room is quiet, save for the steady hissing and humming of the medical equipment, its multitoned beeps and dings. He can't believe how old Nelson looks, his cheeks salted with stubble and his mustache drooping sadly, his head and face badly swollen, like an aged fighter after a twelve-round loss. Jonathan awkwardly reaches for his hand, so cool to the touch, almost cold.

"Hang in there, old buddy," he says. "Okay? You gotta hang in there."

The two men stay that way for about an hour, before Nelson's girlfriend, Lorraine, enters the room, quickly collapsing into Jonathan's arms. He holds her while she weeps. It has been such a long, long time since anyone has wept on his shoulder.

IT IS THE MIDDLE OF THE NIGHT when Nelson's tremulous voice suddenly rises through the silence, waking Jonathan, who now moves closer to his old friend. Nelson holds a hand up, as if signaling him.

"What is it, Nelson? I'm right here, buddy, it's me, Jon. I'm here, buddy." He seizes Nelson's hand only to find a grip as strong as his own—a force, an energy in Nelson's hand. This is a man not yet ready to depart.

"Goddamn right," Jonathan says. "Hang in there, buddy. You took a pretty good lick, but I'd bet a million bucks you seen worse."

"You're always betting," Nelson coughs. And then, "I don't want to go."

Jonathan shakes his head, "You're not going anywhere, buddy. You're fine. Lorraine's here, too. Just went out to grab a cup of tea. She was telling me about Costa Rica. You'll be there soon enough. On some beach. Drinking a cold beer."

"I was dreaming," Nelson whispers.

"Oh yeah? What about, buddy?"

His voice is so weak. "Wilbur's deer . . . and my mother."

"What was that, Nelson?"

"I dreamt about my mother. Dreamt that she was in the kitchen, humming one of her favorite songs . . ." His voice trails off. "And I could smell her cigarette, plain as day . . ."

Jonathan watches as his friend closes his eyes. He looks to the monitors but the machines hold steady. He stands, moves to the curtains, calls out, "Could we get some help in here?" Sits back down beside Nelson.

"Your mother? What else, buddy? Some deer, you said? I'm right here."

"I was just a little boy, and we were sitting together. I was in her lap and she was . . . rubbing my head . . . humming to me . . ."

"All right, buddy," Jonathan coaxes, "she was humming to you. What song was it? Can you remember what song?"

"Then there were deer . . . Wilbur's white deer . . . And I was with them . . . Out in the forest . . ."

Jonathan waits for Nelson to say more, but he just breathes in and out a moment, each intake of oxygen, each exhalation, too, uneven now, ragged.

"Deer? Buddy? Nelson. Nelson! Hold on there, buddy, I'm gonna go to get us some help."

"I was lying down, in the snow, and they were all around me . . . the sound of their hooves . . ."

Again, Jonathan waits for his friend to continue. He squeezes Nelson's hand, but already, the force in that other grip seems to be waning.

"Nelson? Nelson!"

He stands from his chair and reaches for his friend's shoulders. Nelson opens his eyes, narrowly.

"One thing, you got to do for me . . ." Nelson reaches for his chest, below his hospital gown, pulls a necklace free from the patch of white chest hair, removes the chain from his neck. "Give this to Lorraine for me. My good-luck charm."

"Nelson? Oh no—you do it, buddy. No, you ain't going anywhere. Nelson . . ." Jonathan holds the nickel in his hand again, after so many years. A buffalo nickel, of all things.

But Nelson has closed his eyes, and a nurse strides into the room. "Sir, I'm going to have to ask you to leave," she orders. "Mr. Doughty needs to sleep."

HE IS LAID TO REST, a week later, at Whiteside Scout Reservation, on the same hillock as the flagpole that stood like a sundial, for so many days of his life. His headstone is a great granite boulder. The entire parade ground, acres and acres of open land, and all the abutting trails and roads are filled with hundreds and hundreds of grown men and not a few women, too. Children, spouses, relatives. Some of them in their uniforms. CEOs and garbagemen, mechanics and engineers, doctors and janitors, waiters and chefs. Professors, pastors, priests, and rabbis. A sitting governor, several mayors, and dozens of firefighters, policemen, and soldiers—active duty and retired. A retired astronaut, a major-league baseball player, and so many teachers. There are mothers and fathers, children of all ages, and old men in wheelchairs or leaning on walkers and crutches. They have come, literally, from around the world to mourn Nelson Doughty.

The day is warm and blue-skied as Jonathan stands beside Thomas and Rachel. A trumpeter from the New York Philharmonic, a camper at Whiteside some twenty-five years earlier, has flown into Wisconsin for the occasion, and during his playing of taps, Jonathan weeps like a little boy.

》———→

PART IV

FALL, 2019
THE DRAKENSBERG
MOUNTAINS

48

FALL. A SATURDAY AFTERNOON. SCAFFOLDING SUR-
rounds the old farmhouse. Rachel and Thomas standing atop it under
the pouring sun, a radio somewhere broadcasting a Wisconsin versus
Northwestern football game. Two dogs wrestle in what loosely qualifies
as their front lawn.

The first thing she did after being released from the hospital was
drive down a long yellow gravel road not two miles from their house
to a derelict shack of a house, its roof shingles all pancaked, gutters
dangling like broken limbs, even sprouting small trees in places, paint
scabbing off, and a ragged sun-bleached American flag hanging in one
window as a tattered drape. She must have driven by the place thousands of times, even pointed it out to her friends and relatives, joking,
"How much do you wanna bet they're cooking meth there?" But she'd
also noticed a sign sometimes advertising: GERMAN SHEPARDS 4 SALE.

"You sure about this place?" Thomas asked, when she pulled the keys from the ignition and stood on the crabgrass and gravel driveway, spent shotgun shells and cigarette butts near her feet.

"No," she answered, "I'm not."

He disembarked slowly, keeping a constant hand somewhere on the car, even if only the roof, or a side window.

"Hello?" she called out. "Anyone home?"

She was almost relieved when, at first, silence was all that greeted them. But then, the muffled sound of a dog barking, and finally, a big man walked around the corner of the house dressed in a pair of dirty denim bibs, unlaced work boots, coughing into a red handkerchief. He regarded them without saying a word, lumbered steadily closer without any great urgency or curiosity. As he came closer, she saw that he was a giant, well over six foot three. In her peripheral vision, she noticed Thomas take a step back before holding his ground. The man stopped about eight feet away from her, though it seemed a distance his long arms could quickly enough erase. He stared at her dully.

"You got any dogs for sale?" she asked in a firm voice.

He nodded, scratched a place behind his ear, motioned with his index finger, and then moved toward a dilapidated barn some hundred paces or so beyond the house. A dozen Styrofoam deer were all scattered in his lawn, arrows protruding from their sides. Caught in the branches of a dead elm was a very, very old red kite, its streamers ragged with age. He pushed open a sliding wooden door and led them into the barn with its smells of straw and motor oil and something else she could not immediately identify, ages of pigeon shit perhaps—or was it human piss?

In a stall fifteen feet inside the barn door lay a German shepherd bitch on a pile of dirty blankets, surrounded by a litter of six pups, all nuzzling, jockeying for position.

Rachel knelt beside them, reaching to graze her knuckles against their silky little backs. She couldn't help smiling. *Such little things.*

"Which two would you take?" she asked the man, suddenly anxious she make the right decision.

"It don't matter," he croaked, the first words he'd uttered, his voice oddly soft, almost childish. He tilted his head now and peered at the dogs. She wondered who, if anyone, this man had in his world to speak to. Felt she knew the answer already: *these animals.*

"No, really—I want you to choose," she persisted. "They're your pups."

"That ain't the way of it," he protested, almost laughing now. "You're the customer. You choose your own merchandise." He scratched his great jaw.

"I've never owned a dog before," she said. "Thomas?" she called over her shoulder, but the boy was standing out beyond the barn, shaking his head in discomfort. "Come on! Will you please help me choose?"

Thomas wasn't budging, so she turned to the man again. "Won't you please help me make a choice here?"

"Well, am I *you*? Or am I *me*?"

She looked at him. He wore a series of circular scars on his forehead, almost like the marks of several dozen inoculations, but, she suspected, very probably something much less benign. Behind her, she heard Thomas say, "Mom?" *He's just grown more and more protective of me,* she thought. She stretched a soothing hand behind her, as if to pacify the space between them.

"You're me," she said to the monolith. "You're me. And you can't sleep at night."

He smiled a yellow-toothed grin, and reached out, grabbed two pups: both black as coal with brown bellies. They nipped at his dirty fingers with teeth small as needles.

"These two," he said.

"Why?"

"Well, I always think them darker ones is meaner," he said. "But what matters is what we do now."

"What do we do now?"

He nodded his head repeatedly, like a tic, made a popping sound with his tongue, coughed.

"You come back. Every day, for two months. Just before dark. It's important," he insisted. "Every day. 'Round sunset. You make yourself the sunset."

He handed her the two pups, cocked his head this way and that, rolled his eyes.

"You're their mama now," he said. "You bring them food and cold water. And kindness."

She caressed their tiny heads.

"And you?" she asked.

He smiled gravely, reached for another one of the pups, and cradled it in his massive arms. "I'll see you tomorrow night."

NOW THE DOGS ROLL AROUND IN THE DUST, snap their jaws at grasshoppers, and chase mice. She scrapes the flaking paint, and Thomas comes behind her with his paintbrush. They move slowly, and their conversations are halting, rarely carefree. Words come most easily when he is brave enough to ask about his father. He has become more and more interested in Trevor and she suspects it stems from the night of her assault. Thomas was commended for his bravery by the local television channels and newspapers, and *Boy's Life* magazine has even planned an article detailing his exploits, though she has no idea how they'll manage the problematic subject of her rape. So she talks and talks about Trevor, her favorite subject, as the chips of paint fall from the sky down onto the tarpaulins below them.

"Your father was such a twig when we first fell in love," she says, not so much remembering that iteration of him anymore, preferring to re-call the man he was later, thick of chest, coated in hair, standing beside her in the morning cool, in his red-and-black Woolrich jacket, his tired old Carhartt pants, his breath all coffee and mint chewing tobacco, whispering near her ear, waiting for her to pull the trigger.

NELSON LEFT MUCH OF HIS ESTATE to a woman named Lor-raine, living outside the town of Haugen. Another large portion went to the Boy Scouts of America. The rest was left to Rachel. A sizable check and several large boxes of baseball cards, baseball ephemera, most of it seemingly related to the Chicago Cubs. For weeks she pored through the cards. For his part, Thomas does not seem at all interested in Nelson's collection—the cards, the game programs from Wrigley Field, the signed baseballs, glossy photographs, and letters. "It would all weigh me down," he tells her. He wants to leave Wisconsin. Wants to travel the world. Is curious about his mom's time in Africa.

"If you went," he argues, "why can't I?"

"You should," she says. "It's unlike any other place on the planet." What she remembers most vividly are the night skies. A weekend trip when they left Botswana and traveled to South Africa, to the Drak-ensberg Mountains, carrying a bottle of wine out to a rope bridge that swung over a chasm with the soft evening breezes: stars falling and those early kisses stolen from new lips, her old life, her old self, an entire ocean away and here she was now, a stranger, and whatever she cared to be.

SHE HAS TAKEN A LEAVE OF ABSENCE FROM WORK; Nel-son's money has allowed that much. And so she walks the country roads with her dogs, talks to the farmers who drive slowly by in their pickup trucks. They always offer her rides, mystified that a person would intentionally, recreationally walk for miles and miles.

"Your dogs can ride in back," they offer, removing broken-brimmed baseball caps from liver-spotted scalps and scratching white hair with work-mangled hands. "That don't bother me one bit." They stare at her through thick-lensed glasses scratched and scratched. Their foreheads, too, are etched with worry.

"No, thank you," she says with a smile. "I'm fine."

A few of them show genuine concern. "Hey, you doin' all right? Would you like to come on over for supper?"

"Thank you for your kindness," she says, kicking at the gravel, "but . . . I'm managing."

"Well, all right," they say. Or, "One of these days you're gonna get caught out here in the rain." Or, "You know where we are if you need the least bit of help. It don't trouble me at all to plow your driveway or mow, but I don't want to step on your toes." They toss their hands up, resettle them on the steering wheel, guffaw, "All righty, then."

She wonders if these men are capable of evil, were ever capable of evil. Finds herself wondering about their basements and attics. What they store in their barns. What they've buried out in their fields. She wonders how they treat their wives, daughters, nieces. Decides that most of them—perhaps every old-man-farmer she knows—are probably kind, gentle, mostly silent, boring even. Still. She sees their wives sometimes, stooped over in gardens brimming with vegetables and flowers, or standing to stretch their backs. Sees them at the clothesline, pinning up bedsheets to dry. Sees them collecting eggs from their chicken coop, eggs still warm from the breast feathers above them. And sometimes she sees these same wives, rocking a chair in a sun-drenched room, visible through a parlor window, and they are just staring out at the mailbox, or curling their white hair around an arthritic finger. Just staring off.

Day is done, gone the sun,
From the lake, from the hills, from the sky;
All is well, safely rest, God is nigh.

Fading light, dims the sight,
And a star gems the sky, gleaming bright.
From afar, drawing nigh, falls the night.

Thanks and praise, for our days,
'Neath the sun, 'neath the stars, 'neath the sky;
As we go, this we know, God is nigh.

Sun has set, shadows come,
Time has fled, Scouts must go to their beds
Always true to the promise that they made.

While the light fades from sight,
And the stars gleaming rays softly send,
To thy hands we our souls, Lord, commend.

—"TAPS," BY HORACE TRIM

ACKNOWLEDGMENTS

FIRST AND FOREMOST, I AM ETERNALLY GRATEFUL TO my agent, the maestro Rob McQuilkin, for keeping the faith. I am in your debt, once again. For her patience and kindness: Amanda Panitch. Everyone at Massie McQuilkin & Co. Special thanks to Megan Lynch for sound and thoughtful editorial advice. So pleased to be working with you now, and hopefully well into the future. Daniel Halpern, Sonya Cheuse, and everyone at Ecco. In England: Francesca Main and Lucy Cuthbertson-Twiggs. In France: Raphaëlle Liebaert, Camille Paulian, and Mireille Vignol. My friends at Villa Gillet in Lyon. In Italy: Patricia Chendi, Chiara Tiveron, Andrea Coccia, Claudia Durastanti, Giulio D'Antona. La Grande Invasione and Gianmario Pilo. In Spain: Luis Solano. In the Netherlands: the Crossing Border Festival and Louis Behre. All my foreign agents, publishers, editors, and translators, thank you for giving me an opportunity to see the world. Thank you for your curiosity and kindness. Please, come visit us in Wisconsin. We'll have cold beer and good cheese awaiting you.

Thank you to the Iowa Writers' Workshop.

For musical inspiration: Colin Stetson and Sarah Neufeld, Nick Cave, Chet Faker, Jim James and My Morning Jacket.

This was the first novel that I completed after moving back to my hometown of Eau Claire, Wisconsin, a community that has embraced and supported my career. I am thankful to: Nick Meyer and everyone at

Volume One, in particular: Lindsey Quinnies and all the staff at the Local Store. Tina Chetwood. The *Eau Claire Leader-Telegram*. L. E. Phillips Library. Brady and Jeanne Foust. Local literati: John Hildebrand, Max Garland, B. J. Hollars, Eric Rasmussen, Michael Perry, Julian Emerson, Joe Niese, Allyson and Jon Loomis. Racy's and the Nucleus, where many of these pages were written.

My friends: Josh and Charmaine Swan, Nik Novak, Marcus Burke, Scott Smith, Chanda Grubbs, Mike and Hilary Walters, Nicholas Gulig, Betsy and Sheridan Johnson, Chuck and Shannon Stewart, Sara and Chris Meeks, Bill Hogseth and Crystal Halvorson, Mike Tiboris, Tracy Hruska, Erin Celello and Aaron Olver, Ben Percy, Dean Bakopoulos, Noah Charney, Jason Gerace, Tara Mathison, Virgina Evangelist, Zac and Beth Gall, Aaron Rodgers.

A special thank you to the all the independent booksellers who have helped support my career, in no particular order and apologies to those I've clumsily omitted: Between the Covers (Harbor Springs, MI), Saturn Books (Gaylord, MI), Joseph Beth Booksellers (Cincinnati, OH), Boswell Books (Milwaukee, WI), The Reader's Loft (Green Bay, WI), Anderson's Bookshop (Naperville, IL), The Bookstall at Chestnut Court (Winnetka, IL), Parnassus Books (Nashville, TN), The Tattered Cover (Denver, CO), Apostle Islands Booksellers (Bayfield, WI), Prairie Lights (Iowa City, IA), Literati (Ann Arbor, MI), Watermark Books (Wichita, KS), Excelsior Bay Books (Excelsior, MN), Magers & Quinn (Minneapolis, MN), Arcadia Books (Spring Green, WI), A Room of One's Own (Madison, WI), The Book Shelf (Winona, MN), Dulwich Books (London, England), Schuler's Bookstore (Okemos, MI), Mysterious Galaxy Bookstore (Redondo Beach, CA).

To my family: my mom and dad, my brother Alex and sister-in-law Cynthia. Jim and Lynn. Reidar and Kaitlen. All my aunts, uncles, and cousins. My in-laws. But in particular, I feel blessed to have Henry and Nora in my life, and of course, nothing would be possible without Regina. Thanks for believing in me. I owe you the stars.